A STORM OF DOUBT

MASTERS OF THE ELEMENTS

BOOK ONE

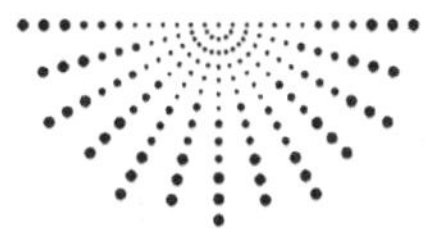

CC SULLIVAN

CD & COMPANY
Canada

ISBN (ebook): 978-1-7382054-1-7

ISBN (paperback): 978-1-7382054-0-0

ISBN (hard cover): 978-1-7382054-2-4

ISBN (audio book):978-1-7382054-3-1

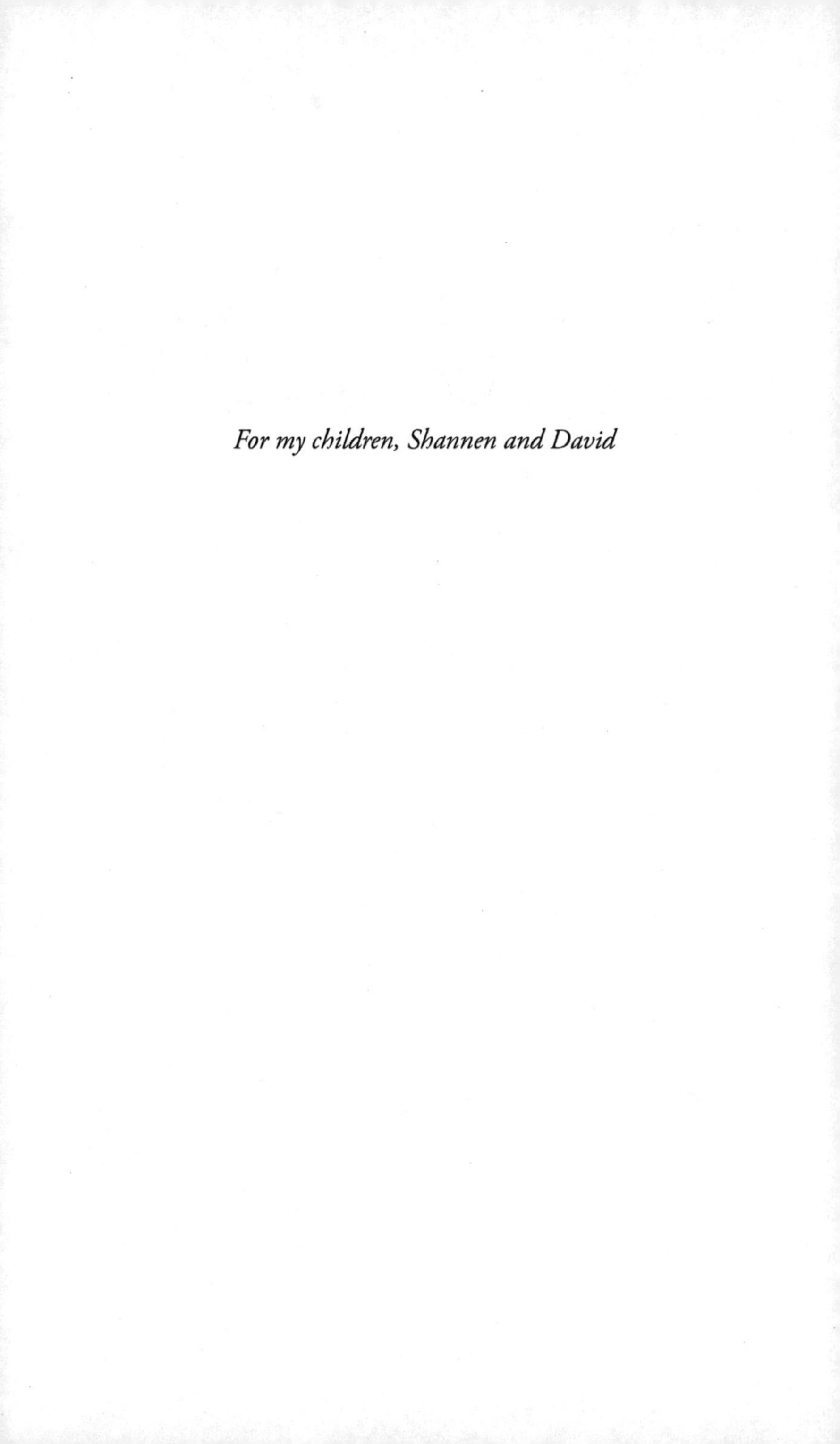

For my children, Shannen and David

ACKNOWLEDGMENTS

I would like to thank all who helped bring my characters and this story to life.

The people to whom I am eternally grateful are my husband, Michael Sullivan, my mother, Rosina Daillie, and my childhood friend, Marika Marcuzzi for their reads, edits, and immeasurable patience.

1
THE MAGIC BOX

I have always had a profound sense
of purpose in my life.
But I was unprepared for the storm
that would test my spirit.
— Lena Bianchi, *Florence*

DANTE ~ FLORENCE, 1489

"*Tre, due, uno.* Whoever is there, I will find you!"

Dante darted through the woodlands while behind him Damiano's faint cry resonated. Under the canopy, his feet tread upon the forgiving earth. He reached a fork in the path and hesitated, unsure which way to travel.

A twig cracked to his left. And beyond the slender trunks of saplings, something shifted. His attention set on the noise; Dante crouched low to the ground to reach for a stick to defend himself. His fingers brushed against a cool, polished surface. *This rock will have to do.* His gaze remained on the underwood. A tree branch rustled. *There!*

Two ice-grey eyes stared at him.

Beads of cool sweat trickled down his back. Dante rose, stone in hand. He awaited the beast's rush and raised his arm, ready to strike.

The wild creature emerged on the pathway, and before his eyes stood a young lady. Dante hesitated, astonished that those unusual and pale eyes belonged to her. She held his gaze, and Dante lowered his quivering arm as he took in her form.

Her long dress fluttered in the light breeze, translucent. The curve of her body sent a shiver skittering through him. She lifted a finger to her lips and shushed him. Though he wanted to, he dared not scream lest she stole away.

Then, she whispered, just above a murmur. Dante cocked his head. He had understood most of what she had said, but one word had stood out: Firenze. With his senses coming back to him, he pointed at the path to Florence.

She carried a shiny silver box emitting an iridescent blue light in her hand. Except for the strange illumination, it reminded him of his mother's sewing kit shaped like a small tin container. Their eyes met for a moment as she slid the peculiar object into the folds of her finely embroidered dress.

A high-pitched voice taunted from a distance, "Dante! Where are you?"

Her expression softened, yet a frown emerged on her brow. "Dante?" And though she stood one body's length away from him, her warm breath caressed his cheek and tickled his ear when she spoke, making the hair on the back of his neck stand on end. How could she feel so close and yet be so far away at the same time?

"*Si Signora,* I am Dante di Ronaldo D'Alessandro."

Something about the fashion in which she wore her hair and the way the sunlight streamed through her dress told him she was not from these parts. He had spoken in his native Florentine dialect because he knew no other language, but he assumed she had understood because she asked him another strange question.

"How old are you?"

He did not answer, and she repeated her question.

"*Quanti an—*"

"Eight." He interrupted her, and a hot flush rose to his cheeks.

The young lady's expression brightened, and she stepped forward. His heart hammered in his chest as she approached him, and he swivelled on his heels and fled as fast as he could.

He ran without looking back. Finally, he glanced over his shoulder, but she had left. He stopped in his tracks and crept back to where they had met. The feathery touch of her breath lingered on his cheek, and he touched his face to capture that memory. Was she one of those magical forest spirits he had overheard his sisters talking about one day?

Ahead, something sparkled. The gleaming object she had held in her hand lay on the ground. With the tip of his sandal, he shoved the metal and glass case along the path, cautious to what it held. He crouched down on his haunches to get a better view. Upon closer inspection, the case had a polished surface.

He picked it up and jiggled it just once. Almost immediately, an image appeared on the glass surface. He dropped the box as if it were ablaze. When he found his balance, he plucked it up again.

Despite his racing heart, he tapped a finger against the slippery glass exterior. The image appeared again: the lady had wolf-like eyes. He gawked at her likeness. How had she fallen inside this box? *Like magic.*

His brother hollered again from beyond the trees. "Dante? Come on, this game isn't fun anymore!" Answering Damian's call, Dante shoved his new treasure deep into his pocket and dashed toward his brother's voice.

LENA ~ FLORENCE, PRESENT DAY

Tears blurred Lena's vision. She stood in the Tribune by herself and gazed up at Michelangelo's *Statue of David.* Memories of her father floated to the surface of her mind, and her throat tightened.

He had held onto her slight hand. It was a soothing warmth inside the frigid interior of the Galleria dell'Accademia.

"Papa, who was this man?"

"His name was David. A young man who stood up to a giant named Goliath, killing him with just a sling and a stone. He saved his kingdom with just *one* shot." Her father's voice echoed in the chamber.

Lena had craned her neck and glanced up at the sculpture's full extent. "I feel like he could step down and walk away with us."

At that moment, she caught a movement in the corner of her eye. When she looked over, a much older boy stood off to the side. His hoodie was pulled back, and through his curly, dark hair which fell across his brow, she saw his crystal eyes peering at her. As she returned her gaze to the sculpture, she sucked in her breath. The statue had the same face as the boy. But when she looked for him again, the boy was gone.

Her father interrupted her thoughts. "Yes, it's true. He looks very real. You know, Michelangelo was an artist and a sculptor who was in a league of his own. This statue captures the moment before David's life changed forever. He grew up to become one of the greatest kings of all time, and his courage symbolized the heart and soul of Florence."

She shielded herself against her father's side. He looked down at her, and his expression sobered as their eyes met. "Lena, the world's not as you know it, but you're still too young for me to explain. One day I will also tell you more about our "*bien-aimée*", and you will also learn about our life—*your* life."

A dark shadow of uncertainty crossed his face, and he squeezed her hand a little tighter than usual. She had only understood the part about being a *beloved* child and had hoped it would chase away the sombre cloud that hung over him.

He patted her back. "For now, I want you to remember that

we'll always watch over you. You are our precious girl—one with special gifts."

LENA SHIFTED on her feet and ran her hand through her hair. She was still unsure what her father had meant; his words echoed in her mind, leaving her puzzled. She looked up, and almost expected to see her father's face, but found herself alone. A tear escaped and ran down her cheek.

Then, a flicker caught her eye, like a butterfly flitting about the statue's feet, fluid and rippling outward. Lena blinked and wiped the tear from her eye. *Nothing.* Whatever it was, was no longer there.

A loud clash distracted her. She turned to see the guard picking up his keys from the marble floor. And as she looked away, something stirred again. Her eyes darted back to the base of the statue. This time, she caught it—an unmistakable undulation. Lena's eyes narrowed. She leaned forward to get a closer look. Had David twitched his toes?

Looking around her, she reached into her jacket for her phone, where she kept it hidden in an inside pocket. She leaned near the glass encasement, which kept *David* safe and hoped to capture something, anything.

Just then, a heavy hand landed on her shoulder. She jerked around and almost dropped her phone.

The guard glared at her. "No photos in the Galleria!"

"I—I wasn't taking any."

The guard held out his hand. "You give me the phone."

"No. I wasn't taking any photos!"

"I telephone the Police."

The *Carabinieri* was never a good idea. She handed it over to him. With her feet dragging heavily across the cold marble floor, she followed him to the office. The guard glanced back at her with a laser beam look that could have burned a hole in her skull. They reached his station, and he demanded her identification.

Her hand trembled as she searched her purse for her student card.

She kept her head down, but she was determined to get her phone returned to her. "I want it back when you're done."

When he had taken her information, he held out her phone.

"Unlock phone!"

Lena did, and a wrinkle emerged in his brow when he found what he was looking for. He shook his head while he viewed it. Had he seen something too?

He hesitated, and his fingers flew about the screen. Then he handed the phone back to her.

"You no welcome at La Galleria."

The guard's tone had a threatening edge to it. He meant what he said. When he reached out to grab her, she yanked her arm away. He stumbled and dropped his walkie-talkie. It fell to the floor with a loud clatter.

Heat rose to Lena's cheeks as a surge of pride pricked the surface of her skin. "I can leave on my own."

A large group arrived at that moment. She took her chance and dashed down the corridor. Just before escaping into the crowd, she looked over her shoulder to see the guard marching toward her. She shoved her way through the group and burst out the front doors onto Via Ricasoli.

On the narrow street's opposite side stood the Libreria Evangelica, a shop spilling out onto the pavement with Christian publications, postcards, maps, and ATMs lined up like mechanical soldiers. This tourist trap was the closest store in which to take shelter, and it was still open.

The afternoon light had diffused into a warm, purple and pink glow. Lena slunk into the store to hide behind the ATMs. From her location, she had a direct view of the Galleria's entrance. If it weren't for the large signs outside, no one would presume this nondescript building housed the treasures it did.

The guard appeared and searched the street. Lena ducked. He mumbled something incoherent into his walkie-talkie and went back inside.

She raced past the gallery with quickened steps and marched up Via Ricasoli as dusk fell. Wrought iron bars secured the lower windows facing the street. Even in the fading light, their appearance ruined the charm of this historic city.

Lena reached Via degli Alfani, but instead of turning toward her apartment, she strode through its small junction and kept walking. Her heart beat at an unnaturally fast pace, and she was not yet ready to head home.

Twilight settled over the city, bringing with it a current of cool air. The day's heat rose off the cobblestone in undulating waves, and from the Arno's waterways, river smoke covered the bridges of Florence, blanketing the piazzas, alcoves, and narrow passageways.

The fine mist descended like a hazy memory. Some lost dream imbued with the perfumed fragrance of a time long forgotten. The city sparkled with a million shimmering diamonds and street lamps glowed like hallowed angels standing guard.

Lena had wandered on much further than she had planned. She stopped at the Ponte alle Grazie—the longest bridge—stretched out across the Arno River. She wiggled her fingers to ease the niggling sensation in her fingertips. To keep them warm, she rubbed her palms together. The prickling changed to pins and needles.

Lena stopped under a streetlamp's misty illumination and wrung her hands with short, jerky strokes. The lamp flickered, and she looked up. Why did they always do that when she stepped under them?

Then, an icy sensation crept up Lena's arms to her elbows, as if she had plunged them into frigid water. Her mouth ran dry and her throat constricted like someone was tightening their grip around her neck. She gasped in horror as the tips of her fingers stretched into a clear, bluish-coloured fluid. Her heartbeat quickened and induced in her a shallow but laboured breathing. Without another thought, she was off and into a full run down the street along the Arno's northern bank.

From one of the dark corners of a home that bordered the river, a hooded figure watched her. Beads of sweat formed on her forehead as she slowed her run and glanced at the cloaked silhouette. She caught the dark curls that escaped the hoodie and the glint in his eyes before fleeing again. Why did he seem familiar? As she approached the Ponte Vecchio, she veered to the right and entered the first street. Lena glanced over her shoulder, but no one followed her.

Yielding to a stream of tourists, it took her ten minutes to snake through the crowds before she arrived at her residence. Lena checked her hands once more at her building's front door. Her fingers had gone back to their original shape.

She fumbled with her large key. After a few tries, she unlocked the door and bounded upstairs. Stopping on the third-floor landing, she entered her apartment.

After she slammed the door behind her, she leaned against it and braced herself against the outside world. Her roommate jumped at this abrupt intrusion.

"Jesus, you scared the crap out of me!"

"Sorry, Portia . . ."

Lena took a deep breath and looked up toward the cathedral ceiling. The calm of being back in her own space settled her nerves.

Portia sat in her own corner of the spacious studio apartment. She was reading in bed, propped up with a pillow against her headboard. She eyed Lena curiously.

"What's going on? You look spooked."

Lena moved to the window to stare out at the avenue below.

"I thought I saw something, but now I'm not really sure what happened."

Though it was getting dark, the Piazza San Lorenzo still had tourists strolling through the square. Shadowy figures walked together, holding hands, carrying bags filled with souvenirs. At the far end of the square, she spotted movement that caught her attention.

A cloaked figure lurked in the shadows. Something in the way the shadow form lingered and stared at her building left her tied up in knots. She nibbled on her bottom lip.

In the window's reflection, she caught Portia staring. Her crystal green eyes glowed in the semi-obscured room.

"Lena, what's going on? Something happen?"

When Lena's focus returned to the square, the shady character had vanished into the night. Lena moved to Portia's side of the room and sat down on the edge of her bed. Her hands shook.

"Check my eyes and tell me if you see anything?"

Portia sat up and leaned in close. Her nose almost touched Lena's. "It's not the best lighting . . . but there's nothing unusual." She leaned back, shrugged, and lowered her eyes to her book. "Just your savage eyes. They're fine."

The click of Portia's tongue made Lena uneasy. Portia only did that when she was nervous. Lena was used to people's discomfort the first time they peered into her eyes.

Her friends had described her eyes as deep blocks of ice, surrounded by a dark blue rim, and they had jokingly referred to them as "The Abyss." But Portia had known her long enough now, so why was she reacting that way?

Lena crossed her arms and huffed. She hoped Portia would look up from her book. Not a chance. Not even a flicker. Portia ignored her, but Lena suspected her friend was keeping something from her.

. . .

LENA AND PORTIA had met at the door of this apartment a year and a half earlier. They were in their last year of studies at the University of Florence.

Their apartment was not your typical university residence. The small, rectangular edifice overlooked the Piazza San Lorenzo, designed in classical Roman style, form, and proportion.

As Lena approached the building for the first time, she admired how pillars carved out of large stones framed the first and second-floor windows. They were topped with a frieze and scroll-shaped corbel.

She loved how the cornice ran along the building's entire facade, accenting the separation between the second and third floors. And a large gold seal on the jeweller's front windows covered the length of the ground floor.

The front door's heavy, black key spanned four inches from the decorative and oval bow to the bit. Moved by its historical context, Lena turned the key and opened the door to a grand entranceway lined with mailboxes on the left wall. A single bulb hung from a wire, providing minimal lighting. Not great for arriving late at night.

At the end of a narrow hallway, a wrought-iron gate opened to a small, treed courtyard. To her right, a wide staircase led upstairs.

Lena climbed the stairs, sliding her hand along the dark, heavy, mahogany bannister. When she reached the third landing, a girl with long, golden curls stood at the apartment's door.

Lena asked, "Is there someone to greet us?"

The girl with cat eyes slid her fingers up along the door's frame, until she found the key. She handed it to Lena. "Nope, and here you have the honour of unlocking the entrance to our new digs."

The girls entered the apartment and gravitated by happenstance to opposite sides of the main room with three windows spaced evenly apart. Lena's eyes widened with delight.

"I love how these large windows bring all this light into our living space."

"What about that wide-arched entry with the heavy wooden double door? Don't you find it fascinating?" Portia beamed as she took in her new surroundings. "And the size of that ancient bolt? I feel as though I've just stepped back in time!"

Lena smiled. At least this girl appreciated art and history.

She reached out a hand to Portia. "Magdalena Bianchi, but please call me Lena." Her new roommate reciprocated by offering her hand. "Portia Rivero. It's a pleasure to meet you."

They threw their bags on the floor and bounced onto their new beds at the same time. Glancing at each other, they giggled, then burst into full belly laughs. That moment defined their relationship.

Portia extended her arms in a welcoming motion. "I think we're both going to love it here!"

Lena agreed and looked toward Portia's side of the room. She would probably need plenty of space—judging by the size of her suitcase.

However, the apartment was larger than Lena had expected, and included a kitchenette in the corner, a tiny balcony overlooking the inner courtyard, and an enormous bathroom.

Lena closed her eyes and breathed in the smell of their new place. Their studio was not too large to create an awkward living space, nor was it too small to share.

Oak hardwood floors warmed up the room, while two fans hung at the highest point of the cathedral ceiling. They had also plastered the walls and given the bare walls a fresh coat of paint.

Portia squealed. "Everything's so beautiful here!" She got up and opened a window that gave out onto the Piazza San Lorenzo.

Lena joined Portia to view the square. "I agree."

Portia . . . Her name rolled off Lena's tongue like the ripple of a mountain stream. This cohabitation idea might actually work out. She had made a resolution to make new connections. But when

Portia turned to her with a smile stretching from ear to ear, Lena shrunk and went back to her side of the room.

As Lena shifted uncomfortably, Portia brushed a curl of hair off her face and let out a carefree laugh. "I suppose it's safe to say we're both Italian."

Lena tittered. There was nothing Italian about them—not in the slightest. "Just in name, I'm afraid. I'm from France, but my family now lives in Canada." She turned to observe Portia. The girl who stood before her looked like she had just stepped out of an American coming-of-age movie.

2
BONFIRE OF THE VANITIES

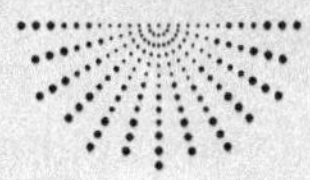

LENA ~ FLORENCE, PRESENT DAY

NAUSEA WASHED over Lena in a rush. With her legs dangling over the edge of her bed, she waited for the queasy sensation to pass. Around her, the walls stretched and twisted, distorting the apartment's objects. Her bed, desk, and framed images spun around the room as if on a merry-go-round. She squeezed her eyes shut, waiting for the whirling in her mind to stop.

She ran to the bathroom and threw open the toilet lid. Her entire body heaved dry, acidic air as she bent over the porcelain bowl. When she collapsed on the cool ceramic floor and against the delicate antique cabinet, the miscellaneous toiletries jostled about inside.

She dragged herself back to bed and glanced to Portia's side of the room, bleary-eyed and rumpled like an old sheet of paper. Portia's bed was empty, made with the sheets tucked tight.

Lena crawled back into bed and grabbed her cell phone from the night table.

— *Hey Portia, where are you?*

She stared at her phone and waited for Leonardo's *Mona Lisa* to blink, announcing a message received. Rolling onto her side, she cradled the cell phone and played the staring game. Who would blink first? Lena pursed her lips. *Mona Lisa* appeared to be winning.

In the shadows of her room, a change in the air drew her attention in that direction. Beyond the footboard, a white, shimmering ray flickered. Lena's eyes adjusted, then focused on where the bright, thread-like wire intersected with other strands of light. It formed a cubic grid, surrounding her on all sides as if she had stepped into a 3-D computer animation program.

She rubbed her eyes. When she looked again, the grid remained—effervescent and sinuous. Some walls had dissolved into the gloom, and the entire room floated upon this lattice—a network of vertical and horizontal lines dissecting each other.

She took a deep breath and surveyed her surroundings where familiar forms took shape. A sentence she had written in her dissertation came to mind.

Memory of form is a vibrancy of energy that exists in the collective consciousness.

The contours brightened like a photograph on a developing tray. She glanced at the niche where the kitchenette stood and saw that the dividing wall no longer existed. The apartment now stretched from the three front windows all the way to the two back windows which overlooked the inner courtyard.

She was certain she had seen this place before. Of course, it was the same location with its matching façade, but this was a warped version of it. She shook her head, curious about its manifestation. Was she dreaming?

A flutter of wings startled her—she turned toward the half-opened window. As the sparrow flew away, it left tiny particles of dust swirling in the air. The withered smell of old books and attics—a strong, musty odour—filled the room. The concrete floor, littered with chipped and broken tiles, had faded to a stained mustard yellow and blue.

The San Lorenzo church bells rang and the sudden clangour startled her. It was seven o'clock in the morning in Florence. She feared she might slip off the web as she wobbled on trembling legs and struggled to regain her footing.

She lifted her right leg and placed her foot along the network of light beams where they intersected. Sweat beaded her forehead as she steadied herself on the web. The mesh wavered and a slow ripple spread outward from where she stood.

She moved to the window, wary and uncertain, and held onto the crumbling frame to peer out at the Piazza San Lorenzo. People dressed in medieval garb walked leisurely through the little square. The women wore simple linen dresses fastened at the waist, and the men were dressed in belted tunics and pants. She cocked her head to one side in disbelief.

A sudden loud buzzing noise in Lena's eardrums made her grimace in pain. She cupped her hands over her ears and shut her eyes. The drone turned into a deafening racket, like a bee caught in her ear. Heavy winds blew around her, then stopped short and abruptly died out, leaving her to free-fall through the pitch blackness of space. In the sudden stillness, her body rattled. A small, faint voice called out to her. Then, it became loud and obtrusive.

"Lena? Wake up!"

Lena blinked and adjusted her eyes to find Portia staring down at her with teary, red-rimmed eyes.

"Why are you yelling?"

Portia's expression went wide with shock. "I've been trying to wake you!"

Lena shook her head. "When did you get back?"

"Get back? I haven't left." Portia's cry caught Lena off guard.

"Calm down. I sent you a text."

Portia's posture collapsed. "What text? I've been here the whole time."

Lena sat up, wide eyed. "Was I sleep-walking or moving around at all?"

"What? Neither. I came out from my shower and you were lying rigid on your bed, your arms glued to your sides. You mumbled a bunch of mumbo jumbo and went into a fit. I freaked out and was afraid you'd hurt yourself."

Lena reached out a hand. The pulse of Portia's heart thundered through her palm as if it were her own. When she pulled back, the sensation stopped.

"I'm okay . . . it's okay. I must have had a nightmare."

Portia's voice rose again. "Nightmare? You were having a fit!"

Lena put her hand on Portia's arm to stop her. "I said I'm okay, Portia." As Lena spoke, she glanced at her alarm clock. "Oh shit, I've got to get ready. We'll be late for class!"

LENA COULD FEEL Portia's eyes on her as they walked. A quick glance revealed they were on the verge of tears. Portia interlaced her arm with hers as if keeping Lena near would protect her.

Portia trembled and her voice broke as she spoke. "I've never . . . I'm sorry . . . The only person I've ever known to react like that in her sleep was my mother."

Lena leaned over and gave Portia a light kiss on the cheek. "I didn't mean to alarm you . . . and thank you. If it helps any, I'd have been scared, too."

Portia's mother was a sensitive subject. Lena never asked about her, finding it too delicate to trouble her with superficial questions. And Portia had never divulged more than a few vague remarks.

Portia's trembling body sent nervous ripples through Lena. Turning her attention away, Lena faced the University building to quell the overwhelming sensation of panic. Her chest tightened. She wanted to let go of Portia but held on to comfort her friend.

. . .

THE GIRLS ATTENDED the same lecture, but in the bustle of the crowd, they had become separated. Lena sighed with relief as she found her seat in the large auditorium. It provided her a break from Portia's rollercoaster of emotions.

However, Lena could not concentrate on the lecture. Under the flicker of the projector light, she replayed the morning's experience in her mind—exploring the circumstances that had triggered the dream and its sensations.

Lena looked at the screen. From afar, the professor's voice described the paintings that appeared side by side. They were replicas with slight differences.

"This painting is Leonardo da Vinci's *Virgin of the Rocks.* He painted two versions. A few theories amongst art connoisseurs explain why Leonardo painted the same scene twice."

With no way to focus, she thought about the previous day's events. They made little sense to her. Was she pushing herself too hard?

"On the left, the Louvre version. Details are subtle. His grotto and rocks stress the sombre tones. The archangel Gabriel looks to the audience, his finger points toward St. John the Baptist."

Lena shook her head at the professor's observation. No, it didn't. Gabriel was gesturing behind Saint John, but at what? Dark shapes of rocks, hills, and valleys filled the backdrop of the painting. Nothing obvious to see there. Why did she think there was a link between Leonardo's paintings and her previous gallery experience? It made no sense.

The professor continued his lecture while pointing to the second painting, and his voice faded into a droning buzz in the background. "That one hangs in the National Gallery in London. In this one, Leonardo's colours are more vivid because the Gallery took the time to restore it to its original version. Also note how Gabriel faces away and how his hand with the pointed finger is missing."

Soon, Lena's stomach growled. As her thoughts about the

paintings faded, she focused on lunch and developed a plan to postpone Portia's impending interrogation.

LENA WATCHED as Portia squeezed through the crowd of the busy cafeteria. Portia's face fell when she eyed Lena's half-eaten sandwich as she slid into a chair across from her.

Portia sat and carefully arranged her plate and cutlery. She cut into her slice of pizza with the small, plastic cafeteria fork and knife as though she were sitting at a black-tie dinner. A smile tugged at Lena's lips, and she tried not to laugh. Portia raised her head. "What? You know I hate it when the toppings fall off!"

Portia liked to have everything in place, and this trait spilled into every part of her life. Lena had observed how Portia compartmentalized her life into neat little sections, and assumed it was to keep herself from falling apart.

Portia looked Lena in the eye. "Listen . . . I need to explain why I reacted the way I did earlier."

"You don't have to if it brings up unhappy memories."

Portia shook her head. "No, I want to tell you about it." She lowered her fork. "Your fit brought back some memories from my childhood. Some which I thought had been long buried; but when I saw you lying there, they burst through as though they'd happened yesterday." She put down her fork and knife and picked at a hangnail. "There'd been mornings where I found my mother lying rigid with her head swaying from side to side. It always scared the daylights out of me. I was much too young to understand . . ."

She cleared her throat and glanced at Lena, who sat listening without saying a word. "One weekend, the fit became so violent, I wasn't able to stop it. I ran to the garden and called for my dad. He didn't know I'd been dealing with this during the week while he was at work. I did my best to take care of her, keep her safe. I just didn't know how to do it anymore—" Tears streamed down Portia's face.

Lena handed her a napkin. "I'm sorry, Portia. That's a lot to deal with at such a young age." She looked down at her hands. "But please don't worry about me. I'm all right."

"My mother always said the same thing."

Lena sat across from her and tried hard to remain calm. She bit her tongue, but what she really wanted to say was, *I'm nothing like your mother.* Instead, she said, "I'm not ill. Please trust me."

Her friend's shoulders slouched. "Okay, I'll try, but I just can't forget the look you had in your eyes this morning."

When Lena placed her hand on Portia's arm, a sudden spasm gripped and held her by the back of her neck. It pricked and burned her skin like nettles. The sensation of Portia's fears overwhelmed her. Lena released her hold and leaned back in her seat.

Lena hesitated as she watched her friend finish her slice of pizza, imagining her flatmate dealing with such a horrible tragedy. However, she was still not ready to divulge her recent discoveries with her friend. She would offer Portia something else, if only to appease and return her trust.

"Thanks for sharing about your mother with me. I can't imagine the guilt you must have experienced while carrying that kind of responsibility so young." Lena stopped, then resumed, revealing part of her own history. "I, too, survived the loss of my parents when I was young."

Portia's eyes stopped and remained on her. "What happened?"

Lena looked away. "My parents died in a boating accident in Venice. My mother died on impact. Papa survived a few days before succumbing to his injuries."

Portia's hands flew up to her face, covering her eyes. "Oh, that's awful!"

Lena shifted in her seat, her left hand tucking a strand of hair behind her ear. "I was supposed to go on holiday with them, but at the last minute, my parents decided it was best that I stay with my grandmother." Her voice must have betrayed the hidden feelings she had suppressed for so long, because Portia reacted almost immediately.

"I'm guessing you weren't too happy about that, but thank goodness you didn't go."

"Yeah, but if I'd gone, they might have lived." Lena blinked away her tears.

Portia gently touched her arm. "You mustn't think that way."

"Anyway, it was a long time ago . . ." Lena pressed her lips together before saying any more.

"How utterly horrible!" Portia drew closer, as if trying to close up the space between them. "I honestly didn't know—"

Lena shifted in her seat. "How could you have known?"

"Who took care of you after that?"

"An aunt and uncle—my father's youngest sister and her husband. They adopted me and I moved to Canada." Lena fiddled with a loose thread at her shirt's seam.

She had unlocked her secret vault of memories by sharing her story, triggering another recollection to emerge—one she had tucked away in the back of her mind.

LENA ~ PROVENCE, 2000

As a child, Lena had lain on her back in the bathtub with her head under water and her legs stretched out, her toes barely touching the opposite end of the tub. She played this game right before the soap and suds soiled the pure bath water.

As she stared up at the ceiling, the clear liquid whirled in front of her eyes. On the one breath she had taken, she lingered below the surface, counting the seconds away. She would try to stay under for much longer this time.

Just as the tickling behind her ear started, her body convulsed. Her mother's loud footsteps pounded on the bathroom floor, and her shrieks echoed under the bathwater. "Lena, what are you doing?"

Lena coughed on the air that filled her lungs when her mother hauled her from the water and wrapped her in a warm towel.

When Lena had finally caught her breath, she patted her mother's arm. "*Maman,* it's okay. I dreamed I could breathe under the water."

"Don't be silly, my little Lena; you can't breathe underwater. You must put an end to your games—"

"But, *Maman* . . . They're not games. They're real!"

Her mother gripped her arms and scolded her. "Magdalena! You must promise you will *never* again play these water games, nor speak to anyone about these silly dreams. Do you hear me? Never!" Her mother's voice had broken mid-sentence, and she pleaded, "Promise me, Lena?"

Lena shook her head, startled by her mother's reaction. She had never seen her tremble like that before.

"I promise."

LENA ~ FLORENCE, PRESENT DAY

It was late in the evening when Lena reached the Dolce Vita. Her friends sat on the patio of their favourite bar restaurant that, like most eateries in Florence, spilled out into the main square. Lena shrieked, overjoyed to be with them again, as they smothered her with kisses and hugs.

These were some of her and Portia's newfound confidantes since their arrival in Florence. They had bonded quickly over their love of the city and their adjustments to the new culture. Since meeting at various university excursions, they had become inseparable.

Christina took her turn and wrapped her arms around Lena, her slim build pulled tight against Lena's in a genuine hug. "We've missed you! You shouldn't stay away so long, Lena."

Lena nodded in agreement. "How's Neurobiology going?"

Christina's auburn hair fell over her oval face, and the roll of her clear, mint green eyes served as an answer.

Gregory snuck in and greeted Lena with a bear hug. He released his hold and drew back, putting his arms up in dramatic fashion. "Don't even ask me how my linguistics and anthropology work are going." The two pals laughed. "Our dear Lena—always tucked away behind your books. You need to come out and play with us more often." Portia smiled and winked at her.

It had been far too long since Lena had gone out with her pals, but a quick glance around revealed his absence.

Christina leaned over. "Marco hates coming out when you're not around. Why don't you visit him?" Her scolding tone had been unmistakable.

Lena's breath caught sharply, as if Christina had broadsided her. "You're right. Tomorrow . . . I'll go tomorrow. I want to spend this evening with you guys. Get my mind off school!"

Christina's attitude softened. "He'll be delighted to see you. But you're right, we're celebrating your return to civilization tonight."

Lena laughed, lifted her shot, and threw it back. She banged her empty glass on the table. "Waiter! We need a refill!"

THE GROUP'S banter became frenzied as the evening progressed, reminding Lena of the early days spent debating literature, movies, travel, art, and other hot discussions on sociological behaviour, religion, and scientific discoveries.

Christina sat forward at some point that night, as if poised to reveal a secret. "I saw a movie called *Flatliners* the other day. Have you guys seen it?"

Portia's eyes widened. "You're referring to the one in which a group of medical students stop their hearts and travel to the *other* side?"

"Yes. I can't seem to get it out of my head, but I'm almost confident it's not possible."

Augustus Reilly laughed. He had once told Lena he had immediately fallen in love with Christina's dulcet Highlander tones when she had called in response to his advertisement for a roommate.

Augustus poked Christina's rib. "Deary, it's only a movie."

Christina protested just as the waiter brought out more shot glasses. "I know, but it's got me contemplating. What if it were possible to separate the spirit from the physical body? We'd be able to capture spiritual energy."

"That's sweet. Our friendly neuroscientist wants to capture someone's soul," Augustus joked, and around the table, laughter erupted.

Augustus touched Christina's hand, letting it linger a little longer than usual. Her cheeks burned to a shade of peach, blending in with her hair's copper highlights.

Lena caught the glint in Augustus's eyes. "You know I'm just teasing you, my sweet Christina."

"Yes, Mr. Quantum, I know." She glared at him with a fake pout.

Gregory snickered. "Ironic isn't it, Augustus? Aren't you researching time travel?"

"To be exact, it's quantum physics," Augustus explained, "and I was only making light fun."

"Now, boys, let it go." Christina always hated confrontation, even in jest.

As Lena listened to the conversation, her left foot tapped under the table. She wondered whether Christina's mention of the movie about out-of-body experiences had been a coincidence, considering her own recent incident. Was Christina having similar experiences? Lena's mind whirled when suddenly Augustus turned his attention to her.

"Lena, what are *you* doing during your time away from us?"

Locking her gaze on Augustus, she stumbled over her words. "Oh, I've been busy doing research. Working on my dissertation."

Lena was a terrible liar. When she reached for her drink, her hand trembled. She wanted to steer away from this line of questioning; however, Augustus was relentless.

"Seems you've been spending time with *David* again. I'm getting terribly jealous!"

"Well, get in line, darling!" Lena imitated Zsa Zsa Gabor's accent as she pointed to an invisible line in front of her. Then she shifted in her seat, her face flushed, not from Augustus's teasing (as he might have believed) but from the memory of the earlier debacle at the Galleria. She did not share her embarrassing incident with them, for fear they would ask too many questions.

When the spotlight was no longer on her, Lena exchanged a puzzled look with Portia, who returned her scowl with a shrug. Without a doubt, Portia had said something to the group in her absence. Augustus's gaze returned to her, and he was ready to say something else when Lena interrupted. "Enough about me. How's your work moving along, Augustus Reilly? What's the latest news in the quantum field?"

As always, Augustus fell for the question hook, line, and sinker. He loved sharing his study on the theories of quantum physics. And he went on and on until Christina interrupted him.

"Enough, you're killing us. You don't know when to stop. Come on, everyone, let's drink up."

But Lena's ears had perked up during one of Augustus's theories. He had touched upon something interesting. Later on, while the others were on another tangent conversation, she tapped Augustus on the arm.

"Do you think we could get together at lunch tomorrow? I need you to explain those theories in more detail?"

"I'm irresistible, aren't I? My place?"

She laughed and shook her head at his flirtatiousness, which she never took seriously.

"Let's connect *here*. Half-past three tomorrow?"
"Oh, all right. Can't blame me for trying!"

After a long night of clowning around and commiserating, the bartender at La Dolce Vita told them it was time to go home. They were the last customers to leave, as they careened down the small streets, giddy with drunkenness.

They sang Beatles songs in reverse, parodying an earlier time when rock and roll caused worldwide protests by religious zealots claiming the songs delivered a message of evil.

Gregory giggled and turned to the group. "*Shh*, we mustn't wake up the watchdogs."

When the group had exhausted their supply of songs defying the gods of censorship, they parted, mumbling their goodnights as they headed home.

Enveloped by the lingering fragrance of jasmine in the night air, Lena became distracted by the sudden scent of burnt paper. A shiver skittered through her. In Florence, past, present, and future remained intertwined, locked within the threads of time.

Arm in arm with Portia, Lena recalled the earlier upheaval occurring close to where they walked—at least five hundred years earlier. There had been a similar attack on creativity fuelled by religious dogma.

In 1494, a monk named Girolamo Savonarola had amassed a youth army to spread his word. In the Piazza della Signoria, he had ordered the burning of art, books, and objects considered frivolous or unorthodox—known as the *Bonfire of the Vanities*.

3
BRAES OF ULLAPOOL

CHRISTINA ~ FLORENCE, PRESENT DAY

Christina sipped on coffee as she sat across from Augustus at their kitchen table. Augustus lowered his section of the morning paper and tapped his fingers. The drumming turned into a loud stampede inside her head. She tried to ignore him, but her own mind was restless.

Something had happened to her, shaking her to the core. Seeing that movie had burst her mind wide open for some odd reason. But why was she even contemplating journeying to other dimensions?

As she nibbled on her toast, she sensed his eyes boring into her. She lifted her head and glared at him.

"What's on your mind?"

"Just curious because of yesterday evening . . . Okay, look, you've never spoken about the metaphysical world. So . . . I'm intrigued."

"Why? Because I'm usually so 'practical'?"

She always hated when people mimicked big air quotes, but here she was with her fingers in the air.

Augustus's face reddened. "Yeah, I guess . . ."

Heat rose to Christina's face as well. "I'll have you know behind all this practicality, I do have a vivid imagination. When I was a kid, I used to dream I could fly and soar above the clouds—"

Her Scottish rogue grew sharper as her irritation intensified. She stopped suddenly, clamping her mouth shut. She had revealed long forgotten emotions, ones she had worked so hard to keep under wraps.

Augustus's lips curled upwards the more she became agitated. "Oh no, no, no, you're not stopping now." He waved his finger at her. "You *must* tell me more about your dreams. I'll only keep asking until you do."

She took quick sips of her coffee, knowing full well he meant it.

"Where shall I start then?"

"It was a dark and stormy night when Christina Carmichael of the Clan Carmichael . . ." He rolled his r's and mimicked her drawl.

Their laughter broke the quiet morning. Augustus could have asked her to read the phone book for all she cared, and she would have done it. She took a deep breath and journeyed back to her childhood with him.

"It was a dark and stormy night in the Scottish Highlands. I was an only child growing up in a small coastal town called Ullapool, where magic, folklore, and myths were borne. And, yes, I was a practical child, a teensy bit beyond my years."

Memories flooded her mind.

"I spent my afternoons playing alone in the hills, in the nooks and crannies of the land." She paused and lingered in the memory of the experience.

"Every inch of that valley lives within me like a breath of air. Without it, I am nothing."

And yet, it had been a while since she had ventured to think about that time in her life. She looked away from Augustus and stared out their kitchen window. The fleeting wisp of a childhood dream floated about her mind like a leaf wafting to the ground, nudged by a gentle breeze . . .

Her toes gripped the cliff's edge. Below, the valley and the sea sprawled out in front of her as far as her eyes could see. The wind swirled around her tiny frame. She extended her arms above her shoulders with fingers pointed. Freedom. If she pushed off, she'd soar above the clouds, swoop into the Lowlands, and skim across the ocean waves. Wiggling her toes further over the stone ledge, she dove into the valley's wide-open air . . .

Christina took another sip and pursed her lips. Her coffee had gone tepid. Her parents' reaction after she had told them about her dream came rushing back to mind. She sat back, pinned to her seat.

Augustus caressed her hand with a gentleness that warmed her heart. "I'm sorry for overstepping my bounds of friendship with you again. Didn't mean to pry. You're upset now, I can tell."

She shook her head. "It's okay, I don't mind. I should talk about it. I'm not sure why, but my childhood keeps coming up lately."

"If you're up to continuing, I'm here."

Christina picked up from where she had left off and recounted her dream to him.

"When I told my parents about my dream, they began to act in a strange manner. Life under their new rules became unbearable. I constantly daydreamed of running away. Of course, I never did." She paused. "In the end, however, my wish came true."

Augustus leaned forward in his chair. "How?"

"Nothing mysterious." She laughed. "I went away to an all-girls boarding school on the coast, and then, later on, to the National Academy in Coventry. I never returned to live with my parents."

The images of her life played before her eyes, and her chest tightened.

"Even now, my visits with them are awkward. I believe when

they sent me away, it gave them the freedom to stop worrying. I'm still unsure why, but I became too much for them. To this day, I have no clue why things changed after I'd told them about my dreams. It was just weird."

"Yeah, that is strange."

Then, like the sun's rays beaming through a dark cloud, Augustus broke into a wide grin.

"Hang on. Did you say the National Academy in Coventry? Um . . . you weren't just *any* child; you were a child prodigy."

She yanked her hand away from his. "Augustus! You're incorrigible. Yes, I went to the Academy, now leave it alone, will ya?"

"Okay, but this conversation is far from done."

Christina wrinkled her nose and flashed him a devilish grin in reply. "You're right. Now, it's your turn. What's your secret, Mister Reilly?"

And Augustus grinned like Lewis Carroll's mischievous Cheshire cat.

LENA

The waning afternoon light settled into the city like a comforting friend. Lena walked through the piazza while couples strolled, giggled, and leaned into each other, talking to one another in private. Wisps of feathery cirrus clouds floated high in the atmosphere. A unicyclist twirled on his lone tire, showing off the art of balance.

In the distance, an ice-cream man pushed his cart, while his eerie chimes drifted through the square. The silver-haired man lifted his head and gazed at Lena. His familiar expression touched her. She searched her memory as children ran past in a frenzy toward his cart, the shrill of their screams echoing in the air. Why was he staring at her like that? Did she remind him of someone?

Had they met before? A recollection tickled at the back of her mind, but she was not quite able to grasp it.

Lena halted and looked around in wonder at the magical aura of colours that swirled around the children. Filaments of bright lights trailed after them like fireflies. She blinked to make sure her eyes were not playing tricks on her.

"Lena!"

She turned toward the call. Augustus stood and waved at her. As she approached the cafe, she glanced back, but the light show had vanished. Augustus followed her gaze out to the piazza.

"What's caught your eye?"

"Oh, nothing. I was just marvelling at the children running toward the ice cream man." Lena greeted Augustus with a kiss on the cheek.

"Ah, I remember those days. It seems like years ago now. So glad to see you." He paused. "Look, I want to apologize for my behaviour last night."

Augustus's cheeks flushed with colour, and Lena clucked her tongue to dismiss his apology.

"Shush. It was a wonderful evening. Really nice to see everyone again. I get busy. . ."

"You do keep very busy." Augustus's almond-shaped eyes gleamed, and despite his constant lightness of being, there always lingered an underlying sadness around his laugh lines. It made her wonder about his past.

After ordering coffee and croissants, Augustus was the one who got right down to it. "Now, what do you want to learn about quantum physics?"

Lena grinned at the abrupt change in topic. Augustus had beaten her to it, and it had caught her by surprise. She had intended to initiate the conversation. While she fidgeted and massaged her palms, uncertain where to begin, the waiter arrived and set down their food. The interruption gave her a moment to pull herself together.

Dropping her hands to her lap, she leaned forward over her steaming cup of coffee. She needed to share her thoughts with someone, and who better than Augustus to tell her the truth?

"Before we go any further, I ask that you please keep our conversation between us in confidentiality. At least till I sort through everything."

He shifted in his seat and lowered his voice to a whisper. "Lena, whatever you share is safe with me, I swear."

Thank God, because she needed Augustus's help with this. And without warning, her father sat at the table in front of her. He leaned forward with his chin rested on one hand, as he awaited her story. It was something he had always done when he was alive. Her chest tightened, and she blinked back the tears pricking her eyes. She looked away to regain her composure. When she turned to face forward again, her father had vanished, and Augustus sat quietly waiting for her to begin.

It all came pouring out of her—the events that had taken over her life and her uncertainty about their authenticity. She paused frequently, worried about Augustus's reaction. Throughout it all, the waiter came back twice with coffee. And, like her father, Augustus listened until she concluded her narrative.

By the time she was finished, the noise coming from the square had faded into the background. She braced herself, afraid her friend would think she had lost her mind. "So . . . what do you make of this?" Her voice rose a pitch higher than usual. "It sounds crazy, right?"

Augustus sat stoic, though she pictured his thoughts bouncing about in his head like neurons firing. He remained silent.

"Augustus?"

In deep thought, he flicked his index finger across his lips. "To be honest, I'm bewildered. The level of detail is incredible." Then, as if to stress his just-rolled-out-of-bed appearance, he ran his fingers through his messy strawberry blond hair. "The web and threads of light you described are both intriguing, but I'm not sure what to say about the experience you had with your fingers." Augustus sipped his coffee, which had probably cooled by now. He grimaced and set the cup back down. "And I apologize if my skepticism offends you, but it's instilled in me."

Lena had expected this reaction, familiar with this kind of response as if it were her own. A wall had gone up, except his walls were porous, and what she had shared with him had filtered through. He would need time to process the information. She would simply have to wait.

A shaft of sunlight pierced through the cumulus clouds, which hovered above. The piazza lit up with a splash of brightness, and a weight lifted from her shoulders.

The waiter came to refill their coffees. Augustus broke his croissant in half and continued on the theories of quantum physics as if she had not just dropped a bombshell on his lap.

"First off, quantum physics is the science of matter and energy and their interaction. It exists in the microscopic realm and changes are so minute we cannot see them with our naked eye." He paused while Lena digested the information. "This is a radical theory suggesting reality is not as orderly nor as predictable as one would think. In fact, it implies we base life on chance and probability."

She had come to the right person. His easy-going nature allowed him to escape the trappings of an arrogant temperament, which often accompanied intelligence.

"For every single event, there are several possibilities and results. In ordinary life, the peculiarities of quantum mechanics are difficult to grasp at the human level since they would allow us to see every probability at the same time. Wouldn't that drive you mad?"

Lena's eyes narrowed. Her mind connected the dots.

"So this theory is like the Butterfly Effect: the flapping of a butterfly's wing in a forest in South America triggers a chain of events causing a hurricane in China."

"Along the same lines, but on a microscopic and unseen scale."

She hesitated before broaching the next question.

"What about going back in time?" She bit on her bottom lip and nervously twirled her hair. "Is that included in these theories?"

Augustus arched a brow at Lena and he leaned back and stretched his shoulders. "Time travel?"

Lena could tell she had startled him with that one. She waited.

"Time travel is a completely different animal. That theory veers off from the idea that—"

Augustus's voice broke midway through his sentence. He looked away, watching as the hustle and bustle of the afternoon's rush hour gained momentum. His eyes glistened, and Lena shifted in her seat. She had never witnessed this side of him.

"Everything okay?"

"Um, yes, yes, of course, it's all good." He cleared his throat and turned back to face her. "I'm sorry. A childhood memory distracted me."

She touched his hand. "I didn't mean to be a bother. Should we do this another time?"

A shadow crossed his expression. "No, I was just remembering my older brother, Seamus. We built a time machine together when we were boys."

"You've never mentioned you had a brother."

But, come to think of it, none of the group had ever spoken about their families. Augustus's bittersweet smile showed he was not ready to talk about it further. Instead, he continued to expound on the theories of quantum mechanics.

"Now, here's something similar to time travel. There's another theory called the String Theory, which suggests the universe is comparable to slices in a loaf of bread. Each slice is attached by strings—too minute for the naked eye—that are like glue, holding the universe together. These strings or loops stretch to a three-dimensional plane similar to large membranes, called *branes*.

"Branes vibrate at different frequencies. They are like slices of bread from a single loaf alongside each other. These *slices* exist without touching, though there are exceptions.

Lena's eyes widened. "You mean like a parallel existence?"

"Something to that effect. It's possible you're vibrating at a certain energetic rate and this dream place or person is also fluctuating at the same frequency, causing a hiccup in the continuum."

The universe weighed on Lena's shoulders again.

"Remember, these are just theories. I can't explain why you're having these vivid dreams without looking further into them." A moment later, Augustus's phone beeped. He read the message and looked at his watch.

"I'm sorry. I have to get going. Let's discuss this further. Will you call me if you have any other incidents?"

"Of course! I apologize for keeping you this long!"

Augustus dropped some change on the table. "*Au contraire,* you have reeled me in with your story. I simply forgot I had to be somewhere else."

Left sitting by herself, Lena watched the crowd in the square. She contemplated whether branes, such as in Augustus's explanation of string theory, could encapsulate unique moments in time, from the past or the future. Instead of slices of bread, she pictured bed sheets hanging on clotheslines, touching at the slight waft of a breeze. As she became lost in her thoughts, she imagined a conversation with her father.

If branes—like two of the wafting bed linens—ever touched another, could it generate a vortex, allowing energy to traverse from one moment in time to another?

Lena leaned back in her seat, as if awaiting a reply. Just then, a sparrow settled near her table. Her eyes widened, and she glanced around her, expecting her father to reappear. But she found herself alone.

Augustus's theories flittered through her mind as she opened her notebook and jotted down: *Thought provokes action, and action invokes reality.*

As THE SUN sank behind the horizon, Lena left the cafe and made her way to Marco's apartment, just steps away from the Ponte Vecchio. Early evening in the streets of this old city always cast a spell on her. In the setting sun's fading light, the leaves on the trees glistened a silver green while the sky took on hues of pinks, purples, and oranges. The building facades gave off a look of airbrushed perfection, as did the stones in the homes' century old walls. An eerie sensation—though, a familiar one—rushed through Lena as if she had walked this same path for centuries.

Lena had not seen Marco in two weeks, but at Christina's prodding the evening before, she paid him a visit. She entered his building, taking in its old and faded walls. While the entrance door stood solid, and the newly renovated ceramic floors shined, the stairs remained ancient—grand and creaky. A fleeting memory eluded her as she ascended the stairs.

At Marco's door, she knocked, and the familiar shuffle of his footsteps resounded on the other side. The door opened wide and the scent of his oil paints flooded the hallway. Marco stood on the threshold, bright colours splattered across his T-shirt and shorts. He always looked glorious whenever she caught him in the middle of an intense period of creativity.

Marco sometimes disappeared for days whenever he became immersed in painting. In the beginning, this had instilled resentment in her. But as their relationship developed, Lena learned to pick up on his cues. Marco needed these moments of solitude to reconnect with himself, and she would reassure him by saying, "I need time too, to work without interruption."

This time, she had been the one who had abandoned herself to her work. As he stood at the doorway, his hair fell across his brow and a shadow of doubt rushed across his face. She stepped forward and leaned against the door's frame.

"Am I still welcome here?"

Marco let out a sigh of relief, as if he had been holding in his breath. He gathered her into his arms and held her tight. "Yes, of course. I've missed you terribly."

She blinked back the tears that threatened to spill over and followed him into the loft. "I've missed you too."

With time, Marco had also learned to invite her into his space as a welcome break instead of an intrusion. "Christina called and told me you had drinks with them last night . . ."

"Yes, I did. You should have come."

Whenever Lena spent time with Marco, an impenetrable cocoon surrounded her, keeping her safe.

Marco took her hand. "I would've if I'd known you'd be there. I-I don't like it when you're not around."

Lena sat on the couch while Marco went to the kitchen to prepare tea for them. Though she shared most of her experiences with him, she kept her recent experiences to herself, trusting Augustus not to betray her confidences.

They made up for lost time by talking and exchanging their thoughts about Renaissance painters, techniques, and books they had recently read. Marco always dove deep into each topic, constantly digging further, never satisfied with just one facet of a discussion or concept. His energy invigorated her.

After they had caught up, Marco led her to his bed. They lay face-to-face, cradling each other in the slight cool of the evening, as church bells rang in the distance. They explored each other while a breeze blew in through his open windows. As evening set, the room glowed with the setting sun, while their shadows danced and melted into one another.

Afterward, as they lay entwined, a perceptible distance wedged itself between them again. Marco enfolded her as if to keep her from slipping away.

"Tell me what's going on."

Lena retreated and attempted to explain, but could not bring herself to reveal the truth. "I can't talk about it right now. I promise I'll share it with you soon, when I figure it out. All I can say is, it's something unique, and much more powerful than anything I've ever known."

"So . . . it's not me?"

Lena put her hand on his chest. "Oh Marco, no, it's not you. You see, I don't even think it's about me."

As he nuzzled her and heaved a sigh of relief, she knew that this questioning was far from over. But, at least for today, it was done.

When his body relaxed against hers, a wave of remorse washed over her. She had never imagined he would suffer from her silences. After all, he had always been the one to retreat first. Marco gazed down at her, and Lena squirmed. As if he sensed her reluctance, he kissed the top of her head and let her escape from his hold.

Moments later, he slipped on his trunks, got out of bed, and wandered over to his canvas. She followed him with her eyes, tracing the contour of his body. Her gaze reached his calves and his feet while her mind drifted back to the waves of energy she had witnessed grazing at the statue's feet.

He looked over to where she lay on his bed. "You don't mind if I continue painting?"

"Not at all . . ."

She was already halfway to sleep when Marco picked up his brushes and continued on his creative journey while she escaped their world.

WHEN LENA AWOKE, she was alone in Marco's bed. The echo of her voice bounced around the apartment's walls when she called out for him. She rubbed her eyes, checked her watch, and stumbled over to his window.

The first rays of sunlight peeked over the rooftops. Florence awoke with the early morning hustle and bustle of merchants. Scents from the street floated upward, invading the cool morning air.

She relished the mornings when the city's residents awakened, a vastly distinct culture in contrast to the throngs of tourists that arrived every day. Florentines walked these streets from birth to death, retracing their steps day after day. If younger generations with restless souls left the city to forge their futures, it was only to return, finding no other place on earth like Florence.

With her head still drowsy from sleep, Lena closed the window and returned to the comfort of Marco's warm bed. The odour of oil-based pigments drifted to her side of the room, transporting her back to her mother's studio.

She turned onto her side and stared at his array of brushes and paints on the narrow table. They acted as a divider between his bedroom and the studio. Her breathing slowed, and she slid into another deep sleep.

A SUDDEN COMMOTION STARTLED HER. Lena mumbled and tried to move, but a pressure forced her down on the bed. A blast and a harsh whistling shrill filled her ears. Lena was powerless against this force. A loud buzz began, like a bee caught in her ear, and the walls caved in as she struggled to open her eyes against the blinding spotlights.

The buzzing in her ear became unbearable. Shielding her eyes with one hand, she observed the gloomy shadows lurking beyond the brightness. With her shoulders pressed back against her pillow, an overwhelming sensation of paralysis pinned her down as if her body had become suctioned against a curved tunnel wall. A few minutes later, silence. The force released and her body slumped, the sudden void making her head spin.

Lena's ears rang, and the odd stillness in the unexpected darkness disoriented her. She floated in a vacuum of nothingness while vertigo removed any spatial cues. With her heart thumping hard within her chest, Lena hoped for some sign of existence—a point of reference—within this dark abyss.

As she searched around her, a yellow line on the horizon glowed, illuminating the grid-like formation she had seen in her other dream. The gradual change in the vast and tenebrous expanse provided her some relief.

Lena squeezed her eyelids together to centre herself. Free-floating within this limitless three-dimensional space, a soothing sensation came over her. A weightlessness. And her worries faded. But where was she?

4
VAGUE NOTIONS

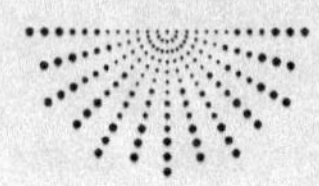

DAMIAN ~ FLORENCE, 1500

THE STUDIO ROOM WAS BRIGHT, with abundant sunlight streaming in through the spacious bay windows. Damian squinted at the glare sparkling off the river.

The buildings on the other bank were reflected in the water, visible from the stage where he stood perched higher than the rest of the artist's workshop. From his elevated position, his gaze drifted from the window to the room's floor, littered with sketches of his likeness.

Damian hopped off and bent down to pick up one of the drawings. When he reached for it, a thin, pale, and feminine arm extended from his body. He jerked upright, shook his limb, and dropped the sheet of paper.

A voice boomed from behind him, and Damian swivelled to face it. The artist peeked from behind his easel and glared at him. "How do you expect me to finish my studies if you keep moving?"

The man bordered on unkempt, his dark moustache and beard in disarray. A solemn expression graced an angular face, ruddy and framed by high cheekbones.

"Excuse me, sir. I don't know what came over me?"

"Just get back to your pose."

Michelangelo's voice sounded curt from weariness. Despite his gruff ways, deep-set eyes underlined an inner sensitivity and a compassionate nature. Only his crooked nose exaggerated his stubborn disposition. And though his lips were full, his rigid mouth betrayed a fickle temperament.

Damian re-assumed the position he had held all morning. Restless, he struggled to keep his thoughts under control. His eyes wandered about the room and caught his reflection in the mirror in the studio's far corner. A peculiar, foreign sensation swept through him.

Michelangelo's eyes bulged as he looked up from his sketch.

"Damiano, I need you to focus. I cannot work like this! Please, you are being well-paid for your time."

Damian's cheeks flushed as heat rose to his face; his heart palpitated. He tucked his hair behind his ear with his left hand and pulled the sling out of place.

"Do not fiddle with your locks and keep your left side still."

In a huff, Michelangelo bustled over and climbed the podium's stairs. "Please hold the sling up to your left shoulder. Let your right arm hang with the stone. Just like every other time."

With a furrowed brow, he rearranged the sling and the angle of Damian's elbow. Damian gritted his teeth while Michelangelo fussed over him until he found the correct posture. Damian frowned as he glanced out at the beautiful day beyond the window.

The maestro clapped his hands once. "That's perfect! Now keep that expression!"

Michelangelo returned to his easel and continued drawing. He sketched with such intensity; Damian did not dare disturb him again. It was midday before the artist spoke.

"You may take a short break."

Damian breathed a deep sigh. He bent forward and held his knees. Stiff, his back ached from hours of maintaining the same position. A sudden increase in dominance on his left side threw his body off balance. Why did it not feel like his own? He tried to loosen the strain by moving around and stretching his limbs.

Michelangelo opened his mouth to speak, but a soft knock interrupted him. They both glanced toward the studio door. The maestro clicked his tongue on the roof of his mouth before responding to the interruption.

"You may enter."

The artist's tone was brusque as he continued to set up for his next drawing. He then motioned with a twirl of his hand for Damian, whose muscles still ached, to resume his pose.

A man entered. He waited in the corner in silence. Michelangelo still had not given this man a single glance. Damian craned his neck for a better look at the stranger.

Michelangelo bristled. "Damiano, stop fidgeting and keep your head still!"

From the dim corner of the studio, the man tapped his foot. Michelangelo, deeply immersed in his work, ignored him. Eventually, the man stepped out of the shadows.

From the corner of his eye, Damian saw a well-groomed man with a distinguished, handsome expression. A vague notion came to Damian that this man was the other master—Leonardo da Vinci.

The man, dressed in loose pants and a short tunic, stood confident and tall. With long and flowing hair, he drew attention to his handsome face. His eyes, although gentle, maintained an intense gaze, and his aquiline nose suggested a proud demeanour. He also boasted a salt-and-pepper moustache and a beard that reached down to his chest.

"Michelangelo, we must speak. In private."

Michelangelo banged his charcoal stick on the table with such force, both Damian and the man jumped.

"Damiano, please give me a moment with Leonardo. We will

continue our work afterward. Run to the Ponte Vecchio and bring us some bread and drink."

Damian's eyes flickered upon hearing Leonardo's name. His assumption had been correct. Michelangelo gave him a tunic and a few coins, and shooed him away.

He wore the tunic Michelangelo had given him and left silently. Closing the studio door behind him, he pressed his ear to it. The masters' conversation began almost as soon as he had gotten out of sight—quiet, but overflowing with passion.

"Micielo, you stay as focused as ever. How I wish I were more like you."

Michelangelo emitted a heavy-ladened sigh, one Damian had gotten used to hearing. He had also caught the endearing diminutive Leonardo had used.

"Leonardo, you are a passionate man, but I am one with a troubled conscience. What brings you here today, interrupting my work?"

Feet shuffled behind the door. One man paced the studio's floor.

"Michelangelo, I have watched you grow and flourish from a distance. In Ghirlandaio's studio, I observed your work. You were already a diamond—a little rough, but cut to perfection. A powerful artist."

While papers rustled, Leonardo continued to speak. "Look at this perfection. You will create the masterpiece of all times."

"Sir, I have not even begun the statue. I wish you wouldn't set me upon that pedestal of yours. I am certain you will cast me aside the moment I am no longer deemed worthy to remain there."

"Never, not in all my lifetime!" The emotion in Leonardo's voice was palpable.

Michelangelo huffed. "My friend, I may be the younger man, but I know you better than you know yourself. We put on this show of antagonism between us, for the world to see, but sometimes I think you take it too much to heart. I don't know whether to believe or trust you anymore."

"Michelangelo, I will always respect you . . . which brings me to the reason for my visit. The majority council wants you to join me and work with us."

Leonardo's voice had been assertive, but Michelangelo pushed back, his answer abrupt and final.

"Leonardo, you definitely do not mince words. I'm telling you, once and for all, I'm fine with who and where I am; well-respected by these people. I have no problem with feigning rivalry, but I will not become involved in whatever you have planned, or the Council, for that matter. Now, there's nothing left to discuss."

"Fine, I'll leave it alone. For now. We *will* confer again at some point. Face your legacy. You cannot avoid it forever."

A creak rippled across the floorboards. Damian, afraid of being caught, scampered down the stairs.

ONCE OUTSIDE, Damian ran toward the Ponte Vecchio. As he passed a group of young men, one called out to him. It was his cousin, Giancarlo.

"Hey Damian, where are you going in such a hurry? You still posing for that crazy painter?"

He turned his head and barked at him. "What's it to you?"

The boys' laughter stopped. Another broke away and ran up alongside him. He took hold of Damian's arm to slow him down. Damian stopped, his mouth rigid.

Identical to his own, his brother's wavy hair blew about his face in the soft breeze and his crystal blue eyes narrowed.

"We were just teasing you."

"Dante, please don't bother me right now."

"What's wrong?"

"Nothing. All is well. Look, I don't have time."

"You don't sound like yourself. Is it the artist? Is he treating you well?"

"What?" Damian glared at his brother. "Yes, the artist treats me better than anyone I have ever worked for."

Dante loosened his grip. His lips curled into a half-smile. "I suppose. You are being paid a good sum of money."

Damian disentangled his arm from Dante's and turned toward the marketplace. He liked to live his life in peace, just the way it was. He did not have time to deal with Dante's facetious remarks. And he wanted to hurry back to the studio to eavesdrop further on the maestros' conversation.

"I have to go."

Damian left Dante behind him. When Damian reached the Ponte Vecchio, he slipped into the crowd. Finding his favourite shop on the bridge, he paid for bread, meat, and drink.

DAMIAN EXITED the crowded Ponte Vecchio and walked along the Arno River's side street. Dante and his group of friends were no longer loitering in the square. He sighed with relief and hurried back to Michelangelo's studio.

After he crept up the stairs, he pressed his ear to the door once more. The mood on the other side of the door had shifted. Leonardo spouted his opinion with vigour now.

"We cannot allow an orthodox bastard like Savonarola to destroy the creative world!"

Even Michelangelo made his voice heard. "Savonarola is an orthodox who believes we are being corrupted by our indiscretions. And, are we not?"

Leonardo fumed. "An artist speaks his truth." There was a silence, and then his voice intensified. "Your frescoes and statues describe your torments, your inner battles, and desires. The truth of your soul. How can that be corrupt?"

"My friend, I don't feel as though I am in control of my

creativity. To be truthful, the reality of who we are overwhelms me. And I don't believe we are any *different* from the people amongst whom we exist."

"We *are* different and must not forget who we are. For the sake of our survival. Please reconsider what I have asked of you."

Even though Damian could not see him, he sensed Michelangelo's reticence. The sound of walking echoed through the studio. Leonardo's tone had shifted yet again, this time to one of resignation.

"We are the keepers of the truth. It is also our duty to pass it on to others like us. Unfortunately, we must do so in secret or it could cause irreparable damage. My friend, I have to leave now but, mark my word, I will be back."

Footsteps marched toward the front door. The door handle jiggled, and Leonardo's voice erupted on the other side.

"Your *Statue of David* will represent the City of Florence, but he will also be the symbol of *our* existence and power."

Damian startled, scampered down a few steps, then turned back. When the door swung open, Leonardo made his way past him. He paused in his step, reached out to touch Damian's arm, and looked deep into his eyes. His voice was quiet, yet foreboding.

"Be careful. For what you witness isn't always the truth."

DANTE

Later that evening, as the city's light dimmed, Dante caught sight of his brother's wild curls amid the Piazza Santa Croce crowd. He had hoped to connect with Damian again, especially after their run-in earlier in the day. Dante caught up to him and nudged his arm.

Damian jolted at his touch. "*Cavolo*, you scared the hell out of me!"

Dante cast a sidelong glance at him. "You're very jumpy lately."

Damian offered no answer, and they strode together in silence.

When they entered their home, Damian moved to the kitchen's fireplace and stood with his back to Dante.

Dante snorted as he paced behind him. "You don't share your thoughts with me anymore, is that it?" Damian kept quiet, and Dante kept on him. "*Per favore*, Damiano, what's going on?"

Damian turned toward him and spat out his words. "I'm at the studio every day, working and posing. Nothing else."

"But you've changed since you started working there."

"I'm exactly the same as always."

"Is there something going on at the studio?"

"Look, if I can't understand half of what's happening in that studio, how could you?"

Anger welled up in Dante's chest. "You're assuming what I can or can't understand?" He could hardly breathe. Damian had never reacted to him in this manner, but when he spoke next, his tone had calmed.

"Leave it be, brother. I can handle it on my own."

Dante cocked his head. "Has something happened in that studio?"

"Just keep your nose out of it. This is my work. I don't meddle in yours, so stay out of mine."

Damian's words stung. A slap in his face. They had done almost everything together. True, their reactions differed, but nothing had ever been so odd that Damian could not confide in him. Dante flinched, but he continued to engage with his brother.

"Damiano, I *will* find out what's going on."

Damian's expression clouded, and he disappeared down the darkened hallway. He yelled at him from their shared bedroom.

"Dante, I mean it! Stay away! It's my life."

Dante remained at the fireplace, stewing over his brother's pointed words. The flames licked at the logs, and sparks crackled and popped where the wood was dry. He must manipulate Damian's schedule and pose in his place.

Dante, who had the same dark locks as Damian, could adjust

his hair in the same way his brother did. The twins had tested this trick frequently in their young lives.

But now, what came most to Dante's mind was the bond they shared, especially the one where they could sense when the other was in trouble. He recalled one such incident from their childhood.

One day, soon after their sixth birthday, Dante had stayed home while Damian went to the river with their mother. Dante had hurried to his father that afternoon, out of breath and his voice hoarse.

"Father, I can't breathe. Something's wrong with Damian! We have to go to him!"

Ronaldo tried to dispel Dante's distress but could not quieten him. They left to fetch Annabella and Damian after Dante became even more agitated.

When they reached the Ponte Vecchio, Annabella came running toward them with Damian in her arms, drenched and dripping with water. Pale and crying, she explained she had jumped into the river to save Damian, who had fallen in. As they walked back through the city, Dante clung to Damian's hand, which hung down from their father's shoulder, until they reached the safety of their home.

Now, as Dante stood before the fireplace, his stomach ached. The longer Damian continued to work for this maestro, the more distant he became. Dante had to find out what was driving a wedge between them.

LENA ~ FLORENCE, PRESENT DAY

The front door flew open and banged against the adjacent wall. Marco entered the apartment, his hands full of groceries.

"Damn door!"

A sudden jolt woke Lena from her sleep. The light flourish of Leonardo's hand on Damian's arm still lingered. Melancholy swept through her as she sat up and looked at her hands to reassure herself she was no longer dreaming. Dreams had a way of interfering with your reality. But had it been a dream? The perceptions, the emotions, and all the scents. Everything had been so vivid.

She fell back onto Marco's bed and stared at the ceiling, stunned by the events unfolding in her dream. Even the bustle of the Ponte Vecchio had been vibrant. Stalls and shops lined the bridge, looking similar to its modern-day version of goldsmith and jeweller's boutiques.

Lena leaned up on her elbow and faced Marco.

"Where did you go?"

"Went out. To get us breakfast."

Lena's stomach lurched, the same way it had the morning Portia had awoken her. Marco took one look at her, dropped the grocery bags, and came to her side.

"You look terrible! Are you sick?"

Her forehead was moist with tiny beads of sweat; her skin cold to the touch. She cleared her throat.

"Just feeling a little nauseous. I—I think I had a nightmare."

"You're pale. Lie back down." He jumped to his feet and hurried to the kitchen. "I'll make you a toast and coffee. Maybe something else too?"

Twenty minutes later, he brought out the breakfast he had made for her and sat on a chair beside the bed. After the feeling of nausea went away, she devoured the French toast topped with fresh strawberries.

After she was done, he sat on the bed and shuffled closer to her, but she scrunched her shoulders together and shrunk away from his touch. He halted and watched her with a sullen expression.

"Why are you pulling away just as we're getting close again?"

Her back stiffened. "What do you mean? I thought we had a great time last night. We reconnected, didn't we?"

"Yes, of course. It was amazing. We always have great energy together. But lately, when morning comes, you close in on yourself and hold me at arm's length again."

"Marco, this is who I am." She clenched her jaw. "I thought that you, of all people, would understand."

"You know I love you with all my heart, but it's hard when you won't let me in."

"What do you mean?" She slid off the bed in a huff. "I let you into my life. Tell you everything." And even as she uttered those last words, she knew she was lying to him.

Marco placed a hand on her arm. "This is what I mean. You always walk away when we talk about what's really going on." He took her hand. "Look, I'm just worried about what's going on with you, but I'll wait until you're ready to talk."

She blinked away the tears threatening to well up in her eyes. Why did she find it so difficult to let anyone in?

He caressed her arm. "Colour's coming back to your cheeks. If you're feeling better, I'll walk you home. It's on my way."

She picked up on the subtle cue. "I *am* feeling much better now, thanks to your breakfast."

When she looked down at his hand, a fleeting memory of her dream came floating back to the surface.

THE MORNING LIGHT had gone from bright sunshine to grey skies. It threatened rain by the time Lena and Marco arrived at her place. He kissed her cheek, and she watched as he rushed off. Why was he so patient with her? She hardly deserved someone like him.

As she crossed the front threshold, Portia arrived, holding a cup of coffee in her hand. She brushed up against Lena as they entered the building.

Portia's eyebrows twitched as she gave her a sidelong glance. "No beauty sleep?"

A hot tingle spread from Lena's neck to her face. Intimate comments about her relationship with Marco always made her blush. This time, though, a surge of regret seized her, and she tried to shake off the residual emotion from her morning discussion with Marco. She breathed in deep, careful to hide her feelings from her roommate. With a thick, chalky sensation in her throat, Lena coughed and let out a forced laugh.

"That's right, none."

Portia poked her in the ribs. "It was about time."

"Yes, I know." Lena lowered her eyes. "But Marco's been busy, too."

Portia took the stairs two at a time to their apartment, and Lena followed behind, relieved the conversation was over. Once inside, Lena settled in to go over her dissertation notes, but Portia danced around her. She fidgeted and rearranged miscellaneous objects on the shelves. Lena exhaled sharply.

"What is it now?"

Portia avoided her gaze. "I saw Augustus this morning."

Lena arched an eyebrow at her.

"You see him all the time."

"True, but he appeared quite curious about how you were doing. More than usual, that is."

Lena could always tell when Portia was determined to get an answer, so she obliged her, but did not give her the one she desired.

"Augustus is just being himself. Mister Curious, you know him. Doesn't he always ask for me when we're not together?"

Lena lowered her eyes to her papers. It was difficult not to share life things—important events—with her best friend. But Portia always wanted to help and get everyone involved. She liked to fix things and find solutions. And Lena feared she would lose the connection she had just made with the past if she shared too much.

Portia huffed. "You're a million miles away again."

"Sorry, my mind is buzzing with all the research I'm doing. My dissertation is taking a lot longer to complete. I'll admit it's getting the better of me."

"No kidding. And you're not taking care of yourself either."

Lena, impatient to get back to her work, approached Portia and gave her a hug.

"Thank you for being concerned about me."

"Why won't you just let me help you?"

Portia's aim had revealed itself. Lena found she had no other option except to placate her. "You help. Just by being my friend."

Portia sighed and reluctantly accepted Lena's response, and returned to her corner of the apartment. As Portia's sewing machine whirred, Lena returned to her work.

THE LIGHT PITTER-PATTER of rain upon the window panes lulled her, and she immediately became lost again in her reading on Michelangelo, Leonardo, and string theories. But the more she read, the further she got from finding any concrete answers.

Most critics were aware of the rivalry between these two artists. That was an obvious fact. She spent hours looking for any evidence of their friendship, but by midday she had still come up empty-handed.

In her dream, Michelangelo had mentioned "feigning antagonism" for the world to see. A bond existed between them. Their connection had been genuine and profound, so why keep it hidden?

The world beyond her window remained hazy, and raindrops snaked down the windowpane as the rain fell heavier. In the opaque world blurred by the storm, distant memories stirred within Lena of classical music drifting from her father's office while she played in her bedroom.

Lena puffed out her cheeks. She needed Augustus's help again but had an inkling he would recommend including Christina, who would leap at the chance to investigate Lena's brain matter. Christina was trustworthy, but Lena still hedged on letting anyone else in. She would give it another week before calling him.

5
KEEPING TIME

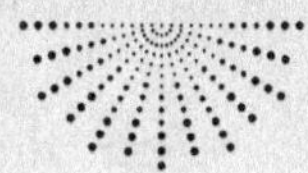

LENA ~ FLORENCE, PRESENT DAY

CALM AS A SPRING BREEZE, the week began without a hint of trouble. Eight days had passed since Lena's dream and she was eager to have another.

She stopped looking for signs and instead explored the realm of her dream. There, in her well of recollections, she discovered more about Leonardo and Michelangelo's friendship. With an inside scoop into their world, she had gained an intimate perspective on these artists through the master's young model. She had crossed the threshold of a potent energy, one she did not quite understand yet. But one thing niggled at her: the more she sought to grasp it, the more it slipped away.

At the Galleria's front entrance, she glanced around and noted that the guard from her previous visit was not there. She breathed a sigh of relief and covered her head with a headscarf, put on some tinted glasses, and walked straight to the Tribune.

The *Statue of David* stood aloof and distant. *David*'s expression reflected such intensity that tears shimmered in her eyes when she recalled Damian's furrowed expression in the studio's corner mirror.

Michelangelo had captured Damian's essence and encapsulated it within this grand pillar of marble.

Lena implored him to reach out to her. Despite her pleas, he stared fixedly at Goliath. Michelangelo's grumbling voice echoed in her mind. *Damian, how do you expect me to work if you keep moving?*

Lena half-smiled to herself and jotted a note on her pad. *I must be losing my mind.*

Just as she lifted her eyes from the sketchbook, the statue's chest rose and fell as if it were breathing. Clearly, her mind was playing tricks. Her forehead furrowed, and then a thought struck her. Was Damian reaching out from the past to deliver a message?

On a clean page, she wrote: *We create the world in our minds. And our thoughts become our reality.*

When Lena arrived home, Portia rushed past her on the landing, leaving her the apartment to herself. As much as she loved Portia, she enjoyed these moments alone at home.

She rang Augustus, and the call went straight to voicemail, so she left him a message.

When she opened the window leading to the square, a cacophony of sounds startled her: a scooter whizzed along the street below, bells finished ringing the hour, and children's piercing cries drifted upward. She immediately shut the window and sealed herself off from the noise of the outside world.

She went to the bathroom and turned on the shower. Letting her clothes fall to the floor, she stepped into the heated, flowing spray. All was quiet except for the shower's rhythmic pulse against the ceramic wall and shower curtain. She closed her eyes and dipped her head back into the cascading stream of water.

As the soothing sensation lulled her into a meditative state, her mind became cleared of all its tensions.

. . .

Lena's head bobbed, and her eyes flew open. She sat cross-legged on the floor of the porcelain bathtub. The spritz of cold water raised goosebumps on her skin. How long had she been sitting there? Her teeth chattered as she stood to turn off the shower and wrap herself in a towel to dry. She had been dreaming again.

On this latest journey, she had stared directly into Damian's blue eyes in the mirror above the washbowl. And his remark had been loud and clear: *Who is there inside my head?*

Had he spoken to her? If so, Lena's quest had reached a whole new level. This visit was brief, but she had remained there until Damian had sat to eat with his father at the shop.

DAMIAN ~ FLORENCE, 1500

Damian splashed his face with the basin's cool water. A sensation fell over him—a lightheadedness—as if he floated just a hair above the ground. His stomach teetered, and he clutched the basin to settle himself. He leaned forward with his nose almost touching the glass and peered into the mirror.

He looked deeply into his own eyes. "*Chi è?*"

Who was there inside his head? Rattled by an unexpected feminine presence, he closed his eyes to centre himself. He took a deep breath, puzzled by this strange development. Were his senses playing tricks on him?

He got dressed in a rush, already late for his father's store. Every year, he assisted the family business by taking inventory at the shop. As he strode through the kitchen, he grabbed a ciabatta and left the house.

A sprinkle of rain and mist greeted him as he made his way through the muddy streets of Florence. He nibbled on the chunk of bread while his mind mulled over the morning's experience. The vertiginous sensation stayed with him as he turned down the narrow pathway to the store.

RONALDO, his father, owned the shop, which was packed with tools and various building and machinery components. In one corner of his store, he devoted a shelf to sundials, hourglasses, and other instruments for keeping track of time—a concept which captivated him. And artists like Leonardo often frequented his showroom in search of supplies.

As Damian entered the store, his brother Dante brushed past him.

"Hey, where are you going? Aren't you supposed to help us today?"

"I'll be back after I run this errand."

Damian watched as Dante took off in a hurry. He let out an exasperated sigh and closed the door. A customer chatted with his father at the counter.

"Thank you for your time, Signor D'Alessandro."

"*Prego.*" His father grasped the customer's forearm. When the robust man swung around to leave, the chain he wore glinted in the candlelight. It was some kind of cross. "Your order should be ready by the end of the week." His father spoke with pride and assurance.

As the gentleman left the store, Damian could see his father had already been hard at work since early that morning. He looked down at his feet.

"I'm sorry for arriving late, Father."

Ronaldo waved off his apology. "It's all fine." He pointed to the basket Damian's mother, Annabella, had delivered for them. "Why don't we sit before you start? I'm famished."

Sitting at the counter, Damian recalled the day his father had announced he would pose for the artist.

"Father . . . How did you learn that the sculptor Michelangelo was looking for a model?"

"You're aware that Signor Leonardo da Vinci pays a visit to the store occasionally?" His father waited for a response before proceeding, so he nodded. "Well, earlier that week, he came to order a contraption for one of his inventions. When you emerged from the back of the store, Leonardo saw you. He mentioned Michelangelo needed a model for his latest sculpture. Don't you remember?"

Damian shook his head. He couldn't recall that day.

"He took one look at you and exclaimed, 'My goodness! I believe your son might be Michelangelo's *David.* He has spent some time looking for the ideal model with no luck. Your son should visit the artist's studio in the Piazza dei Giudici.' Then he said, 'With your permission, I'll leave word with the sculptor to arrange for the young lad's fees.' Later that week, the offer came, and I accepted on your behalf."

Damian recalled his brief visit to Michelangelo's studio. It had meant little to him. Now, his father's knowledge of these men intrigued him.

"Do you know if these two artists are friends?"

Ronaldo shrugged. "I do not know. They compete against each other for commissions. Rivals in that respect, you know? These two artists have distinguished themselves as men with great minds. But, friends? I think not."

"Don't you find it strange that competitors help each other?"

A peculiar expression crossed his father's face. "These men exist in a different world altogether."

Damian's ears perked up at the innuendo. "What do you mean?"

"They see the world with a different mindset. They belong to another world. Leonardo not only paints but researches and delves into the human mind and body. He illustrates and invents machines—the likes of which we've never seen. His mind is brilliant. In fact, I recall when Leonardo was a young man—and I was a little younger than he. See, our families have a long history since—" Ronaldo left his sentence dangling in the air. His face paled, and he clenched his jaw. "Anyway, that's how you became Michelangelo's model."

Damian bit down on the knob end of the loaf, wondering about his father's unfinished thought. He had been unaware that a connection existed between Leonardo and his father, nor that they had grown up together. He opened his mouth, then closed it. Best not to ask him to elaborate. Ronaldo's abrupt tone had marked an end to that conversation.

And as if to detract from the earlier topic, Ronaldo continued to chat about the future of machines, and Damian's mind wandered off. Where had Dante gone? He had disappeared when he was most needed. Then, an unpleasant thought crept into his mind, and Damian hoped he was mistaken.

Dante's insistent prying had bothered Damian, knowing he would try to become involved. His brother liked to fix things, but Damian needed more time to decipher the artists' mysterious dialogues. He wanted no one to interfere. If only he could remain around long enough to listen in on the masters' conversations.

This newfound awareness of life caught Damian off stride, and he developed a fascination for its dynamism. There was a time when he could not care less about the secrets exchanged between two men—especially their private affairs. Now, their liaison piqued his interest. There was some sort of enigma to the situation.

Leonardo and Michelangelo's relationship was adversarial. That was reportedly common knowledge. From the heated conversations Damian had overheard, he deduced they shared a great secret—one so powerful that compelled them to maintain a public facade of discord.

Another strange occurrence caught Damian's eye while he was at the studio. Leonardo's visits to Michelangelo were increasing. Something was brewing.

While he stood in front of his father's time keepers, he recalled

Leonardo's remarks to Michelangelo. What had Leonardo meant when he had said, 'for our survival?' What were they concealing? Who was this majority council Leonardo had mentioned? There were too many questions left hanging in the air.

Another phenomenon had also emerged in Damian's life—a female presence invading his consciousness.

DANTE

Dense clouds dulled the buildings' colours, leaving the streets awash in one monochromatic grey hue. A light drizzle settled on Dante's overcoat as he walked along the Arno River's left bank. The river slithered like a dark serpent through the city.

The Ponte Vecchio's marketplace emptied of its usual mid-afternoon crowd, and a calm settled over the street.

When Dante reached Michelangelo's building, he leaned into the wall and glanced around the corner. His heart pounded in his chest while he monitored the entrance.

Moments later, an old man entered the building with a scroll tucked under his arm. This was the perfect moment for Dante to make his move. With someone else there to distract Michelangelo, he could slip by unnoticed.

He arranged his hair to fall across his forehead like Damian's, hoping that anyone would miss the slight differences between them. He took a deep breath and stepped toward the entrance.

Dante had left the store early, knowing Damian would be busy for most of the day taking inventory at their father's shop, which gave him plenty of time.

He had approached their father about Damian's change in behaviour. His father had hesitated at first, but then agreed to keep Damian occupied while Dante nosed around. He had sent word to Michelangelo that Damian would be available after all. Ronaldo had placed his hand on Dante's shoulder.

"I'll give you enough time to do some snooping, not more than that."

With the recent tide of events sweeping through Florence, including Savonarola's public speeches about morality, Dante and Ronaldo wanted to make sure Damian was not being coerced into any kind of heretical or sexual deviant behaviour.

Although most people in Florence had a deep respect for Leonardo, they had also heard the rumours about his past—the one where he had been charged with an illicit act—even though it had never been proven.

Dante crept into the building and up the stairs. His gut twisted. He squeezed the door handle with cold and clammy fingers, and his parched tongue stuck to the roof of his mouth. As he opened the studio's door, Michelangelo waved and directed him to the stage.

The elder gentleman who had arrived first stood tall at Michelangelo's sketching table, while the maestro leaned over a drawing.

Dante entered the studio and encountered a dismal and unpleasant ambience emanating from the two men. His entrance had cut off their discussion. When he passed by Michelangelo and his visitor, he glanced down at the drawings littered on the floor and made a mental note of the pose he saw there. The younger maestro's harsh voice rang out as Dante walked past them.

"After you change, please open the window on your way."

Fortunately, Michelangelo had gestured towards the screen, inadvertently informing him of the requirement to change into the loincloth. When Dante was ready, he walked to the window and unlatched it. He became mesmerized by the spectacular view. The muted sun hung mid-horizon over the small square and the Arno River.

Under menacing grey clouds, the hills stood guard beyond the city walls. The jagged blocks of dark blue and grey faded into the misty afternoon sky. Dante caught the two men staring at him in the window's angled reflection.

Michelangelo grunted. "I don't have all afternoon, boy. Hurry now, to the stage."

Dante climbed onto the podium. He took his position and mimicked the pose he had seen. Michelangelo groaned and went to re-drape the sling over his shoulder.

As the maestro placed the stone in Dante's palm, the artist flipped Dante's hand from front to back. Dante's pulse raced, and he squeezed his little finger against the ring finger to hide the thin scar that ran along it.

Michelangelo's head cocked, and his frown deepened. With a little tug, Dante freed his hand from the man's grasp and let it hang down to his side. He stood his ground, but a tremor ran through his body, from head to toe.

Michelangelo stepped off the stage and barked at his visitor, his voice rough and dismissive. "Leonardo, please come back another day. With all these interruptions, I'll never finish with these."

Dante glanced at Leonardo and winced as though he were the one on the bitter end of Michelangelo's frigid dismissal. Outside, Dante had not recognized the silver-haired genius. He had heard the rumours, but upon seeing the man in person, he took an instant liking to him.

Leonardo heaved a breath and patted Michelangelo on the shoulder.

"My friend, I will leave you to your work."

As Leonardo turned to leave, an unsettled expression crossed his brow.

Michelangelo disregarded him and muttered to himself, halting every few seconds to frown at his subject and his drawing. He rubbed his chin and picked up previous drawings to compare them to the present one.

Dante did not move a muscle—staying as still as a mouse—afraid Michelangelo might find him out. He was relieved when the artist became engrossed in his work. And as the day progressed, the artist rubbed his hands together, gazing at his own artwork with apparent satisfaction.

When the sun dipped toward the Florentine hills, Michelangelo put his charcoal stick down. The flame of the candle burned straight up within the lantern. He had lighted it to dispel the gloom that had descended upon the studio.

"Thank you, you can go now."

The abruptness in Michelangelo's voice startled Dante. He jumped off the podium, grabbed his clothes from the chair, and changed behind the screen.

Michelangelo called out to him as he went to the door. "Damian, please be here a little earlier tomorrow."

Dante nodded and hurried to close the door behind him before he dared take a breath. His ruse had worked. His back ached in unexpected areas as he hobbled down the stairwell. Even though he was no stranger to long, challenging days, he developed a renewed admiration for his brother's tenacity.

When Dante arrived home, he walked straight to the fire burning in the kitchen fireplace to shake off the clinging cold. His mother worked, bent over to her task, preparing her market wares. Annabella had a big day ahead: cakes and pastries to sell at her stall. She had raised her eyes when Dante entered the kitchen.

"You've missed dinner. Damian and your father have already eaten. They're back at the shop to finish with the inventory. Grab a bite to eat and be quick. They're waiting."

He moved over to his mother, brushed a speck of flour from her cheek, and gave her a gentle kiss. Dante hated worrying her.

"I was working on something for Father."

Since childhood, he had learned to take advantage of her soft spot. Annabella shook her head and pursed her lips. She handed him a trencher. The smoked meat piled on top of her baked bread was his favourite of her recipes. As he took a huge bite, she pushed him away.

"Go! They need your help."

Dante left his home and quickened his gait toward

D'Alessandro's. He looked behind him every two steps, wary of the dark, although torches illuminated his route. This evening, the dancing shadows followed him. He picked up his pace and found comfort in the light emanating from his father's shop.

Ronaldo looked up when Dante opened the front door, with both relief and concern splashed across his face. "Well?" Dante kept his voice down. "So far, nothing." He scanned the shop. "Where's Damian?"

Ronaldo pointed toward a door leading to a small hallway. Dante walked to the back room, and Damian's brow crinkled upon seeing him.

"Where've you been?"

"Helping Giancarlo. Quarry work. Sorry I had to leave."

Damian opened his mouth to speak, but their father popped his head in and interrupted them.

"Let's get a move on. We really need to get this done today."

After the boys had finished helping their father, Dante asked Damian to join him for a card game with their friends. This time, Damian came along.

DAMIAN

Damian and Dante met up with their friends in the Piazza Santa Maria Novella. The comfort of being in a large group eased Damian's worries as they crossed town in the growing darkness.

Giancarlo sidled up beside him. "Hey, Damian, haven't seen you in a long time! Been busy?"

Damian overlooked his cousin's sarcastic tone and the fact that he had heckled him on the way out of the studio the previous day. Hoping to avoid any questions about his work, he nodded. "Yes, it's been a while. Glad to see you again." He patted Giancarlo on the back.

The young men sauntered through the sombre streets. The iron-framed lanterns illuminated the dark recesses, and the flickering flames cast ghostly shadows on Florence's walls.

Damian shrank from the darkness. "I hate the city at night." Then he pushed his cousin off balance. "Why do your parents live so far away?"

Giancarlo shook his head. "Your life is too sheltered. You ought to be more adventurous, like your brother."

Damian remained silent even though comparisons to his twin always irritated him. Dante moved in close and gave Giancarlo a little elbow to the side. "Leave him alone." Then Damian recalled that Dante also feared the night.

The friends chatted and joked with one another as they walked through the city. When the sound of hooves clattered down an adjacent street, they jumped to attention.

Giancarlo stopped them. "Riders rarely enter the city after dark."

Something was afoot, and they rushed to investigate the commotion. When they reached the street where the clamour had resounded, there was not a soul. Even the patrolling night watchmen had vanished.

Damian stiffened. "Where is everyone? I don't like this . . ."

"Come on, it's nothing. The guards must be on their shift change." But the quiver in Dante's voice betrayed him.

The young men glanced up and down the street. Bewildered, they kept their ears cocked for horses, but did not hear them again.

When they arrived at Giancarlo's home, the peculiar incident had already slipped their minds. The boys sat at a long wooden table in the kitchen.

Giancarlo was eager to get started. "Shall we get that game going?"

Dante grabbed the cards. "Yes, let's have some fun."

The night had cooled and the fireplace in the hearth was crackling. Damian watched as his brother dealt the cards and admired his skill at games. Dante had a gift for counting cards and nabbing cheaters—a magician with numbers. Playing Basset was a pleasant distraction for Dante, but Damian detested card games.

They had been playing nonstop since the bells had sounded the seventh hour. At the stroke of nine, Damian stretched from stiffness and stifled a yawn. Dante smiled at him.

"You look tired. Go home. I'll stay a little longer, play a few more hands. Just keep the back window open for me."

As Damian walked home, he strained his ears for any disturbance. He would have preferred Dante with him, but his brother loved his nights out.

Damian's light footsteps on the cobblestones echoed in the night's stillness. The fear of the unknown lurking in the shadows dogged his every step. Each little noise made him jump. A night watchman nodded at him with a look of surprise—or had that been concern in his expression?

Several blocks later, Damian sneaked into the alley next to his house and crawled in through the rear bedroom window. Jumping from the windowsill into his room, he stumbled into the darkness.

His right foot caught the stool's leg, and he yelped from the sharp pain in his toe. He reached for his knee and lost his balance. When he fell, his head struck the stone tile floor.

6
INAUDIBLE WHISPERS

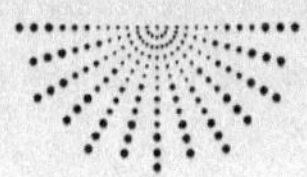

LENA ~ FLORENCE, PRESENT DAY

Lena did not know how long she had been lying there. She rolled her head to the right and stared at a row of perpendicular spindles protruding from the floor. Table legs? She craned her head, and her eyes burned as she focused on the hallway lined with desks to her left and right. In the room's obscurity, a speck of brightness shone in the distance.

The light at the end of the long tunnel expanded to the size of a large ball of fire. She blinked several times to adjust to its brightness. The back of her head throbbed with a heavy pounding.

She moaned, pushed herself up onto her elbow, and waited for her vision to sharpen. It was now clear to her; she was in the Biblioteca of the Medicea-Lorenzo. She recognized it because she had visited the building after discovering that Michelangelo had designed the library for Giulio de Medici.

Though it was a stone's throw from home, Lena could not remember when she had left her apartment or when she had arrived here. She heard a shuffle of footsteps growing louder as they approached. Seconds later, the librarian emerged and ran toward Lena.

"Signorina, are you all right?"

"I'm okay, thank you. I must have tripped."

Lena motioned she was fine. The librarian helped her up and waited a moment to make sure she would not fall again. She thanked him and ambled down the hallway, using the angled tables as leverage. When she got to the hallway's end, she looked over her shoulder. The librarian still had his eye on her as she made her way down the stairs.

She stepped out of the Basilica and walked toward the Piazza San Lorenzo. Her head spun, and she leaned against the wall of the building for support. Had she made her way here, then blacked out? She could not fill the gap in her memory.

Lena's phone buzzed, startling her. She patted her jacket and found it in one of her pockets. A high-pitched female voice came through the speaker.

"Lena?"

With her mind still muddled, she did not respond.

"Lena? You there?"

"Portia? . . ."

"Yes . . . everything okay?"

"Yes, yes. What's up?"

"Where have you been?"

"At the Biblioteca."

"The library?"

"Yes, in the Basilica, next door to our place."

"Um, okay. When did you leave?"

"I had to check on something."

"Now? Anyway, are you going to come and eat with us tonight? Everyone's asking for you."

Lena paused for a second before responding. "Yeah, I'll come."

"I'm still at the apartment. Your voice sounds different."

Lena passed by the jeweller's storefront and jumped at her reflection in the window.

"I'm just distracted. I'll be right there."

Lena hung up. Had she been expecting to see someone else in her mirror image? She glanced about, looking over her shoulder as she arrived at the front entrance of her building.

Before unlocking the large door, she glimpsed at the church and the piazza. For a moment, the Basilica's front appeared vibrant and detailed, as if they had recently constructed it. Then, almost immediately, the walls faded, losing their brilliant hues. A wave of disappointment rippled through her.

Lena shook her head to clear her mind of these conflicting thoughts. What was going on with her? She stepped inside and ran upstairs. After she fiddled with the key in the lock, she rushed in and closed the door behind her with a thud.

A gurgle of running water came from the far end of the apartment. Portia's disembodied voice yelled from the bathroom.

"I'm in here. I'll be out in a second."

"It's okay, take your time."

Lena fell onto her bed from sheer exhaustion. She closed her eyes to stop the room from spinning. A few minutes later, the bathroom door opened and Portia entered in her undergarments. Lena sprang to a half-seated position. She had been on the brink of falling asleep again.

Portia grimaced when she eyed Lena, half-lying on her bed. "We've got to get going. Get into the shower. Everyone's expecting to see you tonight."

Lena gaped at Portia, her golden blonde hair flowing in wild curls down her shoulders to her dew drop breasts and lace bra.

Portia shot Lena a look. "Go on. Move your ass. Stop gawking at me like you've never seen me before."

Lena averted her gaze and hurried to the bathroom, her head still bleary and unfocused. She gave herself a fleeting look in the full-length mirror, and unfamiliar emotions stirred within her. She was definitely not herself.

Portia knocked on the door. "Hey! I don't hear the water running yet."

Lena clenched her jaw. When had Portia become so bossy? She opened the bathroom door a slit. "They'll wait for us."

She stepped into the shower and the spray of hot water immediately soothed her. As the water trickled down the drain, she raised her head and gave thought to its source. She grimaced. Why did she care where this water came from? Annoyed with herself, she left her irrational thoughts behind and dressed in a hurry, for Portia's sake.

When Portia crossed the room to close the shutters for the night, a dove flew off the sill. Lena became dizzy when a noise outside the window triggered a vague recollection. She drew in a sharp breath and held onto the dresser for support. Her eyes widened. Damian was there. His presence was undeniable.

THE GIRLS LEFT the apartment and wend their way through Florence's old cobbled streets. When they arrived at the bar restaurant, the place was dark. Lena's brow furrowed. She found it strange that Portia had been overly eager to get there.

"Is this the right location? Maybe they're—"

Before she could finish, the lights came on. Everyone jumped up and cried in unison.

"Surprise!"

Lena's pulse surged, and she cried out, first in terror, then in excitement as her friends came up to wish her well. In the distraction and confusion of her day, she had completely forgotten it was her birthday.

The DJ turned on the music, and the bartender poured drinks for everyone. "Happy Birthday Lena," rang out from the speakers. Lena chuckled. Leave it to her friends to get a party going.

Friends and strangers danced around her, laughing and yelling at each other over the music. She joined Christina and Portia on the tiny dance floor when one of her favourite songs played. As she swayed to the music, she spotted someone wearing a hoodie in one of the dark corners. The sight of his glistening crystal eyes in the darkness took her breath away. She leaned over to shout into Portia's ear.

"Who is that over there in the corner?"

Portia frowned at her. "Who?"

Lena pointed to the darkened corner, but when she turned to look, he was no longer there.

"Never mind. He must have left."

Despite all the laughter and excitement, she forced a smile, grateful for her friends' attention. However, it was not the same without Marco. She had searched the room for him without luck. Deep inside, her joy waned and left her with a hollow feeling in her chest. What did she expect when she was the one who had been absent for the past few weeks?

As another song started, she caught Christina's smirk. She turned to see Marco standing behind her.

"Happy Birthday! Didn't think I'd miss this, did you?"

Her heart leaped. Marco smiled his big, toothy grin and leaned forward to take her into his arms. In her ear, he whispered, "I'm sorry I'm late." He pulled his head back to look at her and held her face in his hands before planting a tender kiss on her mouth. She broke out in a broad grin and quickly forgot her momentary disappointment.

At that instant, the strangest sensation of déjà vu crossed Lena's mind—as if she had known Marco from another time. Although it appeared ridiculous, her conflicting emotions pushed her to entertain a new thought.

Damian must be the source of this thought. The boundaries between their worlds had become blurred. She suspected the parallel thoughts were his. He had been present since her collapse at the Basilica and now watched everything through her eyes. But how was Marco connected to all this?

Toward the evening's end, Lena learned it was Marco who had arranged for everyone to come together to celebrate. He had wanted to give her a special celebration to remember her time in Florence.

"Thank you, Marco! I truly enjoyed my birthday. It was a genuine surprise." She threw her arms around him.

He spoke in her ear. "Did you want to come over tonight?"

"If it's okay with you, I'll come visit tomorrow. I can't tonight. I have an early class and a lab."

The corners of Marco's mouth turned downward. "I really wanted to spend some time with you."

The look of dismay in his eyes tugged at her heartstrings, and her emotions wobbled.

"I promise I'll come as soon as I'm done."

EN ROUTE, Portia touched Lena's arm. "Can I ask you something without you getting upset?"

Lena looked sideways at Portia, who was still tipsy from the celebration. "Ask away."

"Why did you lie to Marco?"

Lena inspected her feet as she strolled quietly. She bit her bottom lip, and Portia accepted it as a sign to keep going.

"I know you don't have class until later. You could have spent the night. It really upset him you didn't."

She averted Portia's gaze, but this time she spoke up.

"You're right. I should have gone with him, but I have something important to do tomorrow."

"What could be more important than spending time with someone you love?"

Before Lena could stop herself, she blurted out, "Stop patronizing me."

Portia cried out in return. "I'm not!"

Lena glared at her. "Yes, you are."

"I'm just concerned. You're not acting like yourself these days."

"I don't need to be told what to do."

"I'm not telling you what to do. But lately, you've been making it hard for us to approach you. You've been pushing me away."

"Oh, so now I'm a topic of conversation between you all?"

"No, that's not what I meant. I'm just wondering why you didn't go home with Marco. That's all."

Portia had a point, but Lena loathed feeling pressured. She tempered her irritation.

"Believe me, it hurt me not to go with him."

Portia frowned, and it was clear from her expression she did not believe her.

Lena complied. "Look, I really need to do this thing in the morning or I would have gone."

They remained silent for the rest of the journey home, and Portia spared Lena any further discussion because she passed out as soon as they arrived at their apartment.

LENA WOKE UP EARLY. Drowsy from her birthday celebration, she sipped on a strong cup of coffee. Portia slept, still knackered from their late night.

On their walk to the restaurant the evening before, Lena recalled feeling compelled to take a different route. She had shrugged off the sensation, not wanting to delay Portia any further. Now she wondered whether Damian had intended to take her somewhere else?

The last time she visited his world, the dream had lasted until Damian had arrived at the entrance of a shop. As he entered the store, a carbon copy of himself brushed past him. It was Dante. Damian then addressed the man who stood behind the counter as "Father." Somewhere in the dream, in the conversation between his father and a customer, she had caught a name: Ronaldo. Was this their family business?

But she had awakened in the chilly shower tub before she could learn anything more. Frustrated that she had no power over how long she could remain in that dream state, she considered following the road he had taken to see if she could find any more clues.

On her laptop, Lena checked a city map, hazarding a guess as to the general vicinity of the store. She toggled to street view mode, used familiar landmarks to reconstruct Damian's path, and hoped she was not grasping at straws.

With this information, she left the apartment and trekked through the streets. She checked the map on her phone as she walked, sifted through her recollection for the first location—where he had exited from his home. The basic layout of the Florentine streets remained unchanged in five hundred years, despite outward appearances.

She stopped in front of a courtyard's entrance and looked around. It was closed off by a wrought-iron gate with a chain and a large padlock wrapped around its middle bars.

If she was correct, this is where his home would have stood. Lena's throat tightened, and she swallowed hard when the realization hit her. She was not sure what she had expected to find, but there was not even the slightest hint of his parents' home left.

Lena followed Damian's supposed path until she reached a familiar intersection. She turned right onto the narrowed street and passed by an ancient recessed wall fountain until she reached a storefront.

Above her; they had carved a name into a marble slab in the wall: *D'Alessandro.* The ravages of time had smoothed down the lettering, and now appeared almost illegible. But it was still clear enough to read.

She peered in through its front window. And though it was dark inside, she could make out the hanging metal storage boxes and keys which hung on the back wall. On the storefront's glass, a faint etching of that same name appeared below the store's current name. Florentines preserved historical signs and emblems long after their forefathers had died. Sliding her fingers over the lettering, Lena's chest swelled with hope.

Her heart skipped a beat as she dashed home. This quest had led her to crucial information. She chuckled as she climbed the stairs to her flat, overcome by the thrill that surged inside her.

At her desk, she took a piece of paper and, in her left-handed scrawl, wrote three names.

Damiano, Dante, & Ronaldo D'Alessandro.

BEFORE LENA HEADED off to class, she stopped at the town hall for a look at the *Registri Batesimali*—Florence's baptismal records. Luckily, the database registry was available to the public. The microfiches and recorded historical notations had undergone digital scanning. She sat scrolling through the pages, skimming over the entries, hoping to find the D'Alessandro family name.

The birth registries before 1540 were sketchy; however, given its length, Damiano's surname was easy to locate on the list. While skimming over the records, Lena encountered many inconsistent entries that were handwritten, blotchy, and difficult to read.

After she searched for some time, she narrowed her search to the family's patriarch, *Ronaldo.* Starting at the 1350s, she skimmed through the years until she came to the mid 1400s, where she slowed her search. The D'Alessandro surname had surfaced, but she still could not find Ronaldo.

Her eyes blurred as her finger trailed the list and left a streak on the screen. Lena became exhausted and could no longer see the names clearly. She flew past it, but her eye caught the name. With her pulse quickening, she slid her finger back up and stopped. At long last, something.

It listed two names: Vincenzo di Giuseppe D'Alessandro, 1448-1453, and Ronaldo di Giuseppe D'Alessandro di Bagno a

Ripoli, 1450-1515. Ronaldo's name was written in a clear handwritten script. There was a scribble and MCDLXX next to his name, with the name Annabella di Carpezia next to the date. She assumed it announced Ronaldo and Annabella's marriage in 1470.

Lena continued her search. If she had found Damian's parents, surely she would come upon Ronaldo and Annabella's children. Then, there they were: Angelina Maria D'Alessandro, 1469–1530, and Ariella Luisa D'Alessandro, 1470–1532. Next to the girls' names were their parents' names, and nested underneath were the names of their spouses, Giuseppe di Stefano and Sandro Baldini.

But she still found no mention of Damian and Dante.

Losing hope, she resigned herself to failure. How could she find the family but no mention of either of the twins? Had she made them up? Filling in the information to suit her purpose?

Then a curious notation caught her eye, written in a form unlike the others, and almost a decade after the girls. On July 27, 1480, someone had penned Damian and Dante's names in a beautiful script to announce the twins' birth.

She stared at the two entries and traced each handwritten name with her fingertip, unsure whether she was registering shock or relief. Forgetting where she was, she jumped up from her chair, throwing her arms in the air like a marathon winner crossing the finish line.

Overwhelmed, her eyes brimmed with tears. She hugged herself with her hands to her shoulders, bracing herself against the intense sensation that exploded like fireworks in her chest.

"I didn't make it up. I'm not delusional after all!"

Lena glanced around to see if anyone had overheard her, but she was alone. Settling back into her seat, she searched for more information.

Besides a few scribbles in the margin next to their names, nothing else stood out. She could find no names of spouses or children. Just a single entry, scrawled in after each of their names with some other words and the notation, *Primavera, MD—Spring,*

Fifteen hundred, next to them. Curiosity niggled at her as she gazed at it.

She pushed further, comparing the Birth and Death Registries only to discover that in both, they contained the names of the four family members. Ronaldo, Annabella, and the two daughters, along with their husbands and their children, but there was no record of Damian nor Dante's death in the latter.

Lena's watch beeped, a reminder of her morning lecture at the University. She hurried and took photocopies of the pages in the birth and death registries, but ran out of time to ask the clerk for a translation of the notations.

LENA LEFT the University Hall after her lab ended and headed straight to Marco's place. When she rang the bell, there was no response. She rang it again, hoping he would be there. Still, no answer came from the apartment.

She searched her pocket for her phone. When she called, the connection went straight to voicemail. Her shoulders slumped while she waited for the beep. "Marco? It's me, Lena. Could you call me back?"

Lena's voice quivered with emotion. Her vision blurred, and it threw her off balance. She settled herself on the stone step in front of his building. With her stomach lurching, she hugged her knees and leaned her forehead on them.

When she looked up again, the world still spun around her as blood drained from her head. Her body triggered by the same dizzying sensation as on the evening of her party. Sure enough, Damian was there in her head again. Once she realized he was there, her stomach settled, and the dizzy spell ceased.

In front of her, the Arno River glittered like diamonds. In the distance, the sound of sirens pierced the air. Just then, her phone vibrated. She picked up and heard Marco's concerned voice on the other end.

"Lena? Where are you?"

"I'm in front of your apartment."

"I had to step out, but I can head home now. Do you have time to wait?"

"Yes, I'll be right here."

When Marco turned the corner onto the Piazza dei Giudici, Lena's lips twitched and the corners of her mouth raised into a wide smile.

"I'm glad to see you!"

Again, a peculiar sense of connection to Marco—different from her own—flashed through her mind. Marco gave her a peck on the lips and the kiss left her with a strange sensation. She snuggled into the safe comfort of his embrace.

He nuzzled her neck. "It's good to see you too."

She pulled her head back to look up at him and smiled. Despite her earlier reluctance, she knew she had made the right decision to come. Marco looked toward the river.

"Would you like to go for a walk? There's a place I found, and I'd like to show it to you."

"Sure. It'll be good for me to get some air."

Together, they crossed the Ponte Vecchio. Marco's arm hugged her waist as he held her close. On the Arno's other bank, they walked the street that ran behind the buildings. They climbed a narrow throughway until they reached the Museo Roberto Capucci.

"What is this place?"

"It's a hidden garden. I came to it by chance the other day."

Marco and Lena entered the Giardino Bardini, accessible only through the museum. They passed a fountain with a miniature lion sitting atop a monument. A spout jutted out of its mouth, spewing water into a shallow basin. Trees and bushes lined the paths, and statues peered out from their enclaves at passersby.

They reached one of the garden's parapets and leaned against its wall to enjoy the view. From this side of the Arno, Florence took

Lena's breath away. The Duomo rose over the cityscape like a picture postcard.

Marco took Lena's hand, and together they climbed and descended the myriad of paths. Lena exhaled, relieved to be a million miles away from all of her recent challenges.

Her quest could wait until tomorrow.

ON THEIR WAY back to Marco's apartment, they walked past the grand arch of the Piazzale degli Uffizi. Lena had the sensation of walking through two different cities at once as she strolled the streets of Florence.

She stopped to lean against the low-lying wall running along the river to catch the fluorescent blaze of colours splashing across the sky. The river glowed like a fire snake. She could never get enough of these breathtaking sunsets.

They reached his building, and as they climbed the staircase to his apartment, Lena slid her hand along the wooden railing and marvelled at its sturdiness. She rapped her knuckles against it and scanned her surroundings. Everything looked familiar, yet peculiar.

When Marco opened his front door, Lena made a beeline to the window that faced the river. As the sky darkened, the rolling hills beyond the city transformed into blocks of dark blue and violet. The cypress trees looked even more like sentry guards against the landscape's shadows. Lena glanced around with a deep sense of knowing. Again, Damian's observations crowded her head.

"Wow, the studio still looks the same!"

Marco followed Lena with a watchful eye. "What do you mean? I haven't changed a thing since you were last here."

Lena recovered from her *faux pas* by changing the subject. "Did you know your apartment might once have been Michelangelo's studio?"

"Yes. There have been rumours. How did you hear of it? I don't think I've ever mentioned it to you."

Lena flinched and saved herself from the blunder.

"Oh, my professor mentioned today that one of Michelangelo's studios might be in this building. It intrigued me to think it could be your apartment. It would be an interesting coincidence if it was, don't you think?"

She glanced at the corner of the apartment where Damian spent most of his days up on the podium. Her insides wobbled. There was just a settee and a table in the space now.

Marco arched his eyebrows. "A coincidence? You mean because of my artist's studio? Yes, I suppose." He paused and looked around his apartment. "I have certainly experienced an intense energy here."

Lena's eyes brightened. "You have? How?"

As Marco spoke, she scanned the studio where Michelangelo would have stood, hunched over his drawings. And to where his easel had stood. She gasped inwardly. Marco had set up his easel in the same spot.

Marco continued, "I'm not sure how to describe it. Actually, it's a little disturbing, to be honest."

"Really?" Lena leaned forward, waiting to hear more.

"I don't know how to explain it without sounding a little—" He grimaced and spun his index finger beside his temple.

"You won't. I promise. Please, tell me."

Marco paused for a moment as if to compose his thoughts. "Well . . . I've woken up a few times in the middle of the night to the sounds of whispered conversations in this studio area." Marco gestured toward the corner where his easel stood next to the long table with paints and brushes.

Lena's breath became shallow, and a chill settled along her collarbone. "Are you able to make out what they're saying?"

"Yes, sometimes I'll hear entire sentences. Most times it's just odd words. None of it makes any sense."

Lena watched as Marco moved over to his desk, pulled open a drawer, and took out a notebook.

"Let me show you my nightly scribbles."

Lena sat with Marco on the couch, and together they looked over what he had recorded of the conversations. He gestured toward his notes and spoke the phrases aloud to her.

You must stay strong, my friend . . .

They must never find out about . . .

We have to leave clues to our identity for others . . .

I'm afraid for us . . .

"And this is the last entry."

It will remain our secret . . .

Marco tapped his finger on the page.

"It's always the same two people speaking. *Men.* One sounds older than the other."

Lena jumped up and paced the floor in front of Marco.

He looked up, puzzled by her sudden reaction. "What's going on?"

She could no longer contain her excitement. "I think there is a connection between these conversations and what I've been going through."

Marco's eyebrows shot up. "In what way? What have you been experiencing?"

She clamped her mouth. "I—I don't know exactly, but when I find out, I'll let you know." She fidgeted, realizing she had said too much. "Please keep taking notes if you hear of any more conversations."

Marco rose and rested his hands on Lena's trembling shoulders. "I shouldn't have mentioned anything."

Lena stared at him, wide-eyed. "Why? No, it's important you tell me."

"It's just—" He sighed. "You've been withdrawing from us, from me."

"You think my thesis is consuming me, don't you?"

"No. Yes. Look, I just don't want to add more to your current predicament."

"You're not." As she said that, she pulled away. "The more I know, the better."

Marco shook his head. "It's frustrating to see you like this. I don't know what's going on, but—"

"I promise I *will* explain everything when I understand what's involved."

He rubbed his neck. "I knew there was something going on."

She looked down at his notepad. "It might be nothing, but I promise I'll share with you once I figure it out."

Marco patted her arm. "I'm sure you will, and I hope it will be soon because I'm getting worried about you." He got up and made his way to the kitchen.

By the time Marco had dinner ready, she experienced a sense of relief, as if a weight had been lifted from her shoulders. Damian was also gone, no longer present in her mind.

Marco flung open the studio's windows for some fresh air. They ate and talked without bringing up the earlier conversation again.

Later, as she undressed and got into Marco's bed, she reflected on what he had said to her earlier that afternoon. And he was right. She needed to figure out what was going on, and soon.

7
SPACE AND MATTER

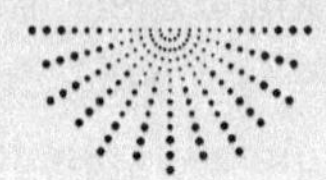

LENA ~ FLORENCE, PRESENT DAY

Lena stepped out of Marco's building and into the chilled morning air. Light pastel watercolours softened the landscape. The city's walls, cobblestone streets, and river wavelets were awash with soft brush strokes of peppermint green, Victorian rose, and aspen blue.

The tapping of her heels on the pavement and Marco's experience of the studio's late-night murmurs became intertwined in her thoughts like a sequence of sound bytes.

The photocopied transcript from the registry remained nestled in her pocket. A wave of guilt rushed over her. She had decided not to show it to Marco. *Or Damian.*

Lena walked toward the Ponte alle Grazie, and took a detour to the Biblioteca Nazionale—the largest library of its kind in Italy. It was still too early when she arrived, so she waited for someone to open up its doors. She sat at a nearby coffee shop with her coffee and toast and stared out the window.

A half hour later, a man with salt and pepper hair appeared and unlocked its doors. She gulped down her last sip of coffee, left some change on the table, and ran after him. At the entrance, she peeked in. The librarian was still making his way in from the entrance. He switched on the table lamps and straightened books on his way to the front desk.

She called out to him and hoped he would have a moment to spare.

"Mi scusi, posso avere un momento del suo tempo?"

The man looked over his shoulder, "What can I do for you, young lady?"

She smiled. "Oh! You speak English."

The man turned to face her.

"Yes, learned from my travels . . . and from speaking with tourists, of course."

By the time Lena reached him, she had pulled out the piece of paper.

"Could you please translate what is written next to these dates?"

He took her transcript, read it to himself, and cocked his head as he pointed to each date. In a thick Florentine accent, he explained the text.

"After the first date, it says, 'Disappeared.' And after that, the year '1500.' This part says, '*potrebbe essere . . . deceduto*.' Uh, how you say . . . deceased?"

"Dead?" Lena's expression turned grim. "Are you sure?"

"*Eh si, ne sono certo.* I am certain. Next to the other name? The same words: 'Disappeared,' and, '1500.'"

Lena's heart sank. She pointed to the list again.

"What's written here? *Before* the dates of birth."

"It says, 'Two little angels born this day in Florence.'" The librarian smiled, almost proudly. "This must be, uh, a celebration because they are *gemelli*. How you say—twins? And . . . not usual for them to live a long time—to survive, I mean."

He looked down at the information again, his voice lowered.

"They live for twenty years!" He pulled at his goatee. "But then they are gone. So young!"

The same thought had crossed her mind. She herself had just turned twenty-one. The librarian held her arm and pointed to the sheet. "Look, the writing. It is different after dates." He joined his two index fingers together as he spoke, then split them apart. "This means they disappear, but not together. *Altrimenti la stessa scrittura, la stessa ora . . .*"

She gestured in the air to mimic writing. "You mean, otherwise, it would be the same handwriting if written at the same time?"

"*Si*, this is my . . . *assunzione*." He tapped on his temple to demonstrate his train of thought. Then he looked at her and a serious expression crossed his face. "*Mi scusi,* is this your *famiglia*?"

She smiled at his valiant effort to speak English. "No. It's just research about a family who lived during the Renaissance."

He had already provided her with a lot more information than just the translation. A chill ran down Lena's spine. Something terrible awaited the twins.

He frowned. "You are upset? Is not information you want?"

She mustered up a smile despite her sombre mood. "Yes, a little saddened, but this is exactly what I needed. Thank you for all your help."

"*Prego.*" He tipped his hat and returned to his work.

The hollow feeling in her stomach turned into a knotted ball of angst. She had to warn Damian and Dante that they might be in some kind of danger. But how could she tell the twins without alarming them? Or, even worse, without altering the course of history?

Lena returned to her apartment. She recalled what Augustus had told her about metaphysics and wrote in her journal: *Thoughts convert into matter through action; space reveals where matter exists; matter determines where and how space alters; and action creates change.*

She next looked for any historical or conspiratorial references linked to either Michelangelo or Leonardo, but came up empty. She jumped when her phone rang. *Augustus.*

"Hey! I was hoping to hear from you."

"Apologies, love, I should have called you back sooner."

"It's okay. I've been busy too." She paused and gathered her thoughts. "I've been thinking about our last conversation. Could we meet again? Perhaps tomorrow? I have more questions."

"And here I hoped it was my company you desired." His constant teasing never failed to put a grin on her face. "But yes, tomorrow works."

Augustus could always make her laugh, but today, his studies on space and time were her focus. They might be speculative theories, but what if she held the key to some of their assumptions? Regardless, if she was losing her mind, Augustus would be the first to tell her.

It was times like these that made Lena wish her dad were still alive. She often spoke to him as though he were there, but it was difficult receiving none of his responses. She needed his support now more than ever. If he had been here, she was certain he would have known what to do.

The trauma of losing him at such a young age had created an emotional void, and it was difficult for her to share her feelings. The friends she had made in Florence had helped her to trust and open herself up to them. But a large part of her heart remained off limits.

Outside her window, the sun retreated behind the cityscape, leaving dark wedges of patrician purple set against a horizon splashed with pink, orange, and lavender hues. Above, soft rays of silk clouds fanned out across the approaching darkness.

Suddenly, a tremor shook the floor beneath her, and the walls undulated like ocean waves. Fragile picture frames rattled, and books crashed to the floor as the shelves rocked back and forth.

As she steadied herself and stood up, her chair toppled and tipped her backward. She reached for the table's corner, but misjudged her distance and crashed to the ground. When her head struck the tiled floor, a searing pain radiated from the back to the front of her skull. She struggled to remain conscious, but darkness won.

DAMIAN ~ FLORENCE, 1500

Damian had spent a long day on the platform, where he had posed for much longer than usual.

He had asked the maestro for permission to leave early, but Michelangelo had his own concept of time. Damian tapped his thigh with a quick tempo, as if doing so would make the day go by more quickly. His father had told him, "Be home early. We're expecting an important guest for dinner." Now, he was already running late.

Another half hour dragged on before Michelangelo finally dismissed him, though it was without an apology for keeping him so long. Damian should have been used to it by now.

He escaped as fast as he could through the streets of Florence. As he got halfway down one street, he tripped and nausea washed over him. He braced himself against an adjacent wall and little black dots swam before his eyes. Though he still could not understand what was going on, he knew the girl's undeniable presence was there within his head.

He arrived home and slipped into the narrow alleyway. Around the back, he climbed in through his bedroom window. As he landed inside with a soft thud, the sound of voices filtered through the house. The guest had already arrived for dinner.

Damian changed from his work wear into traditional dinner attire—dark pants and a white dress shirt. This evening, he added a vest and belt. He also slid on his buckle shoes. His parents had taught him that formal clothing was required when entertaining guests. As Damian combed his hair, he heard a familiar voice in his ear, almost like a whisper.

"You have a lovely and comfortable home."

Startled, Damian glanced from side to side before peering out into the corridor, astounded that he had heard the words so clearly from the other room.

From the kitchen door, which was open by a hair's breadth, one voice resonated above the others. Its melodious and vibrant tone drew his attention. Damian had heard this voice before. *Leonardo?* He rubbed his neck, astonished that his father had invited the maestro. Was he prepared for such an intimate interaction with the artist? He straightened himself, took a deep breath, and walked into the dining room.

Ronaldo looked in his direction. "Ah, my son." The sarcasm was unmistakable. It dripped like molasses from his tongue. "You grace us with your presence. Let me introduce my son, Damian."

When Leonardo stood to greet him, Damian mumbled the maestro had kept him at the studio later than intended and extended his arm.

Leonardo turned to Ronaldo as he grasped Damian's forearm. "Your son and I have met at the studio."

"Sir, I apologize for my lateness."

Leonardo waved off the apology. "Unfortunately, Michelangelo can be demanding with getting his work done. I, too, have experienced the brunt of his exigent nature. And, please address me as Leonardo. Everyone does."

The maestro's intense demeanour softened in the comfort of his parents' home. Damian scanned the room where his entire family sat around the dinner table. Except Dante.

His father forced a smile as his attention followed Damian's gaze to the empty seat. "Now, if only your brother could arrive, we could get dinner started. Have you seen him, by any chance?"

Damian shook his head and sat down. Despite the interruption, the conversation returned to its original thread, and Ronaldo jumped right back in to question his guest.

"Leonardo, what will become of your ideas?"

The family sat still and listened, mesmerized by Leonardo's visions. He oozed with self-confidence as he spoke with passion about his latest ideas and the developing world in which they lived. Ronaldo again asked what he saw coming for them.

"The world is an ever-evolving place. Many changes will occur. Particularly with machines. More than you could ever imagine . . . More than we will ever see in our lifetime."

While Leonardo described his visions of the future, Damian compared them to the big moving machines he had seen in his most recent dream world. He focused on Leonardo's words and descriptions, and a sudden thought caused him to pull in his breath. Was the artist referring to current developments or to a different era?

Leonardo went silent and locked his keen gaze on him, as if he had entered Damian's head and read his mind. But where had that thought come from? Had it been his or the girl's—the one inside his head?

Across the table, Annabella frowned. "Damian, you've gone pale. Are you unwell?"

His pulse quickened, but he answered in as even a tone as he could. "I'm fine. Please go on."

He lowered his gaze and fixed it on his bread bowl before he dared sneak another glimpse at Leonardo. He chewed on his food and hoped his father's next query would divert the conversation elsewhere. The voices drifted into the background until Damian raised his head again when Leonardo complimented Annabella on a lovely dinner.

At that moment, the front door opened and Dante burst into

the house. He muttered about a problem at work. Then there was a pause, a moment of hesitation.

Annabella cried out to him, “Dante, where’ve you been? Come in here at once. We’re dining with a distinguished guest.”

Footsteps shuffled over the tiled floor, and Dante came to a halt in the doorway, a wide expression on his face.

As a family, they didn’t dine in here often, preferring the kitchen’s warmth. Dante examined the room, his gaze inextricably drawn toward Leonardo. Then he made his way around the table to his mother and gave her a peck on the cheek.

“Sorry, Mother—everyone—for my lateness.”

Damian smirked at his brother’s ease and his ability to mesmerize everyone. Dante could calm a disgruntled tiger at will. But even though it was just a fleeting instant, Damian caught Dante’s hesitation upon seeing Leonardo.

Ronaldo glared at Dante. “Let me introduce you to our guest tonight. This is Signor Leonardo da Vinci.”

“A pleasure to meet you, sir.”

Dante’s voice wobbled as he greeted their visitor, and Damian sensed that the maestro’s presence had affected his brother just as much as it had him.

Damian also observed Leonardo’s mouth as it hung open, while Dante settled into his seat. The maestro turned toward Annabella and Ronaldo.

“I was not aware you had identical twins.”

Annabella beamed. “Yes, Signor, it’s a rare thing, isn’t it? They have certain subtle differences that distinguish them, although they are not immediately noticeable.”

Leonardo’s eyes darted back and forth between the twins, but said nothing more. Dante remained quiet, and he was relieved when Leonardo picked up on an earlier discussion with Ronaldo.

Even though the evening continued with lively conversation and humorous exchanges, Leonardo’s earlier enthusiasm had changed. Throughout the meal, Damian pondered Leonardo’s abrupt change in mood. It had happened after he had laid eyes on Dante. What had Damian missed?

Once dinner was over, and their guest had left, Dante made himself scarce. Damian excused himself as well and went to their bedroom to speak to him.

Ronaldo stopped him en route. "May I ask what happened at dinner?" His father appeared to have observed the shift as well.

"I'm about to ask Dante the same thing."

When Damian reached their bedroom, a draft of cool air made his neck hairs stand on end. He groaned when he saw the open window. Dante had escaped once more.

Damian lay on his bed with his arms crossed. His heart thundered in his chest as rage filled him. He suspected what had happened, but first he needed to find out whether it was true. His eyes followed the anomalies in the ceiling, as though he would come upon the answer in its cracks.

He took a deep breath and counted to ten to calm himself. His eyelids grew heavy, and he fought against closing them. Lena, the girl inside his head, had vanished. As the dizziness and nausea subsided, he dozed off.

LENA ~ FLORENCE, PRESENT DAY

Someone opened the apartment's front door and kicked an object on the floor as they walked in.

Through the gap under her bed, Lena recognized the hand reaching for the candle that had fallen from the shelf near the entrance. Her back ached, and she coughed to relieve her parched throat.

"Portia?"

From the other side of the bed, Portia shrieked. "I didn't realize you were here. Why are you on the floor?" She rounded the bed and held her hand out to help Lena stand. "What happened? It looks like an earthquake hit the room."

"I fell over backward." Lena touched a tender spot on her scalp. "Think I hit my head."

"Let me have a look."

Lena sat on her bed, still stunned by the fall.

"Looks a little bruised. No cut, though. Let me get you some ice."

As Portia moved to their kitchenette, Lena rubbed the sore spot on the back of her head. "What t-time is it?"

"It's 5:30."

Lena must have looked at her with a puzzled expression because Portia added, "P.M."

"Shit, I have only a little time left."

"Little time left for—?"

"I'll explain later."

"But—"

She caught Portia's stunned expression as she grabbed her purse and ran out the door.

LENA HAD ten minutes left before the Galleria closed its doors to the public. She sprinted to the statue, certain now that it held a clue to the puzzle. She rubbed her eyes. The images of dinner with Leonardo skipped in her mind like the stuttering frames of an old film. Why had Leonardo's mood changed during the dinner?

You'll find it. Her father's voice echoed in her mind, and she recalled her search for Easter eggs in her parents' garden. She had become fretful, and he had whispered, "Be patient, Lena. Keep looking and you'll discover them."

The museum's closing bell chimed. Her eyes twitched as she stared at the statue. The sensation that something was off still nagged at her. The Galleria's lights grew dim, and the guards made their rounds to close each chamber. But she could not tear herself away. Her eyes grew exhausted from studying each detail as she retraced the statue's sinuous body from head to toe. A guard entered the Tribune to usher her out.

She raised her hand. "Please, just another moment."

Her gaze stopped on the statue's hand holding the stone, and her mouth fell open.

Still in a daze, Lena headed for the exit and stepped onto the street. Behind her, the guard locked the Galleria doors.

Her heartbeat quickened as she examined her hand. In her mind's eye, Damian's hand with the elegant fingers of a pianist lay superimposed on top of hers. How could she have missed this detail?

The statue's sculpted hands were large, knotted, and meaty, like the hands of a labourer. In one of her earliest dreams, Dante had run up to Damian at the Ponte Vecchio and placed his hand on his brother's arm. She had caught a glimpse.

"Damn it, Dante."

DAMIAN ~ FLORENCE, 1500

Damian ran upstairs. When he reached the staircase's landing, he stopped for a breath.

Inside the studio, Leonardo and Michelangelo exchanged heated words. Curious, Damian cocked his ear and leaned in closer to the door.

Michelangelo sounded agitated. "Leonardo, there's something going on."

"Calm yourself, Micielo. I'm sure there's an explanation."

Damian placed a hand against the wall to steady himself and became distracted by a small handprint on the wall above the handrail. As he placed his palm over the indentation, the imprinted hand was small and delicate, just like his sister's hands.

He shook his head and dismissed his nonsensical ideas before they took root.

Damian knocked, a solid rap to announce his arrival, and walked into the studio. The two men fell silent as he entered, and he greeted them with a respectful nod as he made his way inside the studio.

On the way to the stage, Leonardo stopped him and looked him dead in the eye as he shook his arm. Damian cringed at such scrutiny. With a gentle hand against his back, Leonardo walked him over to Michelangelo.

"Look, here is our Damiano. See, everything is fine."

Michelangelo grunted and inspected Damian from head to toe, then waved him to the stage. Damian settled into his pose, convinced that he had been the source of their argument. But why?

Damian searched his memory, back to the last time he had been at the studio, but it had gone without incident. He shrugged off the discomforting feeling and moved his body into position. Leonardo interrupted Damian's thoughts when he addressed the maestro as he made his way to the door.

"Michelangelo, I think you are working too hard. You need to step away. I will come back to get you later to make sure you do."

Michelangelo ignored him. Leonardo took one last look at Damian before he closed the studio's door. In the meantime, Michelangelo had hopped onto the stage and stood before Damian.

"Let me see your hands."

Damian bit the inside of his lip. What was going on? He outstretched both hands. Michelangelo flipped them from back to front, fixing his gaze upon them.

"What other work do you do?"

"With my father, at his shop. On the other side of town."

Michelangelo's eyes and mouth twitched.

"You appear different each time you come to the studio. I cannot work this way."

Damian balked at Michelangelo's implication. "I am unsure what you mean, sir. Is there a problem?"

"Look, *you* are my David." He waved his hands and formed the air into the shape of what could be. "But you change from one day to the next—like a chameleon."

Damian frowned, perplexed by Michelangelo's tone. *A chameleon?*

Suddenly, Michelangelo let out a puff of air and did an about-face. His demeanour changed as if nothing had happened. "Let's try something different today."

The maestro fussed and altered Damian's pose. He grumbled as he moved him around. "I don't understand. It is like you are two different people."

Damian remained in his new position for hours, distracted and perplexed by the artist's erratic behaviour. His back ached, and he pondered over whether he could continue to work in this manner.

As the day wore on, the muscles in Damian's right shoulder burned. His arm grew so heavy that it could fall to the ground at any moment, and he would have left it there. He stretched his back and turned to face the artist.

"Sir, I must pause for a moment?"

Michelangelo waved to a chair and summoned him to sit next to the window. In front of the opened window, Damian closed his eyes and breathed in the cool air.

When he craned his neck to view the Arno River and the houses on the opposite bank, he imagined the scenery he had experienced through Lena's eyes: street lamps that lit up without the use of a flame or fire, carriages that travelled through the streets without the use of horses, and crowds of people dressed in strange attire. He marvelled at how different his city looked from the one in his dreams.

. . .

EARLY EVENING CREPT into the studio. The houses' reflections still danced on the water, while the thin flame from a lone torch flickered in the diminishing light. Outside, the day's activities wound down, and people headed home for dinner. Damian loved twilight except for the shadows that lurked in the corners.

His parents had always been punctual about sitting at dinnertime, especially with four children to feed. Their routine had not changed since his sisters had left. But if the maestro kept working, he would not make it to dinner on time. His stomach growled as he imagined his mother's food waiting for him at home.

As the sky turned a deeper shade of purple, Michelangelo lit another candle.

"One more round. Come now, I've let you rest long enough."

The moon's bright crescent peeked out from behind a distant cloud. Taking a deep breath, Damian climbed the podium and struck the latest pose. When Michelangelo reached for yet another piece of parchment, a knock at the door interrupted him.

Leonardo walked in. "Let us go!"

Michelangelo sighed and nodded to Damian. "Come back tomorrow morning. Early, please."

Damian could not leave the studio fast enough. His body creaked and ached all over. Except for the nagging feeling that something was amiss, it had been an uneventful day.

As the door closed behind him, he glanced at the imprint of the hand on the wall and, again, a familiar sensation crossed his thoughts like a passing shadow.

Damian cast aside his lingering notions and bolted down the stairs, two at a time. All his day's stresses vanished the moment he entered the street, and ran toward home.

8
THE PORTRAIT

AUGUSTUS ~ FLORENCE, PRESENT DAY

Augustus sat in Caffè Gilli, having the corner to himself. Chairs and tables spilled out onto the sidewalk of the Piazza della Repubblica, an open invitation for passersby to stop and enjoy the square.

Despite the late hour, he found himself sipping on a cappuccino. He was looking forward to seeing Lena again. She possessed a mysterious quality which drew him in, and yet there was also a familiar feeling, one he could not immediately place.

He had shared a small but significant detail about his past with her, but she had remained reserved to share more about hers. Whenever she was close, a wave of sorrow and loss washed over him, the kind that pulled him down beneath the calm surface of the ocean. The same kind of agony he had experienced after losing his brother. And though she hid her scars well, he knew she had suffered a deep wound.

Lately, however, he sensed that the familiar ripples of emotions contained a new element. She radiated with new vigour, an untamed power, like a fierce and potent energy about to take flight. And this sparked something deep within himself.

As the light faded, Augustus marvelled at the city's beauty. Across the sea of people in the square, a man stood with his arms crossed and stared directly at him. Augustus rose to have a better look at him when a group crossed in front of them, obstructing his view. By the time the crowd dispersed, the man had vanished. A memory tickled at the back of Augustus's mind. Somewhere, somehow, he recognized him.

Augustus searched the square for the stranger when he saw Lena walking across the piazza toward him. She had a different air about her this evening. Her steps were brisk and, even from this distance, the pale, ice-grey hue stood out within her deep-set eyes. Something in them gave him a chill—an other-worldly sensation—as though she were not earthbound.

Lena looked ready for a fight. Against the encroaching forces in her life, perhaps? He caught her eye and waved. Lena's combative expression immediately melted away, and she flashed him a wide grin.

WITH A PECK TO THE CHEEK, Lena settled in the seat across from him at the little table. Augustus signalled the waiter.

Coffee arrived, with macaroons to nibble on while they caught up on the little details, but Augustus was curious to hear the next segment in this unfolding drama. He was ready to delve further into it, and what it might mean for his research on time, space, and quantum physics.

He had not told the others Lena had been meeting with him—in private. It was obvious she was not yet ready to share her experiences. Lena's reluctance was not something he took for granted. She was studious, level-headed, and down-to-earth. If she was being cautious, there was good reason for it.

At a natural pause in their exchange, he steered the

conversation back to its inception. “Tell me, any further developments since I last saw you?”

Lena turned toward the square, her expression pinched, as if someone watched them. Augustus followed her movement to find what had caught her attention. Had she also seen the man standing in the square?

The piazza was busy with its usual bustle of activity, but nothing out of the ordinary stood out. Augustus leaned forward in his seat. He sensed her pent-up energy, ready to bubble over.

“Lena?”

With his nudge, the dam burst. Lena spilled more of her story and Augustus took in every point, fascinated by her description of the city’s past. She even mentioned Marco’s encounter with the enigmatic voices in his apartment.

“This is everything that has happened till now.”

“So, you’ve spoken to Marco about this?”

“No. It’s a coincidence that he brought up the voices.” Lena pulled out the crumpled photocopy from her pocket. “This is a copy of the registry with the list of names.”

Her hands trembled as she placed the sheet on the coffee table in front of him. Augustus glanced at the handwritten notes, and Lena continued recounting her experiences while he scanned the list.

“I retraced my steps from the episode I had and found a name carved into a marble block on the building where apparently the shop was located. It’s faint, but I took a wild guess it was a family name. Then I went to the registry to search for them.” She pointed to the list. “Look, I found the entire family, as well as Damian and his twin, Dante.”

Augustus’s eyes grew wide. “Twins, huh?”

Lena tapped on the piece of paper and looked him in the eye.

“I know it all sounds far-fetched. You’re probably thinking I saw the name somewhere and created this whole scenario.” She paused. “But does any of this sound plausible?”

He smiled, his lips pressed together. "It is a little 'out there', but you have my complete attention. Ardent support, in fact. Even if your story is a little difficult to fathom."

Lena sighed. "I came to you because you're the *one* person who can help me get some perspective."

He picked up the photocopy and read the translations she had scribbled next to the notations. As he did, Augustus immediately understood why her dilemma had just multiplied tenfold. He looked up to see panic cross Lena's face.

She glanced down at the piece of paper. "If my deduction is correct, this is no longer just a simple matter of proving myself. There are two young lives in question." Her voice broke mid sentence. "I've got to warn him."

A silver lining of tears crested in her eyes and pulled at his heartstrings. Augustus was not one to be swayed by drama, but he had grown up dreaming and believing in the possibility of time travel. He had spent the last five years trying to prove this theory. Still, his own reticence held him back.

"I understand how you feel. But Lena, you can't just go back and change history—"

She cut him off. "Don't you think I know that? Look, I have found out they disappeared—just like that." She snapped her fingers, then let out a deep sigh. "How does that even happen? And I'm not sure why I'm getting caught up in all this, but my gut feeling is telling me to do something."

Augustus laid his palms on the table. "You're talking about events that happened five hundred years ago. What if the twins came back from wherever they went, and they just didn't mark it down? There could be a million reasons there are no more annotations after the twins' disappearance."

"I checked everywhere, and there's nothing in the Death records." Her voice rose in pitch. "What if Damian is reaching out so I can help him?"

Augustus drummed his fingers on the tabletop and his thick

Irish brogue became especially pronounced when he responded to her.

"Okay. You have lots of valid points, but we need to study this with an objective eye. Let's return to the very beginning and go from there. "

DAMIAN ~ FLORENCE, 1500

A single ray of sunlight streamed into the bedroom through the shutter.

The beam of light tickled Damian's eyelashes. In his state between sleep and wakefulness, he shielded the light with his forearm. He sat up in his bed and squinted into the semi-obscurity of his home. Dust particles floated where the light spilled into the room.

He had seen the other world again, and this time he awoke with Lena's image burned into his memory. A single wish ran through his mind as he awoke: he needed to capture her likeness. But how?

By an unusual turn of events, these dreams had given him a glimpse into her world, and he marvelled at how circumstances had shifted for him. As his connection with Lena increased, it also became clear that time played an essential part in it. But what were these visions' true purpose?

Damian recalled Leonardo's words at dinner. He had been vague enough to suggest he could see into the future. Was it possible the maestro had some of these answers?

Damian sprang from bed and dressed. He would approach the maestro and ask whether he could bring Lena to life. His pulse quickened at the thought of seeing her on paper, but he also wanted to see how Leonardo would react to her image. He picked out his best Sunday clothing as he was about to pay an important visit.

In the kitchen, Damian served himself Carbonata—a sweet and salty meat dish spiced with cinnamon, cloves, and parsley, accompanied by a lemon broth. His mother, Annabella, cooked this special dish on Sundays and it had quickly become a family favourite. He sat at the table and watched as his mother moved around the kitchen, busy with her baking.

Damian enjoyed these unaccustomed luxuries to the fullest. There had been a time when his parents had struggled to profit from their hard work. That morning, Annabella prepared her specialty desserts and cakes for another big market event. While Damian ate, he sensed her eyes upon him. He could tell his delicate manners filled her with pride.

He had walked into the kitchen a few moments earlier, impeccably dressed and had only meant to pass through, but the delicious smell of her cooking had tempted him to taste her dish. Before returning to her tasks, his mother beamed a smile that melted his heart, as if she had just filled him with the warm lemon broth she had prepared. Many of his qualities came from her.

But now he squirmed under her gaze. She had a way of peering into his soul, as if she knew what he was thinking. He glanced up at her. Annabella's lips curled upward even though he had not said a thing.

"What is she like, this girl?"

His hand lifted and stopped midway to putting a morsel of bread into his mouth. His mother waited until he found his voice.

"H-How could you know—?"

"How do mothers know anything?"

Damian lowered his hand and gazed at the carved-out loaf which sat on the table.

"She . . . She's the most beautiful girl I've ever seen."

Annabella's eyes narrowed. "Who is she?"

Damian's emotions veered from cheerful to gloomy. "I don't know."

His mother opened her mouth, as if to say something else. Instead, she cleared her throat and turned her attention back to her preparations. She always had a keen sense of when to press further and when to let things be. He kept his head down and finished his food.

When he got up to leave, he kissed her cheek. "I have to go now. *Ti amo*, Mama."

Damian could feel Annabella's eyes on him as he put on his overcoat and walked out of the house. Just before he disappeared around the corner, he looked over his shoulder and caught his mother in the window, watching him with a soulful expression on her face. But something else lay behind her eyes, something she was not telling him.

Memories of his parents murmuring in their bedroom late at night floated to the surface of his mind, of their whispers wafting down the hallway. Even as a child, they had sent chills through him. Now, an icy breeze travelled up his spine and nested between his shoulder blades.

DAMIAN STROLLED through the chilly midmorning air and made his way to D'Alessandro's. Even though Sunday was a day of rest, his father had gone to the shop in search of a tool.

Damian wove his way around the crowds, going about their Sunday obligations. The city always adopted a slower pace on Sundays. Only Damian showed any urgency, setting out to find the master painter. He would ask his father where he could find the artist.

As he reached D'Alessandro's, Damian looked at the marble block lodged into the building's wall. Carved into the stone, his family's name stood out. His chest puffed out with pride. Ronaldo had ordered the chiseled engraving when he had bought the store.

Damian pushed open the shop's front door and peeked his head in.

"Papa?"

All was silent. He called out again. This time, voices filtered down from the back, and his father's laughter rang out. Damian entered and stepped through the narrow hallway. He peered around the corner and saw his father and another man examining a flat piece of metal on a table in the middle of the small room.

Damian coughed to signal he was there, and Ronaldo looked up and smiled when he saw him. He gestured to his customer.

"Ah, let me introduce you to my son, Damian." Then he prefaced his client. "This is Don Camillo from the Medici house."

Damian entered the room and greeted the stern man who stood facing him. "I am sorry to interrupt your conversation, but do you think I could ask you a favour, Father?"

He stammered, unsure whether to delay his request or to ask his father in front of this stranger. But if he waited, the day would be gone and he would lose his chance.

His father's eyes rested upon him. "Well, son, what is it?"

"Could you tell me how to find the maestro Leonardo? I have a matter to discuss with him."

He bit his bottom lip and waited for his father's reaction.

Ronaldo's smile turned into a frown. "Is there a problem?"

"No. I simply need to confer with him."

Ronaldo narrowed his eyes. "I do not know where he lives. It's true he has been our guest and comes by often to order from me. However, I have never been to his home."

Don Camillo, who had remained quiet during the interaction between father and son, spoke up. "If I may interrupt, *I* can direct you to the maestro's workshop. But I am certain you will not find him there most days. Leonardo is like a butterfly, always busy, often flitting around town." He paused and laughed. "I sometimes question how he gets any work done."

Ronaldo rescinded Damian's request. "Regardless, you cannot

visit Leonardo without an invitation. My apologies to you, Don Camillo. My son lacks in manners."

Heat rose to Damian's cheeks, while Don Camillo waved his hands in the air.

"With all due respect, I know Leonardo to be a hospitable fellow who does not require invitations. However, on Sundays, you are most likely to find him in the gardens. I believe he may be in the Giardino Bardini. I can take you there."

Damian's heart thundered like wild horses. Even though his father bristled at this unexpected exchange, Damian's excitement at seeing Lena's image on paper made him much braver than usual. He sensed his father's reluctance to let him go, but Damian would not let it stop him this time.

Facing Ronaldo, Don Camillo straightened his back. "You have spent enough time with me today and should get back to your family."

Ronaldo pointed to the metal bar sitting on the table. "I will see you at this week's end. The part you ordered will have arrived by then. Until then, I will work on this piece."

Ronaldo closed up shop and the three men walked to the Piazza Santa Maria Novella. At the centre of the piazza, Damian and Don Camillo parted ways with Ronaldo.

The crease between his father's brow ran deeper and more visible, even with the increasing distance between them. Damian caught his father's eye one last time before turning his full attention to the formidable man next to him.

As Don Camillo led the way, he spoke on the history of Florence, and revealed himself a knowledgeable man and successful merchant. Walking alongside Damian, he boasted of his association with Florence's Medici dynasty and of his family's status.

"We own large acreages of land around Florence, some of which Leonardo has painted into the backdrop of his paintings.

One painting even depicts *'La Mano di Dio,'* a stone structure found on our lands."

Don Camillo held out his hand in mimicry of the rock formation. *The hand of God.* The visual jogged something in Damian's memory. An unusual sensation came to him because he was certain he had seen those boulders before.

Damian wanted to ask about its location when his companion cut the conversation short, pointing to a labyrinthine path.

"Here is the Giardino Bardini. This is the garden where Leonardo wanders around on Sunday mornings. If you find him, please extend my greetings to the maestro."

Damian saluted the gentleman formally, grasping his forearm, before proceeding to walk up the rocky trail. He glanced over his shoulder and found the man watched him with a grim expression on his face. As Damian turned away, he caught the silver shimmer of light that enveloped Don Camillo. A faint memory skittered lightly across his shoulders, and he shuddered. When he looked again, the trader had vanished from view.

The myriad paths hid lifelike statues, and they surprised him at each turn. In these gardens, Damian stood in awe of the splendour of nature. Throughout this enchanting place, each flower glowed vividly with each petal overlapped in perfect symmetry. He became lost in the wondrous maze as he searched for Leonardo. He recognized the garden, the same one where Marco had taken Lena in his dream of her world.

He ran down another path, and by pure chance, he caught the flap of a short, light-coloured tunic as it disappeared around a corner. *Leonardo!* Damian sprinted to catch up to him and, as he rounded the bend, he almost bumped into him. Leonardo had stopped to peer into a hedge.

Without a hint of surprise, the maestro looked up and put a finger to his lips. He motioned for Damian to approach.

Heartened by the older man's ease and friendliness, Damian moved closer. He peeked into the shrubbery. In awe, they watched a robin feeding her chicks. The nest sat in between two very fragile branches, but safe from the outside world. The baby chicks cackled as they chirped and demanded food from their mother.

It was obvious the world's beauty still fascinated Leonardo. After a moment, the artist turned to Damian.

"Is Michelangelo looking for me?"

It suddenly dawned on Damian that his intrusion had not bothered Leonardo because of his connection to Michelangelo. Beads of sweat formed on Damian's forehead, and he was on the verge of lying. Instead, courage seized him, and he sucked in his stomach.

"No, Sir. *I* am."

Leonardo's eyes lit up with a curious expression. "Then, let's walk." He pointed the way, and they meandered through the labyrinth. Leonardo spoke about his life as an apprentice to his master, Andrea del Verrocchio. "From a young age, I've had the privilege of being part of some of the highest social circles of Florence." Leonardo patted Damian's shoulder. "And at seventeen, I was also the model for Verrocchio's *Statue of David*." He paused, deep in thought. "Damiano, you are a much more formidable *David* than I ever could be. I speak the truth when I say that Michelangelo will create a statue that the world will glorify for centuries. If not for a millennium."

Damian's expression changed to one of astonishment. Was this conjecture, or did he know something more?

Leonardo cast a sidelong glance at him. "My son, what is your reason for finding me today?"

Startled by the question, Damian stuttered. He was about to reveal the reason for this intrusion—a personal dream—and a sudden wave of embarrassment washed over him. Taking a deep breath, he explained his dilemma to the artist. He described Lena as best he could and hoped to persuade Leonardo to draw her likeness. "She is the most beautiful girl I've ever seen. And I would like a portrait of her."

Leonardo's lips curled into a smile.

"When did you meet this wonderful young woman?"

Heat rose under Damian's collar.

"In truth, I've only seen her in my dreams, but I must get her image onto parchment before I forget what she looks like."

Intrigued, Leonardo agreed. "As happens with dreams. Come, let's walk to my studio." And he warned Damian as they walked, "Your description must be precise, down to the last detail, to come close to her likeness. Dreams have a way of washing out details and disappearing just when you're certain you have a grasp on them."

Damian nodded. That was precisely why he had called upon Leonardo for help.

AS THEY ENTERED the Piazza della Signoria, Damian stumbled. With a firm grasp, Leonardo caught him from tumbling to the floor. The maestro's unexpected strength amazed Damian as he was carefully seated on a stone bench beneath the three arches of the Loggia dei Lanzi.

The artist sounded faint. "Your face has paled."

Damian closed his eyes to stop his head from spinning. When he opened them, he looked about him. An unsettling but familiar sensation signalled Lena's presence. Leonardo, who held him by his shoulder, watched over him.

"Shall I take you home?"

Damian shook his head. There might not be another occasion for him. "No, I must do this."

Leonardo helped Damian to his feet and held him up under the elbow.

"It seems your colour is coming back. You seem determined to keep going. Shall we walk further?"

Damian assured him he could go on. They continued their stroll and eventually arrived at Leonardo's workshop. It was a small building with an inconspicuous entrance, hidden amid a nondescript street. Unlike Michelangelo's vast studio, it hardly looked like the workshop of a celebrated artist. Instead, a wild beast of creativity lived here. Miscellaneous objects and bits of ideas were crammed into the room, filling up the space. A veritable chaos.

Damian had heard that the maestros painted in churches and in the homes of the wealthy, who commissioned them to paint their portraits. He looked around at the cramped workspace. If Leonardo had a studio where he painted, it certainly was not here.

As he entered the building, Damian could feel Lena's excitement. In his own belly, butterflies flew amuck, their wings flapping against his ribs. His heartbeat pounded against his temples, his hands shook, and his voice quivered. But something told him he might just surprise *her* tonight. He moved to the drawing table and observed as Leonardo took out a large piece of parchment and his conté sticks.

"Now, let's begin. What shape is her face?"

Damian described Lena, how her face was oval, "with soft edges and high cheekbones."

"Good, and?"

"Thin-shaped eyebrows. Deep-set eyes, intense and expressive."

Leonardo's hand moved swiftly, and his nods encouraged Damian to continue.

"Her eyes are grey—bright, but cold like ice. With a hint of darkness, like a shadow, around the iris. She has a defined nose, pointed and small, and her mouth is not too large, but shapely, and sits above a pointed chin. Her face reminds me of the silhouette of a waning moon, if you know what I mean, maestro." He paused a moment to review the sketch before him.

"Her hair is long, with curls surrounding her face. It falls onto her shoulders and down her back. Her skin is clear, almost translucent." He also mentioned the beauty spot placed just below her lip.

"My dear boy, you speak of her as if she is present and real."

"She is real . . . to me."

Lena's image emerged as Leonardo's conté stick flowed with ease across the sheet of paper. A warm sensation enveloped Damian. His own ability to describe her in such detail amazed him, and Leonardo's skill for bringing her to life before his very eyes flabbergasted him.

"Lena . . . "

Leonardo took a step back and cocked his head at the young woman's portrait.

"Are you sure you have never seen this young lady in person? She looks familiar."

A tingling sensation of prickles began at Damian's nape, and he shifted from one foot to the other. He was now certain of one thing: Lena's portrait had piqued the maestro's curiosity.

Leonardo was about to hand the portrait to him when he flipped it over and rubbed it down onto another sheet. He lifted the original drawing, and on the other sheet, a faint copy remained.

"I like to keep copies of my sketches, if you don't mind."

Damian stiffened, and his hand trembled when he reached for his drawing. Leonardo fastened his grip and held onto it a moment longer before setting it free.

"I understand why you've been impatient. She has exquisite features."

A ball of angst dropped to the bottom of Damian's belly and settled like a lead weight. He was certain his skin flushed bright from the rising heat to his face.

Damian thanked the artist for his time. He picked up his pace as he made his way toward the front door, but Leonardo's strides were longer as he accompanied him to the workshop's exit. Leonardo reached past him and placed his hand on the latch.

He faced Damian, and his deep, penetrating stare turned frigid. His tone became sharp, cracking like a sheet of ice on the Arno River in winter. "Your twin and you are playing a dangerous game." He kept his gaze on Damian. "Be careful where you tread." His voice sent shivers down his spine with its gravelly and ominous tone.

Dante? Damian faltered, bewildered by Leonardo's sudden confrontational manner. But the ominous message that came from this man, who only moments earlier had exuded warmth and generosity, validated Damian's suspicion. Dante had meddled and compromised his employment.

Damian seethed, overcome with a desire to scream. He breathed to calm his nerves, but his body trembled. With a sense of urgency, he had to escape from this place and locate his brother.

Leonardo opened the door, and Damian bolted up the cobblestone street. His heart pumped wildly, almost bursting from his chest. When he glanced back, Leonardo still stood at the workshop's door, surrounded by a glimmer of light, and wearing the same dour expression he had seen reflected on Don Camillo's face.

As Damian made his way back home, he checked over his shoulder every few minutes. Holding on fast to the parchment scroll, he tapped it now and again to make sure he still had it tucked under his arm.

9
SIX HEADS ARE BETTER THAN ONE

LENA ~ FLORENCE, PRESENT DAY

LENA OPENED her eyes to find Portia looking at her, teary-eyed, and shaking. Portia's voice trembled and rose in pitch as she spoke.

"I've been trying to stop you from hurting yourself for the past few minutes. Your body's been jerking around on the floor . . . Lena . . . I can't keep doing this. You've got to tell me what's going on."

The ringing in her ears made Lena cringe as she shoved Portia aside and dashed to the restroom. Her gut wrenched from dizziness and nausea. She mumbled a few garbled words and threw open the toilet lid.

Portia followed. She rubbed Lena's back, handed her a towel and a drink of water, then sat next to her on the bathtub's edge.

"I—I don't think I can handle this anymore. I want to help, but I can't if you keep shutting me out."

Lena wiped her mouth and sank to the floor. She looked up to see Portia's makeup smeared and smudged from the tears that streamed down her cheeks. For weeks, her closest friend had been dealing with her erratic moods and odd behaviour. She had already inflicted too much anguish upon Portia. It had to stop.

When Portia slid down and joined her on the floor, Lena wriggled her bottom to face her. She had to open up to her friend, give her some relief.

Lena divulged her dreams and the events leading up to the fall at her desk. Without interrupting, Portia's eyes grew wider with each elaborate detail. When Lena got to the end of her story, they sat on the bathroom floor, oblivious to the world around them.

Portia slouched, stunned by the overload of information. But a few moments was all it took for her to recuperate; she overflowed with a stream of words, like a flood breaking apart sandbags and rushing overtop.

"I can't believe it! I—I've got a million questions, but—I don't even know where to start. And that's a strange thing for me." She broke out in peels of nervous laughter. "Why didn't you tell me sooner?"

Lena smiled, her lips pressed tightly together. "I should have. Look, I was afraid if I talked about it, I'd lose my connection to him before I had it figured out. I didn't want to risk it."

Portia's lips tightened, and she crossed her arms. "But you told Augustus."

"Yes, only because I needed more information about quantum physics. You can't ask Augustus about his work without him prodding back. You know that."

Meanwhile, Portia took Lena's hand in hers and held it tight. Lena was not sure whether it was out of excitement or fright. Maybe it was both.

Lena waited for Portia to absorb her story, unsure whether she could handle the next part. Suspense hung in the air between them until a flicker of realization flashed across Portia's face.

"What's that look for? What're you not telling me? There's more . . .?"

"Um, yes. But please don't panic!"

"Why would I freak out?" Portia covered her face and spoke through her fingers. "Wait . . . should I be scared?" She was always so dramatic, but Lena loved her for it.

"No . . ." Lena waited while Portia removed her hands from her eyes.

"All right, I'm ready. Tell me now before I change my mind."

Lena let out a chortle at her friend's overreactions. Nevertheless, it was not going to be easy to convince her of the next part.

"Um, well, Damian . . ." She squinted one eye at Portia.

"Ah-huh. What about him?"

Lena took a deep breath. "He's here with us."

"What do you mean by 'here'?" Portia searched the empty room. "Like a ghost?"

"No, not quite. He's inside my head. But . . . he sees everything I see."

Portia jumped up from her seated position and stepped back toward the door. "You mean he's taken possession of you?"

Lena put up her hand to stop Portia. "No, it's more like dual consciousness. When he's dreaming, he's seeing the world through my eyes. The same happens to me when I'm dreaming. I'm over there."

A wave of different reactions flitted across Portia's face at once. She narrowed her eyes and glared at Lena. "What are you saying? He can see me now? Looking this way? With makeup smeared on my face and in my PJs?" Her eyes widened. "He's been here the whole time?"

Lena gasped, half-choking and half-chuckling, all in the same breath. "Portia, *you* are incorrigible!"

Relief spread across Portia's face, but it was not long before her expression shifted again. She paced in front of Lena. "Hang on a second, that day when you were acting all funny and looking at me weird, Damian was here, wasn't he?—My God! He's seen me half-naked!"

"I'm truly sorry about that. I have no control over when he comes and goes. And neither do I. Come to think of it, that was the first night I realized he was *here*."

Portia scrunched her face, and Lena fell over laughing on the bathroom floor. Lena's entire body released the tension locked up inside of her.

"This is totally crazy!" Portia's exclamation let on she had finally registered everything Lena had just told her.

After they had calmed down, an audible grumble came from Lena's belly during a moment of silence. The release of the afternoon's tension prompted another wave of belly-clenching laughter. But as Lena struggled to regain her breath between giggles, a sinking feeling settled in the hollow of her belly. There remained one last vital piece of information she had left out.

After the girls dragged themselves out of the bathroom and dressed, they left the apartment in search of something to eat. Lena pondered if her dreams and connection to the past would change now that she had confided in Portia.

They snaked through the bustling crowd and found a bistro nestled in a side street a few streets down from their building. Lena seated herself while Portia left to use the washroom. When she came back to the table, a shadow crossed Portia's face.

Lena did not have to wait long to find out why. Christina, Gregory, Marco, and Augustus rounded the corner as she and Portia sipped on their coffees.

Lena threw her arms up. "Really?"

Portia's shoulders slumped. "I know you wanted to keep this on the down low, but you really need to trust your friends."

When the foursome joined them at the table, Marco looked at Lena.

"Portia's right. You should trust us to help you with whatever it is you're dealing with."

Lena always kept herself guarded, surrounded by a brick wall. It was second nature to keep things to herself and not let anyone else in, and she found it was a hard habit to break. But she looked around at her friends—the ones who sat with her, the ones who genuinely cared about her—and knew she had to start somewhere.

Lena put her coffee down and stood up.

"Follow me to the Galleria."

She left some bills on the table and walked out of the cafe. When she cast a backward glance, she caught her friends looking sideways at each other. They would understand soon enough.

On the way, Lena contemplated the portrait she had seen of herself, as well as Leonardo's threatening message—a warning of a real danger. It was no longer just about getting caught in a game of switched identities.

Before they entered the galleria, Lena wrapped a scarf around her hair and put on some sunglasses. She waved her finger at her friends.

"I'm banned from the Galleria. Not a word from you guys."

She was about to push the door open when the guard pointed to his watch from behind the door. They had arrived too late. Augustus stepped inside and whispered to the fellow. A brief conversation ensued where Augustus made up some long, convoluted excuse about needing to get in at all costs—university projects depended on it.

The guard rolled his eyes and sighed. He opened the doors to them even though it was getting close to his afternoon break. He tapped his watch again and gave them ten minutes. Once they were inside, he locked up after them.

Lena did not waste any time and led them straight to *David*. In the Tribune, she perceived Damian's rush of emotions as she stared at the statue. Wonder? Awe? He saw himself captured in a giant slab of marble. All the many hours he had spent posing for Michelangelo, recorded into history.

Lena broke the silence. As she spoke, her eyes followed the contour of the statue.

"One day, after I had been here for the millionth time to observe him, I saw a flutter near *David's* toes." She paused, recalling the event. "I tried to get closer to videotape and capture the movement, but the guard on duty caught me."

Gregory shifted from one foot to the other. "Hence, the disguise?"

"Exactly. Unfortunately, he deleted the video before handing me back my phone. I ran out of the galleria and walked around Florence to calm myself. And that's when it all started."

Her friends remained quiet as Lena related her story from start to finish. They looked up at the statue, and Portia stepped forward and swivelled to look at her friends.

"It's possible Damian's here with us now." She turned to Lena for verification. "Right?"

Augustus and Marco stared at Portia like she had grown two heads and waited for Lena to dismiss the ridiculous claim. But Lena nodded, confirming Portia's outlandish statement. The moment did not stop Portia, who continued with an air of authority.

"We can't see him; however, he can see us and hear everything we're saying."

Lena smiled at Portia, ready to show them the evidence of her claims.

"Now I know this story couldn't sound any stranger to you than it already does." Her hands shook when she withdrew the photocopied paper from her pocket. "But, there's more." She unfolded the sheet and smoothed out the wrinkles. Damian also needed to see this information with his own eyes. She swallowed the tightness lodged in her throat.

She pointed to the dates and translated the information. Augustus, who was already aware of her story, remained quiet, but

Marco and the others stared at the dates, doing the math in their minds.

Portia spoke first, breaking the moment of suspense. "Spring? It's spring here too. Do you think it's a coincidence? If that's the case, there's not much time left to save these two boys!"

Augustus touched Portia's arm lightly. "Let's think things through first before rushing to conclusions."

Marco stepped back from the group and mumbled to himself. Lena frowned and watched as he paced the floor.

"Marco, what is it?"

He looked at them and lowered his voice.

"You guys won't believe it . . ."

"What, Marco? Do you know something? Have those voices spoken again?"

"No, nothing else at the studio. But this information you've just brought forward. I think I know the twins' story."

Lena's mouth fell agape. "What do you mean?"

Marco looked back and forth between Lena and Portia. "Is Damian still here? I'm not sure I should say anything in front of him."

Lena nodded. "Go on. It couldn't be any worse than what I've just told him."

"You're right." Before continuing, Marco hesitated for a second to regroup his thoughts. "Okay, this is completely nuts. It could be a coincidence, but I believe you've been telling us the story of my ancestors. *My* family."

Lena could hardly believe her ears. "Your family?" A rush of excitement set her pulse racing.

Augustus and the rest of the group shifted on their feet while Marco explained that Ariella D'Alessandro was his ancestor. She was Annabella and Ronaldo's youngest daughter and the twins' sister.

"What I'm going to tell you is the story passed down from generation to generation. It's the shortened version, of course."

Marco paced the floor as he retraced his family's history to them.

"So, one afternoon, Dante was in the Piazza San Croce with his cousin Giancarlo Baldini—Ariella's nephew by marriage. While they were in the square, someone approached Dante to engage in conversation. Now, here is where the story has lost its thread as it was passed down through the generations of my family. As far as I know, we don't know who that person was, but they believed he was involved in the disappearance.

"After that encounter, Dante worked until lunch, then he left to go to his father's shop. Only, he never showed up there. His father did not worry about Dante's absence *until* Damian arrived looking for him." He took a deep breath. "By the next morning, when Dante still hadn't shown up, the entire family and their friends gathered at the house and went searching for him."

Marco appeared wary about divulging any more of his story, but Lena nodded for him to go on.

"They spent three days and nights combing the area for Dante, but could not find any trace of him." Marco sighed. "And, a few weeks later, to the entire family's shock, Damian disappeared, too. They both vanished as if into thin air and the sad thing is, no one ever found out what happened."

No one spoke until the afternoon guard made them all jump when he announced it was time for them to leave. Lena's breathing quickened as Damian's growing anxiousness rippled through her. She slipped her hand into Marco's as they stepped out of the galleria.

"It's too bad your family never found out who it was that Dante met in the square?"

Marco shook his head. "You know how stories get passed down through generations. They either become embellished or lose certain details, but my family never solved the mystery."

The group walked up the street from the Galleria in silence when Portia stopped them.

"I think we should have a brainstorming session. Figure out what happened. We must find a solution and try to stop this."

A spontaneous overflow of emotions filled Lena. She had indeed found her tribe here in this mystical city that fostered friendships of all kinds.

Her connection to the past had not been severed since Damian was still present, and she instantly regretted her reluctance to confide in her friends. Portia was right. Six heads were better than one.

DAMIAN ~ FLORENCE, 1489

Eight-year-old Damian sat on his haunches, his eyes focused on the ground.

He peered at the large, depressed imprint on the soft earth. A horse's hoof. A warm breeze rustled the leaves and dry grasses in the open expanse of this bright Tuscan afternoon. Near him, the mysterious boulders stood majestic and tall—five enormous towers of stone. They did not seem as frightening up close, but his parents had always warned him, "Stay away from the boulders. They bring bad luck to everyone who goes near them."

Damian reached out to touch the hoof's imprint, which spanned larger than his small hand, when a loud thump reverberated behind him. He figured it was Giancarlo trying to frighten him, and he whirled around.

"Ha! You thought you could scare me."

A shadow fell across him. Startled, he stumbled backward and landed on his hands. A large black horse loomed over him. Bigger than any he had ever seen. A bear-sized man dressed in black armour sat atop the giant horse. In the sunlight, its coat glimmered with sweat. The stallion's nostrils flared and its chest muscles rippled. The knight stared at Damian, with his hand rested on his sword's handle.

"Que fais-tu ici?

The man's voice was more like a deep growl than a spoken language. Damian heard a jumble of sounds, and while the words made little sense, he had gotten the gist of their meaning. When he pushed himself up to stand, he barely reached the horse's muzzle.

His voice wavered as he pointed to the forest stretched out beyond them. "My friends and I are playing there."

The knight dismissed him with a hand gesture. His skin was the colour of hardened leather and, besides his menacing countenance, his deep and sonorous voice echoed in the clearing.

"Go back to the forest. Stay out of here. These grounds are dangerous."

This time, the knight had spoken in the local Florentine dialect, and Damian had understood him loud and clear. He did not waste a minute as he darted past the knight, back to the forest's edge. His heart thumped and beat loudly against his chest.

With his feet light on the ground, he risked looking over his shoulder to see if the knight still watched him. He tripped and his cheek grazed the dry earth as he landed hard on the ground. With a bloody cheekbone, he shook the dirt off and searched the clearing, but found himself alone. Where had the knight gone?

The clearing was a long strip of land rather than an enclosed, circular one. Flanked on one side by a forested area and, on the other, by a steep hill covered with trees and heavy brush. There was no way the knight could have escaped by that route. It was too steep! But Damian explored no further. He ran into the woods and called out to his brother.

Branches snapped underfoot as he thrashed along the path overgrown with brush. The noise echoed amongst the woods' lurking shadows. Through the spindling saplings and branches, a flutter of blue appeared through the leaves.

Damian panted, relieved to find his brother. "Here you are!"

Branches obstructed Damian's view as he made his way as fast as he could. When he reached his brother, a look of terror spread across his twin's face.

Damian's skin prickled with goosebumps. He looked around when he caught a flash of movement at their side. A tall man stood with his gaze upon them—a man unlike anyone he had ever seen before. Not even anything like the knight he had just encountered.

The tall man's crystal-grey eyes mesmerized him as he scanned the area from left to right. Damian observed he had shaved the sides of his head. The man had a braid, and the way his fair hair wound from his crown down to his nape captured Damian's attention. The man cocked his head and stared off into the distance as though he had heard something. Then he turned to face the boys.

Dante spoke up, in a rather confident tone. "Are you looking for the lady?"

Damian looked at his brother with wide eyes. He turned toward the man and a tremor coursed through him. The man glared at them with such intensity. His eyes sparkled and his lips twitched.

Soon, a noise emanated from this formidable apparition. It grew into a loud, penetrating vibration. Damian's eardrums roared as though they might explode. Another curious thing he found: the man's mouth had not moved. The boys let go of each other and cupped their hands over their ears. Next to him, Dante fell to one knee, holding his head. A few moments later, the pain in Damian's ears stopped.

The man spoke to them without an audible sound. "You have seen a lady in these woods by herself?"

As if by magic, Damian understood the words. From where Dante was crouched, he shook his head, most likely the ringing from his ears, before he spoke. "Yes. A lady with long, dark hair and the eyes of a wolf. Like yours." He pointed to the man, and then toward the path. "I showed her the way to Firenze."

The man with the golden braid frowned, and deep creases formed around his eyes. Dante waved his finger at the scroll the man held in his hand.

"Who are you and what is that?"

Damian shoved his brother with his elbow. "We shouldn't speak to this strange man. We don't know him. Let's go."

The man interrupted. "You're absolutely right." He looked from Damian to Dante. "Let me introduce myself. My name is Adrien, and I mean you no harm."

With this introduction, Dante pressed on. "How is it we can hear you even though you do not open your mouth?"

Damian shoved his brother again. "Dante! We should go!"

Adrien smiled. "There'll come a time for answers. I'm simply here to—" He was about to continue when the sound of children's shrill voices rang out. Friends calling out to the twins.

"Where are you? Dante? Damian? Is this how you play hide and seek?" Both boys looked toward their friends' hollers, and when they turned back to the man named Adrien, he was gone.

Dante's voice trembled as his hand came up and crossed his heart. "Damian, we shall never speak of what we saw here today to anyone. Promise?"

"I promise. You too?"

"Yes, I promise. What happened to your cheek?"

Damian had almost forgotten about the knight. "Oh, nothing. I tripped and fell."

Jittery from their encounter, the twins startled at the moving shadows around them. When their friends joined them, Dante announced, "This game is getting boring. Let's go home!"

Giancarlo whined as they followed the twins back to Florence. "But we just got here!"

WHEN THE BOYS entered their home, they laughed and jostled each other as they tried to forget their earlier scare. Their mother scolded and grabbed them both by their ears. "I worry when you're gone for so long. Where have you been?"

She left them at the kitchen table without expecting an answer. Damian jabbed Dante in the ribs after they had sat alone for a moment.

"You saw a woman in the forest today?"

Dante's eyes grew wide with excitement. "*Si!* The most beautiful woman I've ever seen!"

"*Ooh! Una bella donna!*" Damian giggled and poked fun at his brother, who hated being teased.

Afterward, as their mother sat near the fireplace and watched them, Damian was sure he heard her whisper to herself.

"What will I ever do without my boys?"

10
THE FOREST OF THE DISAPPEARING

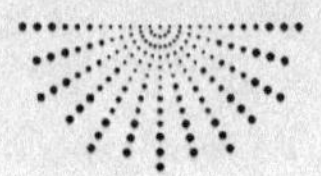

DAMIAN ~ FLORENCE, 1500

In the Galleria, Damian had seen his larger-than-life resemblance sculpted into marble. But he had observed one anomaly. Without a doubt, it had been Dante who held the stone. Of that, he was certain. Damian recognized the bold hands, roughened by masonry work. He was now convinced Dante had been standing in for him.

He inched up the stairs toward the studio, stopping at the landing, and laid his hand over the feminine imprint at the top of the railing. Who had left it there? It had not been there when he had first started modelling for the maestro.

His world no longer resembled the secure place he had always known. If someone were planning to cut their life short, could he and his brother do anything to change their lot?

Growing up, he had basked in the quiet life his parents had built around the family. He had hoped one day to follow his parents' example: complete devotion to each other, to their children, and to the family business.

His understanding of time had now become fluid and

effervescent, and these events had altered his perspective on life. And now Dante's deception had jeopardized his seemingly serene existence.

Damian knocked at the studio's door, opened it, and made his way to the folding screen to put on his loincloth. He took a deep breath before emerging from the private space in the corner. He sensed Michelangelo's eyes boring into him as he moved to the podium. His belly tightened into a hard knot. Damian did not look at the maestro but, in his peripheral vision, he perceived the unmistakable frown. That was enough.

Afraid he would lose his commission, Damian did nothing to arouse suspicion. These men were extraordinary people—the kind who observed small, inconsequential details. Even the public revered—nay, feared them. His hands chilled, recalling the day Michelangelo had turned them over for inspection. Damian bit his lip, fearful to expose his brother's deceitful act.

Damian's hands were no longer identical to Dante's—not after they had pursued different paths. Their mother had been the first to notice the growing difference. She had once remarked, "Dante has the hands of a mason; Damian, those of a musician." It had meant nothing to them—a minor point to the boys.

Now, another minute detail hung above him like a guillotine: a scar which ran along Dante's left baby finger—a gash he had suffered from a fall when they were younger. Though subtle, it was a distinguishing feature that set them apart. He replayed every word he had overheard during his dream, trying to grasp their meaning. Even now, Damian could feel a shiver travel down his spine, the weight of Leonardo's dire warning lingering in the air. *Be very careful where you tread.* Did he mean they would suffer a fate worse than death?

THE FOLLOWING MORNING, Damian awoke to voices coming

from the kitchen. Dante reassured their mother, who complained, "I haven't seen you much these days. What are you up to now?"

"Mama, I told you. Work's been taking up my time."

In the meantime, Damian slipped out the bedroom window and headed down the alleyway. He did not want to confront Dante in front of their mother. That would only worry her more.

Dante had evidently calmed their mother because her laughter rang out as she shooed him out of her kitchen and through the front door. When he stepped out, Damian peered around the corner. Dante was all smiles, but his dimples faded as soon as Damian reached his side.

"We must talk. No excuses this time."

Damian led his brother up the street to the stone bench in the alcove and sat facing the fountain, whose water trickled into a basin. With the morning chill, dank moisture seeped through Damian's clothing where he sat on the stone bench.

Dante shifted from foot to foot and stared down at his shoes. "You've found out I've been to the studio in your place."

Damian's head spun as his mind raced. "How could you deceive me like that?" His words caught in his throat.

Dante avoided Damian's glare. "I'm sorry. I've just been worried about you. You know, with Savoranola burning art in our town square and nefarious activities being punished—"

Damian was tired of Dante's empty apologies. "Your actions have put me in a precarious position. You always want to help, but this time you've made things worse."

Dante's head drew back upon hearing these words. "Why? Has something happened?"

Damian's neck tightened. "Not yet. But if Leonardo tells Michelangelo what he's found out, I'll be out of work."

"Leonardo? What has he said to you? Listen, I'll confess what I did."

"You'll do nothing of the sort. You have done enough harm already."

His brother sighed. “In all honesty, I don’t know how you can pose for such long hours.”

“You’re deflecting, and that is really beside the point.”

Damian fumed and closed his eyes to stop himself from charging at his brother like he used to when they were little.

“This isn’t a game; this is my livelihood we’re talking about.”

He clenched his jaw. He despised losing his temper, but Dante had pushed him too far this time.

Dante rubbed his forehead. “You’re right. Look, I promise not to go to the studio anymore.”

Damian leaned forward as if ready to pounce. “That’s right, you won’t go near that place.” A flood of conflicting emotions rushed over him. Why did his brother always have to get in the midst of everything?

“Whoa, I said I was sorry.” Dante’s eyebrows furrowed. “Anyway, nothing happened while I was there, and I mean, nothing! What’s the big deal?”

Damian shook his head and exhaled. “The big deal? Brother, there’s a lot more at stake than just being caught in some ruse.”

Dante narrowed his eyes. “Did they threaten you? What’s going on?”

Damian rubbed his eyes with the palms of his hands. “The situation is more complicated than that.” He shifted on the stone bench. Did he really want to let him in on this convoluted tale? Telling him would only complicate matters. His brother could never sit back and do nothing. His thoughts waffled back and forth, arguing both sides of the dilemma. Would he be able to figure it all out without Dante? Most likely not.

He drew in a long breath and knew he *had* to explain the situation to Dante, even if it was the worse mistake. Dante would react with disbelief at first. Of that, he was certain. But they would sort through all the details together. After all, he shared everything with his brother.

. . .

DAMIAN RECOUNTED the strange events he had been experiencing. As he told his story, Dante's eyes furrowed with each new revelation. Just as Damian was about to share his latest dream, he halted.

"There is more. But I have to warn you, it's not good."

Dante lifted his hands in the air. "Pray tell me, what could be any more unsettling than this extraordinary tale? Go on, brother."

Damian finished his story, including what he had discovered about their disappearance. When he finished, they both sat in silence. A sense of relief overcame Damian, but Dante's expression had deepened. He squinted his eyes at Damian.

"Let me see if I understand this correctly. You're saying you've learned that we're both going to die?"

Damian swallowed hard. He did not know whether it meant that at all.

"Lena, the girl in my dream, discovered this knowledge. It's noted on the birth registry that we both disappear."

"If I understand correctly, this girl hails from a time yet to come?"

"Yes. She explained that after the notation, there is no trace of *us*. No marriages, no children. Nothing."

Dante stood up and paced in front of him. "Do you think Leonardo and Michelangelo are involved?"

Damian shrugged. Even if they were, he did not want to cause a disturbance at the studio. His work was still more important to him than some arcane conspiracy. Even more important than his connection to the girl . . .

Dante shifted position. "When Leonardo said, 'Be careful where you tread,' was this a warning to stay away from someone or something?" He pursed his mouth. "He must know *something* to say what he did."

Damian preferred to step away from the whole thing.

"Whatever *it* is, it sounds dangerous. We should heed his advice."

"But we need to find out who is involved in our disappearance. If your dream is true, and we disappear without a trace, I don't think I can live with that. We need to do something about it. At least try to stop it from happening."

Damian hated to admit when Dante was right. For the sake of their parents, they had to try.

THE BROTHERS STROLLED about town and mulled over their ideas until Dante offered a plan.

"You will continue working as always, and I will take some time off to follow Leonardo when he comes and goes from the studio."

Damian agreed to his brother's idea. "I am still skeptical, but I think this is our best chance to find more clues. Let's do as you say and tail Leonardo, and we'll see if anything comes of it."

Damian could tell Dante's mind still zigzagged from one thought to the next.

"Did it say on the note *when* we disappear?"

Damian recalled the notation on the piece of paper. "Spring, 1500."

As they crossed the square, Dante looked around the entire piazza. "The magnolia trees and irises have bloomed."

Damian agreed. "You are correct. We have little time left."

Dante's expression changed, and his body jerked to a stop, as though something unseen had grabbed him.

"*Aspettare!* Do you remember the man we saw in the forest when we were little?"

Only a vague memory popped into Damian's mind. However, the memory of a knight atop a gigantic horse came rushing back to him.

Dante did not wait for an answer. "Don't you recall that day? That man materialized out of nothing in the Forest of the

Disappearing. He spoke to us without opening his mouth. Then our ears hurt, and we thought our heads would explode. When the pain stopped, we could hear him, even though there was no sound. Don't you remember? And that morning, we agreed to keep quiet and say nothing to mother and father."

Damian wondered how Dante's mind had veered off to the memory of that day. "I don't see how our current problem is connected to any of that."

"I don't know why that came up. Look, if we work and stick together, we'll understand it better. We'll fix it, as we always do."

Dante was the rescuer. Damian had lost track of the number of times they had gotten themselves into mischief, and Dante had come up with some elaborate plan to get them out of trouble. This time, however, the situation was different, and it was more serious than a childhood prank. It might cost them everything. It might even cost them their lives. A knot became lodged under his breastbone. He put his arm on Dante's shoulder.

"Look, I know we've got to solve this before springtime is over but, please do nothing to put yourself in danger."

"Nor you." Dante tapped his fingers on his thighs. He always did when he was impatient to act. "Anyway, it seems we're already on borrowed time. Now I must go to D'Alessandro's, but let us meet later to go over our plan again."

They grasped forearms in the traditional manner before separating. Dante walked away and yelled back, "I'll be home before dark."

As Damian watched his brother's hurried pace, a heaviness settled on his chest.

DANTE

The cobalt sky appeared beyond the billowy clouds—a typical Florentine spring afternoon.

Dante squinted at the brightness of the day while waiting in the street at Michelangelo's studio. He had taken time off work to spy on the activity around the studio. He thumped his fist lightly against the wall. More than ever, they had to solve this mystery before meeting with the fate that awaited them. He had said to Damian, "You'll work as usual so as not to arouse suspicion."

On this afternoon, Dante kept watch as Leonardo entered the building. Less than a half hour later, the front door of the building reopened and Leonardo stepped out into the square. It had been like clockwork the last few days, with nothing much to report. Dante expected him to turn right and then follow the Piazzale degli Uffizi toward the Piazza della Signoria, where he would stop to pay a visit at the Palazzo Vecchio, where the Medicis lived.

Leonardo had walked the same route all week long, and Dante's patience was wearing thin. Had Damian sent him on a fool's errand? He blew out a puff of air and watched as Leonardo reached the *Lungarno* and waited for him to disappear behind the wall of the Castello d'Altafronte.

To his surprise, Leonardo crossed the street, turned left, and flanked the Arno River toward the Ponte alle Grazie. Dante hung back and counted to ten to calm his jittery nerves. It was not as easy to hide along the riverbank or while crossing the bridge.

Once Leonardo got to the other side of the river, Dante sprinted across the bridge, taking refuge behind the wall of a home. He peeked around the corner in time to catch Leonardo following the road to the San Miniato Cemetery. Dante's eyes darted from left to right and he concealed himself inside doorways as he trailed behind the artist.

When Leonardo reached the city gates, he stepped through the archway and followed a familiar path. Dante had been here many times during his childhood. The unpaved road led past the cemetery to the large wooded area where he and Damian had played with their friends.

Leonardo sauntered past a wash house and reached a knoll where the footpath wound its way around, left, then right. Dante dashed toward the covered stone basin. He peeked around the stone wall as Leonardo rounded the knoll and vanished from view. He waited, fearful Leonardo might double-back. After a few minutes had passed, Dante advanced to the bend in the trail.

There was only one place to hide between the fountain and the knoll if he had to take cover on this unfrequented path. Dante hesitated and peered around the bend, catching the last of Leonardo's white tunic as it faded into the woods. Clearly, this was not some afternoon stroll. The maestro had not once deviated from his path.

The forest was vast, and once inside, it would be harder for Dante to track Leonardo. He ran to where he had seen the man enter. His adrenaline rushed through his body when he realized he would not have a proper explanation if Leonardo caught him, but he kept on.

As he entered the forest, Dante watched for branches or twigs on his path. A noise would carry far in the wood's silence. He stayed low to the ground and stalked the forest like a wolf.

He had not yet caught up to Leonardo when, to his left, dry leaves rustled on the ground. Startled, he expected to see Leonardo, but he was alone. Beads of sweat trickled from his forehead.

He cocked his ear to the soft splintering of brittle tree branches. Footsteps trod gingerly on the forgiving forest soil. The man was nowhere in sight, but it was as though Leonardo tread the ground beside him. Unsure of this gained ability, Dante crept forward and followed the sound of the footfall.

It had been years since Dante had visited the forest. Like revisiting an old friend, he traversed the "Forest of the Disappearing"—a name he and Damian had given to these woods —and felt a rush of nostalgia as he cautiously stepped through the cobwebs of his memory. He ducked below tree boughs and checked for fallen branches. His childhood came rushing back as he wandered further along the track. The forest had been one of his favourite places. He had played there for hours with Damian and their friends with sticks and stones as their weapons, pretending to joust and die as warriors by the sword.

Now certain of the direction they were taking, Dante kept his ear alert for Leonardo's footsteps. He remembered a shortcut and left the path to blaze his own trail through the forest. When he arrived at the opening in the tree line, Leonardo was already halfway across the wide expanse.

Dante crouched and peered through the bushes at Leonardo, who swung his head from left to right until he reached the clearing's other side. Five massive boulders jutted from the ground like a large hand reaching out to the sky. *La Mano di Dio*. The Hand of God.

Dante recalled his parents' warning about those monoliths. "Stay away from *La Mano di Dio*!" There had been stories—nay, myths—handed down through generations about mysterious happenings around this place.

Leonardo glanced around and halted near the giant rocks. It was a curious place for the maestro to bide his time. Was he meeting someone?

Dante heard a low grumble under his feet, then a boom. A blast of light appeared before him and momentarily blinded him. When his sight returned, another deep rumbling noise erupted inside the clearing and voices sounded from the other side.

Two men had materialized in front of Leonardo, but these were no ordinary men. They sat atop two of the largest white horses Dante had ever seen. He became dazzled by the bright silver armour they wore. And underneath the chain-mail armour, they wore white clothing.

Dante did not understand a word they spoke. What dialect could this be? He leaned forward to get a closer look and when he did, a small, dry twig cracked under his footing. The snap echoed against the stillness of the forest, and his heart dropped to his shoes. One horseman turned his head toward the noise. Dante ducked and held his breath, keeping his foot firmly in place.

A stentorian sound came from deep within the knight. It travelled across the clearing and reverberated through Dante's rib cage. Leonardo shook his head and flailed his arms at the knight, who had turned his horse in Dante's direction. Dante's heart raced, but his ears perked up. He heard Leonardo's firm tone as the knight took one last, hard look in Dante's direction before moving back into position next to the other knight.

Leonardo bowed his head to them, and the horsemen guided their horses forward. Dante dared not shift from his position, afraid the branch would splinter again if he moved.

Still peering through the bushes, Dante watched the armour-clad men as they advanced toward the hill. In unison, all three faced the incline that was much too steep for any horse to climb. Dante's eyes narrowed. Another blast flashed and a dazzling white light emanated as the horsemen and Leonardo moved forward. Dante winced and used his arm to shield his eyes.

As the brightness faded, the three men's outlines remained faintly visible. The distant rolling faded into silence. And when the light dissipated, they had vanished.

AUGUSTUS ~ FLORENCE, PRESENT DAY

After Lena's revelation at the Gallery, the group met the following Saturday at Augustus and Christina's apartment to discuss her dilemma. They brainstormed, guzzled coffee, and somewhere in the afternoon's banter, someone mentioned some of the strange occurrences in their childhood.

In the excitement of their similar experiences, the conversation lost its thread. Augustus waved at everybody to stop. It was decided they would pull straws so each could tell their individual stories from start to finish.

On a whiteboard, Augustus drew a chart. Into the columns, he would list important moments brought to light during their discussions to see if there were any common themes.

AUGUSTUS DREW the shortest straw first.

His emotions rushed to him in a cloudburst. "My brother Seamus was my best friend." He choked on his words as sadness pierced his heart like a lightning bolt. It was not until he had mentioned his brother that he realized, even after all these years, he still shared all his inner thoughts with Seamus.

"We grew up in Ireland, in a small house on the outskirts of a town named Killarney. Behind our home, down a slight incline, a forest sprawled for miles where Seamus and I played, almost every day. We found a grotto deep within these woods that we turned into a hideaway. It was our secret place where we stored trinkets and machinery parts to build our contraptions."

His friends glanced at each other, with their lips curling upwards.

"I know. It's pathetic, but I've always been like this." He chuckled. "Anyway, the first machine we built was a go-kart nicknamed *The Reillette*, a play on the Reilly family name. We were terribly excited to try it out. Sadly, our masterpiece met its untimely demise soon after Seamus and I took it out for its first run."

Gregory leaned forward. "What happened?"

"We attached the chariot to our dog in our front yard, like a sled on wheels. But as soon as I fastened the belt around Buster, he sprang forward, trying to shake off the wagon from his back. Seamus, who was in the cart, attempted to straighten it while it barrelled down the hill."

His small audience fell back laughing as he told his story while gesturing left and right.

"At one point, Buster veered to the left and sent Seamus flying into a large oak tree. He—Seamus, that is—suffered a large gash and ended up with a scar that ran from the top of his brow to below his cheekbone. It took fifteen stitches to put him back together. And our go-kart was destroyed."

Portia's hands flew up to her mouth. "That was really brave of you boys, but what about your dog?"

"I'd say we were more wild than brave. And no worries, Buster escaped unharmed."

They heaved a sigh of relief.

"A couple of years later, we started building our 'Time Machine', named after H. G. Wells' novel, of course. We worked over the entire winter, and when spring came, we carted the assembled portions to the grotto to piece them together. We needed just a few more parts to complete our time machine. Now, you're probably wondering where I'm going with this long-winded reminiscence, but this is where my story actually begins . . ."

His friends nodded, confirming they were still with him.

"On my eighth birthday, I lay on my bed, fuming, like a spoilt brat crying over a ruined birthday party. One boy had started a fight, and in a fit, I sent everyone home. I was sulking when I heard a pebble ricochet off my bedroom window. Curious, I went to the window. Seamus waved at me from below and beckoned me to join him. He yelled up, 'Come on!'

"It was all the prodding I needed. I climbed down, using the trellis my father had attached to the house, and followed Seamus toward the forest. When we were halfway there, Seamus told me to close my eyes. 'I have a great birthday present for you!'"

Portia clapped her hands. "Oh, I love surprises!"

Augustus lifted his brow and smiled at Portia's enthusiasm. He resumed his story.

"Seamus had led me to our grotto. I could tell because of the heavy scent of pine and the moist ground into which my shoes sank. The canopy of the forest could make a warm day feel downright cold. But what happened next surprised me even more."

Augustus paused. "I'd kept my eyes closed for Seamus's gift, not wanting to ruin it for him. He'd been working hard to finish our time machine. I heard Seamus's shoes squelch on the wet earth as he walked away from me, and he said, 'Augustus, open your—' but didn't finish his sentence.

"The air became deafeningly quiet, and I wondered why he'd gone silent, so I opened my eyes. As they adjusted to the light, Seamus was making his way back toward me, his footsteps heavy on the damp soil with panic in his expression. And behind him, a man stood next to our time machine, dressed in black tactical gear, a lot like the kind that special forces wear but without the military arsenal.

"He'd shaved his head on both sides in an undercut, with a Viking-style braid extending from the top of his head to the nape of his neck. He stood square to the ground, feet firmly rooted in place, and glared at us with these piercing, ice-grey eyes." Augustus gestured toward Lena. "Much like yours."

Lena made a face and lowered her eyes. The rest of the group sat on the edge of their seats, so Augustus kept on.

"Out of nowhere, this loud electrical static rang out. Both my brother and I had to cover our ears from the unbearable pain. When the noise died down, images, or possibly words, came through the deafening cacophony."

Marco narrowed his eyes. "I'm having a hard time imagining this. Do you mean he was sending you thoughts without speaking?"

"Yes, something like that. After a bit, however, a proper sequence of images came through, becoming more discernible. I was too young to really comprehend what they meant. I just remember being terrified out of my wits."

Augustus paused as he recalled that curious moment. Then he pressed on. "Seamus, who was always a little cocky, pointed to the soldier who held a metal cylinder tucked under his arm. 'Who're you and what's that you've got there?'

"The soldier smiled and opened the container. He unrolled the sheets and held them up for us to see. There were strange illustrations with symbols inside the circular charts.

"This time the soldier spoke out loud. He said, 'My name is Adrien, and one day, you'll understand more about these scrolls. For now, I'll explain what a few of these symbols mean to you. Augustus, based on your time of birth, your strongest elements are fire and earth. And, for Seamus, they are water and fire. You can find this information in your charts.'

"Nothing he said made any sense to us boys, but we'd seen constellation charts before. They looked a little like that, so we let him continue talking without saying a word."

As he relayed his story, the chart's images and this soldier's explanation continued to rise to the surface of his mind.

"'Fire is instinctual,' he explained further. 'Earth is dynamic, water is intuitive, and air is perceptive. You both have other abilities and strengths and you'll learn more about them when the time comes.'

Throughout this time, the soldier had maintained a respectable distance from us. But with each word he spoke, he took a deliberate step closer to us, his eyes narrowing with intensity. "Today, I am only here to warn you about—" he began, but was abruptly cut off by a sudden movement. A shadow crossed the ground between us, almost too swift for the naked eye to see. The soldier's expression changed, and he yelled at us to get out of the forest. Seamus, who was always quick to react, grabbed my hand, and we ran home as fast as we could without looking back."

A lump caught in Augustus's throat, and he coughed to clear it. Christina placed a gentle hand on his forearm. "It's okay if you want to stop." Her warmth touched him.

"No, it's alright. Might as well keep going." He got his bearings and continued his story. "Just a week later, Seamus came down with the flu and our mother thought it was best if he stayed in bed to rest for at least a day. I went to school on my own.

"It was a day just like any other day. Nothing stuck out,

nothing unusual happened. Except that by the time I got home, Seamus had vanished. There had been no warning signs."

Marco, who had been quiet the entire time, shifted in his seat and spoke up. "What happened?"

Augustus shrugged. "All I remember from that afternoon was finding my bed empty, and the sheets rumpled. A tea tray sat untouched on my desk where our mother had left it. He'd always preferred my room because you could see the woods from my bed." Augustus's jaw tightened. "My entire world changed that day, and I don't even remember the last thing I said to him."

His memory took him back to the morning when he had curled up in a fetal position in the same spot where Seamus had left his mark on the bed. The group sat quiet and unmoving.

Christina cocked her head and rubbed the back of her neck. "Did you ever find out what happened to him?"

Augustus shook his head. "No, they never found a body. No clues either. One day, my brother was there. The next, gone. Vanished, like he'd never existed. I never told my parents about the man we saw in the forest. Seamus had made me promise never to tell anyone. When I think of it now, I—I should have said something."

Portia rested her hand on his knee. "You can't blame yourself for what happened."

"I did for a while, but then another strange thing happened. About two weeks later, I overheard my Ma screaming at my Da. 'This would've never happened if we'd just told them.' My da sounded like he was sniffling, but said nothing. After a long silence, my ma said, 'If we tell Augustus now, he'll never forgive us.'"

Christina's eyes crested with tears. She took Augustus's hand in hers and held it tight.

Portia sniffled too and spoke with a reedy voice. "Thanks for sharing your story with us. I can't imagine what it must feel like to lose a brother."

Gregory tapped his fingers against his mug. "What do you suppose they were keeping from you?"

Augustus mulled over his question. "I don't know, but I've always wondered whether that soldier had something to do with his disappearance."

Suddenly Portia's expression changed, and her eyes widened. "Are you suggesting the soldier took him? Because Seamus's disappearance had nothing to do with Adrien."

Augustus drew back. "How would you know anything about what happened to Seamus?"

Portia's eyes darted around at the rest of the group, pleading for support. Lena remained silent, and no one else offered a word.

"You're right. I—I know nothing about Seamus or his disappearance. But you said the soldier's name was Adrien, right?" Portia hesitated and fidgeted in her seat.

Augustus nodded. "Yes, I did."

Portia leaned forward. "I also remember meeting a soldier named Adrien. And I'm certain he's not involved in it."

A deluge of reactions flooded the living room at once. Augustus raised a hand and signalled them to stop the commotion.

"Portia, why don't you tell us your story?"

DANTE ~ FLORENCE, 1500

Dante remained hidden behind the bushes. He craned his neck and searched the clearing for Leonardo. Not a soul stirred. Little by little, forest sounds came back to life, and he released the breath he had been holding. Leonardo and the horsemen had vanished from sight.

He wanted to cut across the expanse, to check whether he had imagined things. Instead, he went the long way to the boulders. As he walked around the forest's inner edge, he peered out into the open space from time to time. When he reached the area where the gigantic rocks stood, an eerie sense of stillness filled the clearing.

Wild shrubbery grew all around, but from this angle he could see the five fingers of *La Mano di Dio* reaching out to the sky. Moss and peat grew on the inner circle of the formation, resembling the garden of Eden. All was still, and only a light breeze rustled the leaves in the trees. As he approached, a swirling motif became visible near its peak, etched into the thumb-shaped boulder.

He sprinted to where the knights had stood. Imprints of hooves dug deep into the soft, dark reddish clay. When he bent down to touch the indentation with the tip of his finger, a powerful jolt of energy shot up his arm. He flew backward and slammed into the ground. For a moment, his soul floated above his body, leaving him in a state of numbness.

When he came back to consciousness, a shooting pain traversed him. He lay in shock, waiting for it to subside. Seconds later, a rush of energy pulsed through his system. He leapt and ran across the open expanse without stopping to look back.

On the wooded path in the forest, he reconsidered everything Damian had told him. He could not make heads or tails of what had transpired before his eyes, but he had to tell Damian what he had witnessed. There was something far more sinister in their midst than either of them could ever have imagined.

The sun hung lower on the horizon than he had expected when he reached the opening to the path back to Florence. He had been in the clearing for much longer than expected. When he exited the woods, he sensed a presence watching him from the shadows. A stirring near the tree line caught his eye. Without a second glance, he picked up speed as he ran along the path.

Dante made it back to the city's gates as dusk settled and shadows bled into darkness. With his coat pockets damp from his sweaty palms, he passed underneath Michelangelo's studio window and whistled his trademark owl call, signalling Damian of his return. The artist had lit a lantern, and the soft glow of its flickering flame illuminated the ceiling.

Dante reached the fountain and waited for his brother. He twitched at the slightest noise and paced back and forth in front of the stone bench.

The sound of Damian's light footsteps drifted down the street before he had even turned the corner. When he came into view, Dante fired a glaring look at his brother for making him wait so long. But now that Damian had arrived, he hesitated about where to begin with his story.

Damian coaxed him. "Well, let's hear it. I can tell you have a lot to tell me."

Dante related the afternoon's events, convinced he had stumbled upon Leonardo and Michelangelo's secret. Damian sat and listened, motionless on the bench.

Dante leaned in closer to his brother. "I think Leonardo and his compadres have found a way to make themselves disappear."

Damian's eyes bulged. "Disappear? For what purpose?"

Dante shrugged and lowered his voice. He repeated almost the same words to Damian as he had when they were children. "No idea. But we must not speak of this to anyone. There is some kind of witchery about us, and we will burn at the stake if we even breathe a word of this."

Damian's feet twitched to go home. "What do we do now?"

Dante trailed behind Damian as they walked home. "I don't know . . ." But when they crossed the threshold of their home, his mood perked up again. "But we'll think of something."

11
THE SOLDIER

PORTIA ~ FLORENCE, PRESENT DAY

PORTIA SAT in Augustus and Christina's apartment, interlacing her fingers and squeezing them until her knuckles grew white. She had blurted out her opinions about the soldier called Adrien, certain she was correct. But now she was unsure where those notions had come from. All she knew was that she had also met him.

As she scraped through the dark recesses of her mind, memories of her mother came rushing to the surface. And of *him*.

"My father and I were at my mother's hospice. I cried when my father put her in a nursing home, but there was not much more we could do for her. I'd been taking care of her at home as much as I could for an eight-year-old—" Portia choked on her words, her heart overflowing with emotion. "I just couldn't do it anymore.

"She had been having seizures, and they were getting worse. Dad no longer had the energy nor the skills to care for her, either."

Portia's heart clenched, and she blinked back tears. "I'm sorry. I hate remembering my mother this way."

Lena took hold of Portia's hand. "You don't have to talk about it if you don't want to."

"I'm all right."

"Okay, take your time."

Portia looked down at her hands. "During one of our visits, my father had to tend to her, so I walked around the home."

She shivered at the memory of the darkened hallways, the wails of its occupants, and the acrid smell of death. A tear ran, leaving a trail down her cheek.

"I couldn't handle the thought that my mother would never leave this awful place. Up to that point, I'd never imagined she would die and leave me. I became overwhelmed by those thoughts and ran out to the hospital's grounds, down a path until I came to a huge pond.

"I kneeled to look at my reflection in the water and saw the silhouette of a man standing behind me. I turned, and there he was, larger than life. Dressed in black with the sides of his head shaved and a braid just like Augustus mentioned."

She wiped her hands over her jeans as she remembered the man's towering presence.

"What drew me in were his ice-grey eyes." She used a dramatic hushed whisper and pointed at Lena. "The way yours do."

The group glanced at Lena again, who kept quiet. Portia sensed Lena's discomfort and went on with her story.

"Anyway, my mother—before her illness worsened—told me I'd meet this man someday. She described him and made sure I knew who he was. She had emphasized, 'It's important you meet him. I don't know when you will, but you will. Don't be afraid of him.'

"Well, that morning I finally met him. I shook to my very core, but he was mesmerizing. What she hadn't mentioned was that he was so fierce looking! A real badass!"

The group broke out in peals of laughter at Portia's dramatic overplay, but it was a welcome break from the intensity of the afternoon. Portia looked off to the side, tracing the window frame to the outside world with her eyes, trying to bring forth more details of the memory of that encounter.

"At first, he communicated with me without moving his mouth in the same manner described by Augustus. And when he did, my inner ears screamed with pain from the loud crackling sound of static, like a train screeching to a stop. The deafening shrill was unbearably loud. I thought my ears would fall off."

Augustus nodded in agreement with her.

"Then the noise dissipated and morphed into images and words. I can't explain how that happened, either. It just did."

She paused, letting it sink in.

"He extended his hand and shook mine. Told me his name was Adrien, and I replied, 'My mother told me about you.' His smile reassured me and made me feel secure in his presence. We walked around the lake together. That's when he told me someone would always be looking out for me.

"He showed me the chart that belonged to me and explained the symbols. I didn't understand what he was showing me, but now, everything he said is coming back to me."

The image of the circular blueprint with symbols crossed her mind. Adrien's message had been clear.

At your time of birth, the air and water elements were on your horizon and at your Midheaven. Air elements can soar higher than anyone, and water elements are intuitive.

"Of course, I did not know what he was going on about." She looked around at her friends. "Oh! And he also told me there were others like me." Portia waved haphazardly in Augustus's direction.

"Eventually my dad called out for me. But before I ran off, Adrien promised, 'I will come back for you when you're older.'

"When I think about what he told me that day, it still makes little sense. My mother only mentioned I would meet him one day. Nothing else. I was going to tell her about him, but I couldn't get in to see her that day, and she passed away the following week before I could visit again."

Lena squeezed her hand, and they spent a moment in silent respect.

Portia dabbed her eyes. "I wish my mother had told me more. When I turned around to wave at him, he had already disappeared. I never saw him again and believed I had imagined it all . . . until now."

LENA

Her five pals remained silent, mulling over everything they had gathered during their conversation. Augustus picked up the straws for them to pull again.

Lena pulled and sighed as she held up the shortest one. The words stuck in her throat as she set the straw down on the coffee table. It was her turn to talk about the past.

Touching her fingers to her mouth, she tapped her index finger against her bottom lip. She had never divulged much of her childhood to anyone, the wound still present in her mind. Marco held her hand in his to reassure her, but she remained hesitant. Where should she start?

Augustus nudged her. "Go back to the beginning. It gets easier from there."

The creamy coffee swirled in her large mug, a comforting sight. Lena closed her eyes, then began her journey back in time.

"I led an idyllic life, surrounded by lavender fields and olive trees. Running through purple fields with childhood pals, playing along twisting trails, crunching mint and thyme underfoot. Those were my early years. If it sounds like a dream, it actually was."

Lena's lips curled into a bittersweet smile. A series of images played before her eyes of home, family, and her parents. A tear threatened, but she coughed it away.

"I was seven the summer everything changed. My parents had planned for us to go on a trip to Italy." She recalled the events as they played out in her mind. "But the night before we were to leave, I overheard my mother tell my father that she preferred it if I stayed with my grandmother this time, instead of going with them. My heart shrivelled, then my insides exploded because until that day we had done everything together. How could she do that to me?

"The next morning, I had a tantrum and yelled at my mother that I had heard what she'd said. I told her I hated her and would rather stay with my grandmother than go on that stupid holiday with her. Yeah, I turned into a real brat.

"Of course, my parents left without me, and three days later, while I was outside playing on the swing set in my grandmother's backyard, I heard a wail coming from inside the house. I stopped swinging and in the pit of my stomach, I knew something had gone terribly wrong.

"My aunt ushered me inside and left me to sit alone on the hard couch in my grandmother's living room. All the while, I could hear their tearful whispers in the adjacent room."

Lena had sat on that couch for what felt like an eternity, with her finger tracing the embroidered design on the dark mustard linen.

"Finally, the door opened and my grandmother entered. She straightened her dress the way she always did when she was about to say something serious. Sitting down next to me, she explained my parents had died in a boating accident in the canals of Venice."

Her grandmother's red, swollen eyes and sobs had been difficult to take. All she could do was stroke her grandmother's hand and gaze down at her prominent veins and age spots.

"My grandmother put her arms around me. 'Thank God your mother wanted to keep you here.'

"I yelled at her, 'No, I should have been with them!'" Lena's voice broke. "I went numb, racked with guilt over my mother."

"The following week, we buried my mother and father near our village, and my world fell apart. I kept thinking that if I'd gone with them, things might have turned out differently, and they'd still be here."

Marco caressed her hand. "What happened to them wasn't your fault."

"I know that now, but back then . . ."

Lena lowered her face to hide the tears that pricked her eyes. "Anyway, after that, it went from bad to worse for me. My aunt announced they were going back to Canada, and since my grandmother was too old to care for me, I would go with them, leaving her, my country, and my parents behind."

Lena stopped for a moment and wiped her eyes. She had spent years suppressing all her emotions, always putting on a brave front. "I'm sorry. I didn't realize I still held on so tightly to all that pain and loss."

Portia patted her thigh. "No need to apologize. I think bringing up the past is allowing us to release our pent-up frustrations."

Augustus nodded as he refilled everyone's coffee mugs. "True. And I, for one, am seeing all of you in a whole new light."

Lena continued with her tale, feeling more assured than when she had first started.

"When the time came to leave for Canada, my heart burst with grief, and I bolted. I ran until I could no longer breathe. I stopped when I reached the cemetery where we'd buried my parents."

Built along one of the loneliest stretches of road between her village and the next, the cemetery lay on an expanse of open land and pastures. There were two gates: one larger double-gate that remained closed except during funerals, and a visitor's gate to the right—narrow and tall, with rust peeking through the crusted paint.

Cypress trees lined the wall's outer perimeter, creating a natural protection against the elements. On sunny days, like this one, the trees cast dark, sentry-like shadows among the tombstones. Peering in through the gate's bars, she had stared at the rows of marble and granite headstones sparkling under the bright blue summer sky.

"A six-foot stone wall surrounded the cemetery, greyed and weathered with grimy streaks. When I pushed open the visitor's gate, it gave a loud screeching wail, like a warning to the dead. I'll always hate that bone-chilling graveyard, but it's the closest place on earth to my parents." Lena let out a deep sigh. "That day, when I walked the gravel path between the tombstones, the hair on my arms stood on end. I couldn't see anyone, but I had the peculiar feeling I wasn't alone."

When she reached her parents' tombs, she fell to her knees in front of her mother's grave. "I'm so sorry, *Maman.* I didn't mean it when I said I hated you." She had spoken in a hushed voice, fearful of upsetting her dead mother. Tears streamed down her cheeks as her fingers traced her parents' names etched into the cold, black marble slabs that shimmered in the sunlight.

"While I sat at their graves, a sparrow landed on my father's stone. It chirped at me, fluttered its wings, and took off. That's when a sudden movement to my right startled me, and I glanced over to see a man standing a few rows over. With his head shaved on both sides, he wore a single braid. Seems like this guy got around." Lena chuckled, and her friends snickered along with her.

Portia chimed in with a remark. "I guess your parents hadn't told you."

Lena shook her head. They had not had the chance. She stared off into the distance, and returned to the events of that morning.

"I got to my feet and when he looked over, it was as if he recognized me. He said nothing, but walked in my direction and stopped a few gravestones away. That's when I saw his clear, ice-grey eyes. He looked extraordinary, and yet frightening at the same time. The two of you know what I mean."

Augustus chimed in. "We're definitely talking about the same guy."

Gregory shifted in his seat, and he rested his elbows on his knees. "This is getting exciting. Please go on."

Lena picked up where she had left off. "He pointed toward Father's grave and said, 'He was a remarkable man, taken from us much too soon.' Suddenly, my head ached as if it would burst. It was a sharp pain, like a dagger. It stabbed at my temples and throbbed between my ears. Just like Augustus and Portia recounted, his lips did not move when he spoke, and then that unbearable sound came."

As though the pain was present again, Lena cupped her hands over her ears as if she could still hear it. She looked into her listeners' eyes, then dropped her hands to her lap.

"Once the static stopped, I could visualize the images he was sending me in my mind's eye, even though he still hadn't opened his mouth. I saw memories of my papa and him.

"Startled, I looked at him. 'You knew my papa?' And he answered, 'That's why I'm here today.'"

Lena remembered the sheen that had lined his eyes, betraying his emotions.

"But when he took a step toward me, my instincts kicked in and I backed off. My parents, just like all parents, always warned me never to speak to strangers. Even the ones who claimed to be your parents' friends. I wanted to run, but terror gripped me, held me by the throat, and I could not move, no matter how hard I tried.

"He spoke aloud this time. 'My name is Adrien.' To my surprise, his voice was much like my papa's. He continued, 'You probably don't remember who I am, but when you're older, we'll meet again. I want you to know as long as I can help it, I'll always keep you safe.' Then, he walked away."

Lena stopped and drew in a sharp breath. Something else surfaced. Something she must have blocked out all these years. "Oh, my gosh! He *didn't* just turn and walk away." She paused. "He carried a cylinder tucked under his arm."

Marco joined in. "Like the one Portia and Augustus saw?"

"I think so. So I asked him, 'What's that?' He opened it and pulled out a scroll of papers. After he searched through them, he unrolled one.

"It depicted a circular illustration with symbols and connecting lines. It was an astrological chart. I know this because my father used to draw them."

Some of Adrien's words floated to the surface of her mind. *You have all the elements' strengths: fire, earth, air, and water. Reach within yourself and you will discover their secret powers. It's hard for you to understand now, but one day you will.*

"He rolled up the chart and inserted it back into the cylinder. 'When you're ready, the information will come to you.'"

Like an old forgotten memory, more of his words spilled out. *You will run faster than a gazelle and swim like a fish in water . . .*

Adrien had rested his eyes upon her for a moment, then he was gone before she could say another word.

"When he was out of view, I scampered to the gate and looked both ways, but there was no one on the road. I ran around the wall's outer perimeter. He had vanished.

"With my heart pounding in my chest, I raced all the way home. And I stayed in my room until it was time to leave and never said a word to anyone about him."

She never saw him again.

DAMIAN ~ FLORENCE, 1500

Damian should not have been out, but he had become restless thinking about Dante's experience in the woods. He left the house and meandered through town.

The encroaching darkness clawed at the walls of the citadel when he found himself on the street that led to Leonardo's workshop. Coming into view of the maestro's humble creative space, he spied two horses tied out front. He jumped back into the shadows and watched as the tail end of a dark coat disappeared into the workshop.

He sprinted across the street to get a better view. Two lone torches lit the street, and with their bright flames rising upward, they cast frenzied shadows against the citadel's stone walls. He slid into a narrow fissure between two adjacent buildings on the narrow street's opposite side. Snuggled into the small space, he leaned out to listen to the ruckus coming from the workshop.

The barking tone made it plain to Damian they were enraged, even though he did not understand the dialect. From the sounds of things, objects were being flung around inside, and Damian became concerned about Leonardo's safety. Suddenly, the noise stopped. Two sizeable men dressed in black armour stepped outside. With brutish expressions, they glanced from left to right.

Damian gasped. He jerked his head back into the narrow fissure and prayed they had not seen him. In the cleft, he waited for them to leave. After their horses thundered past him, he let out the breath he had been holding.

The terror of standing in front of that monstrous horse in the clearing came rushing back to him. And if his eyes were not playing tricks on him, the man on the left was the same knight he had seen in his childhood.

Damian leaned forward to peer out onto the street and watched as the two massive horses turned down an alleyway. He slid out from his hiding place and sprinted to where they had disappeared from view. The alleyway was a dead end. With his heart now beating tenfold, he looked up and down the roadway. The knights had vanished.

With sweat beading upon his brow, Damian scampered back to Leonardo's building. Pushing open the door, he called out to the maestro. He walked in, tripped over an object on the floor, and strained his eyes in the dim light, astonished to see what a shamble the studio had become. He called out again and cocked his ear. When he received no reply, he ran home.

LEONARDO

He jumped up from his nap, startled by a loud noise from just beyond his bunker door. Leaning against it, he listened to the storm on the other side.

At the back of his workshop, there stood an invisible door hidden behind a shelf. This separate space served as a place for him to sleep and work in secret.

He had affixed drawings with numbers and mathematical equations to the walls of the hidden room, alongside images of human body parts. These unlawful images were not for the public to view.

The fuzzy sketches deceived his eyes until he cleared his mind from sleep. The trashing noise beyond the secret door persisted, and what he imagined were his tools and inventions landed on the floor with thunderous crashes. Leonardo hoped they would not destroy too many of his ideas.

They spoke in Old French, confirming his suspicions. The Portal Guards. A dangerous lot, and none of whom Leonardo wanted to face.

One guard voiced some displeasure. "The boy's not here. When I get my hands on him, he'll be sorry."

The other guard responded, "Durand, must I remind you of our orders?"

Leonardo pressed his lips together. He had once crossed paths with Durand—a most aggressive knight. Leonardo's hand trembled as he ran it through his thinning hair. For which boy were they searching? Damiano? Dante?

He sat on the wooden bunk and it creaked as he settled into it. An echo bounced throughout the space—a hollow measure, followed by a high-pitched note.

"Abelard, did you hear that echo?" Durand bellowed, but his companion did not answer.

Leonardo squeezed his eyes, disappointed in himself for being so careless. He hoped they would assume the noise was a creak in the building's old structure.

Two sets of heavy boots stomped down the length of the studio until they reached the back area. Leonardo stayed perfectly still, certain the knights had cocked their ears to listen for more.

Abelard muttered, "The maestro's studio is a mess! I told you to leave well alone."

Leonardo's eyebrows twitched, and he silently mouthed his dissatisfaction.

Durand grunted. "We have orders to find the boy."

Heavy-ladened footsteps marched away from the back of the workshop.

One of the two guards growled. "Let's go. We're wasting our time here."

Behind the shelf and the secret door, Leonardo blessed himself. As he bent his head to gather his strength, the sound of hooves clattered off into the night.

It was still dark when Leonardo emerged from his cocoon. He lit a candle and slid the door to the left, careful not to make a noise. Advancing into his workshop, he groaned at the sight of his work strewn about the floor. After the trashing of his studio; he had heard another voice calling out to him. He had not responded, uncertain of who it might have been.

Leonardo returned to his secret room and opted to remain within its safety until the break of dawn, when he could slip out unseen.

Before getting back to sleep, he sent a telepathic call to Adrien—one of the lords who sat on the Council—to meet with him the next morning.

. . .

AT FIRST LIGHT, Leonardo rolled up the copy of the portrait he had drawn for Damian and tucked it inside his vest. The sun crested over the eastern hills as he made his way out of town toward the clearing in the woods.

Early morning shadows followed him as he traversed the forest, crossed the glade, and waited by the boulders. He paced back and forth. Loitering around here would arouse suspicion if ever a woodsman reported him.

The clearing brightened as a flash of light burst forth from the portal. Through the veil, he observed the tunnel of time. It was a funnel of intersecting grid lines like the ones he drew in his perspective drawings. When Leonardo's vision adjusted to his surroundings, Adrien stood before him.

Adrien silently communicated with him. "Always a pleasure to see you, maestro."

Leonardo returned the greeting with a nod and grasped Adrien's forearm. He knew this meeting would be short, so he wasted no time in confiding in Adrien about the latest events.

Leonardo's shoulders drooped as though the world's weight sat on them. "I'm worried and afraid that someone has stumbled upon the gateway. It's my fault. I should have been more careful. He followed me when I came here last to convene with the Order's knights."

Adrien's eyebrows lifted, and his lips pulled thin. "Are you certain?"

Leonardo nodded. "Michelangelo's young model, Damian, has been questioning things. I thought about explaining certain things to them before they pursued the matter any further but—"

"They?" Adrien sucked in his breath.

"The twins," Leonardo mumbled and looked across the clearing to where the young man had remained hidden that day.

"Who followed you? Damian?"

Leonardo shook his head. "No, I doubt it was Damian. I believe it was Dante. He seems more prone to misadventure than his brother. But I'm almost certain he has shared his discovery with Damian."

Adrien lifted his head and looked up at the sky.

Leonardo did not take his eyes off Adrien. "I don't think Dante understands it's a portal. However, he watched as we walked through it." Leonardo pointed across the expanse. "I had to convince the Knights of the Order that no one had followed me or they would have disapproved of my misstep."

Adrien clicked his tongue and let out an exasperated sigh. "It's too soon for this. I must report this back to the Majority Council."

Leonardo rubbed the back of his neck. "Is this necessary?"

"Unfortunately, it is." Adrien narrowed his brow at him. "We will need guidance."

Leonardo hesitated and shifted on his feet. He had more on his mind. "There *is* another thing of concern."

Adrien arched his eyes at him, and Leonardo continued with a shaky voice. "About three weeks ago, Damian came to me with an interesting request. He wanted me to draw the likeness of a young woman."

"Nothing strange about that. We're talking about a young man."

Leonardo handed over the copy of the portrait. Adrien took one look at it and lowered his head in dismay. When he spoke again, his tone betrayed an underlying dread. "I had a feeling something like this would happen. But how has she become involved?"

Leonardo looked down at his feet. He had more bad news for Adrien. "I do not know, but when I saw her face come alive on the parchment, I was certain I had laid eyes on her before."

"Impossible!"

"Listen, I have searched my mind trying to recall where I had seen her. Then I remembered I had bumped into her in the streets near the Arno River . . . twelve years ago."

Adrien's breath quickened. "Twelve years ago?"

Leonardo watched as images zipped through Adrien's mind as he recalled the afternoon he had visited the twins as well. Young Dante had asked him about a lady running through the forest.

"She has also found the portal." Adrien paced in a tight line. "Leonardo, we must stop this from going any further. The safety of *my*—" He stopped himself. "—of this girl is paramount. It is our duty to protect her from any danger. The Portal Guards have their orders to protect the portals, and they make no exceptions. I must advise the Council immediately."

Leonardo's stomach turned. Nausea and a taste of bile rose from his gut and burned the back of his throat. "The Portal Guards were already at my workshop to question me."

"What did they want?"

"They were looking for the boy, only I don't know which one. Luckily, I remained hidden when they barged into my studio."

"They entered the city?"

"Yes."

As their exchange concluded, Adrien's expression darkened. "This is worrisome news indeed. I will speak with the Council. We must correct this problem before anything happens to *her*—to *any* of them."

GREGORY ~ FLORENCE, PRESENT DAY

The light in his friends' apartment had dimmed, and it was his turn to speak.

Gregory twisted his lips into a grimace. "I'm going to disappoint you all because I don't remember meeting Adrien." He paused mid sentence. "But listening to all your experiences, I have only but a brief story to share."

At fifteen, Gregory Sterling-Darlequin had never left his natal birthplace at the southernmost tip of Burgundy. He had drawn his first breath in the cloister hospital of the abbey and grown up where intrigue lurked in every corner of that small medieval town.

"My parent's ancestral home stands off the main arterial street, across one of the old bridges. It's one of those old restored buildings with a stone face, covered with ivy creepers and white shutters peeking through the overgrown vines. My parents renovated the farmhouse and turned it into a bed-and-breakfast before I was born.

"From the kitchen window, you can see the stone bridge, the murky waters of the canal, and any guests arriving. When I was young, I always loved meeting our visitors. I'd often fantasize guests would invite me to leave with them when their stays were over." His friends stared at him and he chortled. "That's how badly I wanted to leave that place. I'd help them lift their bags into their trunks and wave them off as they departed. Then, I'd stand there for a long time afterward, daydreaming I'd gone with them."

Gregory chuckled at the memory.

"When I got to my teens, things changed. After all those years of feeling left behind, I couldn't stand tourists coming and going anymore. Even the sound of the rubber squelching on the gravel lot would make me cringe. How I loved the quiet days . . ."

One late evening, as he lay in bed, the gritty rubbing of tires in the courtyard filtered up to his second-floor bedroom window—guests arriving after dark. Under his bedsheets, he had crunched his shoulders together as if cowering against the intrusion.

"Little did I know, this late-night disturbance would change my entire view of life. I can still hear my mother's footsteps on the hardwood floors, echoing through the house to greet the new vacationers.

"The next morning, I dragged my feet down the stone steps and entered the kitchen to prepare breakfast. I can still remember the fragrance of bougainvillea drifting in with the cool morning air through the open windows which sent a frisson through my entire body.

"I had not yet seen the girl who sat at the kitchen table, hunched over her toasted baguette and hot chocolate. When I pulled out my chair to sit, she mumbled, 'Bonjour,' and I flinched. However, when I laid eyes on her, my stomach flip-flopped. It was one of those moments when your mind becomes so clear, you know your life is about to change forever."

The girl looked about his age and had the clear, grey eyes of a feline. Lucid and sharp.

"She ate her breakfast like she was angry at the world, then glared at me. 'I don't even know why I agreed to come here with my parents. Is there anything exciting to do in this town?' Funny thing is, she made those remarks as if she had a choice.

"Taken aback by her attitude, I suddenly became protective about the town I'd been dying to leave. 'There is! This town has history and secret places!' Jeez, I must have sounded so nerdy.

"*But* her face lit up and her lips curled at the corners. I thought she'd ridicule me for sounding so geeky, but her response pleasantly shocked me. She said, 'After my parents have taken me around this *amazing* town of yours to see all the humdrum, boring, touristy stuff, how about you show me some of those secret places?' I nodded like a fool and introduced myself. I'd met no one like her before. She walked around the table and shook my hand. 'My name's Em, short for Emmanuelle. See you later.'"

THAT MORNING ADVANCED LIKE MOLASSES, as he awaited her return.

"You wouldn't believe the rollercoaster of excitement zipping through me by the time I heard her calling out for me from the front courtyard. I jumped up like a jack-in-the-box and almost tripped down the stairs."

His friends roared with laughter as he mimicked his enthusiasm.

"That was quite a feeling, unlike any I've had since. I was

flying." Wistfully, he rubbed his eyes and shook off the nostalgia from his heart.

"After a quick lunch, we left on my parents' bikes. Em and I raced each other as I showed her the way. Her slight frame and blonde ponytail bobbed up and down as she stood upright on the pedals and pushed with all her might. We reached a fork in the road and stopped to rest. Her melodic laughter rippled through the air as she parked her bike under the tree's shade.'Where're you taking me?' she asked."

He looked up, and the group smiled at him in unison. Under normal circumstances, their reaction would have jarred him out of his reverie, but he remained lost in his memory of her.

"We climbed to a plateau and hiked across its enormous expanse, with the grasses crunching underfoot in that scorching summer sun. By that time, the heat had chased away the morning scents. Reaching the edge of the upland, we sat at the lip of the downward slope where the landscape sprawled and stretched out for miles around us.

"Em gasped. 'Oh my God, it's heaven up here!'

"I explained to her, 'This aerie goes by the name, *Les Quatres Vents*, after the four winds blowing from the east, west, north, and south.'

"'Up here, trees grow into what we call wind cripples. The ferocious winds, spinning from all directions, and upward toward the heavens, shape the trees' forms into corkscrews. I confided in her, 'This plateau is my favourite place when I want quiet time to think.'"

Gregory flashed his friends a smile that stretched from ear to ear. "I was quite pleased with myself, quite confident I'd impressed Em, but little did I know she would outshine me."

His pals leaned forward, enthralled by his story, and he grinned at their enthusiasm. He had kept this memory hidden for such a long time, but now a calmness came over him as he shared it with them.

"Em let out a long, melancholy sigh. 'I wish you could see where I live. It's as beautiful as it is here. The ocean is temperamental—sort of like me. And like us, made of water and earth. Maybe one day you can come visit?'"

Gregory exhaled. "It was as if we'd always known each other."

At this last bit, Lena nudged him. "Gregory! Where have you been hiding this side of you?"

A forlorn expression crossed Gregory's face. "Tucked away safely, I suppose." He regrouped his thoughts and went on with his story. "My emotions plummeted to the depths of the ocean. My parents would never allow me to travel on my own. And when I'd finally be able to, Em would have long forgotten me." The frustrations of his youth bubbled up inside of him all over again.

"Out of nowhere, Em exclaimed, 'Gregory, you realize that you'll remember this moment for the rest of your life, even if you never ever see me again!'"

She had been right, but he had not understood what she meant at that moment. Regret gripped him by the throat, but Gregory shrugged off this relapse to continue telling his story.

"Later that afternoon, as if she'd read my earlier thought, she entwined her fingers with mine and said, 'I feel as if I've known you forever!'"

Christina's lips curled. "Wow, that's a true meeting of hearts!"

Gregory lifted his finger. "Quite true, *but* just as quickly, her expression changed. Like a light switch had gone off. She whispered in a voice I can't quite express properly, but there was an indescribable sadness in her words when she confided her feelings to me. 'Sometimes I feel like I'm a stranger in this world. Do you know what I mean?'

"I wanted to answer except a lump caught in my throat. I held her hand tight, and we both lay on the grass, looked up at the sky, and watched the cumulus clouds bleat across the heavens like lost sheep. I swear if I could have stayed there forever, I would have."

Gregory looked off into the distance again. Back then, that sort of exhilaration had been foreign to him. "Then she leaned up on an elbow and said, 'Can I kiss you?'"

The emotions of that day welled up inside him again.

Lena reached out to touch his arm. "That's sweet. Did she kiss you?"

Gregory smiled, his eyes lighting up with a twinkle. "I—I can't even explain how thrilled I was. My 15-year-old heart exploded with excitement. I closed my eyes and fell under her spell."

Marco teased him. "Jeez, I knew the French were romantic, but you're putting us to shame!"

Gregory smirked. "We can't help ourselves. However, this is where things became a little strange. The next part is a little hard for me to explain, but I'll do my best to illustrate what happened." He took a deep breath.

"While we kissed, a sudden loss of control took over my senses and the strangest sensation of floating came over me. In that moment, I no longer felt the weight of my physical existence; it was as if I had become pure energy."

Collectively, the group inhaled, surprised by the turn of events, and Gregory caught the looks of astonishment on his friends' faces.

"I opened my eyes to say something to her, but what I saw stopped me. Our limbs had dissolved into this clear, flowing substance and we'd melted into each other. We were one, and I couldn't tell where I began or where she ended. We became transformed and lifted into a liquid spiral, a gentle upward swirl. I panicked and shut my eyes tight and prayed, not quite knowing what was happening to me. To *us*."

To his left, Lena mumbled to herself. "I had the same experience with my hands."

Gregory glanced at her, but went on. "I don't know how much time had passed when I opened my eyes again, but I was lying on the ground with Em nestled in the crook of my shoulder. We were two separate beings again, as if nothing had happened. The only explanation I could think of was that I'd been dreaming.

"When it became late, I nudged Em from sleep. The afternoon heat must have knocked us out. She rubbed her eyes and whispered, 'I'm not supposed to tell you this, but I'm going to anyway because I want to make sure you stay safe.'

"'What do you mean by 'stay safe'? Not much goes on around here.' I laughed, playfully teasing her. I didn't want to believe what I'd experienced was real. Things like that didn't happen. As far as I was concerned, she was being dramatic.

"She got up and crossed the expanse, heading back to the bikes we'd left behind. I ran after her and apologized for my rudeness. After she had collected herself enough to talk to me again, she told me the following.

"'Look, we're not like others. You and me, we have abilities. We are of the earth and water elements, the quickest on the ground and in water. We connect to plant and water life. Don't ask me how I know this, I just know.'

"I must have looked at her as if she'd turned into an alien because she added, 'You think I'm out of my mind, but one day you'll understand. This will all make sense to you.'

"We went home, and I freaked out, to put it mildly. Stupidly, I avoided her the following day. Everything she'd divulged had been too incredible to grasp. The day after that, I woke up ready to ask her for more information. But when I looked out into the courtyard, it was empty. Her car was gone. I'd been in such a deep sleep when she and her parents had left in the early morning hours. I didn't even say goodbye."

Gregory's voice thickened. "Until now, I'd filed those memories into my subconscious." He cleared his throat. "Yet she comes up in my thoughts every day."

LENA

It was late afternoon when the group settled comfortably into the apartment, still captivated by Gregory's tale.

Lena shifted with excitement. She shared with them her own experience of shapeshifting.

"You know, while Gregory told us his story, I remembered I had the same experience a few weeks ago. It was getting dark, and I was alone. I arrived at the Ponte alle Grazie and stopped under a streetlamp to look at my hands. They tingled with pins and needles. I tried to rub them together to get rid of the sensation. Then my fingertips extended outward and transformed into filaments of liquid. I was terrified."

Gregory blinked with surprise. Lena spread her fingers and motioned in the air to explain her experience to her friends.

"They morphed into these transparent, bluish streams of water, a liquid which somehow flowed but remained contained at the same time. Almost like when there's zero gravity. It's hard to explain. I still don't even understand it. Anyway, I freaked out and ran all the way back to my apartment. When I arrived there, my hands had returned to normal."

The group sat quietly, and Portia's expression turned downcast.

"I remember now. That was the evening you asked me to check your eyes."

Lena leaned back in her chair. "Yeah, I was worried I might be hallucinating."

"I'm sorry if I was cool toward you that evening." Portia pressed her lips together. "I should have asked you what was wrong."

Lena snorted. "You asked me, but if I'd told you, you would have thought I was losing my mind."

A ripple of nervous laughter rang out in the apartment, and Augustus sprang from his chair and added this new information onto the board.

A lull settled over the room. The intense energy of sharing their stories from the past had reached a tipping point. Exhaustion replaced their earlier enthusiasm. However, more questions arose now. A chill passed through the room. There was a lot more going on than any of them had expected.

After a few moments of calm, Augustus looked in Christina's direction as he went around the apartment and switched on a couple of lamps.

"Let's take a brief break, and we'll conclude the afternoon with Christina's and Marco's accounts."

Christina agreed and went to the kitchen to make coffee for everyone.

CHRISTINA

A paper napkin became twisted around Christina's finger, pulled tight by her own hand.

Her memories had been returning in more subtle ways, but her friends' stories now evoked a clearer recollection of the events in her childhood.

Shadowy forms floated to the surface of Christina's psyche. She might have caught Adrien in a crowd when she was a teenager, always hovering out of sight. At boarding school and at the Academy, she had been much too busy to notice.

Now, as she tried to remember her own story, she ventured further back into her childhood.

"I was born and raised in Ullapool, a town at the edge of the world. To be more precise, I lived in a cottage in Braes of Ullapool, at the end of a street at the base of an escarpment. This remote and rugged landscape was my backyard.

"One morning I climbed the hill to look out at the ocean, and I must admit that I might have stood a little too close to the cliff's edge that day."

Lena glanced at Christine. "Why were you standing so close to it?"

Christina stared at her feet, blushing. "I had dreamt I could fly and was certain if I jumped off the cliff, I would soar into the valley and over the inlet." The group shifted in their seats, and Christina grimaced.

"I was eight years old!"

Marco puffed out his cheeks. "Well, thank goodness you didn't jump!"

And there it was. She had finally found the memory that had eluded her for so long, hidden in one of the dark corners of her mind. Before Christina's eyes, the recollection played out in a flash. She smiled.

"A man stood behind me."

Augustus cocked his head. "You didn't tell me about him."

"I'm remembering things more clearly now after listening to all your stories."

Portia leaned forward. "What did he do?"

Christina's arms flew forward, and she clenched her fists to show. "He grabbed me by my shoulders and pulled me back. It was so quick I tumbled backward. There was a loud clang and a metal cylinder rolled away from us. He caught it before it fell over the side."

Christina looked to her right as though she were back at the Braes' clifftop.

"That's when he introduced himself. He began with, 'My name is Adrien, and I'm here to tell you a little about who you are. But first, you must promise me you will *never* jump from the cliffs. You have amazing abilities, and that's why you often dream of flying. You *can* jump quite high, but you can't fly off the side of a mountain. Please promise me you'll never try that.'

With her pulse rising and her heart beating against her chest, Christina promised the man. But how did he know she dreamed so often of flying? She moved to back away from him when the cylindrical receptacle caught her eye.

"I asked, 'What's in the cylinder?' The man chuckled and said something like, 'You're all the same.' Then he took out a few sheets of paper and found one in particular to show me. It was a drawing of a circular chart, just like you have all described. He explained, 'Let me show you what I have here. You see these symbols around the chart? This tells us you are of earth and air elements. They are your strongest abilities. This means you can jump higher than most anyone and are quickest on the ground.' I asked him what he meant by that, and his answer stunned me. 'It means you are not like other children.'"

She had stepped away, recoiling from the man's words.

"I couldn't believe what he was telling me. Overwhelmed and scared, my defences took over, and I ran home. He never crossed my path again."

MARCO

In Augustus and Christina's living room, the diffused early evening light seeped in. Energized after hearing everyone's stories, the group sat back, mulling over everything they had heard.

Marco stretched, stiffened from remaining seated for so long. "Let's finish this up. My story won't take long to tell."

When Marco began, memories of the soldier appearing among the trees in the woods flooded back to him. He had been just a little child when he had first seen the mysterious man. Marco's vague images cleared and rushed back as he told his story.

"My first encounter with Adrien was in the forest, where I played during family vacations in Florence.

"Adrien would materialize in a cluster of trees and watch me. I spent many summer hours in those woods, playing with my cousins. It's possible Adrien showed me the scrolls, but I don't really remember seeing them."

However, as Marco spoke, Adrien's message came back to him. *I'm Adrien, and I am here to tell you a bit about you. According to your chart, you have the strengths of water and earth elements. What this means is, you can swim for long stretches underwater and run faster than you could ever imagine. But you won't need these abilities until you're much older.*

"Each summer, I'd look for him. He'd pop up, either in the woods or at a distance in the city's busy streets. But he never approached me again.

"Then, one summer, Adrien stopped appearing. After that, my family stopped visiting Florence, and I forgot all about him."

The man had never threatened him, and Marco had paid no mind to the disturbance. Later, he had determined it had been his mind playing tricks.

Lena cocked her head at Marco. "You know, I've always thought those background shadows in your paintings looked like mysterious figures."

Marco had indeed placed sombre, abstract human shapes into the backdrop of each canvas. He had painted them to add mystery and mystique to his scenery, but had it been a subconscious recollection from his childhood?

Augustus scribbled these recent revelations onto the board. "We'll have a peek at your paintings as well. If you don't mind?"

Marco nodded. "Of course." He now itched to return to his studio to have a look at them himself.

Augustus stood and faced his friends. His face looked drawn. The circles under his eyes had darkened.

"It's getting late. This has been a lot of information to digest. Let's meet again next Saturday."

12
THE CRY

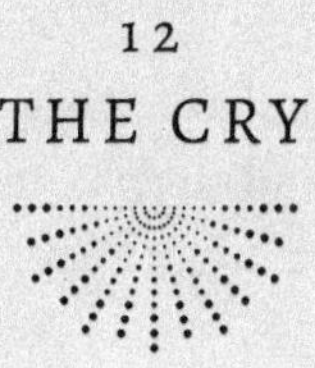

LENA ~ FLORENCE, PRESENT DAY

It had been a week and a half since they had sat around in Augustus and Christina's apartment and shared their childhood recollections.

Lena's cell phone vibrated. *Gregory.*

The text message from him read: *Please meet me at Giubbe Rosse in the Piazza della Repubblica in an hour. It's important.*

Children's laughter filled the air as the carousel spun them around in the centre of the piazza. Organ music spilled into the afternoon air.

When Lena and Augustus arrived at the cafe, Gregory was already at a table with a folder placed in front of him. Lena rushed up to him with a hug and a kiss. He stood to greet Augustus, leaning in for a swift shoulder bump. They settled in, placed their orders, and Gregory explained why he had called her.

"Two strange things have taken place since we last met. I didn't want to wait for Saturday and preferred to meet face to face. It was just too long to text." Gregory rubbed his hands on his thighs. "I have to caution you, it could mean nothing."

Lena reached for his arm. Her cold fingertips tingled at the warmth of his skin. "We need all the information we can gather to help those twins."

He looked resigned to share what was on his mind. "Okay, here goes nothing. So I had a strange dream a few nights ago. Actually, it was more of a nightmare than a dream. Terrifying, actually."

His face turned somber.

"It began with these two Knights Templar. I know this because I did some background check on the web, on their emblems. The emblem in my dream was a redesign, but I can't put my finger on what was different."

Augustus shifted in his chair and drummed his fingers on the armrests. Under the table, Lena kicked Augustus in the shin. Gregory caught her in the act, and his cheeks turned crimson.

"Sorry, I know I get carried away with historical context—"

"And minute details." Augustus grinned at his friend. "Sorry buddy, I didn't mean to be rude. Please go on."

Gregory cracked a smile. "I know. Anyway, these knights were chasing after me on horseback in a forested area. But the thing that was absolutely astounding was the dream's vividness. Everything moved in slow motion. The details were clear, and all my senses became heightened. It was as if I were actually *there*."

Lena interrupted him. "Do you remember where this was?"

"No. Just that I was in a forest. It was foggy, and I was running for my life. The scent of the foliage was so vivid, and I even shivered from the dampness under the canopy. Cool water droplets fell from the leaves, trickling down my arms and forehead as I ran. And the terrifying pounding of hooves on the damp ground followed behind me."

Lena rested her elbows on the coffee table. She sensed Gregory's heart quicken as she focused on him, probably triggered by the recollection of his dream. Beads of perspiration formed on his upper lip.

"While I ran, I suddenly couldn't hear the horses anymore. It had become completely silent except for the sounds of the forest. I remember reasoning—while still in my dream—that the path must have become too dense for them. Still, I kept going, sprinting as fast as I could until I reached an opening in the trees.

"I found myself in a clearing, certain I had evaded them. When I stepped out of the tree line, the knights were waiting for me. It was as if they'd come out of nowhere. I-I guess these things happen in dreams."

Lena agreed. "My dreams have also been as real as that. Go on."

"The knights ambushed me, and as I receded behind the tree line, one of them swung his sword at me, and everything went black."

Augustus tilted his chair backward. "Black? You mean the dream ended?"

Gregory paused for a moment. "No. I'm almost certain it was my *life* that ended there. My heart stopped. I mean, it literally stopped beating."

Lena clasped her hands. "People have had dreams like that, usually when they're under some stress."

Augustus added his thoughts. "Or all your research is catching up to you?"

Gregory waved his finger in the air to show he had more to tell. "Both your points are valid. But I'm not done. I awoke from my dream, drenched in sweat, and just lay in bed, afraid to fall asleep again. That's when I heard a noise outside my window."

Augustus leaned forward in his seat. "What did you hear?"

"Horses' hooves."

Lena shook her head. "You must have still been dreaming."

"Right? That's what I thought. Except my roommate and I, we both leave our street-facing windows open at night. He was still up and working. When he heard the noise, he came knocking at my door. 'Mate, you up? Look below'. When I peered out my window, I saw two men riding horses, and they looked a lot like those same two knights from my dream."

Lena and Augustus glanced at each other while Gregory went on.

"I ran downstairs—with Ronnie behind me—to get a better angle of these guys. When I opened the door, they'd vanished. I found nothing on the street. Not even a hint. I mean, how do two gigantic horses disappear? Even Ronnie agreed it was strange."

Augustus stretched and leaned back in his chair. Lena gazed out at the square. All this made little sense.

Gregory interrupted her thoughts. "I know it makes no sense, and you're wondering how they fit into the story."

Lena laughed. "Did you just read my mind?"

"No, but I asked myself the same question. I wracked my brain to connect the pieces." He explained further. "So this is what I know about these knights. By the end of the fourteenth century, the Knights Templar essentially no longer existed. The church had almost entirely decimated them."

Augustus chimed in. "You're saying you think these guys in your dream were the Knights Templar?"

"I know it sounds ridiculous, but I think they were. *However*, I also realize the idea they'd still be roaming the streets today is impossible." Gregory pursed his lips. "Although it may be far-fetched, I came across a claim in a book called *Holy Blood Holy Grail* that suggests Leonardo da Vinci was one of the supposed Grand Masters of the Priory of Sion. Though I must add that it's a grand conspiracy theory—basically, a hoax. Still, they were pretty convincing. Anyway, I digress . . ."

Augustus's eyebrows furrowed, and Gregory tapped on the folder in front of him.

"There *is* something else. The night following the dream, as I was finishing up my thesis, I got an email from an RSS feed informing me of new material."

His voice rose with excitement. "When the page loaded, it was an article on Leonardo da Vinci's *Virgin of the Rocks.* A comparison of the two paintings hanging in the national galleries of Paris and London."

Lena bolted upright. "My professor presented those two paintings in my class just last week."

Augustus folded his arms. "A coincidence? Or your professor read the same article?"

Lena chuckled at Augustus's dissent. "Weren't you the one who said there are no coincidences?"

Gregory interrupted his two friends. "You could both be right, but that's not why I brought it up. I clicked on the link and discovered something rather interesting."

Augustus burst out laughing. "You certainly know how to tell a story, Gregory. Come on then, spill it."

Gregory grinned. "Upon closer examination, the archangel in the London version bears an uncanny resemblance to Lena."

Lena burst out laughing. "What are you talking about? The archangel Gabriel in the painting is so obviously male unless you're saying I look like—"

"No, I'm not saying that. However, I have also read that Leonardo sometimes switched his subject's genders."

Gregory took a sip of his coffee, and Lena blew out a puff of air. "You're right. I've read that too."

Augustus waved his hand toward the folder. "Are we going to see this painting?"

Gregory opened the folder and set the copy on the table in front of Augustus, who slid the sheet over to face him.

Augustus examined the photo and trailed the image with his finger until he stopped on the archangel. He remained silent for a few seconds, then puffed out his cheeks and blew the air out like a deflating balloon. "I was ready to dismiss the likeness, but the resemblance is eerie."

Lena snatched the loose page from the tabletop to have a look. As she did, she thought out loud, "Damian went to Leonardo to ask for a portrait, and Leonardo kept a rubbing of the sketch. But it's odd. Why would he put my likeness into a painting?"

Gregory signalled to the waiter for more coffee. "Maybe your sketch inspired him?"

Augustus shook his head and pointed to the image. "Didn't you say Leonardo drew you facing forward?"

She looked at it again. "Gosh, you're right. This painting shows my face from a totally different angle."

Gregory craned his neck to get a better look and nodded in agreement. Lena looked at Augustus and recognized his expression. She had seen it plenty of times before, and especially when they sat around speculating on theories.

"What are you thinking?"

Augustus tapped on the piece of paper. "Okay. Just for the sake of argument, let's look at this from another angle. What if you've actually been there?" Lena and Gregory stared at him wide-eyed, and he caught himself. "I don't mean it in the sense of having a past life. I mean, what if Lena travelled back in time from this present one?"

Gregory's jaw dropped. "You're kidding, right? Why do you always have to go to the extreme?"

"I prefaced my question with 'for the sake of argument', didn't I?"

"You are speculating whether Lena has actually gone back to the past? That's an impossible argument. You've told us yourself that quantum mechanics was theoretical."

Augustus glared at Gregory. "I know what I've told you, but what if it's *possible*?" He turned to Lena. "See, you've been crossing over into Damian's body on a metaphysical level. But what if you have done it in a concrete and physical way from *this* time dimension, and we just don't know it yet?"

Gregory balked at the inference. "I can't believe you're even suggesting this?"

"I am, and you just finished telling us about your dream, or nightmare, or whatever you want to call it, and led us to believe that you might have actually seen these knights on our streets."

Gregory stared ahead, then down at his shoes. "You're right. I'm just . . . This is just getting a little crazy, is all."

"Look, when taken out of context and sequence, time can bend, twist, *and* loop around, like a napkin folding in on itself."

Lena set the sheet down on the table and looked at her two friends. "Guys, I don't know what to think anymore."

Augustus pursed his lips and glanced at the two of them. "At the end of all this conjecture, it could just be happenstance, but we need to look at this from every angle." He took hold of the photocopy and the folder. "I'll just add this latest bit of information to our timeline of events."

Lena had charted her nightly adventures onto the timeline board, and kept a rigorous account of each dream. It allowed them to observe whether a pattern existed between the times she went to the past and when Damian was here.

She shook her head. "What if this is just a wild goose chase?"

Gregory tapped the table with his fingers. "If it is, we're chasing it with you, like it or not."

DANTE ~ FLORENCE, 1500

Earlier that morning, Dante had crossed paths with Leonardo in the Piazza Santa Maria de Croce. The maestro stopped him and leaned in to speak into his ear.

"We must meet at the city gates at midday. Bring Dante along too."

Leonardo had mistaken him for Damian, but before he had said anything, the old man walked off.

TIME HAD SLIPPED AWAY from Dante that morning. Now, as he hurried to the meeting place, he found himself caught between finding his brother or being late to meet Leonardo.

He broke into a sprint on his way to the city limits and convinced himself they would miss out on this opportunity if he couldn't find Damian in time. The bells rang when he reached the city gates, but Leonardo was nowhere to be seen.

Dante had time before he was due at his father's shop, so he sat on a low stone wall to wait for the maestro's arrival. He drummed his fingers on his knees as he searched the street for a familiar face.

Leonardo had still not arrived and, against his better judgment, Dante followed the path to the San Miniato Cemetery. He had already followed the artist once and remembered the way.

Outside the city walls, mist surrounded Dante as he wandered further down the path, certain he would run into Leonardo. He went along with the usual route, passing by the graveyard. The thickening fog obscured Dante's view, and he became disoriented. He stopped to gauge his whereabouts when a deep rumble shook underfoot. Dark forms emerged through the gloom, and hooves clattered. The noise thundered toward him. This sudden commotion led him to turn and flee, mindless of all but escape.

Sweat trickled down his back as he bolted. A whistling noise threw him off balance and a lead weight sat in his belly as he fought to speed up. With the raucous close behind, he could tell the horses were gaining on him by the thunderous pounding of their hooves on the packed earth. Racing back up the path, he spotted a momentary break in the haze that revealed the forest's entrance. Without a second thought, he veered to the right.

Droplets from the night rain hung on the leaves. As Dante darted through the weighted boughs, his clothes quickly became soaked. Branches squished underneath his feet on the damp earth. With only a few paces of visibility before him, he half-guessed his way through the Forest of the Disappearing. As he moved forward, the veil of fog licked at his feet and swirled around his ankles. It clung to the trees and played tricks on his mind.

His heart drummed loudly in his ears and kept pace with his footfall. At one point, he jerked sideways when he thought he sensed the horse's steaming breath on the nape of his neck. Further down the path, he peered over his shoulder but saw nothing. They were no longer following him. He slowed and breathed a sigh of relief.

Dante was almost certain he had lost them, but something told him to keep moving because these knights were serious in their attempts to catch him. With the fog thinned in these parts, he tore through the woods. And through the trees, he perceived a brightening.

He reached the forest's edge and leaned against a trunk to catch his breath. His stomach convulsed, and he heaved and retched. As he wiped his mouth with his sleeve, the acidic odour of bile overwhelmed him.

With hardly a chance to recuperate, a heavy thump sounded directly beside him. Its powerful tremor toppled him backward. Dante grabbed hold of the nearest tree when a terrifying vision of darkness towered above him. He looked upward. The knight looked nothing like those he had seen with Leonardo. But the description of the knight Damian had shared with him came back to him—a man dressed in black with a mask of death. His chest tightened as fear gripped him.

The metal glint from the dark knight's blade confused Dante as it whooshed past him. To avoid it, he fell to the ground. His nostrils became filled with the scent of charred skin.

Dante rolled away from the horse and struggled to his feet as he careened toward the middle of the clearing. A scorching fire raced up his arm and seared his flesh. He lifted his hand to examine the wound. There was a gap where two fingers ought to have been, and the laceration gushed with blood. He choked on the vomit rising in his throat and charged forward with all the strength he had. His life depended on it.

As Dante stumbled into the clearing, the fog thinned, evaporated by the sun's rays. The blue Tuscan sky hovered above him. One knight shouted to the other and a second set of hooves pounded the earth. Dante glanced back to see the other soldier closing in on him.

To his dismay, rapid, shallow breaths teased his ear and the impending shadow of the knight's sword rose over him. Then the blade swung down, and the knight delivered one final blow.

For an instant, the deafening noise quietened. Dante's entire world became suspended in that split second of time, and he recalled vivid moments from his life: his carefree childhood with Damian, the echo of his parents' laughter, and his dreams. His hour had come.

Resigning himself to his fate, he threw his body frontward. To his left, he caught a flash of glinting white metal before he let out a bloodcurdling scream. His piercing cry tore through the stillness of the expanse, rippling outward and evaporating into the woods' silence.

13

THE SECRET DOOR

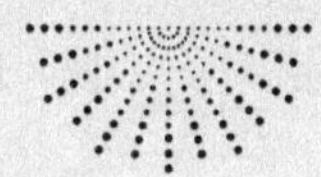

DAMIAN ~ FLORENCE, 1500

DAMIAN JERKED UPRIGHT from his pose. A frightful scream had pierced the air. *Dante?* He had heard his brother's call for help before. But this had been a wail of anguish. He hopped off the podium and moved to open the window.

The thinning fog clung to the rooftops, and an unusual silence hung above the street. Not a soul stirred below.

Despite Michelangelo's usual aloofness, he followed Damian. "What are you doing?"

"Sir, did you hear that cry outside?"

Before Michelangelo could answer, Damian's body tingled, and blood drained from his face. He lost all his strength and collapsed to the ground in a heap. As he fell, a pair of sturdy arms seized him.

A damp cloth cooled Damian's forehead as he came back to consciousness. Michelangelo kneeled above him. With trembling hands, he cradled the back of Damian's head.

After a few moments, the maestro spoke. "The colour has

returned to your cheeks. Luckily, I caught you before your head hit the floor. Can you sit?"

Damian's eyes fluttered as they adjusted to the light. Michelangelo's face came into his view, the blurry podium behind him. Damian's heart kicked in again and thumped like a stampede of horses.

"I have to go!"

Michelangelo attempted to calm him. "Son, what is the matter?"

Damian struggled to his feet. "It's my brother. Something terrible has happened. I must go."

DAMIAN SHIVERED. The sweat running down the middle of his back cooled before reaching his lumbar region. His footsteps echoed behind him, and he tugged at the lapels of his coat.

He burst through the front door, calling out to his mother. There was no answer. He then made his way to his father's store, praying to find Dante there. When he reached D'Alessandro's, he barged in and found his father working up front. Ronaldo glanced up, startled by the intrusion.

"What are you doing here? Why aren't you at the studio?"

"Is Dante here?"

Ronaldo exhaled with a loud huff. "No, I was expecting him, but he hasn't shown up yet."

"Father—" Damian's insides wobbled, and he held onto the counter. "Dante's got some trouble. We must find him."

Ronaldo put down the tool in his hand. "What do you mean?"

"You know how it has always been with us. I have a bad feeling that Dante is in a grave situation."

"Do you know where he's gone?" Ronaldo rubbed his forehead.

"Not for certain, but I've a good idea where to start looking."

MICHELANGELO

Michelangelo's drawing table spread before him in disarray, his conté sticks thrown about with abandon. His mind muddled and disturbed by Damian's outburst.

In a hurry, Michelangelo gathered his drawing tools. There was a knock at the door as he turned to leave.

"Who is there?"

"It's me Leonardo," the disembodied voice answered.

"Come in."

As he waited for Leonardo to enter, Michelangelo did not move from his position.

"I was just leaving to find you, but now that you are here, I must show you something."

Leonardo stepped forward. "What is it?"

Michelangelo rustled through several of the pictures on his table, flustered. "First, look at these drawings. I've been sketching for days and the boy's hands change from one day to the next. At this pace, I'll never be able to finish this statue on time." He took a breath. "Then today, we were making good progress when the boy became distracted, ran to the window, and he fell in a heap to the ground. Something about his brother being in trouble!"

Leonardo paced in front of him. "I had a feeling this was only going to get worse."

"What do you mean, Leonardo?"

Michelangelo became increasingly more troubled, and the conversation progressed from annoyance to apprehension.

Leonardo mumbled to himself under his breath, then turned to him. "Let's go to my workshop and I will explain everything."

They walked through the city and remained silent all the way. Michelangelo had never visited the maestro's studio. When they entered the darkened workshop, Leonardo lit a candle. Michelangelo noted gadgets scattered all over the floor and scratched his head. Leonardo fidgeted about the mess and pointed to the floor.

"The Portal Guards' signature."

Frightful of these men, goosebumps crawled up Michelangelo's arms. He observed Leonardo's every move as he strolled up to a bookcase at the back of his studio and fiddled with it.

Leonardo rotated a device until a sequence of clicks fell into place. Michelangelo gasped when Leonardo pulled on the shelf and slid it over to the side.

Michelangelo cocked his head, fascinated, and waited to find out what lay hidden behind this secret door.

MARCO ~ FLORENCE, PRESENT DAY

In the dead of night, Marco heard feet shuffling on the hardwood floor of his apartment.

He bolted upright, awoken by the sound. Finding his room shrouded in darkness, he glanced at his bedside table. Blinking, his eyes smarted from the clock's LED glare. One-thirty in the morning?

A knock on the floorboards startled him. Someone stumbled around in the darkness. Papers rustled, and a voice spoke. It was the low, quiet tone of the older man he had heard on other nights.

"What is the matter?"

Marco's skin prickled. He opened his mouth to speak when someone else answered—the younger, stronger voice.

"I must show you something."

Marco leaned up on an elbow, keeping still. Now, a faint glow came from a candle in a lantern. Two men faced each other. The taller man had a receding hairline and shoulder-length hair, while the younger man wore short, dark, cropped hair. *Too peculiar to be thieves.* With only a candle flickering in the night's darkness, the scene looked like a Georges de La Tour masterpiece.

"Michelangelo, what is it you want to show me?"

Marco rubbed his eyes in disbelief. *Michelangelo?* Could the other man be Leonardo? In the room's shadows, sheets of paper rustled as Michelangelo searched through them.

"Look at my drawings of Damian. I tell you, something is strange. I've been working for days and getting the drawings all wrong. See, his hands change from one day to the next. At this rate, I'll never complete this statue on time."

Michelangelo's voice strained and grew shrill with anguish.

"And today, in the middle of our session, the boy ran to the window and cried out, 'I must go. Something's happened to my brother'. I tell you, that boy was pale as a sheet. Leonardo, I ask you again, what is all this about? I know you're hiding something from me."

Marco's eyes widened. The other man was indeed Leonardo. He could hardly believe his eyes and leaned in closer to better hear the murmuring between the two men.

Leonardo stepped back, and the visible weight of weariness made him shrink. "I did not want to alarm you. Or cause distress while you were working. But I found out—by happenstance, mind you—Damian's twin, Dante, stepped in for him on at least one occasion."

Michelangelo shuffled his feet and slapped his forehead. "Twins? *Dio Mio*, no wonder I have been reworking these drawings!"

Leonardo's words came out in spurts. "The other day, it seems Dante was waiting outside, watching me. When I left, he followed me to the clearing."

Leonardo cowered as if he expected Michelangelo to strike him. Instead, Michelangelo's hands flew to his own cheeks and his face lit up with horror. "My god, did he see anything?"

Leonardo sighed. “I’m certain he did. But the real problem is, the Portal Guards are now after Dante.”

Michelangelo looked up to the heavens. “I knew this would lead to trouble!” He glared at Leonardo. “I also told you I wanted no part in this. What were you thinking? What are we going to do?”

Leonardo’s shoulders slumped, looking as if he could cry at any moment. Michelangelo paced in front of him. “Do you think they got hold of this young Dante? These gatekeepers are dangerous men, you’ve told me so yourself. You *must* find the boy and secure him.”

Leonardo’s eyes cast downward when he turned to Michelangelo. “Let’s go to my studio and I will explain everything.”

With that, they dissolved into studio’s shadows.

Trepidation crept through Marco as he watched the scene in front of him disappear—like the fine details of a painting fading to black ombre, leaving behind only the dramatic brushstrokes upon a textured canvas.

DAMIAN ~ FLORENCE, 1500

Ronaldo closed the store’s front door. The key clicked, and its teeth turned the levers into place, locking it.

Damian and his father walked together. Ronaldo stopped and put his hand on Damian’s shoulder. “I’ll search around town, then join your mother. She’s working at the marketplace.”

They parted ways in the square, and Damian headed in pursuit of his brother. As he walked through the streets, he hoped Dante had met somewhere with his friends.

He went straight to Leonardo’s workshop after failing to find his brother. When he reached it, he found the studio’s door ajar. All was quiet. He shoved open the door a crack without entering. It jammed and hit something on the floor. With his foot, Damian jigged the door wider.

He checked behind him to make sure the knights were nowhere on the street before he ventured inside.

"Leonardo? Sir, are you here?"

Damian's shout echoed off the workshop's walls. He moved around the room and lifted his feet over the many gadgets and mechanical parts strewn about the floor. On the ground, he found shoe prints leading to the back. They were barely perceptible in the obscure lighting coming through the opened front door.

His eyes narrowed as he studied the rear of the workshop. It lay in the shadows with dusty shelves running from wall to wall amidst the grime and mustiness. They had not been visible the night he had been there for the portrait.

Damian had expected stone when he tapped against the back wall, but his knock revealed instead a hollow wooden sound behind the panel. Why was this back wall made of wood? He jiggled the shelf, but it remained solid, immoveable. Taking a step back, he examined the wall again, checking for a crack or a split, but the frame and the tightly fitted slats allowed no light to filter through. He shrugged, but as he turned toward the entrance, he heard a disembodied murmur.

"You know, if we don't find him, his blood will be on our hands."

Damian's ears perked up, and he stopped in his tracks. He had recognized Michelangelo's voice. It had come through loud and clear. He remained as still as he could to listen for it again and wondered where his maestro's voice had come from.

Damian had gotten used to hearing inconspicuous conversations, but this message had been ominous. Whose blood would be on their hands? Dante's? He waited to hear more, but nothing else came.

A few moments later, Damian headed to the front door with a

heavy sigh. He took one last look around and pleaded out loud as he crossed the threshold of the front door.

"Come on, Dante! Where are you?"

When Damian entered his darkened home, a lone candelabrum sat in the centre of the bare kitchen table with its candle burned down to the last knob.

Ronaldo's face reflected a mix of anguish and optimism when he saw him.

"Anything?"

Damian shook his head. The weight of his parents' worry sat on his shoulders. He found a new candle, lit it, then took Ronaldo outside to speak with him. When they were out of his mother's earshot, he told his father the story that Dante had relayed about the horsemen in the glade, but left Leonardo out of the story.

Damian could have sworn his father staggered at the mention of the horsemen. As the colour faded from his father's face, he glanced sideways at the house and caught his mother gazing at them from the kitchen window. When his parents' eyes met, Damian saw his mother close her eyes, and the curtain fell back into place.

Back inside the kitchen, Damian watched as the sand poured through the hourglass on the fireplace mantle. As dusk seeped into the city, his mother paced the kitchen floor and pleaded, "Our Dante is going to waltz into the kitchen at any moment like he always does." She choked back a tear. "He *must* come home."

Damian's gut feeling told him otherwise, and the evening passed without a sign of Dante.

The next morning, the members of the D'Alessandro family assembled in the kitchen. The gathering included Damian's sisters and their spouses. Word had gotten to them about Dante's disappearance.

The previous evening, they had also reached out to their friends and his sisters' families—the Baldinis and the di Stefanos.

His family had been up before dawn. They waited in the kitchen for the men to arrive. Ronaldo paced around. He sat, then stood up again, impatient to begin the search for Dante.

Damian gazed out the window onto the narrow street in front of their home. Florence was a small city and news travelled fast. By now, Dante should have heard they were looking for him.

There was a shuffling noise. Everyone stopped talking and looked toward the entrance. They held their breaths, and when Damian opened the door, all prayed. He waved his hand at his family with a headshake and let the group of men into his parents' home.

The men greeted Damian and his family, and each of them took turns to kiss his mother's cheek. "We will find him," was all the Baldinis and di Stefanos could promise before they left the house. These were old family friends, whose fathers, grandfathers, and forefathers had been allies, long before this generation.

The men made their way to the Arno River, crossed the Ponte alle Grazie, and walked out of the city gates toward the forest.

When they arrived at the clearing, they marched in a horizontal line, standing at one end to comb the field and search for clues. They stepped forward, inch by inch, throughout the expanse. By mid-afternoon, they still had found no trace of Dante.

At one point, a low rumble shook the ground and the older men looked around the clearing. Damian caught the elders' surreptitious glances. When the ominous tremor faded, they went back to their search, though they steered clear of the large boulders on the clearing's edge. Did these knowing looks arise from superstitious beliefs, or were they aware of something beyond that?

As Damian walked, the overturned ground crunched under his shoes. His faith spiralled when he spotted a deep imprint on the soft earth. A horse's hoof. With his foot, he cleared the tall grasses and found more prints scattered about. He followed the ones that lead toward the forest line and called out for Ronaldo to join him.

Father and son reached a point where two sets of prints veered in separate directions. Picking one, they followed the indentations and stopped short of the forest's edge. A cluster of reddish blotches darkened the loose soil on the ground.

Damian followed the dark trail, which led him back to a tree trunk soaked with deep red blood stains and vomit. Ronaldo remained at his side as they inched toward the tree. He heard a strangled, gurgling noise coming from his father, and Damian lunged sideways to catch him as he dropped to his knees.

As he held his father up, Damian followed his gaze. Where the tree's roots emerged, two fingers lay strewn across the ground. His heart dropped.

"Oh God, please say it isn't true."

Then his father wailed—a cry sharp enough to pierce Damian's soul. His stomach flipped, and he turned aside to retch.

The other men ran to them when they heard the commotion. When they caught sight of the blood and the bone-white fingers laying on the ground, they blessed themselves.

A Baldini man rested his hand on his father's shoulder. "Ronaldo, are you sure these are your son's fingers?"

Ronaldo did not answer, but Damian had seen the unmistakable scar on his small finger—the one he and Dante had always been careful of hiding when they played their deceptive games against others. Damian confirmed they belonged to his brother, as he wiped his tears on his sleeve. Ronaldo's hands trembled as he gathered the severed fingers, their cold touch sending shivers down his spine. He wrapped them in a cloth.

"My son . . . my poor son . . ."

A voice behind them called out, "Separate and search the immediate area. He won't be far."

The men dispersed to cover the grounds close to the

gruesome discovery. They searched until the afternoon darkened into dusk. When it became too dark, Ronaldo suggested they return to their families, but the men argued their families could wait.

One man urged them to keep going. "Dante *must* be here somewhere! We won't stop until he's found."

They lit their torches and combed the forest until late into the night. They walked until their legs gave out, but the trails they followed led to nothing.

With heavy hearts, they made their way back to Florence and agreed to reconvene the following morning.

The search lasted for two days and on the second evening, Ronaldo announced it was over. They had done everything they could and still had not found a shred of evidence leading them to Dante. Damian's tears flowed when his uncle announced, "For Annabella's sake, it's time to put Dante to rest."

Ronaldo had placed Dante's fingers into a box-like container, and they buried the container in the privacy of their garden, since there could be no proper burial without a body.

FROM THAT DAY ONWARD, a dull, heavy-laden weight settled upon them and a stranglehold choked the family's foundation.

One night during the following week, Damian heard his mother's cries as they rang through the house.

He lay in bed and listened as she spoke to Ronaldo.

"We should have told the children."

"We did not have a choice. You know the rules. Anyway, if we tell Damian now, he will never forgive us."

Damian's mouth dropped open.

As the days wore on, Annabella became an empty shell and Ronaldo bore a look of defeat. His parents' pain grew into a gulf too deep to bring up the conversation he had overheard.

His own mind had numbed itself to the pain, and he went

about his life in a daze—a necessity for survival. But how could he go on when Dante had always been by his side?

For the first time, a deep void existed in Damian's inner life. True, they had known that one day they would go their separate ways, but always with the certainty that their bond would forever link them. A bitter tear streamed down Damian's cheek.

He dreamed of Dante every night. And each morning, faced his brother's empty bed. He was adamant that one of these nights, Dante would come crawling in through their bedroom window. He just knew it.

Night after night, he waited for sleep to seize him. And, each time, his dream was the same.

. . . Pushing away the branches that crossed his path, he ran through the forest until he reached a clearing. Across the way, a foreboding monolith of large rocks jutted toward the sky. A loud thump to his right knocked him backward, and he gripped the closest tree to stop himself from falling. A blade swung, and a sharp pain tore up his arm. He stumbled forward and looked down at his hand. Blood spurted where two missing fingers left a gaping hole. He screamed as he ran into a blinding white light . . .

14
THE HAND OF GOD

LENA ~ FLORENCE, PRESENT DAY

The information on the crowded, erasable board loomed over the six friends, with bubbles and notes related to each member of the group, amassed during each of their meetings.

Marco had added his notations of the recent late-night exchange he had seen between Leonardo and Michelangelo. And an arrow pointed to a note regarding Dante's fate—the possibility that he had been attacked and was now missing.

After a long afternoon and late night, the six friends had fallen asleep in sleeping bags and cushions on the floor of Augustus's apartment.

Lena lay snuggled against Marco on the couch. She opened her eyes, disturbed by the clinking of mugs coming from the kitchen. Christina was making coffee while Augustus sat staring at the board full of names and magnets—a spiderweb of strings pointing and joining to each other.

As light streamed in through the shutters, Lena rubbed the sleep from her eyes. She got up and stood next to Augustus. A well of sadness filled her. "Damian's here. And something's not right."

Augustus looked at her sideways. The rest of the still bleary-eyed group joined them at the board. While coffee was poured, Lena looked at them in dismay. "Guys? I think Marco's right about what's happened to Dante. There are images of trees. A forest, perhaps? There's people searching the area and blood is everywhere on the ground and on a tree trunk." She paused for a moment to take in what was flashing before her inner eyes. "I don't know what I'm looking at . . . Damian's all over the place . . . Wait—" Lena experienced a sudden prickling sensation in her ears. Her chest heaved, and nausea overcame her with nausea. "Those are two severed fingers on the ground near the tree line."

The group went silent. If those were indeed Dante's fingers, then the events were rolling out as they had recorded them in history. Lena's knees buckled, and Portia caught Lena by the waist.

Lena's voice was strained as Portia lowered her onto a chair. "I wasn't able to help Dante."

Portia protested. "It's not your fault."

"Maybe not." Lena's heart plummeted. "But we *must* help Damian." She could not let the same thing happen to him.

Augustus slammed his hand on the table. "I don't get it! If we've missed helping Dante, how will we be able to help Damian? What's the point of all this?" Lena sensed his regret as soon as he had spoken those words aloud. "What am I saying? Obviously, we have to do everything possible to help Damian. It must be the reason you're still connected to him."

Her own emotions became a jumbled mess; however, one thing came through crystal clear. "Damian wants us to go to the forest. It's where Dante vanished."

Portia almost immediately posed the question that was on everyone's mind, including Lena's.

"Is it safe? I mean, the real question is, *how* the heck can we help when we're five hundred years into the future?"

. . .

DESPITE HER OWN APPREHENSION, Lena led her friends to the forest. They crossed the Arno River at the Ponte alle Grazie and walked past the ancient city gates, where elements of the ancient decaying wall had been reconstructed with its original materials.

As they walked past the San Miniato Cemetery, Marco looked around him. "This route looks familiar. I came this way many times when I was a kid."

When they reached the woods, Lena warned them to be on their guard. Under the canopy, it was quiet except for the sound of their cautious footfalls on the damp soil. Marco acted as the front guard, watching all around as he walked ahead of Lena. Christina and Portia, who followed behind her, ducked to avoid the low-hanging branches, and lifted their feet above the brush that grew wild on the unfrequented path. Gregory tread on their heels, and Augustus guarded the group from behind.

They trekked their way through until the dense forest gave way to an open expanse. Lena pointed across the clearing toward the monolithic stones that jutted from the ground as they emerged from the trees.

Marco hesitated as the group moved forward. "We shouldn't be here. I remember this place now. My parents warned me that these were hallowed grounds." He pointed to the other side. "Those rocks are called *La Mano di Dio*—The Hand of God. It's dangerous here."

Augustus gazed at the monoliths, amazed by the sight. "Those are the rocks that Leonardo painted. The ones in his background. What was that painting called?"

Gregory halted next to Augustus. "You mean the *Virgin of the Rocks*?"

Lena dropped back and stood next to them. "We have to follow the forest's edge to the other side, and Marco's right about the danger. We should stay near the tree line."

Christina's voice trembled. "Guys, I don't like this place."

Augustus took her hand. "I'm here, nothing will happen to you."

Dense bushes, branches, overgrown moss, and uneven ground cluttered the path. They followed Lena and Marco around the clearing and kept to a tightly moving group.

Gregory had fallen behind, trailing after them. "I'm not getting a good feeling either."

At the clearing's bottom end, they stepped out of the tree line and sprinted into the open space. A quarter of an hour had elapsed by the time they arrived at the boulders of *La Mano di Dio*. Lena put her hand up when they had reached a safe distance from the rocks.

She touched Augustus's arm. "He wants you to come with me. I mean, *him* . . ." She tittered, despite the knot in her stomach. "You know what I mean."

Though it was the start of a bright day, the sun remained hidden behind the hills. In the morning shade, Lena led Augustus to a place near the rocks where she pointed to the ground.

"I think this is where he saw horseshoe prints leading back to the trees over there." She pointed to the other side, where they had stepped out into the clearing.

Damian's vision of a knight zipped through Lena's mind. "I'm not sure what to make of the images I'm receiving because they keep jumping around. But I'm guessing that Damian saw a knight on horseback in this clearing."

Augustus glanced left and right and cocked his head. "Knights? Do you think they're the same knights from Gregory's dream?"

Lena lowered her voice. "*Shh* . . . they'll hear you."

"Who will?"

"Them."

"Them? You mean the knights?"

"I don't know. It's Damian sending me these messages."

Augustus searched the ground. "Look here."

Lena walked over and peered down at the deep depression left by a horse's hoof, imprinted on the soft earth close to where they stood.

"It looks fresh."

He crouched and reached out to touch it. A jolt sent him hurtling backward, and he landed hard on the ground a few feet away from Lena.

She let out a yelp and dashed over to him. Marco and the girls jumped out from behind the trees and ran over to the pair. They helped Augustus to his feet. Catching his breath, he wobbled and his gaze remained fixed at the ground.

"Wow, that was quite an impact!"

Gregory came stomping over to them. "What in the hell just happened?"

"A deep vibration came from the ground. It travelled up my arm and rose in intensity until a flash of energy blasted through me." Augustus breathed in deeply. "I feel like I've taken a sucker punch to the chest. I can still feel my muscles contracting."

Christina gripped Augustus's wrist and checked his pulse. "Those symptoms point to an electrical shock. We should get you home and have a doctor check you."

Gregory agreed. "Christina's right. We should head back to the city and make sure you're okay."

Augustus clenched and unclenched his hands. "My hands feel numb, and I've got this massive headache coming on."

No sooner had he finished his sentence than the ground grumbled from deep below. Lena cast her gaze down the length of the expanse. "That doesn't sound good. We should get out of here!"

Her friends sprinted behind her straight across the open field. They ducked into the trees and did not stop until they reached the other side of the forest. They hurried out of the woods and along the road back to Florence.

A KNIGHT SAT on his horse, hidden among the shadows, and watched them.

IN THE CITY, the group hurried through the streets to Augustus and Christina's apartment. Once inside, Christina found her stethoscope to check Augustus's pulse. The rest sat in silence as they tried to calm their own racing hearts.

Lena gazed out the balcony window and at the street below. "We have to go back."

Augustus fidgeted as Christina listened through her stethoscope. "There's definitely something going on in that clearing."

He freed his arm and went to the board. His hand trembled as he recorded the events of that afternoon, still reeling from the impact of the blow.

Christina stood and paced between Augustus and Lena. "Slow down, both of you. I still want to keep a close eye on Augustus . . . make sure that jolt wasn't more severe than he's letting on."

It was Gregory's turn to remind Augustus of what had just happened. "An electrical jolt is nothing to scoff at."

Augustus turned to them. "You're both right, and I'll go see a doctor as soon as we figure *this* out." He went back to the board. "There's a powerful energy there. I can attest to it. But given Dante's disappearance—and whatever that strange rumbling was—we must proceed with extreme caution."

Lena moved to the board and studied the pinned photocopy of *The Virgin of the Rocks*. Augustus's observation of its background had been correct. The rocks in the scenery behind the Madonna looked like a replica of the rock formation. Her attention shifted back to the angel Gabriel. Archangels were the bearers of secret information, but what was Leonardo trying to tell them?

She pointed to the painting. "We must come up with a plan to get closer to those rocks. There's obviously something drawing us to that place."

Gregory, always the cautious one, piped in. "Should we really be going back to there?"

Augustus's attitude shifted, his tone filled with excitement. "Hell, yeah. I am certain that location holds the answer to our questions."

Lena settled on the couch and hugged her knees to her chest. "I agree with Augustus, but I also think Gregory has a point. It's possible that we're getting in over our heads.

Augustus stood in front of the enormous white board with an erasable marker in hand. He pulled down another opaque plastic sheet and hooked it to the bottom of the panel.

"In order to put everything into perspective, I'm going to create a mind map."

He drew the first circle and inside wrote Lena's name. He tapped his finger on the board.

"She's the centre-point of all these events."

He drew another circle to the left and wrote: *Lena's dreams*. To the right, he filled yet another with *Damian's dreams*.

Augustus pointed to the board. "Now I'll add everyone's name under Lena's inside the larger circle."

He continued to fill in the diagram with circles of information, including all the details they had gathered until now.

Christina narrowed her eyes at the information emerging on the board. "It seems a few threads in common are emerging. The most notable ones, of course, are the experience of the loss of a close family member and the encounter with this stranger named Adrien."

Lena nodded and pointed at the board. "Don't forget to add a bubble that includes the events in the forest."

Augustus drew a new bubble containing the forest's location and its clearing, and marked it as the central place of interest. In a bubble linked to it, he wrote about Dante's disappearance and

Leonardo's depiction of the rock formation in his painting. He also included his own shocking experience with the hoof print.

Marco walked over to the board. "Let's not forget a bubble with our links to the past."

In another space on the board, Augustus included Marco and Damian's ancestral connection.

Portia chimed in. "Don't forget a circle including the knights—the ones connected to both Dante and Gregory's dream."

Once he had completed all the circles, Augustus now wrote abstract nouns around them: history, past, dreams, and time travel?

Lena pored over the words on the board, and noticed the question mark after the last two words. Her mind wandered, and Augustus's story of his 'Time Machine' floated back into her thoughts.

Gregory neared the whiteboard and tapped on it. "You're still entertaining the idea that time travel could actually exist?"

Augustus narrowed his gaze at Gregory. "Well, why not? We mustn't rule out any ideas. I mean, Lena has been going somewhere in her dreams. And now with the discovery of this portrait and the clues in the painting. There's something going on in that clearing."

"I still think that's a little far-fetched, don't you?" Gregory's lips formed a tight line as he nervously picked at a hangnail. "What if it's just some sinister remnant from that era?"

Augustus swept his hands across the various bubbles on the board. "Look, I know it's a crazy notion. But suppose Dante made a significant discovery in that clearing, something with dire consequences or implications that were a matter of life and death. Wouldn't that be worth protecting?"

Gregory raised his hands. "Or maybe it was one of those secret society rituals they were trying to keep hidden?"

"Look, I know this time travel idea is an extreme notion, but Lena has been going somewhere in her dreams. And now with the discovery of this portrait and the clues in the painting, not to mention my bizarre experience. It's worth considering, no matter how foolish it sounds. Plus, I think I saw something when that electrical jolt zapped me."

Lena perked up. "What did you see?"

Augustus shut his eyes as if trying to conjure up what he had seen. He rubbed his forehead. "It looked like a funnel of sorts, but with concentric lines."

Christina interjected. "Could it have been a reaction to the shock?"

Lena's first dream came back to her with a jolt. She had seen a grid as well. "Hm, what do *you* think it was?"

"I don't know."

Gregory cocked his head, his tone incredulous. "You're suggesting it's some kind of portal, aren't you?"

Augustus turned to Gregory, his teeth clenched tightly together. "You said it, I didn't. I'm simply telling you what I saw. You don't think I realize it all sounds a little crazy? I'm the scientist here, remember? How about you come up with a better explanation, and I'll be all ears?"

The group shifted in their seats, but Lena offered some words. "I think we're all on edge. And that's also why I didn't want to share any of this with you."

Portia went to the window and stood with her back to them. She had not said a word all morning and her voice trembled as she spoke her mind.

"So let's say Augustus isn't crazy and something like a portal exists. What are we going to do? Walk through it?"

She had asked another relevant question, and a ripple of discomfort stirred amongst them. All eyes turned to Augustus, waiting for him to provide an answer.

"Well, regardless of what we're facing, we have to analyze our options thoroughly before we do anything. All the risks involved, etcetera. This isn't something to take lightly."

Lena grabbed her coffee mug and took a sip. "There's life and death involved. Let's not forget that Dante has vanished, and we don't know what happened to him. If there's a portal, we can't just stroll into it blindly."

PILES OF PAPER, open books, buzzing laptops, drinks, and food crowded the long rectangular table.

Despite their scepticism, the group worked out the probabilities, the ramifications, the dangers, and the probable outcomes, as if time travel were a common topic to discuss. After they'd listed all the possibilities, they discussed other points such as the clothing they should wear in case they travelled.

Even Christina made a suggestion. "There's a store in town that sells period clothing for the Theatre Hall." She chuckled. "I've never worn a long dress in my life, so this'll be new for me."

Portia interrupted the group again. "Um, what happens to our physical bodies *if* we travel across time?" She cleared her throat as if something had become stuck there. "I mean, until now, Lena's only been dreaming, so there's been no real danger. But what if we stumble through one and can't come back? What happens then?"

Marco spoke up this time. "That's the risk involved, isn't it? None of us truly knows what's at stake."

They stirred in their seats, and Augustus clasped his hands. "Let it be said we'd never dream of asking any of you to do something you're not comfortable with. Given the possibility that Portia is correct, we will do it on a volunteer basis."

Each one of them reacted with a resounding, "Count me in." Only Gregory's feeble voice lingered like a faint echo. He was always the group's most grounded and hesitant member.

Lena looked around at her friends and settled her gaze on Christina. "Okay. Let's plan to go back to the forest at sunrise one day next week. But *only* as a reconnaissance mission."

. . .

On the morning planned, Lena and her friends began their trek before first light. They filled their backpacks with clothing and snacks while Christina brought along her portable EEG kit.

When they reached the forest, they broke off the path, retraced their steps to the clearing, and made their way around to the other side. Augustus, Marco, and Lena approached the boulders and scoped out the location.

In the forest, the three volunteers had changed into the medieval attire. They had bought the clothes from the theatrical store Christina had suggested at their last meeting. Lena wore a timeless dress—eggshell white with swirls of fine embroidery. Augustus and Marco wore loose tunics and long pants.

The trio had volunteered to carry out the recce of the area while the rest of the group remained behind the trees, on the hill's incline to monitor them.

Lena followed behind Augustus, who walked ahead to scan the ground for more hoof prints. Marco remained a few feet behind her and searched the location for anything that appeared out of the ordinary.

As they neared the boulders, the threesome stayed clear of them. Lena looked up at the towering obelisks and spotted a faint signet at the top of one boulder—a Celtic triquetra.

"Hey, look at that signet."

Lena stepped closer to look at the carving, forgetting the protocols they had discussed, and Augustus warned her, "Don't get too near the rocks."

"It's okay. I feel nothing odd here." Lena took another step to peer at it. "That symbol looks familiar, doesn't it?"

She had barely finished her question when an electrical discharge exploded and a blast of wind sucked the air out from around her and sent her whirling into a concentric passage.

15
THE VOYAGE

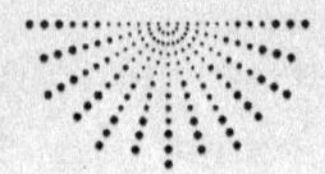

LENA ~ FLORENCE, 1489

LENA BLINKED IN RAPID SUCCESSION.

The sky spanned above her, and its vibrant hue overwhelmed her. Her ears rang. She had received an aggressive pounding when she landed heavily on dry, packed earth. As she leaned on an elbow to tell Marco and Augustus that the fall had not hurt her, she realized that they were no longer by her side. A dozen needles pricked her scalp. She yelled to the others, but her words were carried away by the wind.

When she glanced around the clearing, the expanse appeared untended, and the shrubbery grew thick, lush, and untouched. A faint rumbling shook the ground, and she took no chances. She hoped her friends had found a place safe and raced across the wide expanse toward the forest. As she beat a fresh path through this untrodden land, she crushed plants and herbs underfoot. The scent of mint and tarragon filled her nares—a reminiscence of her childhood.

When she reached the trees, shrill voices came from inside the woods. Children shouted and played in the distance. They must have arrived after the group had made it to the other side of the clearing.

She entered the forest and avoided treading on branches, careful not to make a noise as she wound her way through the trees. Occasionally, she ducked to avoid being swatted by low-hanging boughs.

A child's cry resounded in the woods near her, and she crouched on instinct.

"*Tre, due, uno.* Whoever is there, I will find you!"

From her dress pocket, her phone slipped onto the ground with a thud next to her. She picked it up and glanced at it, noticing the 'no service' indicator at the top of the screen.

She peered through the foliage from behind a coppice and saw a young boy. He must have heard her movements because he stood frozen in place with his eyes darting left to right as he searched the woods.

She stepped out onto the path in front of him and placed a finger to her lips. He stared at her, wide-eyed, his mouth hanging open by a breath. His shock of dark chocolate brown curls and crystal-quartz eyes reminded her of a little wild animal—a stunning sight. For a few moments, she remained mesmerized. At that moment, she observed that the garments and footwear he had on were odd looking—like they were from a different era. Her pulse thundered in her ears. Had she travelled through time, after all?

He still had not uttered a sound, but stared at her hand where Lena still held her phone. She recovered from her lapse and slipped it into her dress pocket. She asked him if he could show her the way to Florence. He cocked his head and frowned, but then pointed to the unfrequented footpath toward the city. "Firenze," he added. She sighed. Fortunately, she was still in Tuscany.

From beyond the trees, a shrill voice called out, "Dante!"

The boy flinched and his body tensed up, but he remained rooted in place.

At the sound of his name, Lena's eyes widened in disbelief. "Dante?"

He nodded, but kept his gaze fixed on her. His eyes narrowed and followed her every movement. His chin rose slightly when he replied in his native Florentine dialect. "*Si Signora . . . Sono Dante di Ronaldo D'Alessandro.*"

"How old are you, Dante?"

Dante's cheeks flushed pink.

"Eight."

She took a step forward for a closer look, but he turned and fled toward the call, vanishing down the path.

LENA DID NOT HAVE time to waste. Her thoughts raced as she jogged in the general direction the boy had shown her. If this child was indeed *her* Dante, she had arrived twelve years too soon.

Lena's reservations did not stop her from taking another gamble. She headed straight to Michelangelo's studio to confirm her assumption. As she ran, her heart pounded against her chest. What if she could not get back home? What if she became trapped here? These questions ran through her mind as she made her way through the foreign landscape.

When she was confident in her safety, she exited the forested area and continued down the pathway toward Florence. She came to a halt in front of the San Miniato Cemetery, astonished that its structure bore such a close resemblance to the one she knew. But instead of the wrought-iron fencing, a stone wall now surrounded the grounds.

Strolling past the last curve in the path, she held her breath. The ancient city of Florence sprawled out in front of her in all of its splendour—recognizable, even with its outer city walls. It nestled along the river like a sparkling jewel, free from the haze of air pollution. She pinched herself hard and yelped. One thing was for certain: this was real.

Her pulse beat a little faster when she entered through the city gates. Rivulets of clay and mud ran between the cobblestones in the streets, giving her a different perspective of the city than the one she had observed in her dreams. As she drew the hem of her dress up over the mud-caked paths, she had not expected the roads to be this sludgy.

She paused in the middle of crossing the Ponte alle Grazie to glance around. It had guard houses at each column and appeared clunkier than the present-day version. She wrinkled her nose. This bridge was not as impressive as the one she had crossed earlier that day.

The sun waned past the highest point in the sky, and the quiet, empty streets created a sense of unease in her stomach even though its residents were most likely at home for their afternoon siestas. Despite the centuries that had passed, routines had changed little.

Her intention was to check on the artist's studio and she did not need to travel far into the city to get there. Downstream, she observed the Ponte Vecchio. They had not yet built the second floor, as it was still just a distant idea in the Medici's plans. She hurried down the street that ran alongside the Arno River and stopped in front of the building that housed Michelangelo's studio.

Her heart sank when she found the structure in extreme disrepair. She opened the front door to find scaffolding on the main floor, reaching up to the cathedral ceiling. Half-dried plaster covered the walls and the dilapidated wooden stairs lay half restored. She ducked under the platform and climbed the stairs.

On her way up, she skirted the broken steps. As she approached the top landing, she slipped and lost her footing. Her right hand lunged towards the wall and smacked against the wet stucco. By doing so, she avoided falling backward and left a perfect handprint on the wall. She grumbled and lifted her dress skirt to wipe the plaster off on its hem as she climbed the last two steps.

She tapped her knuckle against the studio door, pressed her ear against it, and half-expected to hear Michelangelo's gruff response. Her knock echoed beyond the door. She pressed down on the door's lever, and the creaky door swung open.

Lena walked to the window, tiptoeing around the cracked tiles on the damaged floor. Beyond the studio, the Florentine hills were awash in brilliant hues of blue and green. Her eyes welled up with tears at the beauty of it.

Lost in the scenery, a faint cry from below brought her back. "*Pericoloso!*" Below her, at street level, a man wearing a paint-splattered apron waved his arms and yelled at her.

Startled, she hurried to the door, barrelled down the staircase, and sprinted out the front entrance. She scurried toward the Ponte alle Grazie, relieved to escape confrontation.

As the mason entered the building, she quickly glanced over her shoulder and accidentally bumped into someone in her haste to move forward.

"Mi scusi signora," a deep voice announced as she kept her head lowered. Out of the corner of her eye, the man tilted his head and directed his attention at her. As she slid past him, he reached out and rested his hand on her arm—a friendly gesture.

She looked down as a reflex to the warm touch and recognized the hand which had grazed Damian's arm at the top of the studio's staircase.

Lena glanced up, surprised to find herself in the presence of a much younger Leonardo. He addressed her.

"I apologize for my rudeness, but have we met before?"

Her eyes widened, and she sucked in her breath. She shook her head, mumbled farewell, and walked away as swiftly as she could. One of the group's primary rules had been to avoid interacting with anyone.

Despite her admiration for the artist, she reminded herself of his alleged role in Dante's disappearance. Augustus had cautioned her: *Trust no one.*

Feeling Leonardo's eyes on her, she took short, quick steps away from him. When she reached the Arno River's other bank, she checked behind her one last time. Leonardo had left.

LENA HALF-WALKED AND HALF-RAN, frantic with dread. Unsteady on the gravel path, she checked over her shoulder every few minutes. She reached the forest and rushed through the trees without pausing until she found herself under the cover of the deeper woods.

Silence and a soft breeze replaced the shrill of children's voices. The sun had dropped beyond the hill's tree line, lengthening the shadows, and dimming the day's brightness.

Lena broke out in a cold sweat, terrified she might remain trapped and alone in this unfamiliar world. She cut across the clearing, arrived at the five boulders, and ran around to the obelisk —the one with the signet. The etching was clearer now, more prominent than when she had seen it earlier.

She reached for her phone to take a photograph, but found her pocket empty. Lena patted her dress in vain. *Damn!* A flash of movement diverted her attention as she prepared to retrace her steps. To her left, a sliver of light, ethereal and feeble, hovered in the air. The veil floated and tore the landscape in two with its jagged line.

Startled by a distant rumble, Lena rushed forward with no hesitation.

AUGUSTUS ~ FLORENCE, PRESENT DAY

Augustus and Marco were knocked off their feet as Lena hurtled past them. After the impact of her arrival subsided, Lena lay motionless on the ground.

Marco jumped to his feet and sprinted over to Lena. He cradled her in his lap and checked her wrist. "She's got a pulse. Lena, can you hear me?"

Augustus instructed his friends. "Let's get this documented. Gregory, grab your camera and shoot some photos to document her return!"

Augustus turned to Christina and helped her with her backpack. "Check and monitor her brain waves."

Christina pulled out her EEG portable scanner, got down on her knees, and attached a sensor cap to her head.. "Lena! You there? Wake up." She glanced at Marco. "Her head must have hit the ground quite hard."

The machine hummed while Christina surveyed the output, searching it for any telltale activity. With her eyes locked on the sine waves, she whispered, "Come on. Come back to us."

Just then, the machine whirled out of control and began spitting out data with jagged and aggressive strokes on the output sheets as if Lena's consciousness were screaming and clawing its way back to them.

"This isn't good. Her system's overstimulated." Christina jumped to action around Lena. "Help me lie her flat and lift her legs."

Marco followed Christina's orders, but Lena remained listless. Christina reached to check her pulse again. When she removed the sensor cap on Lena's head, she glanced at Portia. "Bring a cloth and some water. Put that on her forehead to bring down her temperature."

Christina's worried expression signalled a problem. "We have to wake her now!"

Augustus dropped to his knees next to Lena. "Come on!" He took a firm hold of Lena and rocked her with a gentle swaying motion.

Marco's voice rose, alarmed by her lack of movement. "It's not working."

Christina put her hand on his shoulder. "Give it a few moments."

In that instant, Lena's eyes flew open. She scanned her friends' faces, clambered to get up, then slumped back against Marco, who was there to catch her. He gathered her in his arms and kissed the top of her head. "You're back."

A bead of sweat rolled down Christina's forehead. "Thank goodness." She exhaled slowly.

Pale and shaken, Portia burst into tears as she hovered and watched from above.

Augustus's voice rose in pitch. "My God! How could you put your life in danger like that?"

Lena rolled her eyes upward at him. "I didn't do this on purpose."

Augustus combed his fingers through his hair, suddenly aware of his outburst. "Sorry. Knee-jerk reaction."

Lena patted Augustus's hand as if to reassure him she was back.

He stood and paced the ground, the corners of his mouth turned downward. "Not sure what we would have done if we'd lost you."

They crowded around Lena and she gave them a shaky smile. "You're all waiting to hear about it, aren't you? I can tell."

They all let out a snort—a release from the fear which had gripped them moments earlier.

"Lena, you terrified us, but if you're feeling up to it."

Augustus grabbed his pen and paper.

Lena smiled. "I knew it."

With Marco's help, Lena stood up. She pointed to the boulders.

"One moment I was here with all of you, the next I was gone, sucked into a tunnel. It's hard to describe the sensation as I went through it, but there was a tremendous pressure in my body, as if the molecules in my body were being pulled apart. But there was no pain. Only a sensation of weightlessness until I was spit out on the other side." Lena waved her hand toward the clearing. "I lay on the ground somewhere around there." She pointed to a spot on the expanse. "It looked like a neglected garden, with brambles, shrubs, flowers and grasses. I called for you guys, but there was no answer. So I ran to the forest to get out of the clearing."

Lena described what had transpired after that, and Augustus scribbled notes as she spoke. When she stopped, Augustus and the rest of them stared at her in disbelief.

Christina was the first to speak. "You ran into Dante?"

Lena looked at Christina. "Yes, I'm almost positive that boy was *our* Dante. He told me he was eight."

"Eight?" Christina frowned.

"Yes. And he looked just like an angel with those bright eyes, wild hair, and dark curls. He was the most beautiful little boy. It was incredible." Lena wiped her eyes to hide her tears. "Anyway, it's obvious I went too far back in time." She swayed as she shifted her weight to get her balance.

Christine jumped to action. "Okay, guys, we should give Lena some time to rest. She's had a hard knock."

"No, wait, there's something else." Lena took a deep breath. "As I left Michelangelo's studio—"

Marco's eyes bulged out of his head. "You went into the city?"

"Yes, I did. I needed to confirm I had traveled back in time. What? I couldn't tell while I was in the middle of the forest."

Augustus shook his head at her. "Jesus. H. Christ. Go on."

"I was looking behind me when I collided with a man. He apologized to me, but then he stopped me and asked if he knew me from somewhere. When I looked up, I realized the man was Leonardo, but a younger version of him."

Augustus's mouth hung open. "Leonardo? The artist?" And as her story sank in, his eyes widened. "He thought he recognized you? What did you say?"

"Yes, the man himself. I said nothing. Just shook my head and took off running all the way to the forest."

Augustus slapped his knee with his hand. "Dang, I was right in my assumption that he'd seen you in real life, but it makes little sense. You said Dante was only eight. That means Damian hadn't yet asked him for the portrait. This is confusing."

"Maybe I should have spoken to him longer. But we still don't know in what way he's involved. Right? I've got to go back there."

Lena met her friends' incredulous glares, and Augustus put his palms up. "Woah, slow down. You're right, we don't know what's involved. First, we have to keep watch on your mental and physical state. It's not like we travel through time every day."

Lena glared at him. "Says the man who hasn't yet gone to see a doctor."

He pursed his mouth. "You have a point. *And* if there's a next time, you're not going alone!"

Portia spoke up. "Can we just be happy for a moment that she came back?" She turned toward Lena. "We went out of our minds when you disappeared. All we saw was a bright flash of light and you were gone. We gave you a half hour and if you hadn't come back, we were coming after you. Luckily, you did."

Lena cocked her head. "Half an hour? Are you sure it wasn't longer than that?"

Portia lifted her arms in desperation. "Did you even hear a word of what I said?"

Lena nodded, but something else diverted her attention. She looked from left to right.

Augustus frowned at her. "What's wrong?"

"I'm getting a terrible feeling. I think we should go."

Marco was about to say something when a low rumble began under their feet. The ground shook.

Gregory, who had wandered off to check the perimeter, yelled at them.

"Over here!"

LENA

They dashed toward Gregory and ducked behind the thick shrubs along the tree line at the bottom of the incline. While the group crouched behind the bushes, the rumble became a deafening roar. After it passed by them, Lena and Gregory leaned out to see two knights on horseback.

His eyes widened. "Those are the knights from my dream. Have a quick look while they're still riding with their backs to us."

The rest stuck their heads out, then at each other in bewilderment. When the knights stopped their horses, Augustus signalled for them to pull back. They remained squatted on their haunches and waited as the clip clop of horses' hooves doubled back in their direction.

As the horses approached; the knights stopped about twenty feet in front of their thicket. One horse became fretful, and Lena watched as Gregory took advantage of the noise to reach into his pocket. He cradled the handheld recorder in the palm of his hand and switched it on to record the horsemen's interaction. The knights spoke in an unintelligible language.

Lena's legs trembled as they waited for the pair to move on. After a hair-raising moment, the men turned their horses and travelled back in the direction from which they had arrived. She poked her head out and watched as the knights receded into the distance. A flash of bright light lit up the clearing, and after the intense flare subsided, the knights had vanished.

"The way seems clear. Let's get the heck out of here!"

They charged across the clearing, through the forest, and back to Florence without stopping. When they reached the Arno, they all stopped for a breath.

Gregory broke the silence. "Those soldiers were speaking in Lingua Franca."

Lena chimed in. "It reminds me of the way they speak in the deep regions of Quebec."

Gregory pulled out his mini-recorder from his pocket. "Have a listen to this conversation."

Christina glared at him as if he had grown two heads. "You recorded them while we were out there?"

"Are you kidding? I had to." Gregory clicked on a button, and the incomprehensible babble played until they heard the clip clopping of the horses' hooves. "I'll give it another listen later and try to translate what they're saying."

Augustus looked at them sheepishly as he pulled out his own cell phone and confessed he had taken a photo of the two knights. The girls looked at him in shock.

"You guys are incorrigible!" Portia scolded them. "Here we were, praying for our lives, and you're recording and taking photos!"

Augustus searched through his phone for the photograph. "When I saw Gregory reaching for his microphone, I figured I'd do the same. I had to get a snapshot of them." Augustus pointed his screen toward them. He had captured the knights on horseback, clear as day.

"I can't believe how close they were to us." Christina shook her head. "We're clearly getting in over our heads, aren't we?"

Gregory put his phone away. "I have to admit, this *was* a little too close for comfort."

As Lena and the group approached the city centre, cries of "Freedom of speech!" echoed through the streets, alive with activity.

Protesters chanted in the square, "We have rights, and you will not ignore us," as they marched into Piazza di Santa Croce with bullhorns and flags.

A wave of contradictory emotions washed over Lena. Her thoughts remained in that other world, from which she had only just returned, but the familiarity of her own surroundings comforted her. She inhaled deeply.

For a moment on the other side, she had doubted whether she could return. But her last thought as she jumped through the portal had been, "Take me home."

Exhausted from the eventful afternoon, Lena and her friends fought their way through the wave of people. Halfway through the crowd, Lena's breathing became laboured and a claustrophobic sensation filled her.

The swarm pushed and pulled Lena along through no will of her own. As she leaned against the wall of people in front of her, she spotted a familiar expression on the sea of faces. *Damian?* She swung her head from side to side, checking to her left and right, but he was gone.

LENA COLLAPSED onto the couch in Augustus's apartment. Marco gathered her into his arms. Her travel through time had zapped her of energy, made her weary, but her mind still raced with everything she had experienced.

Augustus uploaded the day's events to their timeline. He attached magnets with childlike depictions of the knights to the magnetic whiteboard, labelling them as Hugues and Godfrey, after the two founders of the Knights Templar.

Christina peered over Augustus's shoulder as he looked for some material on the internet. He clicked through and searched through many historical sites. "I can't seem to find anything that matches the signet the knights bore on their armour." He sighed with impatience, getting nowhere.

A few moments later, he let out a cheer. "Finally! Here's a

picture that looks a lot like them." He swivelled the screen to show them. "But there's something odd about *our* two knights, don't you think? I'm not sure what it is."

Gregory had been sitting in the corner translating the recorded conversation. "Yes, there is something strange about them. But one thing is clear: those knights definitely guard that portal."

16
DÉJÀ VU

DAMIAN ~ FLORENCE, 1500

DAMIAN REFUSED to believe Dante was gone.

He returned to the clearing every day and half-expected to hear a response whenever he called out to his brother as he walked through the forest.

Michelangelo's studio remained closed, and there was no trace of Leonardo. Everyone had vanished. The only thing left was his family's grief, and the pain written across their faces whenever they looked at him. For his family's sake, he wished he did not resemble Dante.

The other morning, one of his sisters had called after him in town. "Dante?" When she realized it was Damian, she broke down into loud sobs. "Oh, Damian, it's you. I'm sorry! We just miss him so terribly." And he held his sister as she shook in his arms, while his own heart shattered.

DAMIAN SHOVED bread into his pockets and filled a water bag as he prepared for his outing.

Outside the city walls, the path was clear and peaceful. Still, the closer he got to the forest, the more his heart hammered in his temples. He was alone and defenceless, but a desperate need to find Dante drove him forward.

During his latest dream, Damian had led Lena and the others to the clearing. He hoped they would find a clue on their end, but he had awoken before he had found out anything more.

Images of running into the woods with his brother flooded his mind as he followed the old route through the trees. The bittersweet memory of eerie shrills and giggles rang through the forest. *Ready or not, whoever is there, I will find you!* The words echoed in his head. When they played hide-and-seek, Damian had always searched for Dante until he found him. Now, in his heart, he was certain that if he searched long enough, he would find him again.

Nostalgia tugged at his soul, and he wished he could go back to those carefree days. He arrived at the clearing and made his way around to *La Mano di Dio*. The clearing was quiet, with no loud thumping or movement across the wide field. Even the tall grasses stood still. He marched onward through the expanse, finding it strangely quiet.

When Damian reached halfway across the field, the ground trembled. The sound of horse's hooves thundered towards him, and he quickened his pace. As he raced toward the obelisks, the knights on horseback overshot him as their weight pounded the dirt. They formed a semi-circle, doubled back, and rode full tilt to get back to him.

He cast a quick glance backward as he dodged their pursuit. One of the knight brandished his sword and yelled out incomprehensible words. Damian yowled for his life. He sprinted toward the boulders and saw the shadow of the knight raising his blade high into the air, ready to bludgeon him.

A bolt of energy radiated through Damian's body and a burst

of bright lights dazzled him as he spiralled into a dark tunnel to the sounds of a raging storm echoing in his ears.

DAMIAN ~ FLORENCE, PRESENT DAY

Damian landed hard.

Adrenaline coursed through him and numbed his pain. He sat upright and patted himself to make sure his body parts were intact. The rumbling was still discernible, and with no time to explore, he sprang to his feet and ran towards the forest.

A booming roar of hooves trailed close behind again until he escaped into the woods, where he bolted through the trees at lightning speed. Burning leaves and the scent of smoke followed him. On the pathway that led to the city, he glimpsed behind him and kept a constant eye over his shoulder.

When he rounded the bend at the San Miniato Cemetery, the surrounding landscape came into full view. He came to a halt to take in the scenery. The landscape had altered, and it now resembled a well-kept garden.

He caught sight of Florence in the distance and held his breath. His city lay before him—unfortified and vulnerable. He pinched his arm in disbelief. *This* was Lena's world.

His heart thundered in his chest as he ran across the Ponte alle Grazie. As he moved through the crowd, heads turned. He disregarded the strange expressions and continued on his way. Their attire astounded him as well, but his urgent mission remained his priority: He must find Lena. He quickened his pace and headed to the places he thought she might be. In his dreams, the streets were slightly askew, but otherwise familiar. Despite feeling overwhelmed and lightheaded, he persisted on his journey.

Damian sprinted until he found himself at the Piazza San Lorenzo, in front of Lena's building. The large wooden door did not budge when he pushed against it. He stepped away, flustered. Just then, a young woman emerged. A swift glance told him she was not Lena. Despite his disappointment, he caught the door before it closed.

Climbing the stairs to Lena's apartment, he rapped on the door. After the third knock, there was still no answer. He reached up and slid his fingers along the frame's ledge the way Portia had done the last time he had been there. Finding the key, he slipped it into the lock.

The apartment was exactly as he remembered it from Lena's perspective. He trembled as he called out to her and waited for an answer, but none came. Damian took a peek around the room. It was bigger than he had experienced through her eyes. She was not here.

A flutter of wings startled him. Outside, a sparrow flew off the sill, its wings hitting the windowpane. It left tiny particles of dust swirling in the air. Damian moved to the window and leaned against the frame. Looking out onto the square, a rush of déjà vu whirled around his mind, and he scratched his head at the familiarity of it. But he had no time for these distracting thoughts. He locked up the apartment and returned the key to its secret place.

When Damian reached the Piazza di Santa Croce, he ran into a procession. The enormous crowd filled the square. He had seen something similar in his time, and this sort of frenzy frightened him. The demonstrators chanted and waved their flags, jostling and carrying him along with them.

He looked from side to side as the crowd absorbed him. There was a momentary break in the sea of faces, and he recognized a pair of eyes—cold, ice grey, and unmistakable. *Lena?* It was a quick moment. He craned his neck to keep her in sight, but she had vanished. With each wave of movement, the mob pushed him further away.

After he was spit out onto one of the narrow streets that led to the Arno River; he settled on making his way to the forest. He contemplated going back through the city, but the idea of fighting against that mob stopped him. Free from the maddening crowd, his heart calmed. He had hoped to find Lena, but the approaching dusk and its shadows left him feeling uneasy, and he trembled at the thought of being trapped here.

Damian followed the familiar path, entered the forest, then crossed the clearing. Assured the knights sat in waiting for him, he checked over his shoulder and all around him.

The veil remained suspended near the rocks. It reminded him of the one his sister had worn at her wedding ceremony. Dante and he had been so proud to carry its train as she entered the church. Now it was just a bittersweet memory.

With one last look around, he dashed toward the fissure in the landscape. As he jumped through it, he held his breath and prayed it would take him home.

DAMIAN ~ FLORENCE, 1500

The clearing's growing shadows caught Damian as he tumbled through the doorway of time.

He dashed into the encroaching darkness, a route he knew with his eyes closed. There was no rumbling, but he still ran without stopping. When he reached the city walls, he stepped inside the gate, relieved to have returned. There were no crowds or demonstrations as he walked through the darkened streets.

When he stepped inside his parents' home, embers still glowed in the fireplace. He entered the kitchen, comforted by his familiar surroundings. His parents had already gone to bed, and the house lay still. Sparks flew and crackled when he placed a small log onto the iron cast holder. He was home.

His mother had set out some bread and cheese for him. After

he finished eating, he stumbled down the corridor to his room and slid into his bed, fully dressed. As soon as his head met his feather-filled pillow, he fell into a deep sleep.

IT WAS dark when Damian jerked awake. Sweat trickled from his forehead and his clothes stuck to his skin. A heaviness sat upon his chest and the deadweight of fear pinned him to his bed.

Beyond the window, the moon glowed in the night. A ray of moonlight pierced the room through a slit in the shutter. When the weight on his torso subsided, he sat up, placing his feet on the cool floor to clear his mind.

Beyond the sombre shadows, something stirred—a subtle shift in the gloom. Damian rubbed the sleep from his eyes.

In the room's semidarkness, a silhouette lay on Dante's bed. Damian heard the unmistakable drone and got out of bed. He tiptoed to the other side of the room and stared down at the dark form. Had one of his cousins come to stay the night?

Shuffling to his night table, Damian lifted the medallion glass lantern and lit the wick. In the candlelight's flicker, the shape moved. As he approached, the dim lighting revealed Dante in his bed.

Damian gawked down at his brother. How was this possible? Dante's arms hung out over the bed, with a full view of his hands, where all ten fingers spread out without a hint of a scratch. The lantern shook in Damian's unsteady grip.

Shadows danced on the walls, and his heart vacillated between delight and shock. Damian brushed away his tears, and when he glanced down again, Dante's eyes were open.

"Damian?"

Startled, Damian dropped to his knees. His throat tightened as hot tears spilled from his eyes.

Dante lifted himself on an elbow, a wrinkle on his brow. "Are you crying?"

With heat rising to his cheeks, Damian got to his feet and wiped his eyes with his sleeve.

"No. I just stubbed my toe."

He staggered back to his bed. Was he delirious or dreaming? With his head in his hands, he sat on his bed and replayed the events of the last several weeks in his mind.

Dante had disappeared . . . They had found his severed fingers . . . Grief had stricken family and friends . . . Now, Dante lay in his bed as if nothing had happened.

Dante sat up and eyed him curiously. "Has something happened?"

Damian ignored his brother and turned his gaze to the niche on the wall where he had hidden Lena's portrait. It had to be there. If not, he was losing his mind. He walked over to the shelf and looked under the lining. His hands trembled as he frowned at the space. Little beads of sweat swelled on his forehead. He lifted the cloth a little higher and hoped the parchment had simply slid to the back. *But there was nothing.* He squeezed his eyes shut.

"Looking for this?"

Damian swivelled around. In the room's dancing light and shadows, Dante held the portrait. Damian's heart thundered, and a wave of adrenaline blasted through him.

"Give that drawing to me!"

Dante's expression widened with surprise at his outburst, then his eyes narrowed. "*Shh*, keep it quiet."

Damian was still in shock. "When in damnation did you get home?"

"What do you mean? I've been here all evening."

Damian stomped over and snatched the drawing from his brother's hand. He checked it over and sighed with relief that it was indeed Lena's portrait.

Dante sat to attention. "I should be the one asking where *you* have been."

Damian sat down and stared at his twin. He struggled to find the words to describe his experiences over the past few weeks. "A lot has happened since you've been gone."

"Gone? I don't understand."

"You had disappeared. We thought you were dead. But your fingers? How is this possible?"

"Why don't you tell me all about it?"

Damian recounted everything, including the moment they had found Dante's fingers under the blood-splattered tree.

Dante waved his fingers at him. "Look. All here. You must have had a nightmare."

"No, I didn't." Damian huffed with impatience. "By the Virgin's son, it has all happened as I have told you. I just don't understand how you are here again." He leaned forward. "It is all true. I have just come from the future."

Dante scoffed at him. "Did you see any of your *friends*?"

"Yes. Well, no, but—"

Dante snickered, in the way he always did, whenever he thought Damian had said something far-fetched. He lay back on his bed and slid his intact fingers behind his head.

Damian sighed. "I cannot explain—or understand—it all. But I'm warning you. You will run into someone who has a message for me. You must not go alone. If you do, you will disappear."

"Who sent this message?"

"No one knows but you." Damian's shoulders dropped in defeat.

"You're not making any sense." Dante shook his head as he stared up at the ceiling.

Damian lay back on his bed as the room spun. He cast an anxious glance at his twin before turning away. His stomach churned, and he wanted to shout, "*This is my one chance to save you!*" But no words came out.

He closed his eyes when he heard Dante's bed creak and fell asleep to the lantern's diminishing light.

. . .

SUNLIGHT FILLED the bedroom in a brilliant haze of white and golden.

After a moment of rubbing his eyes, Damian looked over at Dante's bed. It was empty. He sprung from bed and raced to the kitchen. Dante stood talking to Annabella while she prepared for her day.

Damian let out a sigh of relief as soon as he saw him, and his racing heart settled back to its regular beat. His mother served him a bowl of soup and sat him down to eat it. She approached him and touched his cheek.

"You look pale. And you weren't around for dinner last evening. Where were you?"

Still thrown off by the time shift, he stared from his mother to Dante. She had uttered the same words on the morning that Dante had vanished.

Annabella frowned at him. "This is not like you. You know it's dangerous to be out at night." She glanced at his brother before she continued. "I hope you're not up to any trouble."

She pressed her palm to his head and pursed her lips. He scowled. Dante was the one who had not shown up for supper. Had his voyage through time altered their situation?

"Your head feels fine. Get some food into you." His mother went back to her tasks. "And don't forget you have work today with the maestro. You don't want to disappoint your father. These men are important people."

Annabella went to the front entrance carrying her basket. She glanced around one last time before heading out to the market. And although Damian's thoughts were a million light years away, he cut her off before she could finish.

"Yes, Mother, don't worry. I'll stop by the store and bring Father his food."

Her brow crinkled again, as though she wanted to add

something else. Instead, she closed the door behind her. Damian waited until his mother's footsteps became faint before addressing Dante.

"Brother, please believe me. I told you the truth last night. Mother has just finished doing and saying everything she did on that fateful day."

"Don't be silly. She says the same thing every day. Look, you thought I was dead, and yet I'm still here—alive."

Damian's cheeks burned like someone had struck him across the face. "That's because it hasn't happened yet! Please listen to what I'm saying. I left and returned the day before you vanished. Perhaps my trip to the future has saved you?" His throat tightened at the thought of losing Dante again. Life without him had been unbearable.

Dante shrugged at his crazy notions. "Fine, I'll keep in mind what you've said. Feel better now?"

Damian sighed. "Promise to be careful." God willing, he had forewarned Dante of the portending dangers. He sat at the kitchen table and watched as Dante put on his overcoat. The weight of worry settled once more on Damian's shoulders.

"Where are you going?"

Dante slipped his arms into his sleeves and buttoned his coat.

"Unlike you, I work every day for my living. But I'll be cautious now that I've heard your concerns. Look, let's meet this evening and figure out what to do next if that will put your mind at ease."

He left the house before Damian could muster another word.

17
BROKEN GLASS

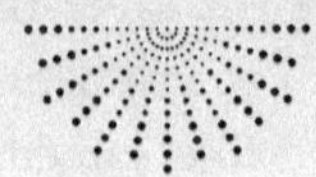

DANTE ~ FLORENCE, 1500

FOG SETTLED on Florence and subdued the midmorning sunlight.

Dante and Giancarlo walked with brisk steps through the market square. They made their way toward the Ponte Vecchio and hastened back to work after picking up some extra trowels.

In the morning's bustle, Dante had already brushed aside Damian's earlier warnings from his mind. But one puzzle remained. He had found the drawing Damian kept hidden in the niche. The girl in the portrait was the apparition he had seen in the forest; he was sure of it. But how was that possible?

To distract himself, Dante chattered about his plans. "One day, I will have my own proper enterprise. I can't work forever for someone who doesn't run a thriving business." Dante reflected on the failings of his current master at the construction job.

Giancarlo protested, "But your father announced you and Damian will take over his store. You have at least something to look forward to, don't you?"

Dante lifted his shoulders in a shrug. "It's possible." He laughed at Giancarlo. "Look, don't misunderstand me. My father has worked hard to get to where he is. He runs a smooth operation, and he likes to be close to his family and his store. I admire his determination, but that kind of life suits Damian. I want more than that."

He imagined conquering many more worlds than just the one in Florence. He loved this city and his family, but here he lived in a gilded cage.

Giancarlo ran alongside, trying to keep up with Dante. "You're always in such a hurry. Slow down."

As they reached the middle of the piazza on this cool, misty morning, Leonardo approached them and he motioned to Dante he wanted to speak with him.

Dante instructed his cousin to keep going. "I'll catch up to you."

Leonardo placed his hand on Dante's shoulder and leaned in. "Damian, I apologize for my behaviour the other evening at dinner. I believe there's something I must explain to you. Let us meet at the city gates on the road to San Miniato at midday." Dante was about to mention he had been mistaken for his brother, but Leonardo cut him off again. "Bring along Dante as well. He needs to hear this as well."

Leonardo left before Dante could speak. He watched as the artist disappeared into the crowd. Was this the mysterious encounter Damian had mentioned to him?

Dante caught up to Giancarlo, who cocked an eye at him. "You're doing side jobs now?"

"Not at all. He's one of my father's client."

With his mind on the strange encounter, he reached into his overcoat to check for the rolled-up parchment with the girl's image. Something had told him to take it from its protective niche. He also patted the secret pocket in his jacket, an old habit to make sure his talisman—the silver box—remained nestled safely in there.

He prodded Giancarlo. "Come on, let's finish this job. I still have to help my father at the store."

DAMIAN

The work session with Michelangelo began as soon as Damian arrived at the studio. He would have preferred to remain close to Dante, but duty had called and his mother's gentle reminder about these men had pushed him to carry on. It was as if nothing had changed, even though he had been to another world and back.

That morning, he went through the motions expected of him. But in his deepest thoughts, he fretted Dante might disregard his warning. However, so far, the day had gone without incident, and Michelangelo worked him harder than usual.

Outside, the fog was ever present and his body ached from the pose he held all morning. It was a little past midday when a knock sounded at the door. Michelangelo responded in his usual gruff tone. "Come in."

Leonardo entered. When he did, Damian caught the shadow of a frown cross his face when he spoke to Michelangelo. "Micielo, I did not realize you were working today." He looked at Damian. "Young man, you did not mention the maestro had summoned you when I spoke to you earlier."

Damian swallowed hard and choked on his words. "I have neither seen nor spoken to you today. Perhaps you bumped into my brother?"

"Ah, a case of mistaken identities. I understand now why *you* didn't come. I don't suppose Dante told you I asked to meet at the city gates?"

"The city gates?" Damian's voice quivered. "I've not seen my brother since this morning at breakfast." His airways constricted, and he gasped for air. He was about to ask Michelangelo if he could leave for the day when the echo of his name reverberated in the street below—as it had on that other dreadful day.

Damian jumped off the podium and rushed to open the window. This time the call had been unmistakable, and its impact crushed him. He had lost him again. His stomach lurched, and his knees gave in. Leonardo and Michelangelo rushed to his sides as he crumpled to the ground.

Damian's soul shattered into a million fragmented pieces—like shards of broken glass strewn across the floor.

PORTIA ~ FLORENCE, PRESENT DAY

At first light, Lena, Augustus, and Marco inched along the edge of the forest toward *La Mano di Dio*.

Portia stood next to Gregory and Christina as she gazed toward the obelisks, and kept an ear out for the horses' thunderous rumble. She watched as her friends grasped hands, counted to three, and dashed through the veil of time.

In that moment, Portia caught sight of the wormhole and its concentric, circular grid. It reminded her of an image she had seen during one of those science documentaries on the universe.

The early morning mist rose from the ground as all three stared at the shimmer left behind where her friends had vanished. After the resplendent display of light diffused, a loud release of pressure sounded, like vacuumed air escaping from a sealed mason jar.

Then, the clearing quietened, and one by one, the calls of nature returned like a volume knob being turned up again: the shrill chirping of birds, the stirring in the tall, pale grasses, and the rustling of leaves. A dove cooed in the distance, answering the call of its mate.

Portia looked at her friends and shuffled her feet back and forth in the dust. "We should go back to Florence." The other two agreed and trailed behind her. Taking the long way around, they hurried back to the city.

Christina quickened her stride as they strolled along the road leading to the San Miniato Cemetery. "It feels like someone's watching us."

Portia kept pace with Christina as she cast a nervous glance over her shoulder.

HIDDEN IN THE MORNING SHADOWS, a knight sat on horseback and watched them. The Cross of the Lorraine sparkled against his tunic, and his silver-white armour glistened.

LENA ~ FLORENCE, 1500

In the tunnel of time, the centrifugal force of energy separated Lena from her fellow travellers.

She fell a significant distance away from her two companions when they arrived on the other side. The abrupt crash landing, accompanied by a resounding roar, gave them little time for reflection. Two riders charged toward them, and Augustus shouted at them.

"Run! To the forest!"

Lena dashed toward the tree line when the riders changed course and steered straight for her. They were the same two knights they had seen in the clearing.

She tore across the wide expanse with her heart thundering against her chest. As she ran, her perception of the landscape became distorted and blurred at the edge of her field of vision. Behind her, she heard the knights as they coaxed the geldings to gallop faster.

The forest line was within reach when Lena stomped on the hem of her dress and somersaulted head over feet. Her hands flew out front when she hit the dirt and skidded to a stop. Her cheek burned as it scraped against the hardened mud. A cloud of dust surrounded her as she struggled to get up.

A sharp pain shot through her upper body when a hand of steel seized Lena by the scruff of her neck and yanked her off the ground. She screamed in agony as her body hurtled through the air and, like a sack of potatoes, the knight dropped her behind him. While his horse continued to keep pace, Lena clung on for dear life to the rider's surcoat. She struggled to draw in a breath and stop herself from crying.

When they reached the clearing's end, the brute jumped down, pulled her off his horse, and dragged her along with him. At the camp's fire pit, he threw her to the ground. The other knight glared at him and barked words in his direction.

"J'm'en fiche si t'n'as aucun respect pour les autres mais nous suivons des ordres et n'lui faisons pas d'mal." Lena recognized the meaning of his words through the blur of her suffering. *I don't care if you haven't any respect for others, but we have our orders and no harm must come to her.*

The disgruntled knight yanked off his helmet, and his disheveled blond hair fell to his shoulders. She wrinkled her nose as the dank, musty sweat of his body odour reached her. He pointed to a flat rock where Lena could sit. At least they had no intention of hurting her just yet. She sat down and followed their movements with a discerning eye. Their helmets were off, but their hands remained by their sides, ready to draw their swords at a moment's notice.

At close range, these men were much larger than when she and her friends had peered at them from behind the bushes. Hardened and boorish, they appeared much too comfortable in these wretched conditions. This might be the only life they knew.

She pretended to give in to capture by accepting drink and a meal from them. However, at the first morsel of food, she gagged from the wretched flavour and spit the chewed piece onto the ground.

"Ugh, this food tastes like crap!"

The knights sat across the fire from each other, paying no

attention to her as they gnawed on their meat. Lena sat in between them and looked from one to the other. Their dour and austere countenance left her with a sour taste in her mouth and a knot of angst in her belly—even worse than the flavour of their food. Lena did not care for what they might be planning.

As she plotted her escape, she kept her gaze on them and wished away all the horror stories of abductions.

MARCO

Marco and Augustus had been running helter-skelter toward the forest, certain the knights were close behind them.

Marco ground to a halt and turned just in time to catch sight of the knights galloping after Lena. The knight who rode in front plucked her up and whisked her away.

Augustus stood with his mouth agape. "What in the hell just happened?"

Marco dropped onto his knees and covered his face with his hands. He was at a loss for words, unable to comprehend how they had found themselves in this predicament. After his initial shock dissolved, he motioned for Augustus to follow him. They darted into the woods until they reached an area with enough dense foliage to conceal their whereabouts.

Marco gulped down the knot caught behind his Adam's apple. "What were we thinking coming here? We have to get her back before they harm her." The back of his throat burned as bile rose. His stomach churned, and he felt a wave of sickness wash over him. "What are we going to do? My god, what if they kill her?"

Augustus stopped him. "If they wanted to kill her, they would have done it already."

"Right. That makes me feel so much better." Marco's tone dripped with sarcasm.

Even though Augustus had made sense, his mind flashed with

worst-case scenarios, and his voice lowered. "What will they do to her in the meantime?"

Augustus rested his hand on his shoulder. "I hope nothing. But we've got another problem. It's getting dark."

They had not expected arriving so late in the day during the planning of their journey to the past. It had been early morning when they had jumped through the veil. Now, it was already late afternoon when Marco paced in front of Augustus. "Wonderful! What a great idea we had coming here."

Augustus scratched his scalp. "Look, we're not equipped to fight against these knights. But we can hear them, therefore they aren't too far away. Those hoof prints must be easy enough to track. For now, we'll get as close as possible to their camp. We'll stay on the lookout and try to come up with a plan."

Marco rubbed the back of his neck and agreed with Augustus. He took the lead because he was more familiar with the forest. They tracked a path toward the muffled sounds in the distance, careful not to step on twigs and branches. As they got closer to the clearing's southernmost tip, gravelly voices echoed. The two knights, deep in conversation.

Marco and Augustus crawled toward the voices, then stopped, and left themselves enough room to escape. Peeking through the bushes, Marco eyed Lena sitting near the fire pit with her eyes fixated on her captors. The knights ate and growled at each other.

From this viewpoint, Marco envisioned the different ways in which he could help her escape. He was certain Augustus was doing the same from the way his friend's eyes darted across the surrounding landscape. As the afternoon light faded, the two kept vigil while huddled against each other to keep warm.

Marco's chin dipped to his chest as he slumped against the tree, his elbows tucked tight into his sides and his shoulders drawn upward. He braced himself against the guilt building up inside him. He did not know why he had let her persuade them to do this.

Augustus tried to comfort him. “It won’t do her any good to feel guilty. We’ll get her back. Rest now and I’ll stay on alert. We’ll need our strength.”

DAMIAN

Light rain droplets fell through the canopy. They floated and bounced off the leaves and plants.

Damian looked down at the two young men resting under the tree. With a fixed gaze, he watched as they slept huddled against one another on the damp forest floor.

A few minutes earlier, he had come upon the knights’ encampment. He recognized the knights as the ones who had trashed Leonardo’s studio. He crept closer to spy on them and could not believe the sight before him. There was no mistake. A young lady lay curled up on the cold ground between the two burly men. They kept her wedged in, like two vigilant sentry guards, making it impossible for her to move without alerting them.

The knights had tied their horses to a nearby tree, and the horses grew restless as he approached. Lena and her captors stirred from the disturbance and he hastily retraced his steps into the forest.

While scouring the tree line for a suitable vantage point, he unexpectedly stumbled upon two young men, fast asleep and leaning against a tree. As Damian moved forward to get a better look at them, he stepped on a small branch.

The sudden, dry pop startled the pair awake. Their eyes flew open, and they gasped at the sight of him standing there. He ducked faster than a sword drawn out of its scabbard and pointed his finger toward the encampment. As he crouched before them, heat rose to his cheeks, embarrassed by his own clumsiness.

The person with hair the colour of sand nodded, displayed no hint of judgment. The three of them peeked through the bushes when the young lady and the guards turned toward the noise and stayed as still as possible. Damian overheard her say something to distract the knights.

When the guards' attention shifted, his two companions turned to face him. Damian extended his arm and spoke in his native Florentine dialect. "Damiano, son of Ronaldo D'Alessandro."

The sandy-haired fellow went from looking tense to visibly relieved. Clasping Damian's wrist, he pointed to himself and his friend.

"I'm Augustus Reilly, and this is Marco Baldini."

Damian's eyes widened. He had not recognized them at first sight, but now he recalled them from his dreams. He shook Marco's arm and added a gentle squeeze. A sensation of familial warmth rushed through him and emotions erupted in his chest like explosions. He saw his sister's features on Marco's face. When Marco lowered his eyes, he resembled Ariella when a stranger's gaze remained on her a little too long. He also had the same dimples in his cheeks as she did.

After the introductions, Damian motioned for them to follow him on the path away from their current position. It was too perilous to stay this close. Augustus and Marco crawled and followed him to a safer distance.

Once they had reached a more secure area, he motioned for them to sit and offered them carbonata and water from his satchel. His two new friends jumped on the food like hungry wolves.

Augustus gestured toward Damian's satchel. "Looks as if you have enough here to travel far."

Damian nodded. It was at that moment he realized he no longer needed to make the journey. And despite their present circumstance, a sense of assurance filled him with hope.

Damian clasped his hands as he balanced on his haunches in front of them. "We must help your friend escape from these ruffians, and I think I have an idea how to do that."

First, he replayed his plan in his thoughts until Marco interrupted him.

"Well, come on, what's your idea?"

He smiled at them and shared his plan. They listened intently, hanging on his every word, and when he finished, his eyes shifted from Augustus to Marco.

"A risky plan, but it's the only one that will work."

THE DRIZZLE CEASED and afternoon crawled in, while the sky transformed from slate grey to cobalt blue.

As the sun began its descent behind the hills, Damian entered the clearing. He motioned to Marco and Augustus to stay behind him as they followed the horses' imprints. They had barely made it ten steps when, to their left, came a loud splintering crack.

Damian and his two companions swung their heads toward the sound. They found themselves with nowhere to run for cover. Seconds later, one of the two spectacular knights burst out of the woods and glared in their direction.

The knight's menacing grimace dissolved into a puzzled expression when his eyes fell upon Damian. His mouth dropped open, and he rubbed his eyes. He stumbled and circled in place. The three watched as the knight regained his balance while he searched the area where they stood.

Damian, Marco, and Augustus stayed still. They had been creeping along, one behind the other, and now stood side by side facing the ruffian.

He was only fifty feet away, yet he made no move toward them, even with his sword hanging at his side. There was bewilderment in his expression as he scanned the area.

Damian frowned and turned to where his new friends had stood, but there was no one there. His pulse drummed in his temples. Where had Marco gone? His eyes darted to where Augustus had been following behind Marco, but he too had dropped out of sight. Damian found himself alone in front of this terrifying soldier. He swallowed the hard lump in his throat.

Then he heard a whisper, a disembodied voice. "Marco, Damian, are you there?" And from somewhere close by, Marco responded, "Yeah, what just happened?"

Damian did not say a word. He could not see either of them, yet he could hear their voices? What kind of witchery was this?

"Damian?"

Damian still gave no response. Then Augustus tried again, his whisper now almost a hiss. "Damian?"

"*Si.*"

Next to Augustus, Marco let out an exhale. "We must all be invisible."

Damian looked down at himself and saw only the ground. "You mean you cannot see me?"

"Nope. And that's good because it means that neither can he."

The knight's eyes moved toward their voices each time one of them spoke.

Augustus lowered his voice to an almost inaudible murmur. "But he can hear us, so we must keep quiet. Let's try to get closer to the camp."

When they made their move to escape, Damian, Augustus, and Marco reappeared in form. Before the knight could react, Damian yelled to his companions.

"*Andiamo,* let's go!"

The three friends bolted away from the knight in multiple directions. Augustus and Marco veered toward the open field, and Damian leapt like a jackrabbit to the encampment. From behind him, the knight hollered to get his fellow's attention.

As Damian neared the camp, he yelled out to the girl, *"Lena, eseguire per la tua vita!"*

LENA

She sat by the fire pit when she heard a cry coming from the grasses.

"Lena, run for your life!"

The knight who guarded her became distracted, and she used the moment to escape. She jumped to her feet and fled until she reached the river, without once looking back over her shoulder.

The thundering of horses' hooves stomped on the hard earth behind her as she hurdled the tall grasses, lifting her knees high while she ran. Damn, those horses were fast.

Though the Arno River was much narrower here, she sprang from the river's bank and soared through the air. A jolt of current stunned her when she hit the icy water. Within seconds, an envelope of heat hugged her body, and she found herself protected from the deathly frigid temperature.

She did not have time to think and dove deeper, swimming beneath the surface of the dark canal. When she paused midway to gaze upward, the knights' forms floated above her. They trotted back and forth, searching as they paced the river on their horses. She pushed herself to swim as far as she could, but ran out of time to escape the knights.

Lena's lungs collapsed. Her body twitched, followed by a succession of sharp jolts. As she slid into unconsciousness, and became enveloped in darkness.

A kaleidoscope of colours flashed before her eyes, and a bright beacon in the distance beckoned her. Was this what it was like to die?

LENA DID NOT KNOW how long she had been floating beneath the surface when she opened her eyes. At least she had stopped convulsing. Above her, the knights' fluid forms still wavered beyond the surface.

As she slowly returned from a hazy, dream-like fog to full consciousness, fragments of Adrien's conversation with her at the cemetery resurfaced. *You have incomparable powers within you. You shall learn of them one day.*

The dark, frigid waters swirled around her as she remained suspended in motion. Treading water to keep herself in place, Lena reached up to touch behind her ears. There had been a tickling sensation, and she slid her fingers over the area. A ridge of skin flapped like jelly between her fingers. Her heart quickened, and she jerked her hand away.

The memory of the bath games she had played as a child came flooding back to her. This had to be what her mother had tried to keep her from discovering?

Looking upward, she saw that the knights' distorted shapes were no longer visible. Lena drifted towards the water's edge and broke through the surface of the river as she peeped out just enough to peer out. The knights had left.

She crawled out and collapsed on the grassy meadow. As her lungs absorbed the oxygen, she gasped and heaved. Her dress clung to her skin and the shock of cool air sent a shudder through her. When she had recovered, she dashed toward the hill to find cover.

18
THE CAVE

LENA ~ FLORENCE, 1500

Carved into the bluff, a shallow cave lay hidden from view.

Lena had found refuge on higher grounds after she had exhausted every ounce of her courage and strength to flee the knights. She sat huddled on the damp, rocky ground, and deep within the grotto. She trembled as she gathered her knees to her chest and hoped Augustus and Marco had fared better than she had in their escape from the brutes.

From the chamber's opening, a faint breeze overwhelmed her with the scents of earthy moss, musky thistle, and minty rosemary, and she dozed off to the sound of light raindrops sprinkling through the forest's canopy.

Lena's eyes flew open to the sound of footsteps. Outside, the rain had stopped, and a shiver shook her body as the night's cool temperatures lingered in the folds of her dress. She crept up to the cave's entrance, convinced she had heard movement.

Her gaze darted back and forth between the trees. Beams of

sunlight streamed through the forest's branches. Birds chirped, insects buzzed, and leaves rustled in the breeze. She held her breath and perked her ears.

The clearing echoed with the sound of heavy stomping and a harsh discussion between the knights. They were on the other side, far enough away from her. She retreated inside, safe for now.

Lena went back to lie on the rugged floor. Though her dress still clung to her skin, she curled up into a ball to keep warm. Her stomach grumbled, but her brush with danger held her back from venturing out in search of food.

She must have dozed off again when a feathery wisp brushed past her arm and awakened her. Her eyes fluttered open. Was she dreaming? A shift in the air alerted her to something—or someone—behind her. A shot of adrenaline rushed through her veins. Warm breath brushed her shoulder and her nape's tiny hairs pricked, sending goosebumps down her spine.

In a single motion, Lena rolled onto her side and pushed herself up onto her knees. With a brusque movement, two hands caught her: one hand covered her mouth to prevent her from screaming, and the other held her from escaping.

The sheer force of resistance sent Lena and her unseen assailant tumbling backward together. They landed on the ground with a loud thud, her body cushioned by the one underneath her. She craned her neck to look behind her, but all she saw was a wave of dark curls.

A breathy but deep voice whispered into her ear. "Do not be afraid. I will not harm you. I am going to let you go, but please do not scream."

She exhaled one long breath to calm her tense muscles. He released her and she escaped from his grasp. Rolling away, she landed on her hands and knees like a cat ready to pounce.

Her gaze fell upon him. A frisson traversed her body, as when she had first laid eyes on Dante in the forest.

"Damian?"

He was as magnificent as she had imagined, with rich, dark curls and crystal eyes. Her eyes stung as she struggled to hold back her tears. She had been going out of her mind for the past week, trying to connect with him through her dreams, and now here he was in the flesh.

He held his finger to his lips and pointed outside the cave. "We must keep our voices low or they will hear us."

She nodded and must have shivered because he took off his coat and wrapped it around her. Seeing him made her feel safe in this unfamiliar world, and she leaned against his side, grateful he had found her.

Damian spoke in a soothing voice. "I searched for you all night. Your friends, Augustus and Marco, are waiting for us. I found them in the forest yesterday."

She exhaled and released the tension that had built up inside of her. "I was so worried about them. But why were you in the forest?"

"Going to your world to look for you. Again!"

"So that *was* you in the crowd!"

"Sì . . ." Damian smiled, but his expression remained solemn. He turned his head toward the entrance of the cave and cocked his ear, most likely for any sounds of approaching danger. "The knights are still out there. We'll wait here to see where they go next."

"Do you think they will keep hunting after us?"

He shrugged his shoulders and put his arm around her to keep her close. Despite her relief, a tinge of sadness traversed her. Yet, an unfamiliar longing rose within her.

Lena looked up and caught Damian gazing down at her. She instantly recognized the traces of Michelangelo's statue staring back at her. She held her breath. *That* expression had kept her going back to the galleria more times than she could count. She coughed and hoped he had not read her thought.

His hand came up and held her face. He leaned forward, and

she closed her eyes. The softness of his lips when they brushed hers sent a shock through her core. She leaned forward for more, but he pulled away.

Her eyes flew open, and she found him facing away from her, toward the opening of the cave. Guilt and shame settled in her chest, and her cheeks burned. She found it difficult to breathe, and her first instinct was to move away.

Damian turned back toward her and caressed her cheek. "Please do not take my retreat as rejection. Believe me, there is nothing more desirable than the thought of kissing you, but I must not fall to temptation." A faint smile crossed his lips. "Our closeness comes from the intimacy we have shared these past few weeks, and I must not let that cloud my judgment."

He was exactly as she had imagined him—honest and honourable—and he had upheld her integrity with such finesse by taking responsibility for the moment between them. And just as he was ready to say something else, his eyes narrowed. He tilted his head again to listen to the sounds outside the cave.

"It seems the knights have gone quiet. Either they have left or they are sleeping. We should take advantage of this stillness to join your friends."

ON THE DECLINE of the hill, the sun's rays poked through the canopy, and the shade of the forest's leaves dotted the ground before them.

Lena and Damian hiked downhill, on edge and alert to every sound and movement. Though she had come up this way, she hardly recognized the route.

Her pulse still pounded from the serendipity of their meeting, making it difficult for her to concentrate. And somewhere inside, the guilt of having such a powerful attraction to him gnawed at her, especially because Marco waited for her.

They reached the edge of the woods, with the landscape spread out before them. To her right, she recognized the river bend, where she had emerged from its dark waters. They crouched and surveyed the area before fleeing across the field.

The now familiar rumble became louder beneath their feet as the horses bolted from the forest's edge and charged straight for them. The knights had been lying in wait.

Damian grabbed Lena's hand and held tight. "Whatever you do, don't let go until we reach the forest!"

The knights were gaining ground on them. With fear pumping through her veins, she held on tight to Damian's hand as they raced toward the woods. When they broke through the tree line, he let go of her. They ran at breakneck speed, both flying between the trees. She followed the incandescent stream of light he left in his wake.

At the forest's exit, Damian peeked out and checked the surroundings. He motioned for her to follow, and they tore down the path toward the San Miniato Cemetery.

They slowed to a jog as they rounded the last bend, and Lena spotted Augustus and Marco off to the right. Marco ran toward her and enveloped her in his arms. "Thank God you're safe!" He turned to Damian. "*Grazi mille* for finding her."

With her arms around Marco, Lena blushed, and another pang of shame surged through her. She shifted and peered at Damian through her eyelashes.

Damian's eyes flickered when they met hers, and he turned to Marco. "In return, I thank you for being here."

DAMIAN

He was certain the knights would stand guard in the clearing, waiting for them to return. Without the maestro's help, there was no way these travellers would make it back through the veil by themselves. At the very least, someone would get hurt or killed. He was doubtful about his next decision, but he convinced himself Leonardo was the only person who could help them.

Damian and his three new friends walked to the city as the afternoon light dimmed toward dusk. The sun kissed the rooftops as they entered through the city gates.

When they reached the middle of the Ponte alle Grazie, Damian looked back. Augustus, followed by Marco and Lena, took in the spectacular scenery of the old city. The sky, ablaze with yellows, oranges, purples, and pinks, cast a fluorescent glow into the Arno's glassy reflection. He smiled at them, but duty called. Twilight in Florence was not as romantic as the picturesque backdrop would have you believe.

"I must get you to our store before dark. It will be unsafe to have you out on the streets."

The little group caught up to Damian and kept a hurried pace behind him until he stopped in front of a small building in one of the narrowest streets. He had grabbed a torch from one of the city's corners to light their way, and in the dim lighting, the sign *D'Alessandro's* was barely visible.

"My father's store."

As they entered the darkened building, Damian led them to a rear room. Embers still glowed in the small corner fireplace. He added a log to get the fire started again. There were no seats, so he brought them crates upon which to sit.

Just a few weeks prior, he had walked into this room to find his father and Don Camillo discussing work on a mechanical part. That day, he had been looking for Leonardo to draw Lena's portrait. He still could not quite fathom how circumstances had changed so rapidly.

Now the girl in his dreams stood before his very eyes, and his heart raced with excitement. Things were moving so quickly, he barely had time to process that his entire life had altered drastically in just a matter of hours. However, he also recalled the terrifying encounter he had survived earlier in the day, and how he had escaped harm. Those knights were a deadly force and posed a serious threat.

Damian looked on as his three new companions huddled close to the hearth. His father's shop would offer them a haven until they could return to the clearing.

AFTER GIVING himself time to recover, he left D'Alessandro's in search of Leonardo, and stopped only when he arrived at the street leading to the artist's workshop. His heart thumped like wild horses, but he was determined to find the maestro even if it meant he had to dodge those menacing shadows. A few torches were lit along the empty street. He leaned out to survey the scene, then ran to Leonardo's atelier.

Fearing the knights' appearance, he hastily peered over his shoulder as he arrived at the workshop's entrance. Damian banged on the door. When he received no answer, he cried out in frustration.

"Leonardo! Maestro, are you there? I need your help!"

Not a sound came from inside the studio. He waited a few more moments, then pounded on it one last time out of defeat before turning away. He had not gone ten steps when the door creaked opened, and Leonardo stuck his head out.

"Damiano, what's wrong? Enter!"

After Damian stepped inside, he recounted the events of the afternoon, including Lena's capture and escape. Leonardo closed up his studio and followed Damian to his father's store.

THE SHOP's back room lay in the night's obscurity, with only the dying fire lighting the space.

Damian invited the maestro into the room. Leonardo's eyes widened as he stepped inside, his gaze immediately drawn to Lena.

The small group stared at him in bewilderment, then snapped

to attention. They greeted him with a forearm handshake, and he gave each a pat on the shoulder.

Leonardo's worry lines deepened, and beads of sweat formed on his forehead as he paced back and forth in front of them. His lips pursed, as if he were thinking of what to say. He looked at each of them while running a trembling hand through his thinning hair.

"Why have you come here?" He had mumbled as if they were not there.

Marco stepped forward to answer. "We came here to help Damian."

Leonardo's head shot up, wearing an expression of surprise. Then he shook his head in dismay. He turned to Damian and placed a hand on his shoulder.

"Keep your friends here. They aren't to leave under any circumstance. I promise to return with a plan."

Damian closed the front door to his father's shop, hoping he had done the right thing by summoning Leonardo. He was still uncertain about the maestro's motivations. For all he knew, they had just entered the lion's den.

When Damian reentered the room, the three friends turned and looked up at him. He had brought extra firewood to rekindle the fire. Augustus spoke his mind first.

"Are you sure we can trust him?"

Damian's answer sealed their fate. "He is our only hope to return you to your world."

PORTIA ~ FLORENCE, PRESENT DAY

The small coffee table stood crowded with cups, saucers, and nibbles. A gentle breeze wafted, lifting the napkins' corners in wisps and curls.

Portia sat with Christina and Gregory, waiting for their friends' return. She hummed a song to calm herself. With her eyes closed, her foot kept perfect time with the second hand of her wristwatch. Where the heck were they?

When she opened her eyes, Christina watched her with red-rimmed eyes, as if ready to say something. Instead, she returned her gaze to her coffee cup and tapped her fingers on the coffee table in a nervous, rhythmic pattern.

Portia smashed her fist on the table, sending the saucers and cups flying. They dropped with a loud clang and wobbled back into position.

"They should have returned already. We have to look for them!"

Startled by her outburst, Gregory answered with an equally high-pitched response. "But we don't know where they are!" He cleared his throat and softened his voice. "Pardon the irony, but it would be like searching for a needle in the haystack of time."

Gregory had a valid point. But she needed to channel her anxiety into something more productive than sitting around waiting.

"They're on the other side of that veil or curtain or whatever you want to call it. We can't leave them there, and I can't sit here and do nothing! What if they're hurt? What if they're being held against their will?"

She turned toward Christina for support, but none came. Only silence ensued. But Christina's fiery, disheveled hair was a sign she had been under some stress.

Gregory leaned over and nudged her. "Christina? Tell us what's on your mind."

Christina caught them both off guard when she let out a cry. "I have to find Augustus!" She had been keeping her emotions bottled up, even though to Portia they were quite obvious.

Portia squealed as if she had discovered the answer to all their problems. "Oh, I *knew* it! You're got feelings for him, don't you?"

Christina's expression turned timid, but she leaned across the coffee table. "No. I'll just never forgive myself if I don't do something."

Portia laughed. "Okay. If that's what you want to call it."

Gregory's eyes grew wide at this unexpected exchange between Portia and Christina, but kept quiet. Instead, he said, "Well, girls, whatever you're thinking, we'd better have a damn good plan."

THE TIMELINE LAY SPREAD out in front of Portia on the whiteboard, with Augustus's notes pointing here and there.

On the way to Christina's apartment, Gregory and Portia had followed her to the theatrical store to pick up period clothing.

When they reached the apartment, Portia glanced through Lena's notes attached to the board. A handwritten note grabbed her attention containing the words, *Ronaldo D'Alessandro—Store—Chiasso del Buco*, followed by *Damian D'Alessandro—Home—Via de Cimatori.*

"I've found something." She pointed to the notation. "That's probably where she would go if they ended up there."

"That's if we find ourselves where they are."

Portia glared at Gregory. "Always the optimist."

"I'm a realist."

She huffed at him. "If every explorer had been a realist, they would have stayed home and the Americas would still be undiscovered."

"Remind me of that when we end up being chased by dinosaurs."

"Can we just pretend we know what we're doing?"

Christina turned to the two of them. "Can you both stop bickering and get on with it?"

It was late afternoon by the time they made their way to the clearing. All was quiet as they changed into their clothing behind a thicket.

They stood amid a cacophony of forest life, peering up at the faded engraving on the obelisk. A gentle breeze rustled the leaves when Portia, Gregory, and Christina faced the portal, which hung in midair near the rocks. Portia glanced at her friends.

"No matter what, don't let go!"

They held hands as their friends had done and sprinted toward the veil.

Gregory muttered, "Here goes nothing!" And Portia prayed. *Please take us to our friends.*

PORTIA ~ FLORENCE, 1500

They landed hard on the other side, the wind knocked out of them. When they rebounded from the lashing, Portia shook off the dust from her clothing and looked around.

"At least we're together!"

Christina and Gregory agreed with her, except that the bright afternoon was quickly fading into dusk. A darkening purple sky seeped into the daylight they had left to see their way around. Portia's optimistic outlook vanished. A forest at night was not her idea of a fun time.

In an effort to calm their fears, Gregory reasoned with them, "One advantage of arriving at night is we're inconspicuous."

Portia now wished she had not ventured into this strange land. "Sure, whatever you say." And Christina laughed nervously at her caustic tone.

Gregory huffed. "I told you I was a realist."

They rushed across the expanse which lay quiet, with no sounds of the rumblings underfoot. With Gregory up front, Portia followed behind with Christina, both almost tripping over him.

He spoke over his shoulder. "Arm's length, please. You're tearing up my heels."

As the gloom descended upon them, Portia muttered under her

breath. "Maybe it wasn't such a wise move to cross over into twilight?"

Gregory glared at her. "Whose the optimist now?"

"I just don't enjoy walking about at night."

"From what I remember of our earlier conversation, we didn't have a choice."

The temperature had dipped, and the chill filtered through their clothes as they stumbled along in the dense forest. Portia said nothing more, and Christina kept quiet and followed him.

By the time they reached the path leading them to Florence, it was pitch dark. With no lights in the distance, Portia trembled. She was deathly afraid of being separated from her friends and clung on to both of them. With each step, she imagined the worst. Dinosaurs. Wild animals. Prehistoric hunters. For all she knew, Gregory was correct, and they had arrived in the wrong time dimension.

GREGORY

Gregory led the way with compass in hand. He had also memorized the map.

In this world, not a speck of light was visible to help them as they inched their way into the unknown. Gregory had ignored the "Don't bring futuristic objects with you" rule and packed flashlights into each backpack. Now, despite his flashlight's beam leading the way, they could still only see a few feet ahead of them.

Gregory groaned, his whole body sapped by defeat. "Is it just me, or is it taking twice as long to get there?"

Portia was about to respond when, to their right, a splinter snapped in the darkness. Beyond the flashlight's beam, something shifted. Gregory sucked in his breath, and Portia squeaked. With lightning speed, Christina covered Portia's mouth.

"Shh!"

Jostled by the two girls, Gregory dropped the flashlight. "Shit!"

As the flashlight rolled away from them, its dazzling beams sparkled in every direction. Flickers of tree trunks, then the ground and a figure, a few more flashes of the ground, tree trunks, and finally, blackness.

The beam switched off, leaving them hanging on to one another in the dark in this unforgiving land. It was the only safety they had left. Gregory's heartbeat hammered and pounded in his ears. The girls trembled as they clung to either side of him.

Gregory whispered to the girls. "Did you guys see that person standing there?"

"Yeah." Christina's voice trembled. "What do we do now?"

A figure emerged out of the darkness as if shined on by a spotlight on the path in front of them. The man gleamed. His straggling white hair spilled to his shoulders, and his beard hung to the top of his chest. He stood a few feet away and raised his hands with his palms facing out. He meant them no harm. At least, that is what Gregory wanted to believe.

The man spoke in Italian. "*Sono Leonardo di Ser Piero da Vinci.* Who goes there?"

Portia questioned aloud. "Am I hallucinating?" And before the other two could respond, the man repeated himself in English.

"No, you are not dreaming. You heard correctly. I *am* Leonardo da Vinci."

He was certainly as confident as Gregory had pictured him. Leonardo bent to pick up the flashlight. The bright beam shot straight out at them after he jiggled it and tightened the bottom. They squinted into the blinding light. He switched off the flashlight, moved toward them, and handed it to Gregory.

"You will not need this."

Gregory glanced at Portia and Christina. "Can you both see in the dark as well?"

Christina's gaze went from Portia to him. "I'm not sure how it's possible, but yes, it looks like I have some kind of night vision."

Portia shifted her weight. "He looks exactly the same as I've always imagined him. I—"

Leonardo interrupted her. "You are Lena's friends?"

Gregory's mouth fell open and the two young women nodded their heads.

Leonardo motioned the way with his hand. "Follow me."

Portia spoke again, but Christina stopped her. She lowered her voice so the artist could not hear her. "Should we follow him? Remember, Lena and Damian weren't sure whether we should trust him."

Leonardo spun on his heel and faced them. His gaze turned icy. "*I* am not the one you should mistrust. *You* are the ones who have broken the equilibrium by using the portal."

The threesome gaped at him until Gregory found his voice.

"Our friends were supposed to come home, and they didn't. So we're here to find them."

Leonardo's hardened expression dissolved. "Your friends are here, and I will take you to them." He paused. "Look, you may believe otherwise, but you *are* safe with me." He hurried them along. "Come on. It is perilous out here, and we don't have time to loiter."

Gregory remained skeptical that they might walk right into danger by following this man. However, the group followed him. As they made their way past the San Miniato Cemetery, they could see its walls, but in the gloom, the place glowed in fluorescent green because of this skill they had gained. They crept along behind Leonardo into more darkness, on a rough path flanked by bushes and shrubs.

Soon, they arrived at the city's perimeter, where two torches lit the gate to the fortified city. Leonardo knocked at the wooden door of the city's gate. He spoke to someone through the small porter hatch, and the gate opened to them.

Within the city walls, the intermittent torches offered weak and softened lighting, and cast foreboding shadows on the citadel's walls. Gregory took mental notes as they walked through this remarkable but unfamiliar city.

As the maestro led the trio across one bridge, Gregory engaged in light conversation to gain some insight into their destination. "Is this the direction of the D'Alessandro home?" Lena's board notes had mentioned that location. Leonardo shook his head and continued walking. He made no further comment, so Gregory kept quiet.

By the time Leonardo and the three friends arrived at the Piazza della Signoria, Gregory's level of excitement was palpable. The rhythm of his racing heart pulsed in his ears. The thrill of walking through the ancient city of Florence had him searching his coat pocket for his phone when he realized they had left their phones behind. He looked to where their café stood in their present day, only to find darkness.

Further along the road, Gregory recognized the place. "I recognize this piazza. This is where Girolamo Savonarola staged the 'Bonfire of the Vanities.'" Leonardo turned to him. "He's not very popular among artists." Gregory registered such events were taking place in this timeline, and he huddled a little closer to the girls.

They turned down a narrow street and walked past an enclave with a fountain. Water trickled out of the stone spout into its rocky basin. When Leonardo reached a small, nondescript building, he told them to stay behind him while he knocked at the door.

After a few minutes, the door opened a crack. Leonardo announced his arrival, and a young man's voice filtered through the gap.

Gregory whispered to the girls. "Did you both hear who Leonardo was talking to?"

Christina nodded. "Yeah, I did."

Portia craned her neck to get a better view of the silhouette at the door. "I heard it too."

Leonardo motioned to the three and ushered them through the narrow doorway into the building. Gregory looked around the hardware store and it matched the description on Augustus's whiteboard.

They followed Leonardo and his young companion down a hallway lit by candlelight. When the back room door opened, a small fire burned in the corner fireplace with three silhouettes huddled in front of it. The figures turned around and the two groups stared at each other. Then, like a vibrant burst of fireworks, Lena and the girls squealed in unison.

Augustus stood and stared at Gregory in disbelief. "My God! What are you guys doing here?"

Gregory's lips curled upward. "You didn't come to the appointed meeting. What did you want us to do?"

Augustus laughed. "We're a fine lot!"

There was a collective sigh of relief. They were together again. The girls talked a mile a minute about their adventures. Portia threw her arms around Lena while Christina gave Augustus a hug and a kiss on the cheek. Gregory smiled, remembering the girls' earlier conversation. He sighed, relieved they had all found each other again.

Portia drew closer to Lena. "Is that who I think it is?"

Near the doorway, Leonardo murmured to Damian, clasped his arm, then left.

Lena turned to her friends. "I can't believe you're all here. I'm sorry I've involved you in all this."

Portia took her hand. "Don't be silly. We're in this with you because we wanted to be."

Lena lowered her eyes. "I was so busy forging ahead, singularly focused on my quest. Now, I've got you all embroiled in something we all know is way bigger than any of us could have imagined."

The group remained quiet and the weight of her words hung

over them. Lena was about to say something else when her stomach growled.

When the wave of laughter died down in the little back room, Damian stood up.

"You must all be hungry. I will go home to get a meal for everyone."

Marco stood up to go with him, but Damian shook his head.

"No, it's best I go alone."

19
QUINTESSENCE

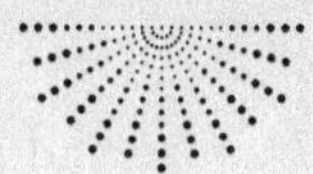

DAMIAN ~ FLORENCE, 1500

DAMIAN SHUT the front entrance and locked it. The loneliness echoed in his steps and surrounded him as he walked down the cobblestone street. Dante should have been there with him.

All was quiet when Damian arrived at his home and opened the front door. As he crossed the kitchen to the hearth, a creaking sound came from his parents' bedroom. He stopped, afraid of alerting them to his movements. Since Dante's disappearance, he had often heard noises through the night—his parents roaming about the house. He listened for footsteps and waited until he heard light snoring coming from their bedroom.

He tiptoed from one end of the kitchen to the other and filled one of his mother's baskets with bread, cheese, and carrots. As he covered the basket, the sound of a familiar footfall sounded behind him and he froze in anticipation.

"What are you doing with all that food?"

Damian shivered when he heard the coldness in his father's voice. As he gazed at the basket, heat rushed to his cheeks, and he swiftly turned on his heels to confront him.

"Papa, I have friends who are hungry, and they need my help."

Ronaldo's gravelly voice hinted at the anger simmering beneath the surface. "You've been coming and going, disappearing, and not coming home at night. Now you're home, and you've packed enough food to feed a small army? Who are these friends?"

Damian grabbed the basket. "Come with me, Father."

IN THE DEAD OF NIGHT, Damian and Ronaldo reached the shop. They traversed the store, and Damian observed as his father's eyes grew wider when he opened the door to the back room.

Damian introduced him to the newcomers. "This is my father."

Augustus was the first to step forward and held out his arm. "Pleased to meet you, sir. I'm Augustus."

Hesitant at first, Ronaldo returned the forearm greeting. "*Sono Ronaldo. Piacere di conoscerti.*"

One by one, the others followed suit, and Lena was the last to come forward. When Ronaldo shook her forearm, he remained speechless, then he bowed to her.

His father's gesture startled Damian, and he recalled overhearing one of his parents' late-night conversation that had involved a family secret. There was apparently much his parents had kept hidden from him and Dante. Damian motioned for Marco to come forward. "Papa, Marco is family. We believe he is one of Ariella's descendants."

Ronaldo took a deep breath and peered into Marco's eyes. "You look like my daughter." He turned to Damian. "I wondered when you would find out about your birthright. Your mother and I—We should have said something."

"Father, you don't have to explain."

And yet, there was still much to understand, but he knew his father and mother still grieved for Dante. Ronaldo pressed his lips together and looked down at the ground as if he were trying to gather his strength. Then he looked up, his eyes watery.

"I will bring more nourishment in the morning, before first light." He pointed toward the basket and gestured for them to eat.

Ronaldo left the room with Damian in tow. When the two reached the store's front door, he turned to Damian.

"I should have told you and your brother, especially about the dangers. We thought you would be safer. Your brother—"

His father's voice broke, and Damian looked into his eyes. "It's okay, Papa. These people will help me find Dante."

Ronaldo's eyes glistened, and a tear ran down his cheek. He hugged Damian. "My boy. Please be careful."

And with that, Damian watched as his father faded into the night.

LENA

Outdoors, the air was crisp and clear, a cloudless morning in the Florentine hills.

With mixed emotions, Lena and her friends followed Leonardo out of the city. She looked around as they walked, in awe of the vibrant, rich colours of the stones of the citadel's walls. The air she breathed in made her head spin, like inhaling pure oxygen.

Earlier, Leonardo had arrived at the store and awoken them.

"Up! All of you. We must leave early to avoid the crowds."

They had slept huddled together around the fireplace in the back room. Lena had stretched and yawned and wondered what this day would bring. Ronaldo had come and gone, and had left them another basket filled with bread, cheese, slices of smoked meats that tasted like prosciutto and capicola, and savoury peaches.

A light, cool wind greeted Lena, Damian, and the group as they arrived at a plateau after a long hike uphill. They marched toward a cluster of trees, out of breath and intoxicated by the scent of apple and cherry blossoms. As they approached the orchard, a man stepped out into the middle of the grove.

Apple blossoms whirled; their white and pink petals floated in the light breeze. The juxtaposition of this imposing soldier amid this floral chaos captured their attention. They stopped, almost colliding with each other. He came forward and stopped about six feet away.

The soldier's intense gaze stressed the brightness of his pale eyes. Lena's chest tightened, and she was suddenly aware of a heightened sense of alertness, and of her surroundings.

Lena found herself caught in a flurry of emotions. This man's shaved head, braid, and piercing look gave away his identity. His innate power was also obvious in the way he stood—bold and upright: She and her companions adjusted their own postures on cue.

Her first conversation with Adrien in the cemetery resurfaced, and then another memory from her childhood came back to her. She had sat upon this man's shoulders, while her father walked and laughed alongside them.

Adrien's gaze softened as he studied the group, perhaps also remembering each of his meetings with them.

"My name is Adrien. By now, I am certain some of you have recalled when I visited you. The information I shared should also come back to you."

Leonardo turned to them. "You must now turn on your other ears."

Lena and her friends glanced at each other, confused, and it took a few seconds before Lena understood what he meant. This time, there was no screeching or pain. The language Adrien used was a language of imagery, scent, and melody—the kind Lena experienced in dreams.

Adrien streamed an array of images, like a movie reel of memories. She watched the moments when each of them had first met him. She glanced at her friends and, from their reactions, they experienced the same nostalgic emotions.

. . .

When the images stopped, Adrien half-smiled. "I will now speak aloud, so there's no room for misinterpretation." He inhaled a long breath, then exhaled. "I didn't think I'd need to explain all this to you so soon since the Majority Council had planned for your initiation at a later time. However, what's done is done. During my earlier visits, I communicated coded messages to you through sounds and thoughts to awaken you at a specific time. Something has sped up the timeline. The knowledge I have to give you now will expand upon what I have already shared with you when you were younger." He clasped his hands together in front of him. "Until now, ignorance has kept you safe. However, as it stands, the more you know, the better you'll be at protecting yourselves."

Unease settled in Lena's gut. *Initiation? Majority Council? Protecting ourselves?* What was he talking about?

"You may have discovered you possess certain heightened abilities." Adrien gestured toward the maestro. "Leonardo and I will teach you how to perfect these skills, as much as is possible for us, considering the limited time we have."

Adrien looked around at the group, who sat listening to him without uttering a sound.

Portia expelled some air and her eyes widened. Her words rushed out before she could stop them. "Are we aliens?"

Adrien tittered, but when no one else laughed, he stopped. "No. "

Portia's voice wavered. "Are we scientific experiments of some kind?"

"You are not that either."

Augustus piped in. "Then what are we?"

"We are earthlings just like *Homo sapiens*. And just like them, we are part of the hominid species, but we belong to another genus group called *Homo regni elementis.*"

Augustus balked at this suggestion. "In all my research, I—I've never heard of the *Homo regni elementis.*"

Gregory's jaw dropped. "That translates to 'Man of the Kingdom of the Elements', doesn't it?"

Adrien squeezed his lips together into a faint smile. "That's correct. We are the Servants of the Kingdom of the Elements. The bearers of true power, both of the mind *and* the elements."

Lena and the others shifted on their feet and in their seats. She wanted to run as far from this place as possible. Her intuitive thoughts were now becoming coherent messages. And with this growing ability to read into other people's minds. She was now acutely aware that her friends experienced the same level of discomfort as she was.

Adrien paused before going into more detail. "Our genotype is more evolved than *Homo sapiens.* Our species also includes all races —the same as our human counterparts. Since the beginning of our time on earth, we have developed and evolved alongside them. It is a specific genetic marker that separates us from *Homo sapiens.* And as far as we know, they aren't aware of our existence."

Christina balked. "How can they not know we exist? What about medical records—"

Adrien interrupted her. "They might have their suspicions, but our genetic marker hides well within our DNA.

"How have we remained so well hidden?"

"Well, they—scientists—would first need to know specifically what they were looking for and where to find it."

Augustus shook his head and glanced at his friends. "I'm having trouble believing this."

Adrien allowed them time to reflect on what they had just learned. "You're skeptical. Understandably so. For now, I need you to set aside your disbelief and put your trust in me." He paused for a second. "For your survival."

If he was going for effect, he had succeeded. Lena perceived her friends' bewilderment through the expressions on their faces. A knot twisted in her belly. She crossed her arms and squeezed until her nails dug into her skin.

"Survival?"

In that instant, she was unsure of how she had done it, but she had grasped onto another thread of thought. This one had come directly from Adrien's mind. *It will not be easy to convince them.* Lena narrowed her eyes at Adrien. Convince them of what?

Adrien pursed his lips and fixed his gaze on Leonardo. "They will understand much faster if we show them." He turned back toward the group. "Let's get moving. I'm going to take you to another place."

Lena and the group followed Adrien and Leonardo to the river at San Jacopo Al Girone, a small village to the east of Florence. At the far end of the village, they followed another path and cut straight through the forest until they reached a steep incline. After a half-hour climb, they arrived at the Convento dell'Incontro—Monastery of the Gathering—built on the plateau of one of the highest peaks in the region.

Here, the Tuscan landscape sprawled out in undulating peaks and valleys, still untouched by the hand of civilization. Trees lined the fields like soldiers guarding their precious land. Below them, a large open area lay beyond a band of trees.

Leonardo pointed to the stretch of land. "That is where we need to go."

As they marched through the tableland, Lena groaned in agony as though nails were being driven into the soles of her feet.

As they kept pace, Adrien spoke to them about the *Homo regni elementis*. "On a superficial level, there is no distinction between us and them. The most obvious difference is, we use the part of our brain which *Homo sapiens* have not yet learned to fully access." He paused, then continued in a tone halfway between despair and irritation. "Unfortunately, our species' survival always remains on the brink of danger. *Homo sapiens* will always see us as a threat if ever they discover us."

Words like "we," "us," and "our" had crept into Adrien's speech indicating a shift towards a more inclusive language.

Gregory had also caught on to the transition in Adrien's wordage and interrupted him. "How many of *us* exist?"

Lena caught the subtle wording of his question, and judging by Adrien's reaction, he did, too.

"Well, let's see. There are approximately 500,000 pure *elementis*, but around 800 million more, give or take, are descendants of *elementis* who have interbred with *Homo sapiens*. Like you, not all *elementis* are currently aware of their abilities."

Lena's ears perked up at this bit of information. "Why not?"

"During the inquisitions, they killed a substantial number of us. After those devastating losses, the Council decided we would stop passing on the knowledge and remain hidden."

"To repopulate our species?"

"Yes, exactly."

The group exchanged wide-eyed glances.

Portia frowned. "*Homo sapiens* outnumber us."

Augustus rubbed his brow. "That's an understatement."

"Yes, exactly." And Adrien continued to provide further clarification. "There are crossbreeds who have certain heightened abilities, such as extrasensory perception and intuitive psychic gifts. Some are senders, while others are receivers, but they are still our weakest link."

Christina straightened her back. "What about us? Are we crossbreeds?"

Adrien pointed to the group. "No. You are pure *Homo elementis*."

Augustus looked up. "So, our parents are—"

"All pure *elementis*. Your parents, your ancestors, and those before them as well." Adrien looked at them. "We are human too, but refer to ourselves as *elementis* to differentiate ourselves from them."

When they had rested, Adrien took the lead and headed toward a pass—a col, of sorts—cradled between two summits. He took a break from talking to let this information sink in further.

Midway between the highland and the open field was a protective zone—a forest belt with a twisted mass of fallen trees, branches, and shrubs—through which they traversed with effort and strain.

Exhausted and irritated, Lena emerged from the deadfall. She looked around at her pals, who appeared just as exhausted as she was.

Gregory mumbled to no one in particular. "Remind me again how we got ourselves into this mess?"

And Christina rode on the coattails of his complaint as she trudged alongside him. "No kidding."

Leonardo overheard them and patted Gregory on the back. "We have a little longer to walk. Don't worry, you will soon learn to use your energy conservatively."

Ahead of them, the col was a wide expanse, covered with tall and short grasses growing over dunes of earth and ditches. A row of cypress trees stood guard on one end while lombardy poplars grew interspersed as though placed there on purpose. The levelled ground looked like an obstacle course, with boulders and mid-size buttes of earth scattered about its surface.

Adrien went on, "I know it's a lot for you to absorb in one afternoon; however, the Council has approved and determined that you should have complete access to this knowledge."

He stood for a few moments as though gathering his thoughts before continuing.

"The *elementis* comprises four classes based upon genotype and the alchemical elements of our planet. The genotypes are categorized based on the four elements: fire, earth, air, and water, and each group possesses unique strengths and physical abilities.

"For now, let me simplify it by saying that we can find your elemental strengths by calculating the position of the planets and constellations at your time of birth."

Lena stopped Adrien. "Those charts you showed us when we were kids depict the groups to which we belong?"

"Yes, that's correct. All *Elementis* possess one main elemental ability. It is speed. You can run and move about five times faster than our human friends."

He looked at each of them, nodding as he read their expressions for understanding.

"Now, there is one class that possesses greater abilities and power. They are the Paragons. The Paragons comprise two groups: The Vox dei and the Quinta noster. The Vox dei can draw strengths from all four elements and they share two heightened abilities: telepathy and invisibility. This group also possesses another ability, but we will not delve into this now."

He pointed to each of them. "You are all Vox dei."

Lena glanced at her friends' wide eyes. This all explained her gained ability to read thoughts, but what was that last ability?

He had caught her thought, and glanced at her as he spoke. "Let's not get ahead of ourselves." His attention then shifted to the others. "In response to your previous question about numbers, there are approximately 20,000 Vox dei."

Christina sucked in her breath. "That's a small number in comparison."

Augustus huffed. "This is completely absurd! Surely we would have been aware of this sooner." His face flushed red from the heat rushing to its surface. His skepticism rushed forward. She understood his dilemma. It was not disbelief as much as a rejection of what was being presented to him. Lena could also feel the refusal building up in her.

It was one thing to find a portal and travel through time, but to discover they were members of another species with unique abilities was something entirely different.

Leonardo stepped forward. "Awareness and knowledge activate this mastery."

Augustus shook his head in denial. "It sounds almost too convenient. I find accepting the fact that I belong to a different species a little difficult and require more than a simple explanation for these abilities I supposedly gained. What am I—we—supposed to do with this knowledge or abilities?"

Adrien put up both hands in deference. "Believe me when I tell you I understand how outrageous everything sounds to you." He pointed to the landscape before them. "So I have brought you here to show you how to use these abilities."

It was Gregory's turn to react. "Earlier, you said we needed to know all this information for our survival. What did you mean?"

Lena's stomach twisted into a knot again. What had she gotten herself and her pals into by crossing through the portal? She looked at Adrien, who responded to Gregory's inquiry.

"I will explain everything. But before I do, let me do some demonstrations. Then you can ask as many questions as you wish." Adrien's answer quietened everyone.

They reached a place where they could sit and rest. Adrien motioned for the group to make a circle while he stood in its centre. "It's going to be a long and physical day. I suggest you stay seated during each lesson. But, first things first." He pulled out a small flashlight. "Gather 'round."

Lena hesitated, but her friends stood, piqued to find out what Adrien had to show them. When he had the group's undivided attention, he extended his arm with his wrist facing upward and told them to do the same.

Lena did not comply, but the rest of the group pulled closer into the circle and turned their wrists to face the sky. She still struggled with her resistance to accept this new information. Leonardo joined them and squeezed in between Augustus and Portia.

Adrien approached Leonardo and shone the flashlight onto the maestro's wrist. The flashlight emitted a ray of black light, a purplish beam, and a neon triangle appeared.

Adrien pointed to the triangle markings. "Only the Vox dei have these imprints."

One by one, the group leaned forward, astonished by the

brilliant shade of tangerine that glowed from Leonardo's marking. A second signet below it, interlocked with the first one, radiated with a bright chartreuse hue.

Fire and earth. Even though Lena stood apart from the group, this information flashed through her mind, and she suspected it was another facet of her increased elemental capabilities.

Lena had been in clubs where they had used stamps with invisible ink and UV black lighting, but had seen nothing peculiar on her own wrist. Before she could say anything, Adrien answered her question.

"The visibility of these signets depends on your knowledge of your ancestry. It's like a switch that gets turned on."

Adrien expounded on the meanings behind the triangle-shaped symbols. "The first triangle shows fire and signifies strength and speed. The linked signet underneath is his secondary element. Here, it's earth."

The group stared at Leonardo's wrist, and Lena craned her neck to inspect it.

Adrien elaborated on the importance of their strengths. "These two insignia show where your powers are strongest. In Leonardo's case, he is a fire element with strong earth power. You'll remember I told you the Vox dei have the strengths of all four elements?"

The entire group nodded in unison towards him, encouraging him to continue.

"Good. Well, for example, Leonardo can also command the air and water elements at will, but he must spend more energy to control them."

Adrien moved the flashlight away from Leonardo's arm, who turned his wrist to face downward.

A few moments later, at Adrien's signal, Leonardo turned his wrist over again. The signets glowed without the beam of ultraviolet light. The group stared at each other and back at Leonardo's wrist.

"You can do the same. However, allow me to present yours using the black light."

The neophytes buzzed, excited to see their own markings. He pointed the flashlight at their wrists, and one by one, neon triangles lit up.

Augustus's symbols glowed with the elements of air and earth, as did Christina's. Gregory's wrist illuminated to show his earth and water abilities. Portia's logos shimmered with its air and water signets. Marco's scintillated with his water and earth strengths; and Damian's triangles radiated with his water and fire energy.

When Adrien reached Lena, her back stiffened. She reluctantly extended her arm, and he cradled her wrist in his hand.

"Lena, you have only one and the symbol on your wrist differs from the others because you have an equal power over all the elements."

Suddenly, she was unsure whether she wanted to know and struggled against his grip. Why was she different from the others? Adrien gave her a subtle squeeze, but released her wrist. Lena withdrew her arm and stepped away.

"It's all right, Lena. Take your time. It's a lot to deal with all at once."

She took a deep breath, came back to the circle, and brought her wrist back up to its earlier position. She nodded at Adrien, and he pointed the black light at her wrist. At once, the Flower of Life blazed with a lavender-white radiance.

"Oohs" and "Ahs" came from her circle of friends. They stared until Lena cringed and pulled her arm away.

Portia cooed. "Oh, that's breathtaking!"

Lena's face reddened. She bowed her head to hide her embarrassment from all the attention. Her mind spun in circles. *This must be the secret Father kept from me.*

But Adrien still had more to say. "Lena, you are not only a Vox dei, you're also a Quinta noster *elementis.*"

Gregory leaned forward to look at it, wide-eyed. "Our fifth element?"

Adrien nodded. "That's right."

Lena shifted from one foot to the other. Her breathing became shallow, as though a boulder sat on her chest.

"The Quinta are the most powerful of the *Homo regni elementis*. They are our last hope for survival if *Homo sapiens should* annihilate us. The birth of a Quinta is so rare that we are extremely protective of them."

Her father's words popped into Lena's mind. He had said this to her as they left the Galleria on the day they had gone to see the statue. *You are special, Lena. You are the quintessence of our species.* She had not understood what he had meant back then.

The revelation that she was a fifth element shook Lena to her core. Even though she was still not sure what it all involved, the foundation of her life crumbled beneath her feet, causing a shift in her consciousness. Her inner equilibrium rattled and pushed her off kilter.

Portia cocked her head. "Were we brought together to protect Lena?"

Adrien nodded. "Yes, exactly. You see, a Quinta is the embodiment and essence of the *elementis* species. They are omnipotent and regenerative. It has been our duty to guard them with our lives."

Lena's pulse raced. Protect her with their lives? She immediately rejected the responsibility thrust upon her and her pals at such short notice. Skeptical of this new information, she resisted against this revelation.

"I don't need to be protected!"

"Your family—" Adrien bit down on his tongue before continuing. "We have always monitored you."

The subtext had not escaped her, but she dismissed it. "Are there others like me?"

"Yes, there are, but only a few. You are rare and our goal—our purpose—is to protect you. As I mentioned, if one does not know of their legacy—like you, for example—it's possible for them to remain well hidden, even from the council. It's a matter which is intrinsically linked to our survival."

Despite his resistance, Augustus spoke up once more. "I can imagine this legacy isn't all bells and whistles. Tell us about the downside to gaining this knowledge."

Leonardo had been wandering about and stopped behind them. Adrien gave him a nod to answer.

"As you said, there is always a disadvantage to learning about things that are better left unknown. Now, before Adrien goes on, I must add that, despite outward appearances, we are essentially a peaceful species."

Augustus pressed his lips together. "Right. So, who are the bad guys?"

20
FLUORESCENCE

LENA ~ FLORENCE, 1500

THE SUN HAD JUST WANED past midday when they sat and devoured the bread and smoked meats Ronaldo had packed for them. They listened to Adrien, who paced in front of them as he delved even further into their new culture's framework.

"The Majority Council is a chamber called the Guardians of the Order of Light. It is our governing body and includes ten councilmen and thirteen masters. I am a master of the council. For each decision, there is a vote conducted.

"Six hundred years ago, a rift formed and separated the Order. This schism resulted in two groups: The Guardians of the Order of Light and the Regni Militis, a warrior faction."

Augustus reacted at once. "An army?"

"Yes. The Regni Militis is a militia group. They train young *elementis* to become powerful fighters.

"What happened to 'essentially we are a peaceful species'?"

"That is where our quandary lies. Obviously, we are far from being perfect. In fact, we are very much like humans."

Augustus's expression became filled with curiosity. "Okay. So why would they need an army?"

"I am getting to that. Let me continue explaining the framework, and then I'll answer your questions. Now, where was I? Oh yes. The Guer'Ombra is a Militis regiment. We call them the Shadow Warriors.

Gregory stretched his arms out, fingers intertwined, and cracked his knuckles. "Something like the Navy Seals?"

"They would like to think they are, but they are more like guerrilla soldiers."

"And they are the ones against whom we have to protect ourselves."

Adrien nodded. "It all started back in the thirteenth century, when a powerful woman named Ysabeau d'Aubervilliers masterminded the idea of building a rebel army. Her son René, who was one of the youngest masters of the Majority Council, stepped forward to present some new ideas for change. When the Council refused them, he immediately resigned. With his mother Ysabeau, they formed the Regni Militis." Adrien's expression soured, as though he had swallowed something that left a nasty taste in his mouth. "You see, Ysabeau's aim was to lead the *elementis* to ultimate supremacy over humans. And how she had planned to do this was to infiltrate the *Homo sapiens* royal lineages and government hierarchies. Fortunately for us, she died before achieving her goal."

Lena sighed. *Thank God!*

He waved his finger at Lena. "Not so fast."

He must have read her mind. She fixed her gaze on Adrien as he continued to explain.

"Her son René continued to expand the Regni Militis just as his mother had envisioned. This rebel army still exists today, and they are just as rigorous and merciless as ever. The only thorn in their side is the Vox dei." He pointed at them. "You. However, you have not yet encountered a Shadow Warrior, but you will. This is our reason for sharing all this knowledge now. Its purpose is to teach you how to use your gifts."

Again, Lena read the thread of his thoughts. *They must learn the practical usage of their powers in order to protect themselves. They will need it to get home.* She looked at her friends to see whether they had read his thoughts as well, but their attention remained fixed on Adrien's words. There was much they needed to know, and he was giving them the information in dribbles. She understood full well he could not tell them everything in one afternoon. But just how much did they need to know to defend themselves against these shadow warriors?

Augustus shifted positions on the rock where he sat. "I think I can speak for the group when I say we're ready to find out what you have to show us. I'd like to get home. The sooner the better."

Adrien pointed to the field in front of them. "Then let's begin because I have a great deal to show you. Mind what I do and remain seated until I call for you."

ADRIEN SPRINTED to the field's east side until he reached a horizontal stretch—a natural runway of clay and dirt—a landing strip of sorts, free of boulders and buttes. His sprint to that position was no faster than any human's.

He sent them a *thought-message*; it was what Lena now called those telepathic communications. *Now, watch carefully,* he advised before he took off, running in a straight line from one end of the stretch to the other.

When he had reached a third of the way, he left a fluorescent streak of light in his wake. He had altered his run to some kind of warp speed. The group let out a cry of disbelief.

A few seconds later, Adrien shifted speed once more, and after a whoosh, a translucent afterglow trailed behind him.

A gust of wind blew all around Adrien as he came to a screeching halt at the end of the path. An enormous, reddish dust cloud formed, and he disappeared behind the shroud of smoke. Before the dirt had settled, Adrien's silhouette reappeared, emerging from the vaporous blur. He walked back to where they waited for him with their mouths gaping.

Damian shifted from foot to foot while Marco whistled with excitement. Augustus punctuated the moment with an ironic but galvanizing statement.

"There's no turning back now."

AUGUSTUS

When Adrien reached the group, he pointed to Augustus and Christina.

"Follow me to the starting line."

As the three walked, Adrien explained the mechanics behind the different speeds. "To begin, the first stage was fluorescence. It is the basic *elementis* velocity. All *elementis* can run at that pace. This includes the Militis and the Shadow Warriors." He glanced at them to make sure they understood.

"Following that, phosphorescence is the earth element's turbo-charged speed—the fastest speed there is. That was the speed I was traveling at when I switched gears the second time. The Vox dei are the only *elementis* who can run at that speed. If the earth element is one of your strengths, you can run continuously at phosphorescent velocity. The Vox dei without the earth element as a chief strength should use this ability carefully, but it can be crucial for their survival when used wisely."

Adrien stood on Christina's left side for her first trial run. He added a word of warning to the two. "Try not to overdo it, because you will feel queasy the first few times."

Augustus sandwiched Christina between him and Adrien and smiled to encourage her. He sensed her mind spinning from the overload of information and squeezed her hand.

Adrien coached them as they faced the long stretch of land.

"Now take a deep breath and begin with a light jog. And increase your speed when you feel comfortable."

Christina began with a sprint, while Augustus and Adrien kept pace alongside her, with Adrien leading them through each stage.

"Now, take your speed up a notch."

Augustus shifted gears and sped up. To his surprise, his feet no longer touched the ground.

Almost as soon as Christina switched gears, she yelped as she lost her footing. Augustus and Adrien caught her under the elbows to stop her from falling.

When they had steadied her, Adrien continued to push them onward. "Okay, now switch gears again."

"What?" Christina yelled. "How? Help—"

Before she could finish her sentence, she shot forward and disappeared into a colourful display of phosphorescent light, and Augustus held his breath.

When they came to a halt at the end of the strip, Christine flung her arms around Augustus. Her heart hammered as she crushed herself against him. When their bodies made contact, there was an intense physical feeling, as if they were one. Without a doubt, she experienced the same exhilaration he did as the adrenaline coursed through their veins.

She released her grip, still out of breath from the run, and gave herself a quick pat. "Am I still in one piece? Oh my goodness, that was exquisite."

His own heart pounded from the intense physical reaction he had just shared with her. They both coughed nervously, suddenly aware of Adrien's gaze on them. His eyes narrowed, but a smile tugged at his lips.

"And this skill is just the beginning."

LENA

As they sat around in the shade of the Lombardy trees, Adrien went over the air elements' abilities in considerable detail. He described all the sensations they would experience. This time, Lena, Portia, and Christina were called up for the lesson.

Lena waited her turn while Christina's laughter rippled through the air as she jumped from butte to butte. Her resistance weakened as she heard the thrill and excitement in Christina's cries. Even though Lena still held on to her earlier misgivings, she surrendered in some measure to her curiosity and was eager to spread her own wings.

When it was her turn, Lena charged ahead. She leapt, catapulted, and somersaulted from a boulder to a tree and back to the ground. Portia soared through the air alongside her. The wisps of her blond curls kissed the air as she ran parallel to Lena's path. Their eyes met, and they shared a moment of pure euphoria.

Lena enthusiastically joined her friends, radiating excitement and a whirlwind of emotions. She recalled that very first evening, her hands had transformed into streams of bluish fluid. It had happened just a few weeks ago. She shook her head, astonished by how quickly her circumstances had altered.

As the afternoon progressed, Adrien worked Lena and her pals through countless drills on how to defend themselves against direct attacks by the Regni Militis.

"These Shadow Warriors will stop at nothing to destroy you."

He charged at Lena with full force and unleashed the various assaults and deadly strikes she would receive from the Shadow Warriors.

With each forceful strike from Adrien, Lena's energy waned, and the afternoon stretched on. Each impact sent shocking pain through her body, yet with each blow, she grew stronger.

To her right, Marco voiced her thoughts. “It’s amazing. The more beatings I receive, the more confident I become. I just can’t feel my body anymore.” They shared a laugh and braced themselves for another round of this gruelling session.

During one of her breaks, she sat on a butte and watched on as he did the same to each of her companions. She gazed around at her pals’ heated faces and slouched shoulders and suddenly did not feel so alone in her agony.

Leonardo beamed at them as they worked on their new faculties. When he spoke to them, his voice was full of wonder.

“Your group is the most powerful I have yet encountered. You’re all learning so quickly. It’s as if you’ve always known about your abilities.”

Lena’s eyes widened at his enthusiasm. Encouraged, the young protégés pressed onward. They fought against the pain they sustained with each blow, and with each new brutal manoeuvre, they learned how to protect themselves.

LATER ON, when Lena stopped for another breath, she caught Leonardo’s grim expression and followed his gaze. At the top of one hill, two shadows stirred.

He confirmed her thoughts. “They are Shadow Warriors. Scouts.”

Lena tapped Augustus on the arm and pointed toward the summit at the two dark figures who spied on them. She rubbed the back of her neck. There was still so much for them to learn. They would *never* be ready to fight against these Shadow Warriors. When she scanned the hill again for the spies, they had left.

Adrien surveyed the higher grounds. “It’s getting late. We should head back to Florence before we’re visited by more warriors.”

The exhausted group staggered through the deadfall behind him as they made their way up the steep ascent. Leonardo’s tenor voice carried over them from the back of the pack as he announced where the group would sleep that night. "You are Michelangelo's guests for the next few days. He may want no part of this mess, but he was kind enough to extend the invitation."

As they glanced at each other with surprise, Lena and her friends opted not to reply to Leonardo, silently expressing their gratitude through a grateful nod. With such a casual tone, he had extended the invitation, as if visiting the home of one of the greatest artists in history was nothing out of the ordinary. Lena smiled with tired eyes.

The afternoon sky deepened as dusk threatened to cast its blanket upon the landscape. As they crossed the plateau, Adrien continued to expound on the training.

"The more you practise, the better you will become at summoning the energy to perform these skills." He looked back at them. "Now, I know you're tired, but we must jog part of the way back. Return you to more secure territory."

The group rushed forward behind Adrien and Leonardo, in order to make it inside the city by nightfall. Adrien left them as they entered through the city gates.

"I'll meet you here again at daybreak."

In Michelangelo's large hall, someone had spread out huge cushions on the floor to serve as temporary beds.

Leonardo ushered them through the house. "Michelangelo has left some nourishment for you in the kitchen. He will not be back until later. Please help yourself."

When they entered the modest kitchen, Michelangelo had indeed prepared a generous dinner for them. A gigantic cauldron of ribollita hung from the fireplace crane, and on the table, he had laid out a feast of fruits for them.

They ate with the little energy left in them. The lessons had given Lena a voracious appetite, but she could scarcely lift her hand. The day's physical activities had exhausted her. When she looked around, her friends appeared just as worn out as she was.

After supper, Lena entered the great hall and collapsed on her cushions. Her mind, however, raced with the possibilities of her newfound knowledge and abilities. She stirred uncomfortably. It had been an epiphany to find out she was unique, and a few things made more sense to her—her parents' paranoia, her mother's warnings after her bath games, and her father's veiled conversation at the Galleria.

She closed her eyes and fell into a deep slumber. She dreamt of flying, leaping, and running; of somersaults and clashing; and of unfamiliar figures charging at her and her friends in this foreboding landscape.

IT WAS STILL DARK when Lena wriggled on top of the padding, sore from remaining in one position all night. Her bones creaked when she pushed herself up off the floor. She rubbed and blinked away the sleep in her eyes.

Marco was no longer on the cushions next to her, and she sensed he had been up for a while. She made her way down the darkened hallway toward the faint voices coming from the kitchen and stopped at the threshold.

Leonardo, Marco, and Michelangelo sat facing the hearth and conversed quietly about art, passion, and perseverance. She leaned against the doorframe and observed the three silhouettes against the blazing fire. No one would believe this scenario, even if she were to capture it in a photograph.

Leonardo shifted in his seat and patted Marco on the back when he caught sight of Lena at the door. "*Vieni, vieni. Avere un po' di cibo, la mia cara.*"

Her stomach growled at the mention of food. She had hardly eaten at dinner, but her thoughts stopped on the words, *la mia cara?* She could hardly believe that Leonardo had addressed her as my dear one. As she made her way closer to the trio, a sense of comfort filled her.

Despite this ease, a peculiar sensation overcame her as she attempted to link the artist she had studied in class with the man gesturing for her to sit beside him.

Marco glanced up at her, his face flush with excitement from the energy of his conversation with the two artists. Lena's own fluctuating emotions jumped from awe to amazement, then settled into a deeper dread for what the day would bring.

One by one, the others made their way to the kitchen, yawning and dragging their feet. They rubbed their eyes and groaned. It was still gloomy, and a chill clung to the walls of the house.

Lena observed her friends as smiles appeared on their faces when they spotted the stewed broth which hung over the fire's flames, hot and ready for them to eat. They showed no sign of distress, or maybe it was too early to tell.

Lena caught Portia's concerned glance out of the corner of her eye.

"Lena, you seem off. What's going on?"

It was a little early for this conversation, but these recent revelations weighed heavily on Lena.

"I'm not sure if it's just me, but I suddenly feel a massive burden of responsibility on our shoulders."

Augustus interjected before Portia could answer. "We've certainly stepped into a snake's pit and there's also been plenty to digest in a short time. I mean, I'm still trying to make sense of it. Me, of all people. But I don't think they're expecting us to save the world *today*."

Lena was less confident than he was about the council's expectations.

Michelangelo had boiled water and filled basins for them to freshen up. He had also stocked another basket of food for their day ahead. His resolve to avoid any involvement remained clear, but he had nevertheless endeared himself to Lena and her companions. The depth of his emotions enveloped her like a security blanket. Like a mother with her children.

Despite their aches and groans, the friends made their way through Florence to the next meeting place. They marched, ready to take on the world, as the horizon's orange and yellow hues faded with the rising light.

They had separated into two groups: Michelangelo, Portia, Gregory, and Christina travelled together and Leonardo left with Lena and the others. He reminded them that "there were always eyes watching."

At an intersection in the city, Lena's group crossed paths with a tall, striking man who stopped to greet Leonardo. She did not recognize him, yet the vibration of his power and energy shook her to her core. When she looked at him, a brilliant white shimmer enveloped him and, with it, the distinct sound of water burbling and rippling. A simple thought came to her: *He is one of us.*

When Leonardo introduced the stranger to them, she caught the slight tightening of his lips. "Don Camillo is an illustrious member of Florence."

Don Camillo's robust and muscular build towered over Leonardo. And when his gaze rested on Damian, a glint of recognition sparkled in his eye. He stepped forward and saluted Damian with a firm forearm shake, but only cast a cursory glance at Lena and Augustus.

Leonardo's eyes widened. "I didn't realize you had an acquaintance with Damiano."

A crease formed in Don Camillo's brow and he looked directly at Leonardo. "And I'm surprised to see you with Adrien's neophytes."

Lena sucked in air between her teeth. She had caught the veiled criticism aimed at Adrien. Her eyes narrowed, and she sharpened her focus on Don Camillo. Goosebumps crawled up her arms. Despite his stylish apparel, a full armour would suit him just fine.

Damian had also caught the terse exchange and turned to Leonardo. "Don Camillo brought me to the garden the other day when I sought your help. He and my father are business acquaintances."

Don Camillo shifted on his feet, while Leonardo's expression relaxed, but only by a shade.

"Well, Leonardo, I see you're busy. I'll let you get on your way. It is always a pleasure." Don Camillo shook Leonardo's forearm and turned to Damian. "Please extend my greetings to your father."

With a penetrating stare, Don Camillo gave a brisk nod to Lena and Augustus. And when he swung around to leave, a necklace slipped out through the opening of his tunic's collar. Lena's breath hitched. She recognized the *Croix de la Lorraine* dangling from its chain.

After they were well away from Don Camillo, Lena addressed Leonardo. "He's definitely an *elementis*. Should we not trust him?"

Leonardo's nose twitched, but he remained silent until they reached the city limits. When he spoke, he kept his voice low.

"Don Camillo is a formidable knight. An impressive warrior. He is also a member of the Chamber's Order and is well aware of your dilemma. To put it mildly, the council is not thrilled with the current situation—the danger you have invited by crossing the portal."

He explained further, "Don Camillo is a well-respected member of Florence. As part of its political strategy, the council likes to place some of our *elementis* members in high-ranking positions. It's good for us to have him there."

At the city gates, Leonardo paused and craned his neck to check both ways. "And his family owns the land that surrounds the portal."

. . .

Veils of light mist spread across the landscape. However, the vast cerulean sky opened up as the sun's rays dissolved the forming condensation particles.

Michelangelo had left them to get back to his work, and the two groups reunited outside the city walls where Adrien awaited them.

"I hope you feel refreshed from your rest."

They groaned in response and followed him as he led them to a different training area.

Leonardo pointed the way. "We'll use this trail, as only locals use it. The fewer eyes on us, the better."

In the morning gloom, a thin fog clung to the trees on this winding, forested path. Lena twitched at the slightest hint of a shadow, and the group huddled closer together as they made their way further into unknown territory. As the haze lifted, the trail suddenly revealed a wide, open area.

At a fork in the path, two figures marched out of the mist. Several paces behind them, a third person appeared.

Adrien directed his group to stop. "Stay behind me. These men are the Guer'Ombra—the Shadow Warriors."

Adrien stood front and centre, and maintained a solid stance as the Shadow Warriors closed in on them. As they drew near, Lena and the group corralled behind Adrien in a v-formation.

These warriors wore long black coats. The man on the left stopped and stood before them, his feet planted firmly on the ground. Tall, slim, and tawny like the colour of leather, with black hair and sombre eyes.

The shorter, stockier one on the right bore a similar countenance, except he had reddish hair, freckled skin, and piercing, amber eyes.

It was the third fellow behind them who caught Lena's eye. A wiry fellow with a crew cut and large, wide-set emerald eyes, which he narrowed almost to slits. He was fairer than the other two, but no less threatening. Something about him bothered her.

To her right, Lena overheard Portia muttering to herself. "How did they know we were here?"

Leonardo put a finger to his lips. Adrien cast a glance over his shoulder and gave them a cold-eyed glare. His not-so-subtle way to let them know to remain quiet. He addressed the Shadow Warriors, and his voice was dark, almost a growl.

"What is your business here?"

Slim, on the left, answered him. "We bring you a message from the Militis."

Lena picked up a sinister energy radiating from them. A dark, suffocating force that seized her by the throat and spread throughout her chest like thick, black smoke.

Adrien contested Slim's reply. "And what is this message?"

"We have come for her." And he pointed at Lena. "The Quinta."

Lena recoiled in response to this hostile provocation. Her stomach churned at the thought of being under their control.

The stocky Shadow Warrior sneered at her. "What's the matter? Don't like that idea?"

Adrien put out his arm in front of Augustus as he stepped forward in Lena's defence. The blonde warrior quickly adjusted his posture upon hearing his comrade's threatening tone, and his back became even more rigid when Augustus made his move. Despite his reaction, his expressionless gaze did not leave Augustus. There was no need for Lena to get any closer. She could see the rough scar from where she was—the one that ran across his right brow and down to his cheekbone.

Augustus's account of the "Reillette" accident flashed through her mind. Seamus had suffered a bloody gash when he had crashed into a tree. She glanced at Augustus, but he was oblivious to this warrior's scrutiny.

Christina nudged her and signalled with her eyes toward the blond warrior who had also captured her attention. *Doesn't he make you think of—?* Lena interrupted her message before Augustus could intercept it. *Not now,* she responded.

Adrien took a confident step toward the warriors, his gaze fixed on them. His jaw clenched. "You can return and tell them they will never get the girl."

A hostile flow of energy collided and vacillated between the warriors and the group. It electrified and terrified Lena at the same time.

The two soldiers sniggered at Adrien and turned away. Within paces, they reached the third emissary, and the three departed together. As they marched away, the blond soldier glanced over his shoulder as the last speck of them vanished into the mist. Lena caught the apprehension reflected in his expression.

21
THE RIVER

LENA ~ FLORENCE, 1500

Following in Adrien's footsteps, the group made their way to San Jacopo.

Leonardo broke the silence as they walked. "Portia's earlier question was a valid one. They knew where we were because once an *elementis* becomes informed of their identity, their energetic signature becomes detectable. We can locate them and monitor their actions using exteroception. Before you leave, we will teach you how to protect yourselves from exposure and how to detect other *elementis*.

Portia cocked her head. "Exteroception? Is that like having an inner motion sensor with a gps system?"

Leonardo smiled at her. "Yes, exactly like that."

Lena tittered. Leonardo certainly knew more about their world than he let on.

When they reached a secluded location along the river, Adrien stopped the group and directed his attention to Lena. "I will leave the water lesson to you. Work with Damian, Gregory, Marco, and Portia."

Lena stared at Adrien, stupefied at his suggestion. "Are you sure?"

"Yes." He looked straight into her eyes. "You're ready, and it's time you learn to lead the others. You'll be fine. Don't worry, I'll send you instructions if you get stuck."

Lena reluctantly agreed, but led her four water friends to the river. She knew immediately how they would respond to this new ability. Despite all the knowledge they had gained, this revelation would shock them. But before she could do that, she had to overcome her first challenge. *Portia.*

Portia had frozen in her tracks and refused to approach the dark waters. "I'm not a skilled swimmer. And I don't like when I can't see what I'm getting into."

As Adrien walked away, he sent a thought-message to them. *You'll be able to see underneath the water as though you were on land.*

Lena responded to him. *You could have been a little more subtle.*

There's no time for coddling, as all he said.

Portia locked her gaze on Lena and furrowed her brow. "*Under* the surface?"

Maybe Adrien was right. Lena sighed and stripped down to her undergarments before she jumped into the river. There was no other way to do this but to show them. After a few minutes, she climbed back out and displayed her gills for Portia and the guys to see.

"Yours will appear once you've entered the water."

Portia gaped as the flap of skin twitched behind Lena's ear. Her mouth fell open at the sight. The boys said nothing.

Marco crouched down and dipped his finger into the frigid water. "We're going in here, are we?"

Lena attempted to reassure him. "Don't worry, you'll warm up. You'll develop a second layer of skin and it will protect you against the cold."

Marco let out an awkward chuckle. "I don't know whether that makes me any more willing to jump in."

Gregory piped up. "Like a bodysuit?"

"Exactly."

Damian's concerned gaze swept over the four of them.

Marco turned to him. "A bodysuit is a type of clothing we wear when we dive under water."

Damian scratched his head. This time, Gregory tried to describe it using some hand signals. "We can swim underwater wearing a suit made of rubber, while carrying a breathing apparatus—"

Portia cut him off. "It's an extra layer of clothing to keep you warm and a machine that helps you breathe underwater."

Lena glared at them. "Are we done?" They all bobbed their heads at the same time. "Good, you guys stay here. Portia and I will go in first."

Portia pursed her mouth. "Really? Why am I going in first?"

Lena reached out and clasped Portia's hand. "Don't worry, I won't let anything happen to you."

On the count of three, they jumped into the water. After a few minutes, they came back to the surface. Portia spat out water and held on to Lena. Her other hand immediately shot up behind her ear and she searched along her hairline.

Her mouth twisted and she let out a nervous laugh. "Oh God, we *are* freaks." She waded in the water for a few minutes longer, and her eyes widened. "You were right. I can't even feel the cold now."

"That's good. Now it's time to learn to use this skill."

Lena remained close to her as they swam side by side down the river. They began with breaststrokes and eventually switched to freestyle.

"Just mimic me, and I'll guide you every step of the way."

On the water's surface, they picked up their pace until they reached a speed almost five times faster than humans.

After a few practice runs, the girls returned to where their friends sat mesmerized by the spectacle. Lena gave Portia a friendly grin.

"Are you feeling better about the water now?"

She responded with a meek smile. "Not really, but I'll survive."

Gregory's expression turned serious as the boys readied to jump in. "By the way, she's right. We *are* mutants."

They joined the girls in the water and took turns swimming up and down the river, while using alternate speeds on its surface.

After completing the exercise, Lena determined they were prepared for the next step. "Now we'll repeat the same exercise underwater."

Portia's expression became gloomy. "But—"

Lena would have none of it. "Just keep your eyes on the four of us. We're right here with you. Mirror what we do. Don't worry about anything else."

Tears sprang to Portia's eyes, and her lips quivered. "I can't. I just can't. You don't understand, I—I am really afraid of water."

Lena relented after seeing how much pressure she was putting on her friend. Not everyone had the same mettle. "I understand. Believe me, I do. But we *must* learn how to use all our abilities and we're short on time. I know this is overwhelming, but have some faith in your new elemental powers. They are there to assist you." Lena put her hand on Portia's shoulder, acknowledging her friend's resistance to the water. "Watch me first."

Lena hovered for a few moments before lowering herself feet first into the depths. As she descended, the portal guards came to mind, and she shivered, remembering her terrifying experience. Looking up, her friends' faces appeared troubled as they peered into the water. When she resurfaced, her friends let out a collective sigh of relief.

"Marco and Portia, it's your turn."

Marco took Portia's hand as they lowered themselves under the water's surface. "If you're afraid, take a deep breath and plug your nose. I've got you." Portia held on tightly to him.

When they were all below the surface, all five formed a circle. They waited until Portia became used to her gills before venturing any further. Luckily for them, they had not experienced the violent convulsions Lena had endured just a few days earlier.

When Portia was ready, she nodded to Lena, who then signalled for them to follow her. Counting to three, Lena darted ahead to a point about one hundred feet ahead of them. She swivelled to face her friends and pointed at Portia to go first.

Portia advanced, and with all her might, blasted forward. She overshot her target by a few feet and slithered back towards Lena like an electric eel. Portia joined hands with Lena, and an electrical charge surged through their bodies, causing pins and needles.

A few moments later, Marco, Damian, and Gregory joined them. They repeated this exercise down the river until all five of them were comfortable with their breathing and pacing technique.

From the surface, Adrien sent Lena a message to signal the end of the lesson. She pointed to her little group, her mind filled with doubts about whether they had had enough time to learn this skill. *Watch what I do now, then follow behind me.*

She swam at fluorescent speed and shot out of the water. When she landed on the riverbank close to her friends, they all jumped back in surprise.

As the group waited for Marco and Portia to surface, he sent Lena a message. *Portia's still scared, but I'll get her to follow the visible trail you've left. Be there when she lands.*

They watched as Portia propelled her body out of the water and landed next to them. She let out a ripple of laughter while steadying herself.

"Wow, that wasn't perfect but it sure was thrilling!"

Within seconds, Marco, Damian, and Gregory landed beside them on the embankment.

The light had dimmed when Adrien ended the session. He patted Lena's arm. "You showed excellent leadership qualities today." Heat surged to her face, and she blushed with embarrassment. Why did he always have to call her out like that in front of her friends?

Adrien faced the gathering. "The skills you learned today will be useful whenever the Shadow Warriors confront you. Remember, they only have the basic *elementis* skills, not the abilities of the Vox dei. With all of your strengths, you can beat them in an attack any day. You just have to be smart about how you use them. However, never ever forget that they are also well-trained fighters and can keep up with you if you're not careful."

IT WAS mid-afternoon when they made their way back to Florence.

Adrien walked alongside Lena and Augustus. "I understand you ran into the Portal Guards when you crossed the veil?"

Lena and Augustus's heads nodded in unison. From behind them, Marco bristled and spat out his words. "Ran into them? They abducted Lena, and who knows what they would have done to her if she hadn't escaped?"

Adrien's brow furrowed, and he shook his head. "You must be mistaken. The Portal Guards are the gatekeepers. They guard the portals. Nothing else."

Gregory put up his hand to speak. "Are you sure these so-called gatekeepers aren't a part of this Shadow Warrior faction?"

Adrien's voice rose. "I am most certain they are not. They apprehend any trespassers and report to the Majority Council." But there had been a hitch in his voice.

Damian, who had fallen behind, caught up with them and heard the tail end of Adrien's comment. "But these knights also attacked Dante. And now he's gone because of them!"

Adrien rested his hand on Damian's shoulder. "We don't really know what happened to Dante, but we are looking into it."

He faced the group. "I assure you, their only role is to protect the portals." Another notion appeared to cross his mind, but he kept it hidden, leaving Lena unable to catch his thought. And after a momentary pause, he resumed his discussion of the guards' function. "The council has very strict rules with the portals and time shifting. Thus, the Portal Guards are exceptionally vigilant. They apprehend, but they don't attack.

Damian spoke up, his voice still filled with anguish. "If those are their only orders, why did they kill Dante and destroy Leonardo's studio?"

Adrien clicked his tongue. "I have heard about that and will have to look into it. It is an unusual protocol for them. But if these guards are taking their orders from someone else, I will find out."

Lena's muscles tensed. In stepping through the portal, they had broken all of those rules. And now they were dealing with the consequences. She had been paying close attention to Adrien and Damian's heated exchange when something Adrien said piqued her interest and her heart rate increased.

"Are you saying there are more portals?"

Adrien's eyes flickered. "Yes, there are other portals, and that's why we must be vigilant about keeping them under guard. *Sapiens* cannot see or use these portals the way we can. But there are exceptions, like some of those who have interbred with our species."

Christina glanced at Adrien. "You mean the crossbreeds?"

"Yes. If they find out these gateways exist, there could be terrible consequences for us—for everyone."

Leonardo shifted and looked at his shoes, as if Adrien had directed his latest remark toward him.

Lena put up her hand. "Have other *elementis* passed through these portals by accident?"

Adrien looked away from the group towards the sprawling hills. His gaze fell back upon Lena, and his jaw tightened.

"Yes."

• • •

As Lena and her companions arrived back at the city gates, they bid farewell to Adrien and ventured into the dimly lit, ancient Florentine streets. Hungry as wolves, the conversation shifted to the feast that awaited them at Michelangelo's home.

Lena had caught Adrien's slight nod to Leonardo as the gates closed behind them. She was about to ask him about it when they arrived at the house, but the thought slipped through her mind. She and the others dropped their belongings in the grand hall and immediately made their way to the hearth.

As she passed through the hallway to enter the kitchen, the sight at the front door took her breath away.

In the entranceway's obscurity, Leonardo and Michelangelo stood murmuring to one another. Michelangelo's pricket held a nearly extinguished candle, illuminating their features in a faint glow.

She halted for a moment to listen in on their conversation.

"Leonardo, do these young folks understand what's involved by engaging in combat with these warriors?"

The candle flickered, and their shadows flitted against the walls. Leonardo put his hand on Michelangelo's shoulder.

"That's why we are training them. The militis will do everything to stop the girl from going back through the portal. It will not happen without a fight."

Michelangelo shook his head, and the lines on his brow deepened as Leonardo attempted to reassure him further.

"I know, Micielo. It's a terrible mess. Adrien and I have arranged a meeting with the Council to end all of this so these young people can go home."

She inhaled deeply, with a sudden understanding of the depth of their problem, then joined her friends in the kitchen. There was no straightforward way out of their current situation. To return home, they had to face the Shadow Warriors. The worry weighed heavily on her mind, but she was prepared to take the responsibility. What would she do if any of her friends were injured—or worse, killed? She could not live with the guilt.

When she entered the kitchen, they sat huddled against each other around the crackling fire. She settled next to Portia, who was in the middle of addressing her little assembly. Her voice was quiet, and she spoke into an invisible microphone.

"Throughout centuries, humans have been searching for other life forms in the Universe."

Then she addressed the imaginary camera. "And all this while, they've been living and breeding right under our noses." She held her arms wide, grinned, and glanced at her friends. "Isn't it ironic that *we're* the other life form?"

They all laughed, except Lena. She could not stop thinking about the maestros' conversation. The look in her eyes did not escape Augustus.

"Lena? What's happened?"

Lena's words came out stiff and disjointed. "I-I don't think I'll make it back."

Portia's smile faded. "What do you mean?"

Lena leaned toward her friends. "I just overheard Leonardo talking to Michelangelo, and it seems it's almost inevitable."

Gregory leaned forward. "What is?"

"We will have to battle these Shadow Warriors in order to pass through the portal." She put her hands over her face, then glanced up at her friends. "Although I knew we had to confront them, I didn't expect it would be a matter of life and death. It's hard to believe that I have put you all in this predicament.

Gregory let out a puff of air. "We really have gotten ourselves into some kind of trouble."

Lena stared into the fire. "Today, those warriors weren't joking. They're determined to capture me."

Christina murmured softly, both to herself and to them. "And we don't have nearly enough training to defend ourselves against them yet."

Marco spoke up, too. "It's going to be them or us, isn't it?"

Gregory rose and paced the floor. "Ha! And here I thought the only challenge we faced was stumbling through a foreign land at night."

Even Augustus's voice shook midway through what he offered them. "If we have to fight them to protect Lena, we'll fight."

While her companions deliberated their situation, Lena knew what she was going to do.

THEY HUDDLED around the fireplace and devoured the delicious meal of carbonara and soup that Michelangelo had prepared for them. The day's work had finally sapped them of all their energy. As Lena took a bite out of her bread, she turned and Leonardo's silent presence at the threshold startled her. She caught his gaze on her.

He entered the kitchen and seated himself next to her. "You are writing a paper about us? Yes?" She nodded with a sheepish grin and wondered how he knew. After a moment, he shared his thoughts on the concept of genius.

"I must tell you, I am no more intelligent than the next person." She begged to differ, but she let him continue. "You see, the essence of brilliance is in all of us. Inspiration leads us to the source of greatness. Anyone can learn to tap into this wellspring and receive divine guidance. And only then can they transform into eternal beings."

She turned toward the hearth, his words now etched into her mind. Tears sprang to her eyes. No one would ever believe—hell, she could not even believe it herself—that he had willingly shared his beliefs with her. Her throat constricted, surprised by her emotions.

Suddenly, Leonardo broke into a song of friendship and love in a deep and soulful tenor voice. While he sang, he joined Damian, who sat apart from the group, buried in his own thoughts. He finished his song, and everyone burst into cheers.

Leonardo clapped as well, happy he had distracted them for a moment. Then he put his hand on Damian's shoulder.

"I have not yet had the chance to tell you how sorry I am about what happened to your brother."

Damian lowered his eyes to the floor, and Leonardo's voice softened.

"The council is investigating the matter and will advise if they find any answers."

Damian's head shot up and tears welled up in his eyes. From across the room, Lena gasped. She sensed his emotions exploding. He bowed his head and clasped his hands together.

"Maestro, I am grateful to the council for their attention to my brother's disappearance."

Lena and the others had overheard Leonardo's message about Dante, and they moved their circle to where Damian sat.

Gregory lifted his cup in the air. "To Dante!" And everyone raised their cup to him.

22
BROTHER O' MINE

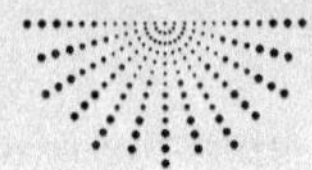

CHRISTINA ~ FLORENCE, 1500

THE FIRE still blazed in the large kitchen fireplace.

Throughout the evening, Augustus's expression remained unchanged when Lena brought up the Shadow Warriors. Christina hesitated to bring up Seamus with him, but considering the council's inquiry into Dante, maybe she could try it?

In the large hallway, she took Lena aside. "Now that Damian has received this positive news about Dante, should we mention something to Augustus about Seamus?"

Lena pursed her lips. "Well, we don't really know if it's Seamus. But it will be better for him if it comes from you. On that note, you'll never forgive yourself if you don't mention it to him."

As the last of the group exited the kitchen, Christina returned and beckoned Augustus to stay behind with her.

She crossed her arms and bit her lower lip while she stood there.

"Can I ask you a question about today?"

"Sure, what's up?" Augustus smiled at her, his expression wide open.

"When we encountered those three Shadow Warriors on the path, did you notice the one who stood in the back?"

Augustus shook his head. "Not really."

Christina frowned. "The tall, blond one?"

"I mean I saw him." He narrowed his eyes at her.

She paused, uncertain whether she should go on. "He stared at you the entire time. You're sure you didn't see him?"

"Where're you going with this?" Augustus raised his hands as he adjusted his stance. "Just spit it out."

Christina shifted her weight from one foot to the other. She was still reluctant to bring this up, but Lena was right; if she remained silent, she would always regret it.

"Please forgive me in advance for talking about this, but the warrior who stood in the back . . . I know it's going to sound strange, but he looked an awful lot like you. Do you wonder if—if he could've been your brother?"

"What?" Augustus's voice rose in panic. "Seamus is dead."

His outburst came so suddenly that Christina's cheeks flushed with shame. How could she have been so insensitive?

"Oh gosh, I'm so sorry. You're right. Never mind. Please forget I said anything."

Augustus bristled and paced the kitchen floor. "After Seamus disappeared, we found no trace of him. Not one clue."

He turned to face the hearth, away from her. Christina's own tensions mounted, but that had been her point.

"Look, it was stupid of me to say anything. With everything happening at once, I should have known to keep my mouth shut."

Christina's heart wobbled at his discomfort, and she headed for the door.

"No, wait! Don't leave. Give me a few minutes to digest what you're suggesting here." He took a few quick breaths, a clear sign of panic. Christina stopped at the doorway, then took a few steps back toward him.

"I apologize if I've upset you."

He shook his head. "I am upset, but it's only because you've caught me by surprise. I have a few questions, though."

Christina's eyes widened. How quickly Augustus's mind could process information always amazed her. He motioned for her to come closer.

"What brought you to that conclusion? I honestly didn't recognize him. But I also didn't really look that closely at him."

Christina swallowed the lump in her throat. "There was just something about him. I thought he resembled you a lot and . . ."

"And what?"

"He had a scar that ran down the side of his face, just like the one you described in your Reillette story."

Augustus's vulnerability gaped at her like an open wound.

"And he stared at you like he recognized you. Even Lena thought so."

"Lena?"

"Yes, she thought the same."

Augustus stared at her blankly.

"Look, I'm going to need a moment alone to think about this. It's a bit of a shock."

"It might not be him, but I couldn't keep this to myself. If it is your brother, you deserve to know what happened."

Christina's heart burst wide open in a wave of sympathy for him. She leaned in and kissed him on the cheek. With a gentle touch to his arm, she left him in the kitchen to contemplate the potential consequences of this unexpected discovery.

AUGUSTUS

Augustus leaned against the mantel of the fireplace. He shrugged off the cold air that crept up his spine. Even though he had secretly hoped to see his older brother again, it had been easier to imagine him dead. But if he was out there somewhere, why had he not come to find him?

His eyes glistened with tears, his emotions a whirlwind of turmoil. If Seamus was a Shadow Warrior, he would have to confront his own brother to protect Lena. However, if he hesitated against Seamus, it could prove deadly for his friends.

These thoughts whirled around his mind as he made his way to his makeshift bed in the large hall. Long, dark shadows danced and flickered on the walls to the restful breathing of his friends. He fidgeted on his cushions as he tried to find a comfortable position when a small, warm hand slid into his own. He turned his head to see Christina's silhouette resting next to him. The comfort and tenderness of her touch comforted him.

AUGUSTUS AWOKE WITH A START. The warm hand, still cocooned inside his, had twitched from dreaming.

Embers in the hall's fireplace still burned, even though the flames had diminished. When he looked over at the mop of auburn hair scattered over Christina's fair complexion, his lips curled and a warm sensation stirred within him.

Christina's eyelids fluttered. Augustus shifted a lock of her hair from her face. Her eyes flew open, and she stared at him. With her hand in his, her racing heart sent a wave of heat through him, intensifying their connection. Somewhere hidden in her gentleness, he sensed a hunger, a thirst. He should have known, but had never wanted to assume she reciprocated his feelings. He leaned forward slightly. Her smile grew wider as she closed the gap between them and gave him a tender kiss. When her lips left his, she glanced around to see if anyone had caught them. He gently turned her face back toward him.

"Everyone's fast asleep."

It was still dark when Christina and Augustus slinked away to the kitchen. The fire was going strong, and an aromatic soup hung in a cauldron to accompany that morning's breakfast. When did

Michelangelo have the time to prepare all this? They hardly saw him.

Augustus plunked himself into a chair, pulling Christina onto his lap. She tucked herself into him, and he enveloped her with his warmth, protecting her from the cold and everything else they had to fear these days.

Even with the heat coming from the fireplace, the night's chill crept up their backs. He folded his arms tighter around her and watched as the flames licked the logs.

Christina looked down at Augustus. "You look tired." She placed her cool hand on his cheek and kissed the dark circles under his eyes. "I can see you've had a restless night after our talk. How are you doing?"

"I'm a little shaken, but I'll be okay. If that guy is Seamus, I'll admit it won't be easy for me."

Augustus gazed into the fire and imagined what this new day would bring. He preferred the idea of staying right where he was with Christina in the comfort of his arms.

From the shadows, Leonardo's signature rap reverberated through the corridor. Augustus and Christina startled at the intrusion. The fire's rhythmic motion had lulled them into a meditative state.

Augustus went down to the front of the house while Christina remained in front of the hearth. He tapped on the door with two quick strokes in reply. Another response came to counter him, with one short, one long, and two shorts. Satisfied, Augustus unlatched the door, and Leonardo slipped in through the narrow opening.

The artist rubbed his upper arms to brush off the chill and headed to the kitchen to warm up. He paced before the fireplace, then faced Augustus and Christina. His expression betrayed his worry.

"I have some news for you, but it will have to wait until everyone is awake. In the meantime, I will lie down in the spare bedroom for a couple of hours."

LENA

The delectable aroma of food wafted through the house and into the vast hall, evoking a craving in Lena.

At dawn, the group stirred and, one by one, they headed to the kitchen. Lena mustered all of her patience to wait her turn. Her stomach growled. Marco and Gregory were ahead of her in the queue for Michelangelo's hearty barley soup. Anticipation had left a hollow pit in her belly. She hoped that satisfying her craving would provide her with some relief.

As Marco served and handed her a bowl of the warm soup, she turned to see a sleepy-eyed Leonardo standing in the kitchen doorway. Had he returned while they slept? The maestro served himself a bowl as if hunger had caught up with him as well. When he finished, he called for their attention.

"Yesterday, Adrien and I went to the Majority Council to negotiate a solution with the Regni Militis." Leonardo heaved a sigh. "However, I regret to inform you that the Commander of the Regni Militis will not negotiate with the Order." He paused again. "An assault is imminent. They will not step aside and will attack if you try to cross back through the portal."

Portia piped up. "I don't understand. Why can't we just make a run for it?"

Leonardo turned to enlighten the group. "If only it was that simple. Look, the Shadow Warriors are your enemy. Now that they know you're here, they will use this opportunity to get their hands on Lena." A shadow crossed his face and his demeanour changed. "Look, the Militis rebels have no morals. The commander tried to counter the appeal with his own solution. He is inexcusable."

Lena perked up. "What did he want?

"You. Of course."

"What were his terms?"

"He proposed a free passage to the rest of the group if you stayed behind. How preposterous is that?"

Lena's eyes widened. This information validated the decision she had made and her voice took on an air of urgency.

"Are you saying if I remain here with the Shadow Warriors, my friends can go home unharmed?"

Leonardo sighed slowly and clenched his eyes shut. She could tell he recognized his error in revealing this last detail.

He faced Lena. "Yes, but that is not why I mentioned it. I was attempting to substantiate the militis's unreasonable requests. We will never cater to his demands. You cannot trust that man to keep his word. Ever."

However, in Lena's opinion, the commander's request solved the problem. She paced the floor and convinced herself it was the right thing to do.

"But if it guarantees my friends' safe passage, I will surrender myself to them."

The six reacted to her comment at once, speaking over each other.

Marco stood up. "Absolutely not!"

And Damian chimed in as well. "We are not leaving you with them!"

Leonardo raised his voice above the others. "I advise against it. And Adrien will never allow it."

Lena ignored their protests. "Look, I came here to save Damian. That was the whole point of this dangerous venture; but circumstances have changed. Six lives for one? It certainly makes sense to me."

Damian moved over to a small window facing the Florentine hills. He brushed his hair back with both hands and cleared his throat.

"Until now, I believed my quest was to find Dante." Damian swivelled on his heels to face Lena. "I now realize my true mission was to save *you*." The group stilled. Damian took another breath and finished his thought. "Don't you see? Everything has led us to finding out who we are, and how important you are. All of this—our connection—was not about me or Dante, it was about you."

Damian stared into her eyes. "Losing Dante was the single worst thing to happen in my life; but now, I believe my brother's actions brought *us* together. I cannot—and will not—let these ruffians win by leaving you here. Don't give them your vital energy for *my* sake, or for any of us. Don't you see? This is so much bigger than any of us?"

Augustus, who stood behind Lena, put his hands upon her shoulders. "Damian's right. Everything that's happened has brought us to this point. Not only do we need to get you back home, we must *all* return."

Portia slipped her hand into Lena's. "Exactly! We shouldn't have come here in the first place, that's a fact. But if we hadn't, we never would've found out we've been living a life of lies. This is *our* truth. And keeping you safe is our responsibility now."

A single tear crested and ran down Lena's cheek. Her chest tightened.

"I still can't ask you to endanger your lives for me."

Gregory stepped forward into the inner circle and cocked his head. "You really have no choice. That's just the way it is. If it were any of us, you would do the same. Now, be the bold leader you are and take us home."

Lena swallowed the lump lodged in her throat. "You're wrong. I'm not that brave, and I really don't think I have it in me. What I want is for you all to get home safe."

Michelangelo's voice called out from behind them. He had been leaning against the doorframe. "It may not be apparent to you yet, but you, my dear, are the symbol of our people and our future."

IT WAS early afternoon when Leonardo gathered the group together in the large chamber.

"Adrien has advised to stay here. It would be an unnecessary risk to step outside the city walls. We will go over your skills and manoeuvres in the large hallway, and how to best defeat the warriors with your abilities."

After they had moved the sprawled cushions out of the way, Lena and the gang sat on the floor. Leonardo gestured to Augustus, Damian, and Lena to stand together in front of the others. "The two of you will fight alongside Lena."

Augustus described each of their strengths.

"My abilities include height, speed, and strength. And Damian has dynamic energy and intuition."

Damian looked at Lena. "Augustus and I can both work together with all of Lena's strengths to keep her safe."

"That's right." Leonardo pointed to Lena. "Skye—one of our light keepers—will join you when the time comes for you to head to the portal. She is one of Adrien's Guardians. You will leave with her and meet me halfway down the decline of the hill. Augustus and Damian will remain behind to prevent the warriors from following you. Portia and Christina, you're up next."

They stood to join Leonardo. "What are your strengths, Christina?"

"Portia and I both have air qualities and along with my earth speed, we will defend ourselves."

Portia's face blanched. "Are you sure I'll be able to do this?"

Christina looked at her. "Of course! Together, we can soar higher, and I'll help you run faster. It will work, you'll see."

Leonardo looked at Gregory and Marco. "You will fight together."

They stood together, and Gregory spoke up. "We both have earth and water qualities in common. It will help with our speed and intuition—"

Leonardo interrupted him. "That's right. Unfortunately, there's no water where we need to travel to get you to the portal, but you can depend on your earth abilities. Speed will be your best asset and, don't forget, you both also have great strengths. The earth elements are vigorous and unyielding."

Leonardo patted Gregory on his shoulder and turned to the rest of them. "I am confident you will succeed in your fight against the warriors. You all have the will to survive. Adrian has called some of his Light Keepers to fight, protect, and guide you back through the portal.

"Remember that you have the energy of all the elements in you, and if necessary, you can use them."

For a split second, he gazed down at himself, disappointment visible on his face. "It is with deep regret that I cannot join the fight because I am too old but, fear not, I will not be far away."

Lena took comfort in knowing that Leonardo was nearby, even if he couldn't join them in the battle. She bowed before him. "You have been of tremendous help to us. I apologize on behalf of everyone for ever doubting you."

They all stood at attention as a sign of respect for Leonardo. Lena turned to her friends.

"We *will* defeat these warriors. Now, let's practise our strategies. "

AUGUSTUS

By late afternoon, the light in the great hall had dimmed. After they had settled down to rest from working on drill exercises to use against all methods of attack, Leonardo took Augustus aside.

"I need to speak with you a moment."

Leonardo waved at Marco to join them. "I need you to translate so that Augustus understands me." He then shifted his attention to Augustus. "Please accept my apology beforehand for bringing this up, but I understand you have discovered your brother may be one of the Shadow Warriors. This must be a shock to you." He paused, and Augustus waited for him to continue. "Do you remember anything about the events surrounding his disappearance?"

This line of inquiry did not wholly startle Augustus, though Leonardo's intention was not yet clear to him. So he recapped the day Seamus went missing, starting with that morning.

"Seamus stayed home on that day. My mother insisted he miss school."

Leonardo cocked his head. "He had an illness?"

"Yes, the flu—*influenza.* I went to school, nothing unusual happened. And by the time I arrived home that afternoon, Seamus had disappeared."

Augustus's voice wavered mid-sentence, and he coughed to clear his throat. Leonardo put his hand on Augustus's forearm.

"I apologize for this questioning, but this conversation is necessary. You will understand later. Now, tell me everything that you saw that afternoon?"

Augustus let out a long sigh, and his nerves frayed. He thought back to that afternoon.

"I walked into my bedroom and the window was wide open."

"*Your* bedroom window?"

"Yeah, Seamus enjoyed staying in my bedroom when he was sick. There was a fantastic view of the forest. You could see it while lying in my bed."

Leonardo scratched his head. "Shadow Warriors rarely take those kinds of risks."

"What do you mean?"

"They would never have entered your room."

"I don't understand." Augustus's cheeks flushed, and his voice rose in pitch. "Are you saying he left with them?"

Leonardo's voice faltered. "I—I'm sorry. I don't mean to upset you, but his appearance yesterday was no coincidence."

"They've done this on purpose?" Unable to believe what he was hearing, Augustus paced the floor before relenting. "Of course they have."

Marco joined in. "To weaken our strategy."

"Yes, all planned to weaken us. Your brother is a Shadow Warrior, and they are planning to attack us. Augustus, we understand you face a quandary here." Leonardo paused once again, and Augustus awaited the rest of his narrative. "If you would rather steer clear of this conflict, we respect your choice, given the possibility of a clash against your brother."

Augustus startled. He stopped pacing and stood squarely before Leonardo. "No way. It would be cowardly of me to step away from the battle because of this one reason. I can handle this. It is what it is. If I have to defend *us* against him, I will."

"I'm not sure you understand what Seamus did that day when he left."

Augustus became irritated. "You're right, I don't."

Marco stepped forward. "Augustus, cool it." He turned to Leonardo. "Please explain what you mean. What are you trying to say?"

Leonardo lowered his voice to a whisper. "Seamus was not the only one they wanted. Your brother must have diverted them from coming back for you, too. He protected you."

Marco's eyes widened. He took a deep breath and prepared to translate. Augustus waved him away and closed his eyes to fight back the tears. He had finally understood the purpose of this conversation.

Leonardo gave Augustus a soft pat on the back. "You'll let me know if you change your mind, and we'll rearrange the formation to accommodate your decision."

"I have not changed my stance."

23
THE STORM

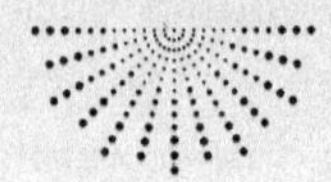

LENA ~ FLORENCE, 1500

DAWN CAST a pinkish glow on the cobblestones and stonework facades. The merchants of Florence had not yet stirred when the team stepped outside the city walls.

Lena looked back and waved at Michelangelo one last time. His face was downcast as he turned, and she saw him make the sign of the cross. She let out a sigh. They needed all the prayers they could receive to get home safely. Her gaze remained on him as he walked away. It was the last time she would see him, and her heart wavered.

As mist rose from the earth, it met the crisp air. On the gravel pathway, they jogged for most of the distance. Leonardo slowed down and held up his hand when they reached the fork in the trail. It was the same place they had encountered the three Shadow Warriors. They came to a halt.

Lena gripped her lapels and hugged her jacket tightly, her palms damp. The night before, Michelangelo had surprised the girls by arriving with clothes typically reserved for boys. "Better suited for a battle." She was relieved to get rid of the dress she had arrived in.

They stood firm in a serpentine formation, with three facing forward and three facing back, and Lena secured at the centre. Her heart raced, and her legs trembled with her nerves on edge.

Finally, they heard the crunch of footfall on the gravel path ahead of them. Lena held her breath when five silhouettes emerged from the light fog.

Adrien led the pack, and she let out a slow exhale. Behind him, four soldiers marched in a V-shaped formation. The chrononauts stopped a few feet from Lena and the rest of her companions.

Adrien introduced the Guardians, referring to them as light keepers: Sven, the Viking; Skye, the avant-garde rebel; and Altair and Al Faris, the Arabian gladiators.

Adrien had explained that the light keepers came from all walks of time, summoned by the Order for specific missions. Each unique in appearance, they shifted in and out of position to greet them with the traditional *elementis* forearm shake.

When it was Lena's turn, the light keepers bowed instead of extending their arms to express their respect. Lena squirmed at this formality. She would *never* grow accustomed to it.

After the introductions, Adrien got down to business. "The four Guardians will remain in the lead, while the others will cover and support our defensive positions."

When they all moved into their positions, Adrien pointed to her.

"Stay in the middle."

She understood she was no longer simply 'Lena'. Her species' survival depended on her. She had to be protected and defended as if she were a separate being—an entity. Despite that, she still loathed the feeling of isolation she experienced whenever he singled her out.

Adrien took the lead and transmitted a thought-message to

them. *We'll travel at a slower speed to preserve our energy for the inevitable confrontation.*

Along the route, Leonardo broke off from the pack and headed into the woodlands. Lena and Damian exchanged glances as they watched Leonardo disappear into the trees.

Lena read Damian's thought, *Adrien's taking a longer route. I think his plan is to approach from the elevation on the southeastern side.* Unaware of Adrien's plan, she continued to march steadily with the group until they arrived at the ruins of a castle.

The dilapidated estate lay on a hilltop, eerie and majestic in the early morning fog. Leaves blew about the broken structure like stray memories of its earlier occupants. Trees lined the path to a stone archway marking the entrance. The castle's name—*Chianti*—was carved into its keystone.

The group advanced around the inner courtyard without breaking out of their tactical formation. *We won't let our guard down until we're all back where we belong.* Despite Lena's courageous and defiant nature, she still resisted the idea of her friends going against these seasoned fighters to protect her life.

As they began their descent through the trees on the ground's far side, she heard the muffled pounding of footfall in the distance. Adrien confirmed her assumption. *Shadow Warriors are arriving at the ruins. Be watchful.* These Shadow Warriors had not shown themselves yet, and a knot tightened in the pit of Lena's stomach. These merciless soldiers were coming dangerously close.

The gang should have split off here, which would have given Lena the chance to prove herself, but Adrien would not risk it. Instead, he sent his booming order as a thought-message, *cloak yourselves!*

The seven pals had sat around the fireplace the evening before, perfecting their cloaking technique. The Vox dei's air ability allowed them to disappear, leaving their forms visible only to each other. At first, they could only maintain invisibility for a few minutes before their appearance began to jerk and flicker like the dust and scratches on old film reels. They had worked through the afternoon to master this new ability. By the time it was dark out, they had grasped the technique and could now remain covert for far longer.

Adrien reminded them, "Remember to use this ability sparingly. It uses up a lot of your energy, and you're going to need it."

As they dashed through the woods, Lena and her guardians faded from sight and used their advanced energy sensors to keep tabs on who went where. It was here that her protection mattered most. Adrien explained, *if your guardians fall away from you, you'll be easily cornered. In the forest, it's not a good idea.*

Ahead and behind her, trails of fluorescent lights illuminated the forest. The elemental colours of light blue, green, grey, and yellow-orange streamed behind Lena's pals as they ran.

Within minutes, they had reached the checkpoint and became visible again. Adrien sent another message. *Hostile entity on the right. Stay vigilant.*

In the shadows, a warrior lurked behind the trees. Adrien nodded to the two Arabian gladiators who had taken up positions in front and behind them.

The group reorganized itself, and Lena, Portia, and Christina took their places at the centre of the circle, while the others formed a barrier around them.

Seconds later, the mysterious entity came barreling toward them and hurtled into Altair, the gladiator guarding their backs. The altercation broke the ring of protection.

Lena glanced over her shoulder as Altair tumbled into a roll with a fiery crash. He immediately rose to his feet and countered with a vicious assault on his rival. The gang continued on their journey.

Al Faris, the second Arabian guardian, dashed forward at lightning speed to ensure that the path ahead was clear, then returned to the group and relayed a message to Adrien. *To the left, there's another one along the path.* Lena intercepted his thought-message.

She warned her friends. "Prepare for another attack."

The Arabian gladiator led the way, then swerved to the left, and allowed Adrien and the others to go. Al Faris struck the dark entity with an explosive crash. And by the sound of it, he had delivered a fatal blow to their adversary.

Lena pictured the gladiator smashing into the Shadow Warrior and hurtling him through the air. The sounds of bones cracked as his body smacked against a tree trunk. Then, nothing more. A few moments later, Al Faris caught up to them.

As they travelled farther along their route, Lena recognized the area. They were getting close to *La Mano Di Dio*. The morning sun's rays poked through the hillside's foliage and dotted the shadowed ground with bright spots of sunlight. When they reached the upland, the walled city of Florence lay nestled in the Arno valley. At the far end, a steep descent marked the final approach to the clearing.

Adrien led them across the tableland. Skye and Sven, the two light keepers, followed up front while Altair and Al Faris shielded their backs. Time slowed down as Lena made her way with the pack. Her gaze wandered across the area.

Rocks, mounds, and trees lay scattered across the landscape, forming many paths towards the far end of the field. She and her guardians could twist and catapult themselves over and around these obstacles in their attack against the warriors. Using the strategies and techniques they had practiced the days before, Lena visualized how they could take advantage of this terrain.

As she looked around at her friends, rays of energetic beams radiated from them like tentacles reaching out and drawing strength from one another. Despite their lack of training time, they might even defeat the Shadow Warriors and return through the portal unscathed. This goal instilled both anxiety and excitement in her.

The sky darkened behind them while they moved across the plain. As they marched, dandelion clocks exploded, releasing their seeds into the air. This scenery gave Lena the surreal impression of floating.

Wheat chaffs bowed their heads along the plateau's perimeter, succumbing to the increasing force of the wind.

In the distance, the Shadow Warriors marched toward them across the tableland. *Foot soldiers.* Thick strands of black auric smoke swirled about the troop, their tips sharpened into spikes. Her hopes faded, and the acrid taste of bile burned the back of Lena's throat as she pushed the impending feeling of doom from her mind.

The Shadow Warriors tread through the thick mist rising from the ground. Lena's skin crawled when her gaze fell upon their commander. Her stomach tightened into a knot, and her courage waned under the pressure to perform.

The expressionless Shadow Warriors marched toward them until they came to a stop. The tall, blond warrior—Seamus—scanned his opponents' faces, and he paused on Augustus. For a split second, his composure wavered. His demeanour softened and his eyelids fluttered briefly in recognition. But as soon as Augustus's eyes met his, the inscrutable mask reemerged.

Lena pursed her lips and glanced at Augustus, who faltered under his brother's scrutiny. She picked up on Augustus's shallow breathing and sensed his hesitation. Under different circumstances, he would have rushed to his brother. Instead, he looked away and the muscles in his jaw tensed.

Adrien brought them to a halt and moved forward alone towards the dark army's leader. He met his foe halfway between their two groups. Lena focused her attention on their conversation.

"Julian, it's been a while." The icy tone in Adrien's voice reverberated across the plateau, each word piercing the quiet like the deep resonant snapping of icicles.

"Yes, Adrien, it has."

Julian's voice was thick, like a rock dropping to the bottom of swampy waters. His charcoal-coloured clothing emphasized his dark aura. With a deep, sinister timbre, Julian spoke and got right to the point.

"We are *here* to collect the Quinta."

Though Lena could only see the back of Adrien's body, a distant memory flashed through her mind—a myriad of images of these two men in their youth . . . *Julian and Adrien in a fighting arena . . . The two young men walking together, laughing . . . and then again, Julian, antagonistic and aggressive, while Adrien grimaced in pain . . .*

As if it were her own, she sensed as Adrien's heartbeat quickened, and his voice turned into a deep growl.

"She will return through the portal, and we shall fight you to the death to keep her safe."

Julian let out a snort. "Funny, considering we captured her the other day. Where were you then when she needed your protection?"

"She was under the Portal Guards' care."

Julian's tone became slimy and unnerving. "I wouldn't be too sure about that."

A chill ran its icy fingers up her Lena's spine. He was the one who had given the Portal Guards the order to seize her.

He sucked in his breath—a vile, slithering sound. "Anyway, they were a trifle negligent since she escaped them. We certainly won't make that mistake again."

Adrien's back stiffened and his voice sharpened, like the blade of a knife striking a whetstone. "You weren't ever able to convince me of your plan, or Charlotte, for that matter. And you won't *ever* have that power over the Quinta, either."

Julian shifted and a dust devil picked up around him. "Didn't I once own you? And Charlotte was *mine*, remember?" He took a brief pause before inserting the knife further into Adrien's heart.

"But the easiest target of all was Gabriel. It's almost laughable now that I think about it." The sarcasm dripped off his tongue.

Lena cocked her ear. Gabriel? Her father? What did he have to do with any of this? Why did this Julian bring him up?

Before Lena could react, Adrien spewed out this venomous threat. "One day you will pay for what you did, mark my words!"

Julian laughed. "My, it seems I've struck a nerve. But let's be honest here, you're not really the all-knowing, all-powerful leader you imagine yourself to be. You couldn't even be there for your brother. What makes you think you can keep *this* Quinta safe, hm?"

Julian's words bore deep into Lena's consciousness. These two men had a long, antagonistic history together. Blood rushed to her cheeks, and her heartbeat thundered in her temples. Adrien's ties to her were now clear. He was her father's brother. But who was Charlotte? And had this Julian murdered her parents?

The realization of what she had overheard struck her like an icepick thrust at the centre of her heart. The sharp pain in her chest knocked the wind out of her, and she gasped for air. And just as quickly, vengeance coursed through her. Her eyes pricked at the rage building within her. She raised her hand to her mouth to keep herself from screaming.

She glared at the two men and caught the tremor that shook Adrien, and the strength it took to restrain himself from launching his own savage attack on Julian. Her leg muscles tensed. She must have flinched because Augustus extended an arm to stop her.

"This is not the time."

Augustus's authoritative tone halted Lena, and at the centre of the field, Adrien turned away from Julian, keeping his fists at his sides. He marched back across the expanse. His face had turned a shade of crimson, and his nostrils flared. When he reached them, a visible vein throbbed on his forehead.

Adrien clenched his teeth. "Let's destroy them."

Behind him, a loathsome noise came from across the field as Julian rejoined his men. He turned and glared across the field at them. An ominous laugh emanated from his throat—a high-pitched raspy sound, like a sander being dragged across rusty metal.

As HIS SQUAD marched across the plateau in serpent formation towards its enemy, Adrien transmitted a thought-message—a distinct advantage they had over their foe.

Remember, these warriors are skilled fighters. They fight to the death. Stay on your guard, keep steady, lead from the front, and work together to defeat them. When your turn comes, take your leave as planned. No deviation.

Against the backdrop of an approaching thunderstorm, their first adversary—dressed like a Kheshig warrior—charged toward them as though he had just arrived from a Mongol battle led by Genghis Khan.

The Shadow Warriors had also recruited militis mercenaries, just like the Vox dei had summoned their Light Keepers to help in the battle.

As the serpent reared its head, Sven the Viking rushed forward to face the first attack. The two clashed against each other, erupting into a brilliant explosion of sparks.

Glints of shimmering specks of light burst, like embers crackling against the wide horizon. Dazzling streaks illuminated the darkening sky as the battle raged across the Tuscan countryside.

In one corner of the tableland, Adrien and Julian engaged in a duel. Adrien twisted, altered speeds, and shifted from place to place while Julian fought back with a formidable and steely resolve. In contrast to Adrien's deliberate and planned manoeuvres, Julian was as volatile and unpredictable as quicksilver.

In response to Adrien's war hammer fists, Julian delivered precise and lethal blows. Anger and resentment raged in a battle of wills. They traded deadly bursts of hostile energy and inflicted devastating attacks against each other. But neither went down in this epic battle of wills.

Adrien launched an aggressive offensive technique to drive Julian further into the corner. To counter this attack, Julian skillfully propelled himself off a boulder, spun through the air, and escaped Adrien's grip.

At the other end of the field, Portia and Christina fought hard against a swift opponent, lithe on his feet. But the girls' air abilities thwarted his rapid footwork and flexibility.

Christina grabbed Portia's arm just as the warrior lunged forward. They used a mound to launch themselves upward and held onto each other as they somersaulted through the air. As they descended, Christina's heel contacted the warrior's jaw, and knocked him clear off his feet. He crashed to the ground and remained motionless.

Portia and Christina found the opportunity to escape. They reached the end of the plateau and fled down the hill, leaving a trail of light behind them.

As Lena advanced toward her adversary, she watched as Augustus's focus became distracted as Christina vanished down the hill. Just then, another warrior charged toward him.

Lena cried out. "Augustus, watch out!"

Augustus jerked backwards, almost lost his balance, and narrowly escaped the swing aimed at his head.

On Lena's left, Damian confronted a bulky Shadow Warrior who was making his approach. Using his speed, Damian darted back and forth, shifting positions to confuse his challenger. Then, he slammed into the warrior and knocked him to the ground. From behind, Damian grabbed the warrior, wrapped his arm in a chokehold around his neck, and held on until his opponent went limp.

Lena fought like a sharpened sword alongside Augustus and Damian against a ginger-haired fighter who was a challenge to vanquish. Lena's confidence waned as she still had trouble transitioning between all her elemental abilities.

When Ginger charged at her, Lena shifted and extended her arm to defend herself. But she missed, and the force of her swing launched her forward. Taking advantage of this mistake, Ginger spun around and shoved Lena from behind.

She put her hands out to protect herself, yet still scraped her cheek over the hardened earth. As she shook her head to clear her mind, she choked on the dust cloud that Ginger had kicked up around her.

Augustus sprang to Lena's defence, to protect her from the harm that Ginger was about to inflict upon her. He distracted Ginger while Lena regained her equilibrium.

A yell from behind alerted Lena and Augustus. As she turned to look, she caught Damian hurtling himself against an opponent with a clash so powerful it sent them both crashing to the ground. As he rolled away, Damian grasped his sides. He had deflected another powerful blow meant for Augustus, but had received a critical hit to his ribs. Augustus ran to Damian. He kicked the fallen warrior in the ribs and in the jaw to keep him down.

While Lena continued her battle against Ginger, Marco and Gregory fought against a clever and masterful combatant. They wore him down with their speed and strengths, but he kept getting back up.

With one final manoeuvre they had practised the day before, they finally knocked the tall warrior to the ground with a combined blow to the chest and gut. Assured he would stay down, Marco dashed in Lena's direction while Gregory bolted toward the horizon.

As Marco ran toward Lena, Adrien sent him a thought-message. *No, Marco. You must go. Stick to the plan.* Marco hesitated, so Lena sent him her own message. *Go! See you on the other side.*

Earlier, Adrien had admitted to her, "I trust no one else. Your friends must be on the other side when you arrive."

Upon Lena's instruction, Marco changed direction and joined Gregory at the plateau's edge. Lena glanced over at Marco as he reached the edge of the plateau, and their eyes met for a flicker of a moment. Marco nodded, then took off, leaving a streak of light in his wake.

On the plateau, the battle raged on. The Guardians had put three more Shadow Warriors out of commission, but only after severe blows from both sides. These warriors were as strong and skilled as Adrien had predicted.

Finally, Skye, the light keeper who had been summoned to accompany Lena to the portal, unleashed a megaton of force against her own opponent and knocked him off his feet. When he remained on the ground, she joined Lena to help her bring down Ginger.

Lena could not catch her breath from the onslaught of hits from Ginger. But now, with Skye's help, Lena's vitality returned, and she fought Ginger with jabs, strikes, and kicks.

The wind had picked up when Skye threw Ginger to the ground. She had been certain she could take care of it herself, but now she questioned Adrien's confidence in her abilities. To her left, Skye yelled, "You have to go! I'll finish her."

The order to leave snapped Lena back to reality, and she took advantage of the moment to escape. Dust and leaves blew across the plain as she ran. She looked over her shoulder and saw Julian steering himself around Adrien, who once again had him cornered.

When Lena reached the plateau's edge, she spotted Skye and Ginger soaring through the air toward each other. While up high, Skye stuck her arm out and knocked Ginger over with a blow that looked strong enough to bring down someone three times the redhead's size. Ginger's body landed on the ground with such force, a cloud of dust lifted off its surface. Ginger lay unmoving, and Skye caught up with Lena.

Julian whistled to his soldiers and motioned toward them. "Don't let her get away!"

Adrien sent Lena his own instructions. *Just keep moving until you're home.*

TINY DROPLETS of rain dropped from the darkened skies overhead. The storm was fast approaching.

Leonardo waited for the girls on a secondary landing partway down the hill, just above the tree line. Lena and Skye descended and leaned into the slope to break their stride. Their cadence increased with each step until they came to a stop in front of him.

He stood beside two identical hang gliders, looking suspiciously similar to modern day designs. The hang gliders, made from light wood, each had a sail. "My beauties!" He pointed to his inventions. Above the roar of the wind, he yelled at the girls, "Quick! Strap yourselves in!"

Skye gave the contraptions a dubious look-over, but Lena had already climbed into hers. She secured herself to the glider and wrapped the leather belts and hooks around her. Skye pursed her mouth, then jumped into her hang glider to do the same.

With another cry from Leonardo, now barely discernible above the wind, they sprinted down the hill and leapt off the lip at the jump-off point. Lena prayed that Leonardo's experiment would work. He hollered at them as they rose into the turbulent sky. "Use the control bar and levers to direct your path!"

Lena's heart lurched as she juggled to balance her hang glider in the twitchy, unstable wind, and Skye let out a nervous yelp as she pulled up into the air. As they floated above the forest in Leonardo's inventions, Lena glimpsed *La Mano di Dio* at the far end of the long expanse of land before them.

Raindrops pricked Lena's face and arms when her glider was lifted skyward by a gust of wind. With a knot lodged in her throat, she fumbled with the bar to find her balance and stay afloat above the clearing.

Nearing the portal, Lena looked over and mirrored Skye, who

pushed her bar as far forward as she could to lower her craft. On Lena's attempt to land the hang glider, its wings caught a downdraft and sent her into a tailspin.

Lena shrieked as the hang glider jostled her about in the air as she desperately tried to correct her position. Before she hit the ground, Lena flipped the glider over to cushion the landing. She slid along the ground upside down until the glider skidded to a stop.

The rain prickled Lena's face when Skye came into her view.

"Are you hurt? For a moment, I thought you wouldn't make it."

"Oof. Neither did I." Lena drew in a breath and when she exhaled, pain seared her ribs. It became unbearable as she tried to move. Bruised and battered, she wondered whether she was going to make it out of this place alive.

As Skye untangled her and helped her ease out of her glider, Lena grunted with pain. Despite her discomfort, she narrowed her eyes as she focused down the field's length.

"Augustus and Damian are on their way with two warriors behind them."

She recognized the tall blond warrior who chased after her friends.

Seamus.

AUGUSTUS

The warriors were steadfast in their pursuit of Lena.

Augustus and Damian had been quick to follow Lena and Skye. He looked up, followed their path, and yelled at Damian, who hugged his body with one arm.

"If you can manage it, we should run at fire speed!"

As they made their way up the expanse, Augustus's stomach lurched as he witnessed Lena's crash. Luckily, Skye was there to untangle her from the glider, and he was relieved to see Lena stand on her own. As he geared up and shot ahead, he caught a look of horror on Lena's face, and Skye held her hands up to her mouth.

Augustus glanced back just as Damian collapsed and hit the ground. When he got back to his feet, a short, stocky warrior charged toward him. As Damian tried to regain his speed, he stumbled again. He had not yet recovered from the blow sustained on the plateau.

Augustus ran back to help Damian. As he ran toward him, he watched in horror as the burly warrior reached him first and smashed into him. Augustus watched in horror as the burly warrior reached Damian first and delivered a powerful blow that sent him flying into a tree. The hit struck him unconscious, and he slumped to the ground.

Lena's cry rang out behind him, and Augustus turned to look. She rushed for Damian, with Skye close behind. He shouted, "Lena, no!"

The stocky warrior shook off the blow he had just delivered to Damian and stormed headfirst toward Lena. Without hesitation, Augustus also tore a path toward Lena, but the warrior reached her before he and Skye did.

Lena shielded herself with all the strength she had left, but her crash had left her defenceless. Her ribs burned with a searing pain as the warrior grasped her wrist. Despite her efforts to break free from his grip, he struck her with a single blow to the chin, and she sagged to the ground.

Augustus lunged at the stocky warrior. From behind him, Seamus yelled a warning to his partner, "Regan, on your right!"

With all the strength Augustus possessed, he drove hard into the warrior and sent him barrelling skyward. When Regan landed, he hit his head with a thunk against a small, rounded boulder and slumped over, inert.

Skye rushed to Lena's side as Seamus raced toward Augustus and stopped a short distance from him.

"Augustus, before you go, we must talk."

Augustus turned to face him. "So, it *is* you, brother."

"Yes, it is."

"You want to talk? You just warned your partner against me!"

"I had no choice but to do that. It would get back to Julian if I didn't."

Augustus kept a safe distance. He had dreamed of this moment since the day his brother had disappeared, but it was unlike any scenario he had imagined.

Seamus ran a hand through his hair. "I'm sorry to meet you again under these circumstances."

Augustus blurted out, "What are you doing with these people?"

"I'll explain one day, just not today. But listen to me, you must leave. Julian will continue his attack until he gets his way. He wants *her* at all costs."

Augustus's throat closed, and his heart pounded. He blinked back tears. He stepped forward and met his brother halfway. They clutched forearms, and Seamus pulled him closer. They stood almost nose to nose and brought their foreheads together as they had done as young boys. It had been instinctive. Augustus could not believe he had found his brother again.

"Why did you go with them? You shouldn't have—" Augustus's voice broke as the overwhelming emotion lodged itself in his airway.

"I did what I did because you, little brother, are the one with the brains." Seamus explained. "Now go! I'll stay here until you're gone. We'll be together again one day. Don't worry, I'll find you."

Tears blurred Augustus's vision as he tore away from Seamus. He did not turn to look back, afraid he would crumble from the emotions exploding inside of him.

Skye moved off to the side when Augustus dropped to his knees near Lena. He placed his fingers on Lena's throat. Thank God for the pulse. She stirred at his touch and mumbled, "Damian," before she passed out again.

Behind them, Seamus called out to them, “They’re coming. You must go through the portal.”

Skye agreed. “I’ll take care of Damian. Let me help you with her.”

Together, they lifted Lena. As they hoisted her up onto Augustus’s shoulder, he spotted another warrior stepping out of the bushes.

“There’s another one.”

Skye looked at Augustus, then at the warrior, but this one stood his ground and let them be.

“I’ll take care of him. Now, go!”

24
KNIGHTS OF THE ORDER

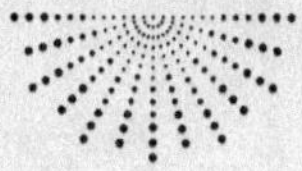

LENA ~ FLORENCE, PRESENT DAY

AUGUSTUS CARRIED Lena to the portal, draped across his shoulder, as they left the old world behind.

It was almost twilight when Augustus thumped to the ground with Lena. She rolled away from him, spurred by the hard landing, and its force jolted her back to consciousness. Augustus dashed to her side.

It was strangely quiet in the clearing. Dusk had extinguished the last of the sunset's orangey glow, and the last rays of light disappeared behind the thickening clouds on the horizon.

They brushed off the dirt and dust from their clothes and peered around. Lena was still wobbly from the blow when she heard the low, familiar rumble as it began beneath her feet.

"We have to go."

Leaves and branches rustled in the trees behind them, and they heard Gregory's disembodied voice before he and Marco emerged from the darkness.

"Hey guys, it's just us."

Augustus looked relieved to see them.

"Let's hurry. We have to help Lena. One of those brutes knocked her unconscious on our way to the portal."

Marco and Gregory rushed to Lena's side, slipped their arms around her waist, and supported her weight on their shoulders.

Marco gave her a side glance. "Can you run?"

Her mind was still foggy, but she did not want to stay in the clearing.

"Yes, I believe so…"

With a quick reminder from Augustus, they switched to night vision and the obscure landscape turned into a fluorescent display of forms and contours before Lena.

As THE FOREST's edge was within reach, the sound of horses' hooves thundered toward them. In a dazzling burst of light, two knights in silver-white armour rushed by on large, white stallions.

Lena cast an upward gaze and recognized the aura that surrounded the first knight—a brilliant shimmer and the distinct sound of gurgling water. *Don Camillo.* He rode atop his horse and looked exactly as she had imagined him.

Another set of hooves pounded the ground and reverberated in the clearing. The deep thumping grew louder as it approached them. Don Camillo's resonant voice bellowed in the dark. "I order you to stop at once!"

A moment later, a thunderous clangour rang out with metal clashing upon metal, and the clearing lit up with sparks. The resounding crash of swords snapped Lena out of her daze. The Order's knights arrived and launched an assault on the Portal Guards.

This intervention gave Lena and her friends the chance to flee. As the foursome approached the tree line, one of the Portal Guards broke free from the assault and charged at them. His unexpected approach forced them to scatter. Marco, Lena, and Augustus swerved left, while Gregory darted to the right.

Lena glanced over her shoulder as the dark steed reared on its hind legs, and the Portal Guard swung his blade into the night. As she bolted into the forest, a bloodcurdling scream echoed across the countryside.

Lena, Augustus, and Marco heard the cry and screeched to a stop. They turned on their heels towards the sound and ran through the trees back in that direction. Inside the tree line, they found Gregory on his knees and covered in blood. Lena rushed to his side despite still feeling disoriented herself.

"Where are you hurt?"

He raised his head towards the sound of her voice, looking confused and in shock. His voice and hands trembled.

"I can't see."

Lena's eyes widened at the sight. The knight's blade had nicked Gregory's forehead at the bridge of his nose, and had just missed his left eye.

"Blood is covering your eyes."

She jumped to action and tore off her sleeves. With one, she cleaned his face as best she could, and with the other, she made a compress for the cut.

Under her fluorescent vision, Gregory's blood looked like tar, dark and viscous. Marco searched for any other signs of injury.

"Did he get you anywhere else?"

"I don't think so. Just my face."

When Lena finished wrapping the compress around his head to protect his face, Augustus looked down at them.

"I don't want to hurry you, but we should get out of this forest."

The three of them lifted Gregory to his feet and made their way through the woods.

ALONG THE PATH TO FLORENCE, Christina and Portia ran out to them from their hiding place. Christina let out a gasp when she saw Gregory's bloodshot eye, bruised face, and the blood-soaked bandage.

"These sword-wielding maniacs slashed Portia's arm, too."

Lena turned to Portia and drew in a breath when she saw the red-stained cloth Christina had tied around Portia's upper arm. Her friend's lips quivered.

"They thundered after us, and his sword tore at my flesh. I knew I was as good as dead if I fell or stopped."

Lena draped her arm around Portia's waist. She held her close as Portia trembled.

"As I ran, I could hear his horse inching closer. When his sword struck me, I didn't even feel it at first. I just ran and ran until I reached the forest, certain he'd kill me if he caught up to me."

Lena's throat tightened. The realization that her friends could have died gripped her. This would not have happened if she had remained behind. The mortal danger Portia and Gregory had just averted shook her to the core.

Christina put her arm around her. "Don't blame yourself. We chose to be here." She looked at Lena, then to the others. "Thank goodness we're all back. Now, we'd better get Portia and Gregory into the city before they go into shock. They'll need to go to a hospital."

Augustus looked over his shoulder at the dark path behind him.

"Yes, let's go. These guys are unpredictable, and we don't want to run into them again."

Here, at least, there were street lamps to guide them. As they made their way to the city, Lena overheard Marco's whisper as he leaned in to speak to Augustus.

"Where's Damian?"

Augustus shook his head. "He didn't make it across . . ."

Lena glared at him as his words trailed off. Her chest tightened. "He didn't make it because you were too busy tending to me. We should have brought him back with us."

Augustus let out a remorseful sigh. “I couldn’t carry you both. He was unconscious when we left him. I’m sorry.”

Lena looked away and fell into silence. She hated herself more.

“If only I had fought harder, Damian would be with us now.”

“Lena, it’s not your fault. We did our best.” Augustus shrugged, but she could also hear the guilt in his words. “We were just following Adrien’s orders and couldn’t risk losing you. And I’m certain Damian would have agreed with us leaving him behind under the circumstances.”

Lena’s new role and its responsibilities overwhelmed her. “I don’t care. You should have taken him and left me. What makes me so special we couldn’t save him?”

Augustus shook his head. “If it makes you feel any better, I don’t really know why we didn’t leave you and take him instead.”

Despite their frayed nerves, they all laughed. Even Lena tittered at her own ridiculousness.

Lena closed her eyes to gather her thoughts. Deep down, the nagging sensation she had failed Damian gnawed at her. When she lifted her eyes to the darkening landscape, her focus returned to her injured friends.

“Let’s get Portia and Gregory home. We’ll need to figure out how to explain their injuries.”

THEY HAD JUST SETTLED in at Augustus’s place when a knock at the door echoed in the apartment. Everyone froze. Augustus was the first to move. He tiptoed to the entrance and checked through the peephole. The stranger rapped again. This time, a little harder.

Without opening the door, Augustus stood his ground. “Yes?”

A voice came, thin and curt. “The Council has sent me. You have injuries?”

Augustus looked at his friends with a questioning shrug.

“How do we know you’re from the Council?”

Lena sensed the man's impatience despite the door between them. She walked to the door and peered through the peephole.

"Show us your signet."

On the other side, the man lifted his arm. The signet glowed on his inner wrist, and Lena opened the door to him.

The man's stern expression matched the severity of his height, slim build, and greying temples. Dressed in a dark charcoal suit, he carried a silver case.

The man walked in, wasting no more time on conversation. He placed his case on the kitchen table and opened it, allowing the trapped vapours to release with a loud, whooshing sound. The container held a sterilizing compartment, syringes, and other portable medical paraphernalia. Lena had seen nothing like these instruments before.

The doctor began with Gregory by freezing his nose and forehead before he stitched him up. His movements flowed without hesitation. Gregory wriggled with discomfort and his hands grasped the chair's armrests, but he did not emit a sound. When the doctor had finished suturing him, he moved on to Portia.

He examined Portia's arm and pursed his lips. "You were very lucky." His voice was nasal and flat, as if he'd done this one time too many. "The blade just missed your brachial artery." Then he turned to Christina. "We'll have to put her under general anaesthesia to deal with that deep wound properly."

Portia's eyes widened, and she protested. "By *her*, you mean me?"

Lena flew to her side and held her hand. "It's all right. I'm right here."

The man prepared his suturing instruments, while Christina placed a portable scavenger mask of nitrous oxide over Portia's nose and mouth. Portia squeezed Lena's hand until she passed out. When the man in the grey suit had cleaned the wound and stitched up Portia's arm, he covered her gash with a bandage.

On the counter, he left bottles of pills, antiseptic cream, and instructions for Gregory and Portia's care, then exited the apartment as quickly as he had arrived.

THE STARS GLIMMERED in the night sky and the full moon left night shadows in the streets.

On the couch, Lena nestled into Marco's arms while Christina and Augustus sat together and watched over Gregory and Portia. A deep sleep seized Lena, and each torturous dream overlapped the last as she relived her battles against the Shadow Warriors.

A loud bang interrupted her fitful sleep, and she sat up, terrified of another attack. She rubbed her eyes to clear them when she heard Marco's familiar, raspy voice.

"Adrien and Leonardo are here."

"What . . .?"

Still groggy from sleep, she got to her feet and greeted the two men who stood in the middle of the living room. Christina and Augustus joined Lena and Marco near the couch.

Adrien ran his hand over his head. "It's good to see you all here —safe."

Leonardo shuffled over to Gregory and Portia, who remained on their cots, and fussed over them. He caressed their hands and spoke with a gentleness that tugged at Lena's heartstrings.

"You have done well, my young fighters."

Augustus reported on their wounds and informed Adrien of the doctor's visit.

Adrien clenched his jaw. "We sent him here as quickly as we could." His face turned a deep crimson. "I swear I'll find those rogues and have them face the Council's jury, if it's the last thing I do."

Lena pressed her lips together. "What about Damian?"

Adrien's expression darkened, and he looked her in the eye.

"He suffered severe internal damage, but Skye's taken him with her. He's in excellent hands."

Lena's gaze swung from Adrien to Leonardo. "He will survive, right?"

Leonardo gave Adrien a brief glance. "We believe he is strong enough to heal. The rest is all up to him."

She was uncertain whether they meant to appease her with their assessment, but she backed down from asking any more questions.

With a quick inhale of breath, Adrien looked in Lena's direction and uttered the following command to all of them. "The council is relieved you made it home safe. However, you have explicit orders not to go near the portal again."

Aware that the command was specifically directed at her, Lena dropped her gaze to the floor.

Adrien pursed his lips. "I also suggest you keep a low profile and return to your regular routines. Go on with your daily lives, your plans . . . Granted, it's easier said than done, but it's imperative you do as I say." He paused. "Keep in touch with each other. Work on your skills because we *will* send you a message to meet again."

Augustus spoke, his question mirroring Lena's thoughts.

"Will we have to face the Shadow Warriors again?"

"Yes. Where and when, we do not know." He shrugged his shoulders. "Look, I'm proud of you all. You've proven yourselves to be formidable fighters in such a brief span of time. I know without a doubt you can take on the best Militis warriors and defeat them, at any time and place."

But Adrien had not convinced her. How could he be so sure of her abilities? Her adversary had put her unconscious before she could even cross the portal.

Their voices filled the room as they urged him for more specific answers. From behind them, a weak voice asked, "Is all this trouble connected to that evil man, Julian?" It was Portia, from her cot.

Adrien's eyes slid past Leonardo to Portia, and then back to the group. "Yes, there's been trouble brewing among us for a few years. A time of reckoning, so to speak."

Marco stepped forward. "What about Lena?"

Lena squirmed and glared at Marco. "What about me?"

Adrien had immediately comprehended the reason behind Marco's inquiry. "Lena will be on constant watch. Julian seems to be even more determined in his pursuit of her."

Marco pursed his lips as though not altogether reassured. Still, he turned to Adrien and offered his arm. "Thank you for everything. Will we see you again?"

Adrien's expression softened. "I'll see you if time and fate allow it. And don't worry, we will always have two Guardians monitoring Lena."

Lena cocked her head slightly at this mention. She opened her mouth to speak, but Adrien beat her to it.

"Altair and Al Paris are on your guard now. And don't worry, you'll hardly notice they are there. We will keep in touch. In the meantime, stay out of trouble."

With that, he and Leonardo headed for the door and left. The six friends were alone again. Undoubtedly, a single concern circled the room. The realization that they were no longer connected to humanity made the idea of returning to their normal lives seem utterly inconceivable.

WITH THE MORNING clear and bright, the six bruised and battered friends decided on an early stroll into town.

Portia hesitated at the thought of staying alone at the apartment.

"I'm too nervous to stay here by myself. What if they find us?"

Gregory agreed, and they tagged along despite their appearance.

Before they headed out to the Piazza de Repubblica, Lena and the girls changed into Christina's dresses. Augustus wore jeans and a t-shirt, but was too tall for his friends to borrow his clothes, so Gregory and Marco remained in medieval garb. If anyone asked, they were on their way to a rehearsal.

As they roamed the streets, they were still bleary-eyed. They had each taken turns to watch over Portia and Gregory throughout the night. Lena struggled to find some sense of security in what had now become an uncertain world for her.

The group walked into the café looking like a motley crew. Lena hoped they would not run into anyone they knew. They ignored the other patrons' surreptitious looks and called the waiter over.

As they waited for their order, they made light conversation to suppress their discomfort. Vulnerable and anxious, this extraordinary event had shifted and redefined the entire meaning of their existence. Lena grappled with how her own life would move forward, especially knowing that she was continuously being guarded. She glanced around the square, curious where the two gladiators could be hiding.

Gregory spoke his mind first. "How will we work as a group to support Lena and each other when our lives are going in all different directions? I mean, I'm off to Prague, Lena's off to London." He pointed to Augustus and Christina. "You guys are off to Scotland, Marco has work in New York, and Portia—"

Portia interrupted him and winced when she moved her wounded arm. "As difficult as it is, I think we should just go on with our lives the way we had originally planned. There's not much else we can do."

Christina gathered the plates into a pile for the waiter. "And they'll get in touch if they need us. That's the way I understood Adrien's message."

Gregory lifted his shoulder in a half shrug. "I suppose we can continue practicing our skills on our own. And I can always take a trip to Scotland or London every once in a while."

Lena laughed. "Yes. That would be a wonderful idea." She stared down at her hands and cracked her knuckles. "I'm just wondering how I'm going to go about my daily life, pretending I'm not being followed by two gladiators. Like nothing's happened."

The group remained silent, and Lena picked up that each was contemplating the same thought. She could not help but laugh at the way their conversations had changed. "It's all so crazy, isn't it?"

Augustus took a deep breath. "You know what? We've been through a lot. I think we should go home and rest. Let's regroup tomorrow."

Lena cast a nervous glance at the others. Her friends' presence provided a sense of safety for her. However, the group agreed, and they each made their own way home.

LENA WALKED WITH PORTIA, holding her by the waist to protect her wounded arm. As they approached their building, Lena's brow crinkled, and she stopped in the middle of the San Lorenzo Piazza. Tears sprang to her eyes.

Portia took her hand. "You still think you could have saved him, don't you?" She sighed. "We didn't go through all this for nothing. His role was to protect *you*, and he signed up for it. And though I can't say for certain, I think he will pull through."

"Yes, you're right. He's a fighter." Lena forced a smile. "Anyway, right now I'm worried more about you. Let's get you upstairs to rest."

Portia leaned against Lena as they climbed the stairs. "I could use the rest. The pills are wearing off, and this pain's returning with a vengeance."

Upstairs, Portia swallowed two more pills from the container the doctor had left for her and lay down on her bed. She was asleep as soon as her head hit the pillow.

. . .

It had been three weeks since their return, and Lena's life had returned to its normal rhythm—as normal as Lena could feign. The memory of the battle they had fought was receding into the background of her mind, but she was still restless and easily frightened by sudden loud noises.

She became busy once again, clearing up unfinished projects, and only saw her friends when they convened to practise their skills. Portia's and Gregory's jagged and purplish scars were the only reminders left from their dangerous journey to the other world. On some days, she had the impression it had all been an illusion, a bad dream.

Now, Lena's mundane days robbed her of any feeling of urgency, and time moved at a torturous pace for her. Late-night studies replaced the hours she had spent contemplating ways to save Damian and Dante. And she gradually slipped back into the life she had known here, attending lectures and completing her thesis. Yet there was an undeniable sense of emptiness in her life.

Her natural inquisitiveness had lost none of its intensity. She had lingering questions that continued to go unanswered. Had Damian survived? Had he found his way back home? It took everything she had in her power not to return to the portal.

She passed by the registry to double-check the baptismal records for Damian and Dante, but to her disappointment, nothing had changed. *Disappeared and never found* remained inked in the same flourishing medieval script at the registry. His family considered him lost forever without a trace.

The weight of her responsibilities settled on her shoulders. She looked up from the scattered papers on her desk and stared out the window.

Lena visited Marco as often as she could. The future of their relationship loomed like a dark cloud hanging over them every time they met. Her love for him had remained as strong as ever, but she struggled to readjust to her new life. And Marco continued to plead his case.

"You're sure you can't find something in New York City?"

"Marco, this London Tate position is a once-in-a-lifetime opportunity. I could ask you to do the same and come to London."

After debating all their options—or lack of them—Marco finally conceded. "You're right. But I *will* come visit as often as I can. You too." He had spoken as if their lives together could go on as usual. But circumstances had already altered their relationship. Lena looked away to hide the tears welling up in her eyes. Nothing would ever be the same again—at least, not for her.

THE MORNING LIGHT seeped into Marco's studio, and the sun's rays cast a rosy hue across the room.

Lena had awoken at the crack of dawn to complete the final chapter of her dissertation. Leonardo's words had motivated and provided her with the answer to her central question.

Marco had painted through the night and he had only just slipped back into bed when she stirred awake. She cast a glance at him where he lay curled up, facing away from her on his side of the bed. Her heart cracked at the thought of being apart from him. Even if she changed her mind and followed him, the chasm had already formed, and the feelings of helplessness, remorse, and fear only helped to make it grow wider.

During the time Portia had gone to visit family in Rome, she had been staying at Marco's and now needed to retrieve more of her clothes.

After outlining her conclusion, she dressed and sat down next to him. "I have to go to my place, but I'll be back." She brushed aside his hair and kissed his forehead. In his half-sleep, he smiled and mumbled something unintelligible. The thought of leaving behind these languid Florentine mornings with him made her heart ache.

She stepped out of the apartment building to an awakening city. Under the lingering glow of the street lamps, she found solace in the tranquil stillness of the morning. As she walked, the echo of her footsteps on the cobbled stones lulled her back to her memory of old Florence. Sadness breezed through her like a cold draft in an empty room. She had not helped either of the twins, and it was still a bitter pill for her to swallow.

She was nearing the end of the street when an odd sensation—butterflies, or maybe moths?—flitted in her gut. The scent of burnt rubber wafted to her nostrils. She scanned up and down the narrow street and caught a shadowy figure lurking in a door's recess. In the distance, a gloomy silhouette watched her. *Julian.* Despite the distance between them, his menacing gaze made her skin crawl.

Lena's racing heart triggered a flight response, and she dashed down the narrow streets towards Augustus's apartment building.

When she reached the top of Augustus's street, she glanced behind her and her nostrils flared. The sharp odour followed her. She should have remained calm, but something about that man always put her off balance and doubting her abilities. Despite knowing the Council's strict rules, she took off at fluorescent speed to the other end of the thoroughfare. It was a risk, but she needed to get away from *him.*

She was never certain her guards were around and with this uncertainty, her confidence waned. When she reached the apartment building, she looked back to where Julian had caught up with her. He had come to a halt near a street lamp, but made no further attempt to approach her. Instead, he gave her a menacing glare and emitted a low, ominous growl that sent shivers down her spine.

"One day, when you least expect it, I will capture you."

His words clung to her like thorny vines, coiling around her and pricking her with each movement. She clenched her jaw. As she pressed the button to ring Augustus's apartment, Julian's gaze shifted away from her and up to the top of the building on the other side of the street. Something had caught his attention. She peered upward but saw nothing.

Augustus's hushed voice came through the speaker. "Yes?"

"It's me, Lena. Can I come up?"

The buzzer sounded, and she opened the front door and closed it behind her with a thud. In a flash, she was up at the top of the stairs to the safety of her friends' home. Augustus sat her down at his kitchen table. He prepared coffee and brought over toast and jam for the two of them, then settled in the seat across from her.

Christina still slept, so he kept the conversation to a hush. "What's going on? You seem spooked. And why are you out so early?"

"I saw Julian again when I was headed home from Marco's to get some things." Lena sighed. "I should be used to this by now, but it still freaks me out to see him following me so closely."

"He won't do anything to you with Adrien's guards watching over you like hawks. These are just scare tactics."

"I guess . . . but *that* man killed my parents." She rubbed the palms of her hands on her thighs. "What's stopping him from doing the same to me? On the plateau, I heard him say to Adrien, 'Eventually, we *will* get our hands on your Quinta.' What could he possibly want from me? And I don't know how these guards are following me because I never see them. But . . . if they ever slip up, he might just succeed."

"Lena, you keep forgetting you are a Quinta. You're much more powerful than he is. Plus, you're worth more alive than—"

"Thanks! *That* makes me feel so much better." She clenched her jaw, then snorted when she realized he was joking. "I suppose there's not much I can do except get used to that creepy man following me all the time. Ugh. I'm sorry. Thanks for ringing me in. You're a good friend to put up with my hysterics."

Despite her apprehension, she smiled at Augustus, and he patted her hand.

"You'll be just fine. Now stop letting that bogey man get to you. Glad you stopped by, though. That's what we're here for."

She twitched. Was that what their relationship had become? A responsibility? A sadness creeped into her heart.

Augustus hugged her, and she descended the stairs towards the entrance, as if she floated on air. She enjoyed taking advantage of her newfound abilities when she could.

She stood on the building's front stairs and looked up and down the street. There was no more sign of Julian.

THE CEILING FAN twirled and pulsed to its own rhythmic cycle.

Lena reclined on her bed and followed the fan's circular movement, which thrummed in time with her heartbeat. It had been a week since Julian had followed her to Augustus's apartment, but she had awakened from another nightmare in which she ran to save her life from a dark entity.

She supported herself on one elbow and watched Portia's figure rise and fall with each breath. Her friend's return from Rome had brought her comfort. And while Portia slept, Lena crept out of the apartment. She walked the streets until she arrived at a familiar location.

It had been too painful to revisit, and she had not gone there since her return from the past. But now she was leaving Florence and might not get another chance.

IN THE GALLERIA, her steps faltered as she approached the statue. Damian stood before her in all of his splendour—all fifteen feet of him. She gazed up at his familiar, stubborn expression, and a bittersweet feeling trickled through her.

A cool breeze wafted past her, and a frisson skittered up her spine and settled between her shoulder blades. Her nerves stood on high alert. A presence stood behind her, almost touching her. Their warm breath brushed her bare shoulder and chilled her to the bone. She had been standing in front of the statue for much too long, and this unexpected intrusion had startled her. The person shifted closer, and she quietened her breathing. Her eyes darted from left to right. Where could she run? She was about to bolt when she heard a murmur.

"He's a wondrous sight, isn't he?"

Lena swivelled on her heels and stared at him, hardly believing her eyes. Leonardo wore a dark blue bomber jacket, a white t-shirt, cuffed jeans, and white converse sneakers. Sunglasses rested on his nose and his hair was in a ponytail. He grinned at her, and she recalled the day she had seen the silver-haired man pushing the ice cream cart in the piazza. She stifled a laugh.

"Yes." He winked at her. "That *was* me."

Her brow furrowed. "How—"

He cut her off with a finger to his lips. "Shh . . ."

Lena relaxed and gently slid her hand into his arm and they both turned toward the statue.

"I gather you've heard news about Damian?"

"Indeed." He turned toward her and smiled. "He is on the mend."

Her eyes welled up, and a tear rolled down her cheek. Leonardo put his arms around her and pulled her close. He gave her a comforting smile.

She could not resist seizing the opportunity. "I don't suppose you can tell me where he is."

"No, but I am happy I could bring you this good news."

"Thank you, maestro. Truly."

He left her in the tribune and waved as he exited the building. Relief flooded her as her eyes scanned the statue one last time. She wiped away her tears and walked out of the galleria without looking back.

THE GROUP of six ambled in from all parts of the city to their favourite cafe. Lena observed her friends as they made light talk of their plans, fiddled with their pastries, and avoided any mention of their adventure. She listened, but struggled to accept their impending separation.

When they had exhausted their conversations, she and her friends walked away from the cafe. Arms entwined, they left behind their empty coffee cups and crumb-filled plates.

They came to a halt, formed a circle, and clasped their hands in the centre. Beside them, the carousel stood still.

"'Til we meet again."

They exchanged affectionate hugs and quiet farewells before parting ways to begin the new chapters in their lives.

As they walked away from each other, they turned around one last time and waved at each other. Lena's heart burst with a wave of sadness, and she blinked away her tears. The one thing that held her together was that they would meet again, at some point.

As Lena and Portia headed home, she needed to make one more stop.

The corners of Portia's mouth drew down. "Don't be too long. We still have to finish packing."

"No worries, I'll be back soon."

ABOVE LENA, the sun's rays crested over the rooftops.

Lena reached the fountain near the D'Alessandro shop and watched as the water gurgled out of its spout and hit the basin's shallow pool. The morning shade cooled her skin and sent goosebumps up her arms.

A family strolled behind her, and a child's shrill laughter pierced the morning's stillness. Lena shrunk away from the noise when a young boy ran past her to the fountain. On tiptoes, he was just tall enough to reach the lip of the basin. His giggles echoed as the water sprinkled on his face. A shimmer glistened on the surface of his skin. Lena's breath hitched, and her chest tightened as she watched him.

As he hurried back past her, he shot her a quick glance, then unexpectedly stopped. He sprang up onto the bench and joined her there. His chocolate brown eyes looked up at her.

"We're the same, aren't we? But you're different."

Lena's eyes grew wide. She wanted to respond, but the words caught in her throat.

From behind them, his mother called to him. "Roman, come here!" At the sound of his mother's voice, he sprang up like a jack-in-the-box and jumped off the bench. He ran to his mother, who scolded him.

"How many times have I told you not to speak to strangers?"

He looked back at Lena. "But, mama, she's not a stranger."

Lena stared at the boy, whose lips curled upward when he waved at her. His smile made the hairs on the back of her neck stand on end. There was something eerily familiar about him.

As THE SOUND of the water trickled from the fountain, Lena tucked away this unusual encounter into the back of her mind.

From an opened window, the notes of Bach's Ave Maria floated into the morning air. Her thoughts wandered to her father, who had often played this piece on the piano while her mother painted. Tears pricked her eyes as she recalled all the long afternoons she had spent in the studio painting by her mother's side, mimicking her movements.

Along with the music, the familiar scent of lilac wafted down the narrow street toward her, bringing with it another forgotten memory to the surface.

That last morning, before her parents left on their vacation, Lena found her father in her grandmother's garden. Lena hugged and kissed him goodbye, but her mother's betrayal lingered in her thoughts like a bitter taste.

As she stepped inside the house, her mother's soft voice echoed through the living room, filling the space with warmth. Lena's longing to run to her was overshadowed by the bitterness that wrecked her. Instead, she hid behind the nearest door to listen in on her mother's conversation.

"Please tell Lena I love her with every bit of my heart. I know she's angry now, but one day she will understand why I thought she'd be safer here. Tell her I'll miss her terribly, but that we'll soon be back."

The pitter-patter of water droplets in the fountain brought Lena back to the present, and a bittersweet tear rolled down her cheek. Ever since her parents' death, she had pushed everyone away. She had kept others at arm's length for fear of being betrayed or abandoned again. Now she understood that her mother's actions had come from a place of love. Lena had completely misread her mother's protective instincts as a rejection of her.

However, the real challenge wasn't that, was it? In truth, she simply could not trust herself with others, always second-guessing her words and actions. The weight of the pain she had caused her mother consumed her, filling her with apprehension.

But life serves you with challenges, not to alienate yourself from others, but to teach you to reach out to them—to trust you are not alone. She was finally learning to have more faith in herself, in her friends, and in her family. There was still a distance to go, but this was a start.

She had also resigned herself to her duties. After all, it was her legacy, and she had little choice but to accept it.

Her inability to help Damian was another burden she needed to release. Ultimately, she understood that their connection had served as a catalyst. One that had prompted her and her friends to discover who they were.

SHE WALKED AWAY from the bench and stepped out of the shadows into the sunlight.

Goodbye Damian. Goodbye Florence.

25
GOODBYE TUSCANY

LENA ~ FLORENCE, PRESENT DAY

LENA BOUNDED up the stairs to find Portia already putting her things away into boxes. Their overnight train to Paris was leaving at nine thirty that evening, and the movers were due to arrive mid afternoon. By lunchtime, with the apartment packed, they had an entire day ahead for last-minute details.

When the shadows grew long, Lena went to the windows to close the shutters. Outside, a flutter of wings startled her. A sparrow landed on the sill. It hopped and nodded its head at her. Then the bird batted its wings, lifted into the air, and left a swirl of dust as it flew away. *Papa! Here you are again. What message do you have for me today?*

Lena smiled and opened the window. A rush of emotions flooded her. Portia sidled up beside her and rested her head on her shoulder.

"I know."

. . .

TOGETHER, they closed the shutters to the Piazza San Lorenzo, took one last look around the apartment, and locked the door behind them.

Through the narrow streets, they wheeled and dragged their suitcases over the cobbled stones. The tourists' excited chatter filled the air as they walked past. Even without them, life in Florence would go on.

At the Santa Maria Novella Train Station, they boarded their train. Lena plopped herself down on the bench in their assigned compartment and stared out the window.

She watched as travellers scrambled to carry or shove their luggage up the train's narrow metal staircases. Her eyes struggled to capture every detail and store it to memory. Her chest tightened, and she squeezed her eyes shut. She did not want to let go just yet.

A rapping on the window made her jump. Outside, Marco stood on the quay. She dashed down the corridor and jumped off the train. He wrapped his arms around her and squeezed her tight. She nuzzled into him, inhaled deeply, and the familiar scent of oil paints flooded her senses. His lips grazed her ear.

"We'll see each other soon."

Marco's husky voice had cracked and left a hollow echo in her ear. Lena swallowed the hard lump in her throat. He leaned down to give her a soft kiss on her mouth and a rush of emotions overwhelmed her. She pulled away and ran back toward the stairs to escape the unbearable pain threatening to overflow from her. On the first step, she turned for one last look at Marco, but her vision blurred from the rush of tears.

When her eyes regained focus, she observed a movement in the people behind Marco. A guy craned his neck, struggling to get a better glimpse above the heads in the crowd. She wiped away a tear so she could better examine the departure gathering, but she lost sight of this stranger in the sea of faces. Her gaze returned to Marco, and she lifted her hand slightly to wave at him.

As she stumbled through the train's passageway, the train jerked forward, screeching to announce its departure. When she arrived in her compartment, she stepped past Portia and pressed her forehead against the window. The train lurched as it pulled away, and Marco lifted his hand and waved. Her heart shattered as she watched him recede into the distance.

In the background, something stirred again. A mop of dark curls caught Lena's eye. *Damian?* Despite her efforts, she searched the mob of people in vain, straining her neck until the quay disappeared from view.

THE CYPRESS TREES vanished from the sprawling landscape as they sped out of Tuscany toward the rugged north. Lena drifted in and out of sleep, lulled by the rhythm of the train. Visions and memories filled her dreams.

The loud whoosh of another train on the opposite track startled Lena. She sat up, groggy and feeling out of place. Portia lay asleep on the other bench. Outside, darkened shapes blurred past the window.

Her phone beeped. She hoped it was Marco and clicked to activate her screen. In her half daze, she noted her own name sat at the top of the sender's message. She frowned and read the text.

— *Lena?*

Was she still dreaming? Why would she send messages to herself?

Her phone beeped again.

— *Buonasera. Questa è Lena?*

The message read, *Good evening. Is this Lena?* She typed furiously and sent her reply. What kind of sick joke was this?

— *Che scherzo è questo?*

Without waiting for a response, she aggressively tapped another message on the phone's keyboard. Who is this?

— *Chi è questo?*

Tapping her foot nervously, she had to know who was sending

her these messages. Was it Julian taunting her? Would he ever leave her alone? Butterflies flitted about in her stomach as she waited for an answer.

Her grip tightened around the phone with each passing second. When the beep went off, it made her jump. The phone wobbled in her palm, and she nearly dropped it.

Her finger shook as it hovered over the button that would reveal the new message. Her neck muscles stiffened. She held her breath and tapped on the glass surface, her eyes fixed on the screen as it lit up. The answer was a single word.

It took a moment for its significance to sink in. When it finally registered, shock rippled through her. The word on the screen blurred. She rubbed her eyes and reread the message.

.

.

.

— *Dante.*

THE END

THANK YOU!

Dear Reader,
Thank you for reading *A Storm of Doubt* of *The Masters of the Elements* Series.
If you enjoyed the book, please take a moment to visit my author website at http://www.ccsullivan.me
or join my mailing list by clicking on
SUBSCRIBE.

MORE TO COME FROM THE AUTHOR:

To continue on this journey with Lena and her friends, CC Sullivan is currently working on the following titles:
Book 2—A Rush of Malice
Book 3—A Blaze of Glory

To find out more about the author, check:
Web Site: http://www.ccsullivan.me
IG: @ccsullivan_writer
TikTok: @the.write.artist
Email: thewriteartist711@gmail.com

ABOUT THE AUTHOR

CC Sullivan is a writer and graphic artist from Canada with roots in France and Singapore. After many years in the publishing and design industry, her focus and attention turned to writing fiction. She enjoys writing in the new adult, low fantasy, paranormal fantasy, and romance genres.

A few years ago, she started writing the *Masters of the Elements* series. She drew from a trip to Italy during her young adult years to describe the Florence found in her first novel.

In Book 1, *A Storm of Doubt,* she hopes to inspire her readers to discover her young protagonists, Lena and Damian, as well as the city of Florence, and the two great Renaissance masters, Leonardo da Vinci and Michelangelo.

The author introduces these artists into her story through her own impressions of them, and they become involved with her characters and in their adventure on the journey to discovering their true identities.

In her series, she weaves in themes of astrology, cartomancy, and the supernatural.

She is currently writing the next instalments of the *Masters of the Elements* series, *A Rush of Malice,* and *A Blaze of Glory* where Lena and her friends continue to face many challenges while on their journeys through time.

If you would like to get in touch with CC and correspond with her, please write to thewriteartist711@gmail.com

www.ingramcontent.com/pod-product-compliance
Lightning Source LLC
LaVergne TN
LVHW091139150826
845672LV00005B/984